I0760423

# Spencer

Bomb/Guns Omnibus

# Hija HUSS

Spencer – Bomb/Guns Omnibus
Contains the books Bomb and Guns

ISBN: 978-1-950232-35-2



Edited by RJ Locksley
Cover Design by JA Huss

# Bomb

Rook & Ronin Book Six

JA HUSS

# CHAPTER ONE

***"Spencer! Fuck, dude!*** Watch the fucking road!" Ronin grabs the wheel and I tap the brake to stop for the light at College and Laurel.

"Ronin, was that Ronnie back there?" I'm trying my best to check the side view to see, but it's no use. The girl went into the restaurant. "I think that was Ronnie walking into Anna Ameci's."

"How unusual," Ford replies dryly from the back of the surveillance van, "for a woman to be going into a restaurant at dinnertime."

I check the rear view so I can talk shit to his image. "Well, that woman was with a man. A man who is not me, so uh, yeah, asshole, it's pretty fucking unusual for Ronnie to be having dinner with someone who is not me."

"Since when?" Ford asks as he types away on that stupid keyboard. "I see her out with men all the time."

"*What?*"

"Ford, goddammit, what'd I tell you?" Ronin interjects.

"You know about this?" I ask Ronin.

"She's not your girlfriend, Spencer. Rook says she's got a few other good prospects."

"A few other… what the fuck? Since when?"

"Since you ignore her and treat her like shit," Ford says, still tapping away.

A horn honks behind me and I look back to the road. The light is green so I move forward with the rest of traffic and then turn left on Elizabeth. "Eye on the prize, Spence," Ronin says from the passenger seat. "Just focus on what the hell we're doing. You can figure out what's going on with Ronnie later."

Yeah, easy for him to say. Fuckass. He's got Rook at home. And hell, even Ford has a fucking girl at home. And a baby for Christ's sake. And my best booty call is out on the town with another fucking guy!

"Turn left, turn left, Spencer!" Ronin yells. "Fuck."

"I was gonna turn left all along, calm down, Larue."

He shoots me a dirty look at the nickname but I don't give a shit. I love calling his whipped ass Larue.

"Spencer, you can go home if you want to act childish. Ronin and I can do this alone."

"Fuck off, Ford. Get your toy ready, we're almost there."

"I'm ready," he says, leaning up to the front cab. He's holding the little robot that looks a lot like a two-pound dumbbell with antennae. "Where's he now, Ronin?"

Ronin looks down at the tablet in his hand. "Same place. At the bar, just ordered another drink."

"So we have a little buffer then, right?" I ask. "He's gonna nurse that thing?"

"Dunno," Ronin says with a huff. "He's got a shot and a beer, which means it could just be a chaser. Better get it in quick, Ford. And I swear to God, Spencer, if we get busted for this stupid shit, I will have your ass."

"Stupid shit? This asshole stole seven fucking bikes out of my showroom! That's like eighty grand! It's not some stupid shit."

"Allegedly stole. You have no proof. And eighty grand is not worth the attention this close to the trials," Ford replies back. "But I'm clean on this."

Ronin laughs. "Ford, we're using a military-grade robot to spy on Spencer's competitor, you really think if we get caught we're clean? Please. We're the first people they'll pick up."

"Anyway… we're here. This close enough, Ford?" I pull up a few blocks down from the warehouse that Drake Cikes calls home base. "Cikes Bikes. What the fuck is that?" I ask, pointing up to the sign near the entrance to his part of the complex. "And he just has to open up shop in Fort Collins?

You know what he's doing, don't you? Trying to confuse people. Cikes Bikes and Shrike Bikes sound the same, and if you look us up online, he comes up Fort Collins and I come up Bellvue. People think his stupid bikes are mine! He's getting my business and now he stole from me! Hell, I bet you anything he's chopped up those bikes and has my fucking parts on his custom shit right now!"

"Calm down, Spencer," Ronin says. "We don't know any of that yet. And there's no way anyone can mistake you for him, so just relax."

Well, that is true. Because I'm all tatted up in black and red. I've got the body of a Greek god, and I own this fucking town. Drake is one of those rockabilly types, with his skinny-ass body, thick black glasses, and white t-shirts. "Thinks he's Fonzie or something."

"What?" Ronin asks with a weird look.

"Drake. Thinks he's Fonzie with those white t-shirts. And him stealing my bikes is his version of jumping the shark. He's desperate, so he's gotta steal my shit."

"You're crazy, Spencer." Ronin goes back to his tablet.

"Crazy enough to come up with this plan, *yo*."

I might've gone too far became they're ignoring me now.

"OK," Ford says, "I'm gonna drop it." He opens the back door of the van and tosses the robot out. Ronin switches feeds so he has the bot cam on one side of his tablet and Ashleigh manning the Drake cam on the other. She's new in town and no one really knows her yet, so she was the only one who could keep an eye on the guy while we tapped his shit.

The bot's all-terrain tires start to roll and it travels down the alley to the warehouse. The bay door is closed. We've been watching this place all week and it's the same routine. Drake takes off about four-thirty and heads over to the Cat Call for dunch and a few brewskies. Then he comes back and locks the place up. We've looked at every possible way to get in here without resorting to the stealth and stalk we're doing now, but the place is tight. Ford even hacked the blueprints of the building from the city, and no dice. The place was remodeled before he moved in last month and it's like these guys are stashing guns and gold in there.

But Drake always pulls into the bay when he comes home, he likes to work on his bike in the evenings or something because he stays late every night. So the bay will open to let the bike in and that will be our window to drive that bot right into his lair, the mechanical hum of the tiny motor covered up by the roaring of the motorcycle.

He's got quite the setup for a man who came out of nowhere. Warehouse, employees, production schedule, advertising. It's like he's got a backer or something. But Ford checked him out. There are no obvious ties and no covert ones either. None Ford can see without taking risks that are not warranted for this particular annoyance.

At least as far as Ronin is concerned. And since Ronin's the one who has to dig us out if we fuck up, he always gets the final say on shit like that.

The radio in back crackles and then Ashleigh's voice comes in. "This is Mama Likes a Spankin', come back good, buddies."

I look at Ronin. He shakes his head. "You don't want to know," he says.

"Go ahead, Red Cheeks," Ford replies.

"Playtime's over, time to get busy. ETA"—her voice is drowned out by a loud motorcycle starting up and driving away—"five. Mama out."

"Someone's been watching a little too much *Dukes of Hazzard*."

Both my partners in crime ignore me now. Figures. I'm always the bored one on these jobs. I never have anything to do unless someone needs to be roughed up. And this guy can't be roughed up. He's too close to me. But that guy with Ronnie back at Anna Ameci's can.

I crack my knuckles and pat my leather jacket until I find the outline of my little Smith and Wesson Bodyguard. Love this little gun. It fits everywhere. In a pocket, in a boot—and shit, my hands are so big, I can probably conceal it in my palm. It's always there, inside left pocket of the leather, ready to go when I am.

A motorcycle roars by and the van shakes a little from the wind and the rumble.

We watch the bike on the bot cam, then it inches forward into the bay with the bike. "We're in. Now all I gotta do is find a place to park it."

"Find that place now, Ford. Else we're fucking busted." Ronin says with urgency.

I lean over and watch the feed as Ford tries to maneuver the bot under a tool bench. The little cam picks up the bike and Ford backs the bot up and does a neat little three-point turn until it's concealed. "One and done," he says. "Let's go. I can come back later when the place is locked up to reposition."

He doesn't have to tell me twice. I start the van and pull out, taking the long way around the block, and then head up towards Mulberry. Ronin's truck is parked on Laurel, but I drop Ford off first. Ashleigh is waiting for him at the FoCo Cinema where Rook was watching their kid until her job was done. Rook's already walking down the road towards the prearranged meeting place for Ronin to pick her up.

After I ditch everyone I park the van in the alley behind Big City Burrito and head back up towards Anna Ameci's. I enter through the back door where the bathrooms are and sneak up towards the dining room. It's not a fancy place, just a family restaurant, but that sure the fuck is Veronica having dinner with a dude. And they are both dressed like they work on Wall Street.

I let out a long breath and wait it out, because the waiter just dropped off the check. They get up and the guy puts his hand at the small of her back, guiding her away from a large group who are jostling everyone near the door.

What a player. That's my move.

I can't see them after they go through the door, so I slip back out the way I came and walk the wall down the alley that takes me back out to College Ave.

I'm just rounding the corner when the guy slams into me. He backs off, apologizing, then keeps walking. I peek around the corner and catch Veronica getting into her little Mini Cooper parked in front of Sick Boyz Inc., the tattoo shop she runs with her father and brothers. I turn back to the scumbag trying to bag my girl and walk silently down the alley. He's looking at his phone, standing next to a dark-colored sedan. I slip the gun out of my pocket and walk up behind him and place it against his head.

"Do not move," I whisper.

He freezes and I pat him down until I find his wallet, and then slip it out. I want to ask him so many questions, but I can't. Not without risking my identity. I clock him on the head and he crumples against the car and then folds until he's on the ground. I take his ID and throw the wallet down as he moans and starts checking his head for damage. I walk off, calmly. He never comes after me, but even if he did, he wouldn't find me. I know this downtown well enough to make it back to the alley behind Big City Burrito without being on the street.

I don't loiter when I get to the van, just start it up and head back to the shop up in Bellvue.

Fuck, what a night. I palm the guy's ID and wonder what the hell he's doing with my Ronnie.

He's not her type, but she sure didn't look like my type tonight. Not in that tan skirt-suit and trench coat.

This throws me. Ronnie has never looked the part of tattoo artist. She's wild and she's got big hair and bigger boobs, but she has no tats. Not even one. She's got a severe blood aversion and I've always been surprised that she can put up with the little pinpricks of blood that bubble up when she's working. So maybe a businessman *is* her type.

I chew on this the whole ride back to Shrike Bikes, my thoughts as twisted and unsettled as the Poudre River that's raging with an early spring thaw right alongside the road. And when I get home and park the van in a locked building at the back of the property, I come to the conclusion that Ronnie's type just might be a businessman after all.

But I'm a businessman too. I might not look like one, but I am *all* fucking business.

And if she wants to play a game to see if I'm serious, well, I can play as well as anyone.

In fact, I'm a damn good player.

I'm the best fucking player this town has ever seen.

So game on.

# CHAPTER TWO

***I jingle my keys*** in my hand as I walk back up to the house. I pass by the shop and sigh. We're moving into town for Shrike Bikes Season Two. Biker Channel has had about enough of Bellvue—too fucking small. And really, this isn't even Bellvue. I live ten miles north of the intersection that thinks it's a town.

But I like it out here. It's quiet. Too quiet for some, but not for me. I spent a lot of time here growing up because this was my gran's house. So it's always felt like home.

I brokered a deal with the Biker Channel people though, got them to foot the cost of renovation of the new shop if I bought the building. They do get to put a bunch of promo material in the shop, which is fine, I guess. The more people watching the Biker Channel, the more people watching the Shrike Bikes show. That's more money for me. Win-win.

Last fall Rook was annihilated in the media when she took her story public and outed a huge human trafficking ring in Chicago. She got a lot of publicity for the show because she's been part of this project since the beginning. First as my body art model for the Sturgis pilot show, then as the Shrike Bikes receptionist for Season One. But no one knew that Season One would be almost all about her. No one knew all that shit would go down and change the whole production schedule. But the publicity worked in my favor and I renegotiated the contract with the Biker Channel to get the building remodel paid for.

I key in the security code to the house and let myself in the kitchen, throw my keys down on the granite counter top, and open the fridge. Empty.

I haven't eaten at home in a while. We've just been too busy in town getting ready for the new season. In fact, I haven't even built a bike in over a month. I slam the fridge door closed and open the pantry.

Mac and cheese. And Campbell's Soup. I'm living like a fourteen-year-old who has no parents.

Fuck. I take the businessman's ID out of my pocket and study it. He's got his hair slicked back, and not in that *I'm dangerous* way like Ford does it. No. This guy's hair says *I use product.* In fact, this asshole's hair says *I have a stylist.* Not a barber, a stylist. I bet he gets his fingers done while he's there. And his toes.

Asshole.

I'm on fucking TV and I don't even let the makeup girls touch my fucking hair. I just buzz that shit off when it gets too long.

I check him out again. Banker. I bet he's a fucking banker. He looks like one. Wearing some fancy suit like he's important. Plus, he's got beady eyes. Beady brown eyes, says his ID. That's a sure sign that he's no good. Every cartoon connoisseur knows that beady eyes are a tell.

I study him for a few more seconds. He's even got a suit on in his driver's license photo. I glance over to his name. Carson. What kind of stupid name is Carson?

Last name of Reed—Veronica Reed? Nope. Ronnie Reed? Fuck, that one sounds pretty good. But Veronica Vaughn has always hated the fact that her names start with the same letter.

I happen to like it, myself. And my name is the shit. Spencer Shrike. It's got a nice ring to it.

Veronica Shrike? Maybe.

Ronnie Shrike. Better.

Ron the Bomb Shrike? I laugh at that. Fucking girl makes me smile even when she's not here. I sigh. Fucking Ronnie. I fish my phone out of my pocket and flop down on the couch. I press her number in my contacts and wait as the phone rings.

Voicemail. "*You've reached Ronnie Vaughn. I'm either working or playing. If you need me for either, leave a message and I'll get back to you!*" She makes a slurpy kissing sound and then the beep.

"Hey, Ronnie. You should come over. Call me back." I sigh again and pocket my phone, but it buzzes an incoming call before I can release it, so I pull it back out. I look at the screen. "Yello, baby! Wanna come over?"

"Oh," she says. "It's you. I was expecting a call from the bank. I deleted your number and didn't recognize it, sorry."

"What? You deleted my number? For why?" I'm stunned. Like my hand is up in the air and I'm mid-shrug with wide eyes.

"Why? *Why*? You have some fucking nerve, Spencer. I haven't talked to you since fucking Halloween!"

She's on drugs. She might need a blood test. "I took you out for New Year's, you hot little amnesiac."

"No, you did not take me *out*. You *saw me* at Antoine's. Dates pick up their girlfriends, Spencer."

"We ate, we drank, we fucked. How is that not a date?" This is what dates usually entail.

She growls at me though the phone. "The food was free, the drinks were free, and I was too drunk to remember most of the fuck, so it hardly counts. I definitely don't recall an orgasm."

"Ha!" I pull the phone away from my ear and find the voice memos, then push play on the one dated New Year's.

"*Ohhhh, Spencer!*" Veronica wails in the recording. "*Baby, yes!*"

My phone does the three-beep thing that says the call ended. I laugh and call her back. It rings through again. "Ronnie, come on! It was funny, you know it was. Since when does this shit piss you off?" I stop talking. And wait. I'm not sure why, it's a fucking voicemail, she's not gonna respond. I frown and let out a sigh. "Well, fuck. You're mad, I guess. Sorry, Rons. Seriously. Call me back, OK?"

I end the call and slump back against the couch. It hasn't been that long since I saw her, has it? I know we were pretty drunk on New Year's but I spent the night with her down in Rook's old garden apartment. What more does she want? She knows I'm busy and I've got shit going on. I can't have her hanging around too much or people will think we're together.

I can't have people thinking we're together.

My phone buzzes in my hand again and I look at the screen with some hope. "Arrrgh. Fucking Ford." I press his ugly mug to answer the call. "Yeah?"

"Meet me tonight at midnight so we can take the van back over to Fonzie's and reposition."

"I don't wanna go out at midnight. Can't you just do it?"

"Spencer," Ford says in that new parenting voice he has. "You're worse than Kate. You're the driver in this scheme, so drop your balls and do your job. Pick me up at my place at midnight."

I get triple beeps again.

"God!" I slam my fist down on the coffee table. I'm just the guy everyone gets to shit on tonight. And I'm starving. I pocket Carson's ID and get back up, grab my keys, and head outside to my Shrike Bikes truck. Might as well go into town and get something to eat. Then I can stop by Ronnie's and sweeten her up with some love. She's so damn excitable. She's always been like that, from the first moment I saw her.

Not met her. *Saw* her. Because I saw her weeks before I finally made my move.

I had just started up fall semester at Colorado State after transferring from University of Denver to get away from Ronin senior year. This was after all that shit went down with Mardee and the Boulder asshole ended up dead. Our team was in desperate need of a break. And I was walking by the CSU bookstore heading into Engineering for my mandatory science class, and there she was.

Throwing a fit.

*"Who the hell died and made you king?" the bombshell blonde screams at a huge mother all tatted up with dragons down his arms. She pushes him in the chest, straining to make the mountain of a man move. He folds his arms and yawns.*

*I figure this is her boyfriend so I stop dead in my tracks to see if the guy makes a move to hit her back. She's irate, he's calm. No one's paying any attention to them whatsoever. In fact, even though it's between classes and there are probably more than a hundred people walking the path with me, these two have a nice big circle of space around them.*

*And being the smart motherfucker that I am, I deduce that's because these two have a reputation.*

*So I cop a seat on a cement planter and pull out a smoke. She pushes him at least a half dozen more times, she yells at him. Some professor comes over and tries to intervene and the bombshell whirls around so fast the poor nerd has to step back from her fury.*

*The campus police show up after that and break it up, but then Bomb and Tat guy walk away—together, how ridiculous is that after all her stomping—and I notice they have the same logo on the backs of their shirts.*

*Sick Boyz Inc.*

*A tattoo shop on College in downtown Fort Collins.*

I had one tattoo back then. And it was fucked up. I told Bobby Choo down at Choo's Tattoos in Capitol Hill in Denver I wanted a raven on my back. He gave me a hula girl.

I beat the everliving shit out of Bobby Choo. I tattooed his eyes up black and blue.

Hey, I rhymed.

So I was looking for an artist and I figured that if this bombshell worked at Sick Boyz, I needed to check that out because I could certainly enjoy her hands all over my back a helluva lot more than fucking Bobby Black and Blue Eyes. I stalked her good. I'm an accomplished stalker. Recon is part of my team job. Ford does the virtual things, but I'm the guy on the ground.

So I reconned Bombshell. She was an art major, senior year like me. She had four brothers, all of whom worked at Sick Boyz, and she had just started out there as well. I learned that from the website. They have a bio on all the artists online and a fifty-year history of the shop from the time her gramps started it in the sixties.

And the website gave me another vital piece of information. That guy she was yelling at was her *brother*.

Game on.

I liked the Bombshell immediately. Her hair was long, so blonde it was almost golden, and her eyes were big and blue. She did wear a lot of make-up, but I'm not one of those guys who thinks that's a bad thing. I like fuck-me eyes and her lips could be green for all I cared back then. And the Spencer Shrike of today knows damn well those lips are magical.

And from the second I walked into Sick Boyz to check her out in person, I knew.

I wanted her. Bad.

# CHAPTER THREE

***Sick Boys Inc., Three years ago***

***The Stray Cats*** blares out of hidden speakers as I push through the entrance to Sick Boyz and the sounds of downtown Fort Collins are muffled once the door swings closed behind me. Bombshell is at the register, ringing up some guy who has a small square of red-speckled white gauze covering the top of his left wrist. He's got full sleeves, so this is acceptable in my opinion. The wrist is not something you do alone if you're a guy.

The guy pays, tips, flirts, and leaves as I peruse the art on the wall. There's a lot of pictures of Bombshell in here too. Starting with her in bouncy blonde pigtails looking to be about six. I laugh a little just as the music is turned off.

"Something funny?" Bombshell asks from behind the register.

I turn and watch her shuffle though the day's receipts. It's late, just about closing time, so I'm not here for a tattoo. I'm here for a date. Otherwise known as an appointment.

"This you in the picture?" I ask, using my polite Catholic-school manners.

"Yeah," she replies, not looking up at me. "That's me. All twenty-seven pictures of the little blonde girl on that wall are me. Can I help you with something? I'm just about to lock up."

I walk over to her and lean down on the glass counter, checking out the aftercare products they have for sale. "I've got some fucked-up work I need fixed." I stand up straight and look down at her. She's not short—average height, really. Maybe five six or seven. But I'm tall, so I tower over her. She looks up at me and this makes her big blues look even bigger. God, this girl is like a pin-up from the good ol' days. Her tits are like melons. Big, round melons that are practically begging for my giant hands to manhandle them.

"Eyes up, perv," she says dryly as she traces a line from her cleavage to her chin. "I'm up here, big boy."

I grab the hem of my t-shirt and slowly drag it up my body, exposing my chest, then pull it forward over my head.

Her eyes are plastered to my abs. Actually, I'm pretty sure they're darting back and forth between the v line and the happy trail.

"Hey, Bombshell," I say. She swallows and looks up at me. "You can look at me all night long. Fuck me with your eyes for all I care."

She recoils a little, like I might've insulted her. But surely a girl who is not only a tattoo artist in a college town, but also grew up with four brothers, could not be that easily offended.

"Watch your mouth, asshole. Or I'll stuff my fist through your teeth," she snarls.

Or maybe she is. I hold my hands up in an *I surrender* gesture and turn around so she can see my back.

"What the fuck is that?" She snickers down a laugh and I roll my eyes and sigh.

"A mistake, hence the need for a fix. Can you make anything out of this?" I jolt a little when her fingers touch my left shoulder blade, and then trace down what I think is the hula girl's leg.

"God, I've never seen an uglier tattoo."

I look over my shoulder at her, kinda irritated. "Can you fucking fix it or not?"

She smirks at me and then traces it again, making me shudder. "I can," she whispers, and then clears her throat. "But my brother Vic is probably your best bet."

I turn around and her fingertips drag along my arm and stop on my chest. "What if I don't want your brother to do it? What if I came in here specifically to get you to do it?"

She stares up at me, her chest heaving a little, making her tits expand. As if that was even necessary. Her tits are spectacularly large. She blinks at me a few times, like she's coming to some kind of realization. Like she's deciding I might be hot.

"My brothers will beat the shit out of you if you think you can come in here and flirt your way into an appointment with me. I'm not on the books for new appointments. I only see regulars. So, if you'd like me to set up a consult with Vic, I'll be more than happy to do that for you. Otherwise, get the hell out of the shop. It's eleven o'clock and we're closed."

"Well…" I stretch my neck a little as I lean over the glass case, clasp my hands together, and get comfortable. "I can see I'm gonna have to unleash the charm on you."

Her hand is a blur of motion and the next thing I know, the blunt end of a pink .38 Special is pressed up against my skin. And yeah, she's got a gun against my head but the only thing I can think about is how her tits are being squished against the glass in front of me as she leans over.

"Fuck, Bombshell, that is the hottest shit I've ever seen." And it is. I'm hard right now as I play that move back in my head. I laugh.

"It's not hot or funny," she growls at me. "I'm dead serious. Get the fuck out of the shop."

I grab her wrist and twist until she drops the gun. It clatters to the ground as I pull her over the case, swing her over my shoulder, and then twirl her around and set her ass back down on the glass. I hold her wrists for a few seconds and then step back and take in her reaction.

She screams.

I slap my hand over her mouth and laugh. "Shit! Stop already. I'm not gonna hurt ya, Bomb, I'm playing." Her muffled screams have made my palm moist and this is weirdly erotic to me.

She stops screaming and just stares at me.

"You OK?"

She nods her head.

"I can remove the gag order and you'll be calm?"

She shrugs.

"I'll take that as a yes." I remove my hand and she stays quiet, so I lean down to pick up the little pink gun and get the feel of it. "Now, you care to explain to me why you're pulling out a gun that's not loaded?"

"It's loaded," she retorts, scowling.

"Nah," I say back as I twirl the little pink gun on my finger. "I know what a loaded .38 Special feels like, and this isn't it, sweetheart. If you're gonna threaten someone with a gun, might as well keep the bullets where they belong." I offer her the gun but as soon as reaches for it, I pull it back. "Let's make a deal, how about that?"

She snatches the gun away from me and scoffs. "You're in no position to make any deals, buddy. My brothers are gonna kick your ass."

I smile and study her intently. "Is that right? Because the way I see it, all I gotta do is tell them how easily you were overtaken tonight and your ass will be banned from any alone time at the shop for good." She gasps and looks shocked. "So let's make a deal and you can get some shop-time freedom and I can get your talented hands on my back, fixing that ugly-ass tattoo."

Her hands come up at the same time and she shoves me hard on the shoulders, trying to get me to back up and give her space. I don't even move an inch. Instead, I grab each of her knees and open up her legs so I can slide right between them.

"Back off!" she growls.

I press my palms on either side of her faded-jean-covered thighs and lean in until we're face to face, her blue eyes looking up at me in surprise. "No. I want an appointment with you. Give me one."

She kicks out and struggles, then tries to scoot back across the glass and escape that way, but I grab her calves and slip my hands behind her knees and squeeze until she squirms, stifling down a tickle laugh.

"Don't," she says through her squealing. "Stop it!" She laughs.

I ease up so she can stop wiggling against my grip. "Give me what I want, Bombshell. And I'll walk out of here and I won't come back until our date."

"Date?" she scoffs. "An appointment is not a date. There's no fucking way I'm dating an asshole like you. You think you can come in here, manhandle me, threaten me, and get—"

I kiss her. I crush her mouth silent, slip in my tongue, slide my hands up to her tits, squeeze hard enough to make her moan, and then grab her hair and keep her there.

She kisses me back, her pouty red lips pressing against mine. She's panting hard as I pull us apart and she actually moans.

*Fuck yeah.*

"I want a tattoo appointment, Veronica Vaughn. Give me a date and a time, right the fuck now."

"Tomorrow at four," she breathes, her spectacular chest once again heaving.

I shoot her with my finger and wink. "I'll see you then, Bombshell. Be ready for me." And then I turn and walk away.

"Wait!" she calls. "What's your name? And how do you know *my* name?"

I don't turn, just open the door and call out, "You'll know my name soon enough. And the rest is recon, baby. It's my job to know."

## CHAPTER FOUR

***I chuckle to myself*** as I live that memory over again in my mind. I had her. Man, I so, *so* had her the minute I walked into that place. She was feisty with her little pink .38 Special, but my lips are irresistible. They call to her, they suck her in places she's never dreamed of, they whisper dirty things in her ear and make her blush, tremble, and come all at the same time.

But her lips. Fuck. My bombshell's lips make me explode every single time. She's got a pucker that won't quit. She's got a tongue that can swirl a pattern in my mouth so erotic, I just want to throw her down on the ground and fuck the life out of her. She uses her teeth with such skill, it makes me hard just thinking about them. And when you combine all of those things with the wetness of her mouth and the heat of her breath…

Fuck. I need her right now. Why the hell did I leave her alone so long? The commotion leftover from the human trafficking shit in Chicago died down months ago. Veronica was not pestered once during the whole debacle, I made sure of it. She's right about New Year's. She was pretty fucked up, but we still had a good time. We always have a good time, I just need to remind her how good it gets.

I press on the accelerator of the Shrike truck and speed towards Highway 14 that will take me into FoCo, then ease on into downtown and strain my neck looking down the street to see if her Mini Cooper is outside Sick Boyz. I hold out hope until I've passed it. That damn deathtrap always hides out among the trucks everyone else drives around here.

But no. I see her oldest brother Vic's bike, her father Vern's bike, her twin middle brothers Vinn and Vonn's bikes, and her baby brother Vann's Vespa.

I laugh at that. Poor Vann. The Vaughns are ruled by traditions. Everything they do has precedent. And in that family you cannot get a motorcycle until you build it yourself. Vann is only seventeen, and tradition also says you can't build your bike until you're eighteen. So the dirty, primer-covered classic Vespa is all he's allowed.

Sick Boyz must be going off tonight if the entire family is working at the same time, so it's interesting that Veronica isn't there to help. I swing a right on Mountain and head over to her house. She still lives at home. I pull up along their old brick monstrosity and scowl to myself. No Mini Cooper.

Gramps opens the door and waves at me to come inside.

Fuck. You don't say no to Gramps. He might be nine hundred years old, but he's got a mean streak. A sneaky mean streak. I park the truck in front, get out, and walk up to the open door. "Yo, Gramps! I'm looking for Ronnie, ya seen her?"

He comes out of the kitchen wearing a red-checkered apron around his waist, no shirt on, and flashing his five-hundred-year-old tattoos.

"Ahhhh, put some clothes on, ya old fart! No one wants to see your saggy shit."

He holds up a spoonful of pasta sauce and shoves it to my mouth. "Taste," he demands.

I slurp it and nod. "Yeah, it's good. It's always good. Tastes the same as last time. Ya seen Ronnie? I'm looking for her."

"At work," he barks as he goes back into the kitchen.

"No," I call out, walking after him. "I went by there, her car's not there."

"She walks now. Gonna sell it, so she parks it and walks."

"What?" She loves that car. "Since when? I just saw her in it like two hours ago." Gramps is busy stirring the pot on the stove. The whole place smells like an Italian restaurant. "Gramps," I try again. "Why does she want to sell her car?"

He looks over his shoulder. "I'm not allowed to tell you."

"What? Why the fuck not?"

"I'm not allowed to tell you that either. Go ask her, she's at the shop. And tell that son of mine to bring me some smokes on his way home."

"You quit smoking forty years ago, Gramps."

"Not for me, I have a date tonight, dumbass. Who you think I'm cooking for?"

I let out a long breath and feel a little sorry for myself as I walk out and get back in my truck. Ronnie's got secrets. Lots of them. She's having dinner with guys who are not me, she's selling her car, and she's slapped a gag order on Gramps.

This is adding up to something.

I swing the truck back out, flip a bitch, and head towards College Ave. I'm not sure what's going on with Ronnie, but I'm about to find out. I park next to Vann's gray primer-coated Vespa and head into the tattoo shop. I swing the door open and I'm accosted by frat boys all waiting around like idiots and looking at the sample art on the walls. That's one bad thing about living in a college town. College kids.

Of course, when Ronnie and I were in school together, we were the shit. But now that school is a distant memory best left forgotten, these kids annoy the fuck out of me. I've always lived out in Bellvue, even when I went to Colorado State for senior year, so I never had to put up with them much. But the new shop the Biker Channel and I decided on for Season Two is located a couple blocks up. Unlike my shop at home, this new shop will also have a showroom. So I expect the college kids will be dropping by often.

"Well, if it isn't Shrike fucking Bikes!" Vic's loud welcome blasts over the roar of excited frat boys and everyone turns to look at me.

"Where's Ron?"

Vic smiles that big-brother smile and that can only mean one thing. "She's not interested in talking to you, Shrike. Told me to tell you that if you came by."

I flip him off and walk down the hallway. Vic is not going to mess with me unless I ask for it. And a friendly *fuck you* is not enough to get us brawling. Because we've been down that road before. Once we start, we don't stop and there's always medical bills involved.

I look into each of the tat rooms as I pass. Vern's room is first, then Vic's, which is empty now since he's up front, then Vinn and Vonn—they share the biggest room—and finally Ronnie's room is last.

Her gun is buzzing, so I know she's got a customer. Her back is to the door so I slip in and lean over her shoulder. The customer is some wimpy eighteen-year-old, obviously a brother from the frat house since he's getting Greek letters on his non-existent bicep. "Beautiful, Ron. Love it, babe."

She never even flinches. Her machine never slows. She draws and wipes, and then draws again. Like I never said a word and I'm nobody.

I point to the other wimpy frat boy sitting in the only chair in the room. "Get the fuck out." He gets, and I sit, rolling my eyes as the plastic covering over the seat of the chair crinkles under my ass. Ronnie never even huffs. Usually that's what she does if I come in to her work acting like a caveman, but tonight I get nothing.

She's pissed.

I bide my time until she's done. She leaves and I stay put. I can hear her talking out in the lobby, then she tells her next victim to wait until she cleans the room and she'll be right back for him.

Ronnie is a freak about blood splatter from the tattoo machines. She wears scrubs to work. She has both a facemask and a visor with a clear plastic shield that covers her face. She wears gloves from the minute she walks into the shop until the minute she leaves and there's an air ionizer in the corner to clear out any microscopic bacterial byproducts that may or may not be floating around in the air.

Everything in this room is covered in plastic. From the tattoo chair to the cord on her tattoo machine. Even the flat screen mounted on the wall is covered in sheeting. You really have to use your imagination when you watch TV in Ron the Bomb's room.

It takes her a good thirty minutes to remove all the plastic and apply new between customers. We've all learned to love this about her, even if she's constantly behind schedule.

She returns to the room crumpling her mask up and holding her face shield in her hand. "Why are you here?" she snaps at me.

I shrug. "I want to see you tonight."

She busts out a long low laugh as she shakes her head and starts pulling plastic off things. "Well, that's not going to happen, Spencer. I've got a date after work."

"I know," I say back calmly.

She looks over at me now, her eyebrows all scrunched up in confusion. "How do you know?"

"Because," I say sweetly, "your date's with me."

She whispers under her breath as she turns back to her room duties. "I'm busy, Spencer. Go away. Vic!" she yells over the music and buzzing of tattoo machines.

"Veronica," Vic says in his *how-can-I-help-you* voice. He must've been right outside the door. Asshole. "You need me to give him the boot?" Vic says with a smile in my direction.

"Please," she sighs. "I'm busy, Spencer. Just go away."

"Out, Spencer," Vic says. "She's working until eleven."

"Vic!" Ronnie screams. "What the fuck?"

Vic motions for me to follow him so I get up and grab Ronnie by the waist and haul her sexy little body up against mine. "Veronica Vaughn. You're mine tonight, baby. I'll be back at eleven. And don't think you can duck out early, because I've got my recon hat on right now. I've got a lot of questions for you and I'm just gonna spend the next few hours between now and then trying to answer them myself." I kiss her on the head and pat her ass gently as I leave.

I can hear her stomping her foot and growling out obscenities after I leave. Vic is waiting for me at the front door. He opens it and I walk through, then he follows.

"What's up?" I ask as I walk to my truck.

"You ever meet that new guy in town, Spencer? Drake what-the-fuck's-his-name?"

"Cikes," I hiss. "Drake Cikes. Is she going out with that fuck tonight?" Fucking Drake, I'll kill that mother—

"No, she's been sorta seeing an accountant or something. Real boring guy, she's into the boring ones right now."

"What?" She really is dating that fuck from the alley. "Wait, the boring *ones*? She's dating more than one?"

"Spencer, that's her business. I'm asking about that Drake fuck. Because I saw him over by your new place the other night. Stalking around the building. I was walking home from a fun night out with that redhead from Cat Call, and he was nosing around. And I know your showroom in Broomfield was just robbed. So—you know. He might be your guy."

I grunt a little but I don't give anything away. My team is in too deep with this shit to be copping out to some bullshit spouted off by Vic Vaughn. "Nah," I say. "I got a lead on that other incident, and it's not him."

Vic nods. I'm not sure if it's a conspiratorial nod or just a regular nod, so I let it go. "OK then. Take it easy. And Spencer?" I'm already turning to go when he calls me back. "Stay the fuck away from Veronica until she says otherwise. I will kick your ass over this. She's happy. I'm not sure what she's doing, but whatever it is, she's happy. Leave her alone."

And then he turns and walks back into the shop.

# CHAPTER FIVE

***Leave her alone, my ass.***

I repeat that in my head over and over again as I wait for the girl at Big City Burrito to make my dinner. Fucking whatever. Ronnie is mine. Ronnie has always been mine. I own her ass. She's belonged to me since that very first night at the shop. And if she thinks I'm just gonna give her up after all these years, she's on some pretty powerful drugs.

I won't.

I might ignore her, but I have my reasons and that life is almost wrapped up. I can feel it. We're gonna wrap all that illegal shit up and move on. Ford's fucking married and has a kid, Ronin will have Rook roped in very soon, I can already see that shit coming. And I'll be damned if those two assholes think they're gonna become all mature and shit before I do.

Fuck that.

I'm the mature one on this team. I'm the one who has a real career. I've got three businesses, plus that little campground out in Nebraska. I'm on TV, I have my own line of custom bikes, and I've got the whole body art painting thing going. I'm bona fide. I'm on my way up. I've got plans, I've got big, big plans.

And Ron the Bomb has always been part of it. Shit, has that woman no memory? How could she have forgotten our first date?

"Shrike!" the burrito girl yells as she hands my dinner to Carla, the girl who runs the register.

I walk up to the counter and grab the bag. "*Gracias*, Carla."

"See ya *mañana*, Spencer."

She winks at me and I wink back and shoot her with my finger. "Tomorrow, baby. We're on. Pick you up at eight."

"I'll have my boots on, handsome!"

I chuckle as I walk out. Fucking Carla, gotta love that girl. She makes all my Thursday nights better. We've had a Thursday night date for almost two months now. I kinda like it too. She's one helluva cowgirl. Fridays I hang out with Renee from the Cat Call while she's at work. I got a new regular for Saturday. Kim from the Harley store down south in Broomfield. I don't usually go in there since I own my own bike shop and we sell or make everything I need custom. But I was looking for a specific set of pegs for the new bike I'm thinking about building, and I found a guy from Craigslist who had them, and he just happened to work at the Harley shop.

Sunday I go home to see the folks for dinner. It's a thing I can't get out of even if I wanted to. My old man would kick my ass if I didn't show up for family shit on Sundays.

So yeah, I haven't had much time for Ronnie, but I'm a busy fucking guy. What does she want me to do? Change my whole life around? I will, eventually, but not yet. I'm not ready for that yet. Too much shit to get done.

I get back in my truck and head home. Once I get past the little town of La Porte there's nothing else around, so I grab my burrito and start chowing. When you live thirty minutes away from the nearest real town, you learn to eat your take-out on the road. By the time I get home and let myself into the kitchen, my food is gone, my mood is even more sour, and I'm totally unsatisfied. I will go see Ronnie at eleven when she gets off, I do not care what Vic says. Ronnie and I have history.

I walk down the hallway towards my office and key in the code that controls the locks. This was Ronin's brilliant idea. And it *is* pretty brilliant. Key codes instead of keys. You always have a key and you always have a record of when the door is accessed.

I flip the light on and take it all in. Every wall is covered with pictures of Veronica. She was my body painting model for almost three years. I have touched every inch of her beautiful body with my paintbrush. And I do mean every inch. I even painted her hair once. She hated that and I laugh just thinking about it.

Our life together started the moment I saw her and Vic arguing outside the CSU bookstore. And while I did have to wrangle a gun out of her hand to get the first real date, the second time I talked to her, things went a whole other way.

### *Colorado State University - Three years ago*

"Miss Vaughn," I say sweetly as I saunter up to her. She's walking fast because she's late for her early morning art class.

"Go away, you caveman. I'll fix your stupid tattoo, but I'm not going to be nice about it. You kissed me, you know. Without permission."

"You liked it last night."

"Yeah, well, I was tired. And caught off guard. And manhandled." She quickens her pace to try and give me a hint, but I don't take hints. Besides, my legs are longer than hers. She can't out-power walk me.

"You liked all of that last night if I remember correctly."

She pulls open the door to the art building and I follow her in. We weave through the various displays in the shadowed room. "I like the art building," I tell her casually. Like we're just friends walking to class. "It's dark and moody. Like the artists who study here."

"Why are you following me?" she stops and asks in a huff, her foot stomping on the polished concrete floors.

"I'm going to class. I'm not following you."

She looks over at me and scowls. "You have class here in this building at seven AM? Not likely. There's only one class in here and it's by invitation only," she says with an air of superiority as she begins walking again.

I walk again too, then smile at her when she checks to see if I'm still following. "I've been invited, don't worry."

This makes her stop and whirl around to face me. "You're in my class?"

"I am," I say smugly. "I'm a transfer from DU. I major in business, but I take art on the side."

"Oh." She flips her long golden tresses over her shoulder. "A hobbyist."

"Yeah." I smirk and shrug at the same time. "You could call me that."

She turns again and resumes the power walk. I catch up, pass her, and then hold the studio door open and wave her through.

"Thank you," she says under her breath as she passes close enough for me to breathe in her scent. She smells like sugar. Seriously, like a fucking cookie or something. I watch her head across the room to gather her things. The studio is filled with students. At least forty of them. Everyone is setting up, getting ready for life drawing.

"Mr. Shrike," the middle-aged voice calls out to me from across the room.

I look over at Bombshell and she's watching me very carefully. I wink and shoot her with my finger, then turn and walk towards the professor with a smile. "Miss Aberdeen, thank you for fitting me in the class. I can see what you mean now, it's packed full."

She blushes at me. Yeah, I have that effect on women of all ages, so I shoot her a winning smile and tilt my head a bit. Ronin taught me that move. I might not be on speaking terms with him these days, but that guy knows all the fucking charm tricks. He has the women lined up like groupies.

I'm not a groupie gatherer, but this head-tilt thing works well enough on the professor in front of me. Her look says, *I'm an artist.* She's got the earthy clothes that hang off her skinny frame, the glasses, the put-up hair that's falling out all over the place, and the Birks on her feet.

She's so earthy, I was sorta shocked when she named her condition for letting me join this class.

"Mr. Shrike—"

"Please, Miss Aberdeen, call me Spence." I smile again and chance a look over at Bombshell. She's set up in the front row. I already knew this. I've been doing recon on the Bomb since I first saw her in that fight with her brother in front of the bookstore.

"Very well, Spence." Aberdeen blushes when she says my name and that's sorta cute. "Next week your space is next to Miss Vaughn—"

She continues talking about what will happen next week. But I'm more concerned with what's happening this week to give a shit about a time so far in the future, so I tune the rest out. I'm too busy looking over at the Blonde Bomb as she tries to process what's being said.

I chuckle as Aberdeen walks away and Veronica Vaughn walks up. "You planned this. You're stalking me, aren't you?"

"Recon, baby. Not stalking." And then I grab the hem of my shirt and pull it straight up over my head. Not too fast, Ronin taught me this too. He said the slow-mo shirt removal was one of the easiest ways to snag a girl. When I look back at Veronica her mouth is gaping open.

"What are you doing?" she hisses at me. "Put your shirt on!"

I drop the shirt to the floor and go for the pants. Veronica gasps when I pop the button and downright chokes when I go for the zipper. I hear a few cat calls from the back of the room as I slip my pants down.

I'm commando today, so His Highness just pops right out.

Every girl in the room explodes in laughter. It's the good kind though. I know the difference. This laughter says, *Holy fucking shit, I cannot believe he just took off his clothes*!

"You look more like a cherry than a bombshell right now, Blondie," I joke with her.

She shakes herself out of her silent stare and turns on her heel.

"Well," Miss Aberdeen says as she claps her hands together in delight. "Mr. Shrike—err, Spence." She smiles big as she says my name. "It's too late now, obviously, but next time—"

"Next time?" Blondie says as she peeks out from behind her easel.

"—please use the dressing room over there in the corner. And put on a robe until we're ready for you." She bats her eyelashes at me, then steals a glance down.

"Sure thing," I say as I wink and shoot. "Where do you want me, Miss Aberdeen?"

Veronica blushes the entire fucking class. Her face is this sexy shade of flush for ninety minutes. And every one of those ninety minutes, she thinks about nothing but me. She traces every line and curve of my body onto the paper in front of her. She licks her lips seventeen times. She sighs twenty-two times. She groans and whimpers when she makes five mistakes, and she even has a pouty frown on her face for the splittest of seconds when Aberdeen announces that class is over.

I wait for her as she cleans up. I'm wearing clothes again and all the girls, and a few dudes as well, are coming over to introduce themselves and ask who I am and where I came from.

I have that effect on people. I'm blessed in the body department. Ronin has his charm, Ford has his brain and I've got this beautiful body. *Plus* charm and brains. I'm the total package. Almost six foot three—I'm taller than both Ronin and Ford, and that's all muscle. I played a little football in high school and got two scholarship offers. But I stayed in town with Ronin and we both went to University of Denver.

The team comes before everything else—and DU is a great school anyway.

Ford was already in Boulder studying film, he's two years older. So Ronin and I started college together. He continued to model with Antoine, his sister's lover who runs Chaput Studios out of a remodeled six-story building near Lower Downtown. I continued to build bikes and learn how to run the business so I could take over Shrike Bikes from my old man. My mom was desperate to get him to retire after a heart attack a few years ago.

We roped Mardee into doing some cons with us. Some basic shit. Little bit of hands-on stealing from scumbags. Then she overdosed on heroin and died.

We didn't take it well, it was a huge blame game. Ford blamed Ronin, Ronin blamed me, I blamed—fuck. I blamed all of us. We were all at fault. We took it out on the local drug dealers using every skill we had in our arsenal. Namely Ford's savant hacking abilities. And all that ended abruptly after the Boulder job. The job that would change our lives, send me to Colorado State in Fort Collins and Ronin to University of Colorado in Boulder after we were kicked out of DU.

Of course, DU never said we were kicked out. But there's no way an institution of that caliber would allow us to stay.

We saw the writing on the wall and Ronin and I don't come from the big shots around town. We have money, but not that kind of money. Not Ford money. We can't just donate enough money to purchase entire academic buildings to erase our mistakes.

I shake my head. I'm pretty surprised that these kids up here in Fort Collins have no idea who I am just by my face. I was all over the Denver news last spring. So were Ronin and Ford.

We fucked up. Bad. And the only reason we're not sitting in prison right now is because the cops in Boulder fucked up worse. They accessed one of Ford's computers illegally and obtained evidence that would put us away for a long time.

Luckily the grand jury was honest. They refused to allow that evidence and all the charges were dropped.

I let out a long breath at that. I hate thinking about it. It makes me sick. I close my eyes for a second to make those thoughts go away, and then continue playing nice with the art students. I love the art people. I'm a business major because my father was not about to pay exorbitant private university prices for an art degree. So we compromised. I'd take business—which I'm actually fucking stellar at—and he'd pay for a summer internship in France with a famous *trompe l'oeil* artist. That was two years ago. She taught me how to paint three dimensions in 2D and I used that to start my body art hobby.

I paint naked girls.

And that bombshell I'm waiting for, she's about to become my new canvas.

# CHAPTER SIX

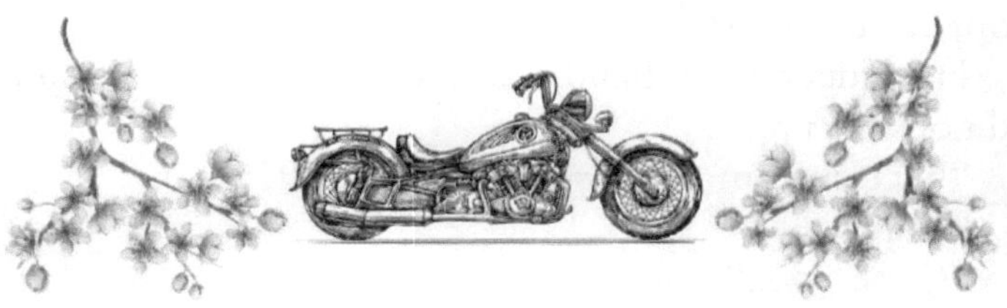

***Veronica ditches me*** the second she leaves the art building. I let her go. I have a date with her at four anyway. Plus, she's done for the day. She only has one class, but I have three and mine are all across campus, so I have no time to stalk her ass or chase her down.

I walk out of finance class at three forty-five and smile all the way to my truck. Bomb's tattoo shop is just down the street, and technically I could probably walk to her shop faster than it takes me to get back to the parking lot over near the art building where my truck is. But that girl's coming home with me tonight. I'd hate for her little feet to become weary after hoofing it all the way across town to get to my truck.

I pull up in a space in front of Sick Boyz at three fifty-nine.

Her brother is waiting for me when I walk in, giving me a not-so-nice look. "Hey, man," I say casually. "What's up? I have an appointment with Veronica."

He gives me the once-over. Maybe the twice-over. He's a big guy. Bigger than me, and that's saying something. He might not be much taller, but his muscles say he works out daily. Possibly several times a day. He's wearing a white t-shirt with the shop logo on it—which is a rockabilly guy and a pin-up girl who could be a redhead version of his sister or a biker version of Jessica Rabbit. And both figures are tatted up and sitting on a badass bike. There's a few custom bikes out front, so I'm getting the feeling these guys are into the rides.

I make my befriend-the-brother move and stick out my hand to shake. He accepts it. "Spencer Shrike. That your chopper out there?"

He squeezes my hand, I squeeze back, then he drops it and nods. "Yup."

"Nice custom work, you do it yourself?"

"Yup."

"Cool, cool." I want to get more into it, talk about the custom shit my dad and me do, but something tells me he knows who I am and he's waiting for it. So I turn away and look at the pictures on the wall.

"I'm ready," Blondie says as she turns the corner of a hallway. "Follow me," she huffs as she turns her back and walks away.

I shoot Big Brother a smile, then do as I'm told. There are several tattoo rooms and hers is at the end. I watch her ass as she walks. She's wearing those scrubs that doctors wear in surgery. Hers are pink. That makes me smile. She looks like a pink girl. A real girly girl. I bet she wanted to be a princess when she grew up. She turns the corner into her room and beckons me inside with a sigh.

I stop short. "What the fuck?" Every surface of her room is covered in plastic. It's like the dentist, times a bazillion. The TV is covered, the chair is covered, the counters have plastic over them, and when I turn around to ask her what's up, she's got on a pink face mask. I laugh.

She flips me the finger. "Fuck you! You should be happy I'm so hygienic. You will never catch a disease in my room. Sit your ass down in the chair and don't say another word unless I ask you a question."

I chuckle under my breath and take a seat. The plastic crinkles underneath me and I slip around a little. "So, Veronica. I never properly introduced myself this morning. I'm Spencer."

"I don't need to know your name. Besides," she says as she slips a visor over her forehead that has a long clear plastic shield attached to it. "I already know all about you." Her last few words come out muffled and with an echo from behind the mask and the shield.

I smile and wink. "Don't believe everything you hear, then, OK?"

She ignores me. "Take your shirt off and tell me what you want that awful thing you're calling a tattoo turned into."

I slip my shirt over my head slowly, just like I did it this morning. She pretends to be busy with her machine and ink, but I catch her looking out of the corner of her eye. "I'm thinking I need a whole back piece to cover that little lady. I'm thinking ravens, and skulls, and smoke. I'm thinking Blackbirds, of the mechanical variety. I'm thinking all done up in black and red."

"Ha," she fake-laughs. "That's a month's worth of appointments. I want to know what you want me to do today."

"A Blackbird, Blondie. I want a Blackbird today. The hula girl can wait until we get the design right. Today I want you to start the piece. Give me that paper over there, I'll draw it out for you."

She looks at me skeptically, removes her face shield and mask and walks over to the counter top where she's got a spiral notebook. She grabs it, and a pen, even though there are pencils in the jar she's keeping her writing utensils in, and hands them over.

I open the notebook and realize it's her personal sketchbook. I look up at her and she's got her hands on her hips, like she's waiting on me to perform. I do the head-tilt smile and page through, trying to look at each of her drawings without being obvious. They are all very detailed with elaborate shading and perspective. She's a talented artist and I'm dying to see the sketch she did of me this morning.

I find a blank page and uncap the pen with my teeth and start to draw. I can sketch this image with my eyes closed, that's how often I've drawn it, both in real life and in my mind. I was drunk when I let Bobby Choo tat me up with a hula girl.

Out-of-my-mind drunk, celebrating after the grand jury refused to indict me and my team for murder. That's the only way I'd let his dumb ass tat me up. Especially my first time. Because I've been planning this bike since I was a little kid and I was still handing my old man tools in our garage as he was building the business.

I'm not sure how much time goes by when Bomb whispers over my shoulder. "Thunderbird."

I laugh and turn my head. I don't have to turn it far, her cheek is practically right up against mine. "Yeah, baby. Thunderbird, American-style. The 1956 Triumph Blackbird. I want ravens and rooks. And skulls and smoke. All done up in black and red. But first, I want the Shrike Bikes version of the Blackbird. And this is it." I stop talking so I can stare at her lips for a moment. She licks them and I almost die. I reluctantly drag my eyes up to her heated stare. Her opinion of me has changed since I came in this room. I rip the page out of the notebook and set it on the counter. "Will you do it?"

She lets out a breath, like she was holding it in. "I'd need to plan it properly, Spencer."

The sound of my name coming out of her mouth gives me the chills. "Of course."

"You'd need to help me," she continues in a whisper.

"I'd have it no other way."

"I might need a model." She licks her lips again.

"I have the perfect specimen at home in my garage."

"You have a '56 Blackbird?"

"I do. You should come see it, get a feel for it between your legs. Get a feel for me as well."

She's undressing before my eyes. I almost have a heart attack and start looking for Monster Bro before I realize she's got shorts and a girly top on underneath her scrubs. Her hair comes down out of the pony tail and flows over her gorgeous breasts that are accentuated by the tightly stretched fabric of the Sick Boyz shirt. The next thing I know she's applying some red lip gloss and snapping her compact closed. "I'm ready."

"I have to admit," I say with an air of admiration as I slip my shirt back on. "I'm fucking impressed with that little display." I hold my hand out to her and she takes it, then snags the drawing up off the counter as I pull her out of the room and down the hall.

Monster Bro is about to bark at her when we appear holding hands, but Bombs just slaps the drawing down on the counter. "He's got this in his garage, he wants me to tattoo it on his back, so I'm going to see it in person."

Monster Bro is stunned silent so we make our escape and practically run to my truck. I open her door and she quickly slides in as I go around to my side. Her brother is just opening the door to object to what's happening when I start up the truck, check for traffic, and pull out into the northbound lane of College Avenue.

"I live out in Bellvue, that OK?"

"Why would it be a problem?" She's got her foot up on the seat, her elbow propped on it, just looking at me. Whatever I did back in that shop, it changed her mind about me. And I'm not sure if it's the drawing or the fact that I have a '56 Bird in my garage, but at this point, I really do not care.

"You hardly know me. I'm taking you to a farmhouse in the middle of nowhere. I'm a known criminal."

She frowns. "So you are guilty?" It's a question, like she wants to believe I'm innocent, but she also wants to hear the truth.

"They dropped the charges for a reason, Bombshell. Let it go. I'm not the guy they made me out to be on the news. I'm not that guy."

She chews on her lip for a moment and then digs through her purse and pulls out her pink .38. "I've got my gun. So if you mess with me, I'll just put some bullets in it and make you sorry." She's laughing before she finishes her sentence.

I shake my head. "You should never carry an unloaded gun, Ronnie." She blushes at the nickname. I'm not sure why, I've got a shitload of nicknames for her a helluva lot more erotic than Ronnie. But I note this for future reference. "You might only get one chance to save your life with that gun. It needs to be loaded so when opportunity knocks, you're ready."

"I don't know how to shoot," she reluctantly admits after a few seconds' pause. "My dad and brothers never taught me. I bought the gun to piss them off, but I never learned how to shoot it. I don't even know what kind of bullets it takes. I've been wanting to learn for a long time though."

"Oh, baby," I say wistfully. This is a girl after my own heart. "You're talking to the right guy. I've got a shooting range on my property. I'll teach you the basics, then I'll put you on my gun club membership and buy you some marksmanship classes."

Her eyes light up. "OK," she says through her smile. "Wow." She laughs a little. "I think you just changed my life, Spencer Shrike."

"That was the plan, Bombshell. That was always the plan."

We drive in silence after that. She looks out the window as I make my way across the countryside until I come to my driveway. "Who do you live here with?" she asks as I pull past the house and park the truck next to the shop building out back.

"Just me. I inherited this house last year. I figure my life could use some slowing down, so I decided not to get an apartment near school and just drive in every day."

She jumps out, her hair waving in the wind. "What do you do out here all alone?" She follows me to the door and I unlock it and wave her through, flipping the switch for the lights as I pass in behind her.

She gasps in surprise as she takes in the room.

"I build bikes, Veronica Vaughn. I make custom bikes. You recognized a Triumph Thunderbird from a drawing, and at least one brother rides, so I know you have some knowledge about bikes. But what I don't know is if that interest is really you or just a byproduct of your upbringing."

Her fingertips caress the cherry-red tank on a custom piece I've been working on all summer and then she walks straight over to the Blackbird and swings her leg over. She looks damn good on that bike. "I could ask you the same question, Spencer Shrike." She grips the handles and leans over like she's pretending to ride. How fucking cute is that?

"I learned to love them as a kid, but these bikes are my future. Can you ride?"

She shakes her head no. "My dad and brothers." This seems to be a common theme with her.

"So they run your life?"

"Yes," she laughs. "They do. I live at home. I don't make enough to move out and get my own place, I don't have a lot of clients yet. I just started at the shop a few weeks ago."

"Well, I can't blame them, really. If I had a sister as perfect as you, I'd never let her leave home or ride a bike either."

She smiles up at me from under her blonde hair. It's covering her bright blue eyes. "What about shoot a gun?"

I walk over to her and swing my leg over, sitting behind her. She hisses out an exhale, like I just surprised her. When I wrap my arms around her waist, she moans. "Guns are a lot safer than bikes, Ronnie," I whisper in her ear. "Shooting is something you should know how to do." I flatten my hands against her belly, then slip them inside the bottom of her tank top.

She draws in a breath.

"Do you want me to stop, Ronnie?"

Veronica hesitates and I pull back, but her hands grab mine and hold them to her body, tightly. "No, I don't want you to stop." She looks over her shoulder at me, her mouth open, her chest rising and falling faster than it was a few seconds ago.

I lean into her neck and kiss the soft skin, right under her ear.

She shudders.

"Oh, hell," she sighs. "Maybe you should stop."

I pull back immediately. "I will if you really want me to. But Veronica—" I reach up to turn her chin towards me. She has to reposition herself a little to look me in the eye. "Don't say no because it's expected of you. Or because you're afraid I might hurt you. Or because it's too soon. Because you're mine, baby. I knew the moment I saw you last week, outside the bookstore having it out with your brother over something. I watched you stand your ground and toss your hair at the same time. And I told myself, *She's mine. I need her. I don't know her, but I will.* And now I do. And I want you. Not just for tonight, not for just a weekend, not for just this semester to pass the time, not just to get some kickass ink on my body. I want you for all those things, but I want them indefinitely."

She lets out a long breath. "Holy shit, that's sorta deep. What's that even mean? Indefinitely?"

"It means I'm here, for as long as you want me."

"But you don't even know me, Spencer."

"I've watched you for weeks. I know all I need to know."

She's silent for a moment, and then she stands up and turns around and straddles the long black leather seat, facing me. "What do you want me to say?"

I smile. "When I ask if I can touch you tonight, I want you to say yes. When I ask if I can kiss you tonight, I want you to say yes. When I ask if I can have you tonight, I want you to say yes. Just say yes, Ronnie. I want you to say yes. One word, that's it. One word is all it takes. And I really will change your life."

Her eyes dart back and forth, searching my face. I can almost hear her thoughts. Running all the questions through her mind, past conventional expectations. Past her father's opinion of her. Past her brothers' reactions if they find out she gave in to me after knowing me less than twenty-four hours.

And then she closes her eyes and whispers, "Yes."

I rub her bare thighs, causing her to shiver, and then I grab the hem of her tank top and lift it over her head, revealing her breasts, perfectly cradled inside a lacy pink bra. "I knew it would be pink," I whisper as I toss the shirt and pull her chest right up to mine. "I've pictured you in this moment a thousand times over the past few weeks, and those fantasies don't even come close to how beautiful you look to me right now."

Her perfectly manicured fingernails grab the hem of my shirt next. I let her do it herself because she drags those nails up my abs and then pushes it over my head, leaning in, pressing her breasts up against me. I grab her around the waist again, pulling her fully into me, my mouth on hers, probing with my tongue. She parts her lips, allowing me entrance, suddenly panting from her rapidly racing heart.

My hand goes to her chest so I can feel the thumping I've created, then I slip her bra down over her soft mounds and squeeze. "Your tits are fucking fabulous. I'd like to stick my dick between them and fuck your mouth at the same time."

She gasps as her eyebrows hike up. "Oh, my God!"

"Do you like the dirty talk, Bombshell? Does it turn you on?"

She looks like she wants to reply, but words evade her, so she simply nods.

"I'll keep it to myself if it bothers you, but you should know, my mind will be thinking these dirty things every time I'm around you, Bombshell. Because once I have this"—I look hungrily down at her body—"I'll never forget it. I will undress you, reliving the scent of your pussy, every time I see you. My fingers will be reliving how I make your nipples bunch up against my touch. My cock will be reliving how good it feels when you clamp yourself around me."

"Oh, my God!" she moans. "Don't stop talking. Holy fuck, Spencer. Please, don't stop! I like it."

I unbutton her little jean shorts and smack her thigh. "Stand up and take these off."

She stands up and swings her leg over the bike seat, then shimmies her hips until the shorts fall to the ground around her wedge-heeled sandals. She kicks them off to the side and stands in front of me. "Now you, Spencer."

I shoot her a crooked, devious, filthy grin. "Now me, what?" I growl. "If you want something from me, you have to ask for it. And if you expect me to deliver, you better be descriptive."

She blushes and my wood is petrified, that's how fucking hard I am for this girl. She doesn't ask, she just takes. She slips out of her panties and straddles the bike again, her legs open and her wet pussy exposed. She goes for the button on my jeans and I stop her hand.

"You want my cock, Ronnie? You want me to take it out and fuck your tits and your mouth?"

She pants harder now. "Yes."

"Say it, Bomb. Tell me why you want it, or I won't give it to you. I'll tease you and leave you to suffer. If you want me, you have to ask for it. You have to ask for it the exact way you want it, Veronica. If you want my cock in your mouth, tell me. If you want my cock between your perfect tits, say it. If you want to suck me until I come down your throat—fuck, baby. Just ask. I'm ready."

She stares up at me, her ragged breath a total betrayal of her desires. But I stay still and quiet as I wait her out.

"I want you," she finally whispers. "I want—" She stops to swallow hard and closes her eyes. Her cheeks flush red with embarrassment, but she forces the words out anyway. "I want your cock between my tits, Spencer. I want you to fuck me in my mouth." She squeezes her tits together and wiggles her pussy against the hard thickness pressing up against my jeans.

I can't take the restraint anymore, so I get off the bike and strip off the jeans. I'm still commando from this morning's modeling job, and His Highness is ready for battle.

I sit back down and look down at her pussy. It's so wet her juices are almost flowing out onto the black leather bike seat. I grab her hips and pull, bringing her beckoning sex within easy reach of my throbbing cock. "Lie back, baby. I'm gonna take you now. I'll get to your tits and your mouth later, but right now I'm gonna fuck you good. I'm gonna make you squirt. Are you a squirter, Bombshell?" I push her until she falls back against the tank. "I bet I can find out right now." I slip two fingers inside her and thrust, fast and hard. She buckles and screams, wiggling against my palm, which probably stimulates her more. I pull my fingers out quickly once her muscles begin to clamp. "You are, baby. You are most definitely a squirter. But I'm not gonna let you off that easy. If you want that, you can ask for it next time."

"Oh. My God," seems to be her standard answer tonight. I've got her off balance. She's not sure what to make of me, but her wet pussy says she's OK with that for now. I ease forward and she moans out, "Please, Spencer, just fuck me! Please!"

I do fuck her on the '56 Blackbird. She screams my name four times. We almost topple the damn thing over with our antics and I could care less. That bike can be repaired, but this first dirty fuck with my Bombshell, that's never gonna happen again.

It's a once-in-a-lifetime thing.

It's a change-my-life-forever thing.

It's a falling-in-love-and-lust thing.

It's a recognizing-my-best-friend thing.

And it's the day I decide—this girl is mine.

Forever.

# CHAPTER SEVEN

***I pull myself*** out of the past and sigh. It's not going to end this way, that's for damn sure. It's not. I've been planning for my moment for years and that shit is just about in reach. I refuse to submit to circumstances.

I glance up at the clock on the wall and realize it's already ten o'clock. I might as well go back into town early, just in case Ronnie thinks she can duck out and evade me at closing time. I grab my keys and my phone and head down to the buildings on the far end of the property where I keep the surveillance van. Ford's robot shit is in there and I won't have time to come back to the house before meeting him at midnight.

I key open the garage and walk into the darkness. A stray beam from the outside security light bounces off a chrome fender and distracts me for a moment. I reach over to the wall and flip on the light.

My old Chevy truck—the same one I drove around town when I first moved out here, the same one I met Ronnie in—is staring back at me. One of my mechanics borrowed it last week when his truck was out of commission. He must've parked it in the wrong bay.

I suddenly have an overwhelming need to drive this truck into town to see Ronnie. Maybe I can talk her into going for a drive and it will spark a memory in her? A memory that reminds her that we're good together. I fish around in a drawer where I keep an extra set of keys, then reach inside the surveillance van and pull out Ford's case. I think there's a computer in there, but I really have no idea. He locks that shit up tight. It's not really a briefcase, it's a portable safe. You'd break whatever's inside opening it up without a key, and even if you ever did access Ford's computer, he's got an automatic kill switch on the drive if you get the password wrong just once. We learned our lesson the last time his shit was breached. Almost cost us life in prison. We don't make the same mistakes twice so the password kill is more than a just-in-case precautionary measure. And Ford never forgets a password. There is no need for a second chance.

I check the back of the van for anything else we might need, but it's clean back here, so I get in the old Chevy, set the case down on the passenger seat, and pull out of the garage.

The ride back into FoCo is nothing but a whole lot of time to stew in all the mistakes I've made over the past few years. I'm second-guessing everything. The team, the jobs, the revenge, the bailouts. All of it had consequences we never saw coming.

But there's nothing we can do about that now. We just need to move forward and clean it up as best we can.

The only thing I don't regret is how I've handled Ronnie. In her case, I did everything right. I made sure of it. I covered all my tracks, I left no trace, I have kept her as far from me as possible for as long as possible. New Year's was the first time I slept with her in months. And that was a private party. We stayed the night in Rook's old garden apartment. We never left the building together. I made sure I was gone in the morning when she woke up.

The time before that it was just after Rook spilled her guts about her life on national TV and got more than a hundred people arrested in the process. People lined up outside Chaput Studios with giant signs. One proclaimed her a lying whore. And that was one of the nicer signs. She wasn't even living there, she was here with me. But as soon as those monsters found that out, they parked at the end of my driveway.

I smile. They made the mistake of assuming that the road leading up to my house was public. It's not. It's my road, all three miles of it. It's on my fucking land, which makes that land my fucking home. Which means I can shoot those fuckers if the right situation arises and it's totally legal according to Colorado law.

I never got my chance to shoot anyone, but I did beat the shit out of a reporter who was hiding in the trees near the river in back of my house.

The county deputies pretty much had it after that. They cleared them all out under the pretense that it was a fire hazard. A few years ago this whole area was up in flames, so people tend to take that fire talk seriously around here.

Rook survived. Ford was here, Ronin was here. The Biker Channel hired security. She never had to leave if she didn't want to, she worked in my shop while we were filming and did her classes online. Ford fired that piece-of-shit tutor who ratted us out and helped Rook in her college math class himself. I even got Ronin to do her delivery duties.

We protected her one hundred percent. But her situation was unique.

For instance, Ronnie works in a tattoo shop downtown. If she doesn't work, she doesn't make money. She can't pay her bills. Her family is not rich. Hell, they're not even middle-class. They might be the token white trash of Fort Collins. They do have a big-ass house in the historic district, but they have that house for one reason only—Gramps won it in a poker game back in 1958. It's not in good repair. The place is freezing-ass cold in the winter because the furnace is so old it hardly functions, and the roof has been leaking since I met her.

And Ronnie might have a pack of badass brothers and a father who'd drop you with one kick to the throat, but the doors don't even lock on that house. The windows barely shut. The only reason it's never been robbed is because the Vaughn clan scares the shit out of people.

If Ronnie was thrust into the public eye like Rook was, she'd never make it. The entire family would be annihilated. They'd lose their business, they'd be hounded day and night. And there's no way to restrict picketers on a public sidewalk in downtown like I can do on my little backcountry private road.

There's just no way to keep her safe other than the way I've been doing it. Ignoring her.

The minute anyone finds out this girl is my future Mrs. Spencer Shrike, people will pounce. And while I can handle that at any other time—I could get her out of here and put her somewhere safe, I could make sure the Vaughn clan gets Sick Boyz' rent paid on time, I could drum up business for them with some word-of-mouth buzz—I cannot do any of that shit right *now*.

We've got a major trial happening in two weeks. Rook will need to testify about the most horrific details of her previous life. They will try their best to link Ronin, Ford, and myself to a shitload of crimes that took place several years ago. I cannot be worrying about Ronnie and her family.

It's just not a good time.

I turn off College Avenue before I get to Ron's shop and park the truck on Maple, right next to my new building. It used to be an auto repair place a few years ago, but that went under and no one picked it back up. The Biker Channel loved the location, just past all the cute shops in downtown so we won't offend anyone with our loud bikes. Plus, it's already set up for a shop.

I get out of the truck and walk up to it, just checking shit out. The windows are all boarded up still. No one's supposed to see inside until the grand opening and the crews won't even start painting the outside for another week.

Not much to see, so I head down the street towards Sick Boyz. It's still packed when I get there. All those frat guys are milling about outside waiting on their brothers to be finished. They're drunk and I don't like it.

I check my phone for the time. Ten forty-five. And just as I look up, Ronnie comes plowing through the doors in a rush. I slink back against the building, hiding in the crowd of guys as she looks up and down the street, probably checking to see if I'm doing recon on her ass. One of the guys outside the shop whistles at her and she flips him the bird and tells him to fuck off as she walks off towards home.

I start to laugh, but it dies in my throat because she stops at Mountain Avenue and hits the walk button. This is where things get interesting. Because her house is west, and that signal is for crossing College Avenue to the east.

My legs are in motion before my brain fully understands what's happening. I'm an act-now-think-later kinda guy, so I take off after her. Where the fuck is she going? It's late, it's dark, she's got no car—she should not be walking around downtown alone. Not that this town is unsafe *per se*, but bad shit happens everywhere. Even here. And it's a college town, which means there's always the threat of predators.

She walks briskly on Mountain, then turns abruptly into an alley. I hang back. My Ronnie is not stupid. She never looked back at me, but I taught her to keep walking if she ever thought she was being followed. Keep quiet for as long as possible and get that gun ready. I stalk up to the corner and wait. I know she's on the other side, ready to pounce on anyone who appears. I can feel her when she's this close. Like we're connected. I can almost hear her heartbeat, that wild heartbeat that drives me crazy beating against mine as she lies on top of me after sex.

I hear an exhale, then the pounding of her Chucks as she beats a retreat. I poke my head around and catch her disappearing around another corner. But this is not a street, it's a building. I cross the alley and stalk the wall, getting to her corner just in time to hear a screen door slam.

What the fuck is she doing?

I peak around the corner just as some lights flip on in an upstairs apartment over an old building.

That little sneak got her own place. Her car is out back, parked. And sure enough, there's a For Sale sign on it. And she's dating some rich guy. I bet she's got new panties on as well! That uptight fuckass banker is enjoying my Bomb's new panties!

I'll kill him.

I walk over to the stairs and try my best to be quiet as I ascend, but they are wooden. And old. And squeaky. Suddenly the door is kicked open and a gun is pressing against my cheek. "Move one inch, motherfucker. I'll blow your teeth out the other side of your head!"

"Whoa there, Ron, it's me, baby."

She pulls the gun off my face. "Holy hell, Spencer! You scared the fuck out of me! I thought you were gonna break in and rape me!"

"Well…" I chuckle a little. She does not find my joke funny. At all. "Sorry, Veronica. I was waiting for you outside the shop and saw you walking the wrong direction. I just needed to see what's up."

"It's none of your business what I do." She pulls the screen door open and walks into her place.

I follow her in and stalk her to the kitchen, where she grabs a beer from the fridge and then pushes past me and plops herself down on the raggedy thing some might call a couch.

"So… you moved out? Why? And what's this shit about you selling your car? I bought you that for graduation. "

She kicks her Chucks up on the battered coffee table and twists off her beer cap. "I'm twenty-three, Spencer. It's about time I left the nest, don't you think?"

"Uh…" No, not really. That's not what I think at all. I like her at home. I like her surrounded by Gramps and her father and little brother. Three related men in the house. Yes, that's something I can live with for a long time, thank you. But I say none of that. My Shrike Sense is tingling. I feel a declaration of independence coming from my little Ron. So I sit down next to her and try to be reasonable. "Ronnie, this place is a dump. You can't stay here."

She takes a swig of her Fat Tire and lets out a long, "Ahhhhh." Totally ignoring me.

I decide on the subtle approach. "So how long is the lease? Please tell me it's a month-to-month."

She flips the TV to Comedy Central. There's an *Ab Fab* marathon and I get a little distracted for a second. But then I snap out of it and take my attention back to her. "Veronica, answer me. Why are you living in this dump?"

She laughs as Patsy smokes a joint on TV, then drags her eyes over to me. "If you're here to fuck me tonight, the answer is no. I have a boyfriend."

"What? Yeah, me! I'm the boyfriend!" I stand up and pace. This has gone too far now. "Please tell me you're not seeing that banker asshole. Because I swear—"

"Dammit! Who told you that? Ford? Did Ford tell you? I'll kill his ass."

"I saw you together at dinner, Veronica. What the fuck is up? And I still want to know why the fuck you're living in this alleyway shithole."

She snorts out a laugh and shakes her head. "You have no clue, Spencer. None." She looks over at me again, only now her eyes are filled with anger. "You really think that you can saunter in here and demand my attention?" She stands up and points at me. "You really think I give a fuck what you think about my home? Fuck you. I'm not ashamed of this place." She looks around the apartment and points to the art affixed to the walls with thumb tacks, and then looks back at me. "I love this place. I *love* this place," she repeats with the emphasis. "You wanna know why I love this dumpy little shithole? I'll tell you. It's because it's *my* dumpy fucking shithole, you giant prick. I wasn't born to a wealthy family. I wasn't given a private education growing up. I didn't even have a fucking mother, you insensitive jerk. I had to claw my way through dinner every night. Fighting back four brothers for food. I had to submit to them at every turn. I had to fight them, for fuck's sake. When they got the itch to pick on me, whether it was in play or not. My life has been nothing but one long fucking struggle. And this"—she pans her hands wide to include all the space within her little apartment—"this is my reward. And maybe it's not up to your goddamned standards, but no one gives a fucking shit about you in this room except *you*, Spencer Shrike. And you do not deserve me. You don't. I'm a good person. I worked hard to get what I have. And maybe it's not a lot compared to what you have, but at least I got it honestly."

I just stare at her. Unable to move or even form a sentence.

"So fuck off. I've moved on, asshole. Get it through your thick skull. I'm not interested."

"Veronica," I say calmly. "You don't—"

My cheek is suddenly stinging with heat and Veronica is staring at her red palm, stunned that it actually struck out and hit me across the face.

She shakes herself out of her daze and points her finger at me again. "Don't you dare tell me what I think or what I feel. Don't you dare. I'm so fucking tired of people telling me things about myself they have no clue about. Every damn day I walk into Sick Boyz and swallow down the vomit. Do you know that about me, Spencer? You think you know me so well. Do you know that the smell of blood makes me sick? The sight of blood makes me sick? Not sick as in I might faint, or I might feel a little queasy, or that's sorta gross. But sick in a way that makes my heart beat so fast I think I might drop dead. It gives me panic attacks, Spencer. Every damn day I fight it off." Her whole body is shaking.

"Ronnie—" But I have nothing to say. "I didn't know that, no. I thought you liked it. It's art."

"*Art?*" She laughs and then the tears spill out. "Art? It's a fucking tattoo shop, you dumbass! I went to school for four years to study art and three years later I trace line drawings on skin. I have to cover myself head to toe in personal protection equipment because I am obsessed with the idea that I'll contract hepatitis through some innocuous cut on my arm. Did you ever once ask me why I cover the room in plastic?"

She stops her rant to let me think about this. Have I? "I don't need to ask, Ronnie. I know why."

"Why? Tell me why, then, if you're so fucking smart."

"You hate the blood and—"

"Wrong." She cuts me off. "That's not why. Do you realize no one—*no one*," she reiterates—"has ever asked me why I cover the room in plastic?"

I move towards her to bring her in my arms. She struggles against me but I'm so much bigger, it's hardly a problem. I wrap her up and pull her close to my chest so I can lean down in her ear and whisper, "You cover the room in plastic to protect people, Veronica. I've always known that was the reason."

She starts to cry and I just hold her close. This is an end-of-the-line meltdown my little Ronnie is having. She's good and strung out. Bad.

"I don't want to go there anymore, Spencer. I need this, OK? I need this so fucking bad. I can't think straight when I'm at work. All I see is the blood. And I finally have a chance to make a real change. This banker, Spencer. He's my chance. Please don't ruin it for me."

We stand there in silence for a few moments. I'm not enough for her right now, I can see that now. I can't give her what she needs because of my own stupid mistakes. This is her personal struggle and it's got nothing to do with me. "What do you want me to do, Ronnie?" And even though I already know what she's gonna say, it hurts me so fucking bad when the words finally come out.

"Leave me alone, Spencer. Just go. Leave me alone."

I swallow hard and shake my head. She doesn't try and pull away, she gives me this moment at least. "Veronica, if that's what you need, I'll go. But before I do, I'd like to have my say too." She stays silent so I push forward. "The day I saw you, my life started. My chest swelled with this feeling. A feeling I'd never felt before. When I watched you that first week before I made my move in art class, I realized something. I realized that the day I saw you my heart started to beat a whole new way. It was like all these years I had no idea what my heart was for, and then bam—you were there in front of me. And by the time I followed you to art class that day we got together, I had finally figured out what it was."

I blow out a long burst of air, not sure I should even be telling her this.

"Say the words, Spencer," she pleads through her soft sobs. "Because if I don't hear them, I'm gonna explode."

Her eyes are searching mine, pleading to make this better. Just begging me to fix this.

"It was like… it was like…" I take a deep breath. "It was like I was listening to some scratchy classic vinyl and then suddenly you appeared, and my whole world went digital. It's like life *shifted.* Everything became real. You make me real, Ronnie. You started my heart. You are the missing piece of me. We're partners, Ron. Soul mates. We are, I swear it. But—" She cries into my chest again and it stops me dead. I can't stand to see her cry. God, it hurts me to see her cry.

"I can't listen to the 'but', Spencer. I can't. Please don't make me listen to the 'but'. I just want you to say you love me."

"I love you, Veronica. I've always loved you."

She looks up at me, her eyes all red and watery. "Then *be* with me! Please!"

Fuck, her misunderstood sadness breaks my heart. "I want to say I'm with you, baby. I'll never leave you. But I can't say that. Not yet."

"Why?" She's a mess now. Her tears are spilling down her face like mad.

She pulls away and I bring her back. My hand comes up to cup her face. I tilt her chin up so she has to look me in the eyes when the words come out. "Because Veronica Vaughn,

I'm guilty. Every single thing they said about me on TV that year I met you…" I pause to try and gauge her reaction. But I have no idea what she's thinking, so I have no choice, I just have to say it. "Every single thing they said about me was true."

I can hear her stunned swallow and then she wriggles until I let her go.

And I do let her go. I have to let her go.

"It's all true, Ronnie. So if you need this banker to get what you want, then go do that. Because I am *this guy*, Veronica. This guy right here, this guy who did all those things all those years ago. This guy is me. And you're absolutely right. This guy doesn't deserve you."

# CHAPTER EIGHT

***I have to walk away***, so I turn towards the door.

"Spencer," she whispers.

"Veronica, I'm sorry, OK? I just need to go." I pull the screen door open and walk though, taking the steps two at a time, and then walk briskly around the corner of her building. When I get to the alley I lean against the wall and bend over to try and calm my racing heart. "Fuck!"

She probably heard that. I stand back up and walk down the alley towards Mountain Ave, then cut over and take Jefferson back up to Maple where my truck is parked at the shop. If she stays in that apartment at least she'll be close to me.

When I get to the truck I just sit there, trying to process what my life will be like without her around the edges. Frayed. That's what my life will be. Even though she wasn't in my life all the time, everything I did, everything I do, I do with her in mind. Every decision I make. Every person I spend time with. Every cent I spend. The first thing I do is ask myself, is this good for *us*? Will this make Ronnie and me stronger in the end? Will this make her happy?

I punch the steering wheel and my knuckles split open. "Fuck." My phone rings and I pull it out of my pocket. "Ford," I say. "On my way, dude."

I hang up before he can say anything and start the truck, then I head west and cut over to Mountain Avenue. Ford lives down the street from Ronnie's family house, in an old Victorian across from City Park.

He's waiting on the corner of Mountain and Frey so I pull over. He's dressed up in dark jeans and a black t-shirt, looking like a cat burglar. He pulls the door open and slides in. "Where's the fucking van? I have shit—" He sees the case on the floor. "Well, that does not explain why you're driving your personal vehicle while we're doing a job, Spencer."

"I just wanted to, Ford. No reason." I follow the road past his house and look hard at it. "You sneaking out tonight? That tiny wife of yours cracking the whip already?"

He flashes me a sardonic glare. "Right. The fucking dogs will hear the vehicle and have a hissy fit if you came to the house at night."

"Dogs?" I almost choke. "Since when are you an animal person?"

"I've always loved pets, Spencer," he says with a grin. And then he laughs that diabolical laugh of his and growls, "Don't be an idiot. They're not really *dogs*, they're employees. Security. I paid forty grand apiece for these fucking dogs. One wrong look at Ashleigh or Kate and they eat your face off."

"That does not sound safe, Ford."

"I'm half kidding. We had them trained and bonded specifically to us while we were in New Zealand. They are the best-behaved employees I've ever had." He stops for a moment. "Aside from Pam, of course. I cannot allow Ash or Kate to be hurt because our past is rushing up to greet us. I wanted to send them away, but I'd go out of my mind with worry if I didn't know where they were at all times. So I got dogs. They have service jackets, they can go anywhere a human can and they are trained to work as a team. One dog attacking you is frightening, two are formidable."

"I'd just give her a gun, Ford. Quicker and no shit to clean up."

"She has a gun, Spencer. But when you've got a baby in your arms, a gun is not practical."

"Security guard?"

"I have those too, but they need to stay hidden. Ashleigh has no idea what we're really into, Spencer, so keep your fucking mouth shut. I've got it all under control. We've moved into a normal house and I want them to have a normal life."

"Nice house, by the way. How the hell did you get all that shit organized from New Zealand? You've only been back for like three days."

"Pam."

"That personal assistant chick? Must be nice, eh? Have her to take care of things for you."

"It is, Spence. You know the Biker Channel wants you to get one, right? They've been hounding me about it for weeks. They say you hardly ever answer their calls and ignore the emails completely. You should just hire someone to take care of that shit."

"Yeah," I say. "Maybe I should. I could use the help. How close do you need me to be, Ford?" I hang a right on Elizabeth and then cut up north to where Drake's shop is.

"Just about the same place we were before. I didn't get the long-range option for this bot. That model was out of stock." He pulls the case up from the floor, keys in his passcode to disengage the locks, and then pops it open. When I glance over he's got a tablet in there and some smaller things tucked away in a bulging pocket on the inside of the lid. He fires up the tablet and then accesses some app on the home screen that controls the bot. A camera pops up in a new window, but the image is black.

"Night vision is standard," Ford says. Like I was actually wondering how much he pays for the fucking robot add-ons. "OK, here we go." The bot screen flashes green, and then some details start to emerge. "We're under a workbench, I think. Hold on, let me look around a little and see if this is acceptable. You might have to tell me where a good place will be, Spencer. A place that's in plain view, but not near something he needs every day. I don't mind losing the money

I paid for this should things go bad. But I certainly don't want this bot in the hands of that stupid fuck Drake. He will blab all over about it and even though I had Merc cover my tracks, Homeland will be called in and they will immediately know it was me. I'm already on a list for hacking."

I wince. We're doing this job because I asked for it. "Maybe we should just pull it, then, Ford? Maybe I should just eat the money and drop it. He won't last, I'm not really worried about him taking my business, I'm just excitable. I'm an artist. People buy my bikes because I made them. And he's not me."

Ford just stares at me. "Who are you?"

"I'm serious, Ford. Let's just come back tomorrow and—" A knock on the glass stops me cold and Ford's eyes dart to the window behind me. "Please tell me that's not the pigs," I say without turning my head to look.

Ford laughs under his breath. "It's Drake."

I turn in my seat so I can see and then slide the window down about an inch. "Can I help you?" I ask, peering out at him.

He's not as tall as me when I'm standing, so when I'm sitting in a big-ass truck, he looks minuscule. He's such a skinny little fuck.

He scowls at me, squinting his eyes as he tries to make out if it's really me behind the tinted glass window. "Shrike? I should've known. You're out here like a loser, spying on me? What the hell?"

"I'm sorry," I say politely. "Do I know you?" Ford chuckles off to my right. "Do we know this rat, Ford?" I lower the window another half an inch. "Oh, wait," I say sarcastically. "Yeah, we know this asshole. He's the poser who moved into my town, pretending to be me. You're not even worth my time, Fonzie." I catch the sound of the little bot being maneuvered from the tablet.

Drake squints his eyes and gives those thick black frames a push up his nose as he considers this. "Then would you care to explain why you're sitting outside my shop in the middle of the night?"

"We're smoking a doobie, Drake. And you're killing my fucking buzz, so shoo, little man. Just shoo."

Ford laughs again.

Drake sniffs the air, trying to smell me out. "You're not smoking in there."

"It's that new odorless blend out of Boulder, you idiot. Now scram."

Ford bursts out laughing, "Scram," he mutters. "What are you, a character in *Scooby-Doo*?"

I look over at him and laugh. "Yeah, scram. That's such a great word, isn't it? So underused." I turn back and Drake is still there. "Drake, if you have an opinion on the merits of the word 'scram', let's hear it. Otherwise, get the fuck out of here."

He does that little two-finger to the eyeballs gesture, pointing at me, then his peepers, and I laugh like a girl.

"I'm watching you, Shrike. I know you're up to something and if I catch you around my shop, I'll take care of business."

I roll the window back up as Drake walks away. "You get it parked, dude?"

"We're set," Ford says. "He really is annoying. I'm pretty sure he's not your guy though, Spencer. He's so stupid. How the hell did he get past your security outside the showroom, let alone move seven bikes through the back fucking door? It makes no sense. This guy is backed, that's for sure. But he's not the one who stole your shit."

"Maybe not. But he's part of it, whether he knows that or not. Whoever is behind Drake Cikes is my guy. And I'm not sure who that might be, but I'm gonna figure it out."

I pull the truck forward, do the double honk to Drake—who is still standing in the alleyway entrance to his shop—and turn right at the next street to go back towards town.

Ford lets out a huff as he thinks in silence for a few seconds. "I might've been wrong earlier. This might be something after all. And I'm with you on figuring it out. Maybe it's not connected to the trials coming up. Maybe Drake is just some guy who fell into some money and decided to give you a run for yours. And maybe those missing bikes are just bad luck on your part. Some past employee getting revenge or some shit like that."

I look over at him as I wait for the light at Mountain and College.

"But somehow I doubt it. I think whoever is backing Drake is absolutely the one we should be looking at about the missing bikes. But I also think that somehow, some way, all of this is tied to Rook."

"Rook?"

"Yeah," he sighs. "They might be sending messages. And your bikes might've just been the initial greeting."

We sit in silence as I make my way back down Mountain to Ford's house. I pull over at the corner of Frey, and he opens the truck door. "Just keep an eye out, Spencer. And for fuck's sake, don't do anything stupid without calling Ronin and me first."

I laugh. "Yeah, if we do something stupid, we should definitely do it together."

"That's what teams are for, brother."

"Later, dude. Tell your little dudettes I said hey."

He flashes me a two-finger salute and slams the door closed. I watch him walk up to the house and when he gets to the porch, the light flicks on. Ashleigh appears and for a minute I expect them to fight. I really did figure he had to sneak out to do this shit tonight. But she leans up on her tiptoes and plants a kiss on his cheek. He smiles broadly, and then ushers her back inside and the porch light goes dark.

I sigh.

How ironic is it that Ford has a fucking family before the rest of us? And even Ronin has Rook. At least he has her.

Me? I have no one.

# CHAPTER NINE

***I park the truck*** over by the shop and walk back down to Ronnie's alley once again. I know this is probably the wrong thing to do, but I can't help myself. When I reach the parking area below her apartment, I lean against the wall of the building next door and I dial her number.

She's awake, I know that for sure, even though it's almost one AM and all the lights are off save for the flickering bluish tint that comes from a TV. It rings. One… if she doesn't pick up I'll leave. Two… if she doesn't pick up, I'll go knock on the door. Three… her shadow walks across in front of the apartment window.

"What do you want, Spencer?" she answers curtly.

I swallow down the feelings her words evoke. Because it's crystal clear that she's really done with me.

"Hey, uh…" I clear my throat. "I've been thinking, ya know. How you work so hard and everything." I pause to see if she'll say anything. But all I hear is her soft breath. "And I was just talking to Ford. You know how he has that assistant who's been working for him in LA?"

"Spencer, get to the point, OK? I'm tired."

"Pam, right? You remember me talking about Pam? She works for Ford long-distance. You know, she does everything virtually. They almost never see each other."

"I'm hanging up."

"Bombshell, please." I hear a smile on the other end, I know it. "Just calm the fuck down for a minute, OK? I'm trying to tell you something."

She walks past the window again, then pulls the sheer curtains aside and peeks out. The moonlight hits her face and illuminates her blue eyes for a second before she drops the curtain and walks away. "Just tell me then, Spencer. I'm tired."

"Pam works as Ford's personal assistant. She runs his email and shit. Schedules things and, well, shit like that. You get it?"

She huffs. "Spencer, I know what a PA does, just fucking spit it out. What's Pam got to do with this conversation?"

"Ford and Pam go way back. Since college. But the Biker Channel has a budget for a PA, so she got a raise when he started working for them. They have a small budget for each of us. Rook included. And they've been on me for a while to hire someone since I ignore them most of the time. And I was wondering if you'd like the job?"

She laughs. "You're kidding me, right?"

"It's not a huge deal, my budget is only forty grand a year—"

"No, thank you."

"—and benefits—"

"No."

"—and paid holidays."

"I said no, Spencer. I'm not interested."

"It starts next Monday. Hours are variable—"

"What fucking part of 'no' do you not understand?"

"I'd need you on call almost all the time, but I wouldn't be unreasonable, ya know?"

"I'm really hanging up now."

"I'd let you do your thing. Work the tattoo shop. Or—" I stop to wait and see if she's gonna hang up. But I hear her breathing. "Or whatever else you'd like to do. You could quit the shop, Ronnie."

Silence.

"You could do something else. Date someone else. Start a new life, if that's what you want. I won't interfere."

I get the three quick beeps that says the call is dead and I look up at her window. She paces back and forth a few times, and then her shadow disappears. There's no more movement, but the TV stays on.

I sit out there for more than an hour, leaning back against the wall. Watching her get up and occasionally grace me with a shadow. And at two thirty the place finally goes dark and I walk back to my shop. I open the side door, go inside, and flip on the lights.

This place is my dream realized. Everything in this shop is all I've ever wanted in a bike business. There's six bays with bike lifts, custom tool kits with more than a hundred thousand dollars in equipment. The cinder block walls are painted red and black and there are reproductions of my tattoos covering every inch. Blackbirds, rooks, crows, and ravens. Everywhere.

Ronnie says she traces line drawings on skin. Fuck, she could not be more wrong. To me, the art on my body is just as beautiful as any classical piece hanging in a museum. Veronica Vaughn is the Renoir of the tattoo world.

I walk past Rook's reception area. She's gonna run the showroom and the desk this season and she won't be answering calls. The showroom is open to the public, but bike appointments won't be made over the phone. In fact, we've got the entire year scheduled. Everyone had to put up a fifty grand deposit to get a Shrike bike this year and Season Two will tape on and off for almost six months instead of the three months we've been doing. We'll deliver a new bike to one high-profile customer each episode, and we'll do that twelve times.

This is it. This is what it looks like.

Success.

My eyes sweep to my office door and I walk past the reception area towards it. My name is on the door, done up in the fancy Shrike Bikes font. Yeah, I have my own font. People will be able to download it for free from the website. I open the heavy maple door and wave my hand in front of the light sensor so I can take a good long look at my future. I turn back to my bay, which is even more tricked out with a custom-airbrushed tool chest that has the Shrike Raven painted on the front.

I turn back to the office and walk around the massive stainless steel table that's been custom-fabricated and welded into my throne. This is where I'm going. This is where I've been headed since I turned eighteen and decided I would take this business over. This is the pinnacle of my dream.

And for some reason, it's just not that sweet.

I drop down into the soft black leather chair. It's so fucking luxurious I actually feel myself relax.

But none of this means anything to me right now. Because the only reason I was working so hard towards this future was so I could share it with Ronnie.

And she wants out. She's done. I see it. I'm not delusional. I'm not one of those guys who wants to force himself on a woman and make her submit to his advances. Trick her into telling him how she feels, how she can't live without him.

I'm not like that. I want my Ronnie, but I only want her if she wants me.

And right now, she hates my fucking guts.

I lean back in my chair, looking up at the ceiling. Thinking about how this might go.

I snap back to the present after a while and reach into my pocket for Carson Reed's ID. He lives up north, not that far from me actually, but in a new neighborhood filled with those up-and-coming professional types.

Carson Reed is the key, I figure. I get up and walk back into the reception area, then scribble a note on the work order board telling the guys I won't be in tomorrow. Today. When I look up at the new Shrike Bikes clock with my face staring back at me, it's just about four in the morning.

They can live without me for one day, because I've got business to take care of.

# CHAPTER TEN

***I sit inside*** the backseat and just bide my time, tired as fuck, but amped up at the same time. It's almost six AM now. Pretty soon. After I'm done here I'll just go home and crash, because I am dog-assed tired. Then I'll have my date with Carla tonight and life will move forward.

Whether I want it to or not.

And I do want it to move forward. I really do. This in-between shit is wearing me down. I need this trial to be over. I need this bullshit to be put behind me. I need to be able to look myself in the face again.

The door to the garage opens and I sigh.

Finally. The guy takes his goddamned time getting ready. He fumbles with his remote key and doesn't even notice when the alarm doesn't chirp. He's got his arms full of folders and crap and he sets all that down on the roof as he pulls the door open. The dome light stays off, but he's too preoccupied with his phone to notice that either.

Man, this guy is dumb.

He shoves his shit over on the seat next to him, then closes the door and starts the car. It's not until he presses the button on the garage door opener that he finally figures out something is wrong.

I point the gun at his head and say, "Bang, motherfucker. You're dead."

He stiffens and takes in a sharp breath, but he keeps his mouth shut, and that's the first smart thing he's done since I saw him yesterday.

"You know why I'm here, Carson Reed?"

He eyes me in the rear-view and nods.

"Why?"

"Uh…" He clears his throat and tries again. "You're Veronica's… friend. You own that bike shop."

"Well, you got the who down, but I asked you if you know the why."

He swallows hard. "You love her?"

"I do love her. That's exactly why I'm here. What time were you gonna call her and tell her no?"

He squints his eyes at me. "What?"

"Time, motherfucker. What time were you gonna call her today and tell her no?"

"How do you know I was going to call her?"

"Carson, do not fuck with me, OK? What time?"

He stares at me, and maybe it's possible he doesn't know what I'm talking about, but somehow I doubt it. "Four."

"Right before closing? That's a dick move."

"Mr. Shrike, I'm not sure what you think is going on with her and I—"

"She wants a loan, right? To start a business? I'm not sure what, but something that is not tattoos."

"Uh, yeah." He shakes his head. "Then why are you here? I thought you wanted to kill me for finding us together at dinner."

I laugh. "Oh, I do. Believe me. I do. But I need you and there's that little matter of murder being illegal. So no, I'm not going to kill you. I need you."

"For what?" he asks, his voice cracking a little.

"How much money did she ask for?"

"Twenty, why?"

"Twenty grand? And you were gonna tell her *no*?" Fuck, twenty grand. I have that stuffed in my fucking sock drawer at home. I sigh. "Well, Carson, you're not gonna make that call at four, OK? You're gonna make that call at nine AM. You're gonna get her on the phone and you're gonna tell her yes. With conditions."

"I can't, Mr. Shrike! She's got no co-signer, she makes less than two thousand dollars a month, and she's got no down—"

"Carson," I interrupt him, using my angry voice. "Shut the fuck up and listen. You will call her, you will tell her yes. But then once she's all happy and screaming with joy, you tell her the conditions. She needs to have a full-time job. She needs to make thirty-seven grand a year. She needs to buy something big to establish her credit, like a car. And she needs to have all that in a week, or your boss will yank the application and make her reapply. You tell her the reapplication process is more grueling. Tell her once she gets turned down, it's a black mark. You tell her she needs to hustle this shit up pronto, you got it, Carson?"

He just stares at me.

"Carson? I asked you a fucking question."

"Uh, yeah. But… *why*?"

"Why?" I laugh. "You got it right the first time, asshole. I love her. I want her to be happy. I can't be with her right now for obvious reasons, but that doesn't mean I'm gonna let her go. So you're gonna do me one more favor. You're gonna take her out on dates. Nice places, dinners—"

Carson Reed throws his hands up. "No. Absolutely not. I can't do that, Mr. Shrike. She's…" He stops and physically turns all the way around. "She's…"

"What? She's what?"

"Intense, Mr. Shrike."

"Dammit, quit fucking calling me that. It's Spencer."

"Spencer," he says hurriedly. "She's way out of my league. She's not my type. I mean, she's gorgeous and she's got, well, you know what she's got. But I don't like the wild ones, I like the quiet ones. And Veronica Vaughn is always on the verge of exploding, that's how wound up she is. She's the opposite of *calm*, Spencer. Wild isn't even a wild enough term to describe this girl. She's like a loose cannon, she's like fireworks, she's like—"

"A bomb," I say, cutting him off. I smile. I love this characterization of my Bombshell. She's feisty.

"She's not into me, I'll tell you that right now. I'm not into her. We went on one real date awhile back, but I pretty much knew it would never work right away. She just needs a loan and I've been stringing her along because I didn't want to hurt her feelings. And I'll tell you now, my boss will *never* approve her loan. She's risky—"

"I'm the fucking bank, Reed. God, you are dumb for being so fucking smart. I'm giving her the money, asshole. Just do as I tell you and I'll have that dough deposited into her account in thirty days. It'll look like it came from your bank. All you have to do is make the call today, tell her the conditions, and take her out somewhere fancy and treat her nice, once a week."

"What if she won't go out with me?"

"Make her go, Reed. You tell her you're just friends if you want, but you will take her out and treat her nice once a fucking week."

He squints his eyes at me and then turns so he's facing forward again. "Well, what do I get out of it? You're obviously not going to kill me, so what's my motivation?"

So he does have a spine. That's good to know. "What do you want?"

He smiles in the rear-view, like a kid grinning ear to ear. "A custom bike."

I laugh. "A custom bike? From me? That's like a hundred grand, Reed."

"Welllll," he says, drawing the words out slowly. "She's worth it, right?"

Damn. The pencil-pusher's got me.

"I want one of those bikes you make and I want to have a say in what it looks like. I think that's fair."

I shrug. What do I care. He's doing me a business favor, I can do him one back. "OK, stop by my house shop tonight and we'll work out the details. But Carson, I need her to understand she must have a job, OK? I offered her a job working for me as my personal assistant a few hours ago. I need her to call me *today* and give me a yes. Push that. Get her to make the call and accept my offer, without letting her know you know about it, and we're on. I'll make you any bike you want."

He turns around in his seat again and we shake on it. "Deal."

# CHAPTER ELEVEN

***It's six o'clock*** by the time she makes the call. "Spencer?" she asks after my cheerful, "Yello."

"I thought you hated me, Bombshell? You love me again?"

She sighs and I beam a smile over at Carson. He thumbs me up as he peruses the catalog of accessories for his fucking custom bike.

"Spencer, I've been thinking about your offer. It was very generous. And—" I can actually hear her swallow, that's how loud it is. She's having trouble eating her crow, but I let her stew. She needs to eat the whole bird tonight. Feathers and all. Because she's just not seeing the big picture and I need to her pay attention to what the fuck I'm trying to accomplish here. "I'd like to take you up on that job offer. If it's still available," she adds quickly.

"Well, I was gonna offer it to Carla, the burrito girl at Big City, but I haven't talked to her yet. I don't pick her up for our weekly date until eight."

I can almost feel Ronnie's seething anger over the phone. I look over at Carson and he's shaking his head at me. I put up a hand and wink.

"Well, I want the job. So is it available or not?"

She's mad now and I smile. I like my Bombshell on the verge of exploding. That's the only way I know she's OK. When she's quiet and contemplative, that's when I know she's having trouble. Ronnie is tough as nails, and while *I* understand she really wants to be treated tenderly, she's just not there yet. So the bad-girl routine is all she's got.

"Veronica," I say softly so I can set her back a little.

"Yes?"

"Even if I did offer Carla that job, I'd never choose her over you, baby. Never."

She snorts. "That's funny. You have a date with her tonight though, right?"

"Yes, that's right."

"So if I ask you to take me out instead of her, would you?"

"No, baby. I can't."

"But I can have a job?"

"Yes. The job is yours."

"That makes no sense, Spencer Shrike."

"That's because you have no details, Veronica Vaughn."

"Enlighten me."

"Someday, Bomb. Someday I'll tell you everything. From start to finish. But not tonight." She's silent after that. She might even be crying. "It's a virtual job, remember?"

"Yes," she squeaks out.

"I'll text you all the info to access my email accounts on Monday. We'll start there for now. We don't need to see each other, just texts and phone calls. Got it?"

She's silent for almost ten seconds before she manages to acknowledge me. "Got it, Spencer. I'll talk to you Monday then."

"Right. Oh, and Ronnie?"

"Yeah?" she comes back with some hope in her voice.

"I think you should date that banker. If he's still interested, that is. Because I had Ford check him out, and he's a good guy. I'd like for you to find yourself a good guy, Ronnie. So if I've screwed anything up, I'm sorry. Maybe try and explain I'm just a dick and you're done with me."

This time when she answers I know she's crying. She manages an, "OK," and then the phone beeps three times and the call is over.

"Shit, Shrike," Carson says from his perch on my crappy desk. "That was fucked up."

"She'll get over it, Reed. Just do your part and I'll do mine. You got an idea what you want? Because I really do have to meet Carla soon."

Carson shakes his head at me. "What the hell? Why are you seeing other girls if you love the Bombshell?"

I sigh. "Carla and I go line-dancing on Thursday nights. Ronnie loves to line-dance but I've never gone with her because I just can't afford to be seen with her in public like that. But soon, I *will* be dating her, Carson. Soon. So I'm getting ready for that day. Carla offered to teach me and every Thursday night we practice at the Sundance Saloon. Fridays, I hang out with Renee from the Cat Call. I watch the strippers so people think I'm available. And Renee is the bartender. She flirts with me and I keep an extra eye out for her when the bar gets crazy. They have shit bouncers over there. Saturdays I hang out with Kim from the Broomfield Harley store. She's on a bowling league down there. Ronnie's brothers have a bowling league up here in FoCo. And as soon as life settles down, I'm in. I want to insert myself into Ronnie's life. I want to be accepted by her family and I figure bowling with them is a good way to do that."

Carson laughs a little. "So you're not fucking any other girls?"

"Hell the fuck no. I haven't had a bit of fucking fun since New Year's when I saw Ronnie last. This trial shit, Carson—this trial shit is big fucking time. These people are not playing around. My friends and I are in deep, man. I do not have time to fuck, or drink, or worry about shit like that. Hell, I barely have time to think about the show."

"You really do love her?" He looks at me hard now. Like he's changing his opinion of me on the spot.

"I really do. But by the time I get my chance to tell her, she might not love me back."

"Well, fuck. I really had no clue."

"That's how it has to stay, Reed. You got it? No one can know I love her. No one. Did you see what happened to Rook Corvus last fall?"

Carson nods his head. "Yeah, I felt sorry for her."

"Well, my Ronnie will not survive that. OK? She won't. I cannot have those filthy reporters following her around like animals, trying to ruin her life and make her freak out for the cameras. Rook has no ties to anyone but us. She was easy to protect. Ronnie has all kinds of family. There are so many ways to get to her. So many people she loves who can be hurt to get even. I need to keep her and her entire family safe."

He nods at me. "OK, then. I get it. I'm in."

"In?"

"Yeah, I'm in. I'll keep your secret for you, Shrike. I'm in. I don't know the whole story and frankly, I do not care. But what you guys did last fall… that was some brave shit. Those assholes all need to go to jail. So if keeping my eye on Ronnie helps you finish them off, you can count on me."

I let out a long breath.

I am one lucky motherfucker.

Not because I got away with murder.

Not because I have a TV show.

Not because I came from a good family or was well-educated, or because I can build bikes or paint naked girls.

I'm a lucky guy because I have friends.

And I'm gonna need every single one of them, because the shit is about to get ugly.

# Guns

Rook & Ronin Book Seven

JA HUSS

# CHAPTER ONE

***"The first rule*** of Shrike Club is never talk about Shrike Club."

"Aw, Spencer," Ronin complains. He's standing in my new Shrike Bikes office looking out the window that faces into the bays of my new garage. It's a nice big place, beats the shit out of the old shop in back of my farmhouse in Bellvue. "Stop, man. It's sad."

"Yes, I have to agree with Ronin," Ford says in his dry tone that makes me roll my eyes. Like he's so mature. "It's not funny."

I look over at Carson, the banker-turned-Club member who is helping me keep Veronica out of trouble while the Team cleans up the mess we've been dragging behind us for the past several years. "Don't listen to them. That joke was perfect. And the timing—"

"I don't get it," he says.

Ronin drags his attention from the window where he's keeping a lookout for Rook, and Ford glances up from his computer. "Don't get what?" we all say together.

"Shrike Club. It's a joke? I don't get it."

I look over at Ford and he's got his eyebrows up towards the ceiling. "It's a book," he says with disbelief.

"Book?" I say, laughing. "Carson"—I grab him by the arm and push him away from Ford—"don't listen to him. It's a fucking movie. *Fight Club*? How could you have never heard of *Fight Club*?"

He squints his eyes a little. "Yeah, I've heard of *Fight Club*, but I don't get it."

"'The first rule of Fight Club is never talk about Fight

Club?'" I ask, still slightly hopeful.

Carson gives me nothing.

"Did you see *Fight Club*?" Ronin asks.

"No."

"That's it," Ford says, slapping his laptop closed. "We can't work with a guy who's never seen *Fight Club*. It's absurd. Real men watch *Fight Club*. It's like *Full Metal Jacket* or… or… *The Godfather*. It's something we all do as men. Carson." He pushes past me and stands in front of the banker. "You're out of the Club. Sorry."

Ronin turns back to the window and Carson begins to leave.

"Carson, sit the fuck down. You're not out. He's joking."

"He doesn't look like he's joking," Carson replies.

I sigh. Carson is not on the Team. Only Ronin, Rook, Ford, Ashleigh, and me are on the Team. But we have a new JV version of the Team that we're calling the Club, and Carson is the first official prospect. He's my spy. I need him. And I need Ronin and Ford to be on board with this.

Rook has been demoted to honorary Team member only. We're done getting her involved in shit. In fact, all the girls are out. Ashleigh and Rook will not be a part of our little schemes from now on. And Ronnie was never part of the Team, so she's never even gonna get close to being involved. I need Carson to pull this off, because I've got Ronnie working for me as my personal assistant to keep my eye on her without getting too close, and he's my key to keeping her semi-in love with me until Agent Abelli's trial is over. Abelli is the FBI asshole who wrongfully imprisoned Ronin, tortured Rook's ex-husband, and threatened to sell her to a Columbian drug lord. Most of that happened here in Fort Collins, so the federal judge decided the trial would stay in Colorado.

None of the other defendants require Rook to be a witness because they all made deals. We just have this one trial to get through, then we can put all this bullshit behind us.

"Spencer," Ronin interrupts my thoughts. "When did you say Rook called? You did hide the keys, right?"

"Ronin, I'm trying to work here. She wants the motorcycle back, let her pick the thing up and bring it here."

"No," Ford says emphatically. "Ronin, do not give in. Be strong. She's much safer with no car and no motorcycle. You never know when she'll get the urge to go save someone and take off. Take Ashleigh, she walks everywhere. I love it. No car. She's totally localized. I've got no fewer than five guys on her at any one time. She has no clue she's being guarded day and night. You should let me set this up for Rook too. Ashleigh is predictable, Rook is… not." He stops and looks over at me. "And Ronnie," he huffs. "Don't even get me started on how explosive *she* is. You need more than this guy to keep her in line, Spencer. Face facts here. This guy is not enough. He's clueless."

"Anyway." I shake my head. "Carson, you will go home tonight and watch *Fight Club*, got it? That cool with you guys?" I wait.

But Ronin is still peeking through the blinds and Ford is checking his fingernails.

"OK, that's a yes."

Ronin turns to object but that's when I see Rook storming down the aisle, blowing past all my mechanics as she fumes her way towards my office, trailed by a three-man camera crew. "Shit, Ronin. Here she comes."

Ford pushes Carson until he stumbles backwards and ends up sitting on the edge of a metal table in the corner of the room, then he and I stand in front of him as Ronin takes point.

Rook does not knock. She doesn't have to, she's Rook. So she bursts through the door huffing mad. "Ronin," she says through clenched teeth. "I need those truck keys. I know you told the guys not to give them to me, but I'm going to get that motorcycle right now."

She stomps her foot and we all laugh. Fucking Rook. She's adorable.

She points at Ford and me and we zip it.

"Rook," Ronin says calmly. "I told you, we'll go get it tomorrow when I'm free. Today I have to go down to Denver and work with Antoine on something. In fact"—he looks down at his watch—"I'm late. I gotta go."

"Ronin, do I look helpless? I can get the bike myself. Besides"—she stops to look over at Ford—"Ashleigh said she'd come help."

Ford is shaking his head no before Rook even finishes her sentence. "No, Ashleigh never mentioned that to me."

"Ashleigh doesn't tell you everything, Ford."

He laughs. "I'm pretty sure she does."

Rook smirks and we all start to squirm. "You'd be wrong. I have coffee with her every day now. I know her *secrets*."

I chance a glance over at Ford and he's thinking hard about this. I smirk a little at his discomfort.

"And you," Rook says, pointing to me. "You think you know Veronica? Well, you don't. Now hand over the keys or I will call a taxi, go down to the nearest dealership, and buy myself a fucking truck. Hell, maybe I'll buy myself a motorcycle instead. And ride it home."

She stomps her foot again, only this time we're not amused. We're all scratching our chins.

And then we all remember there's a fucking camera crew here. Damn.

"OK." I grab Ronin by the arm. "Give her the keys. She's being taped today, so she can't get into any trouble with the camera crew with her." I stop and the three of us look at each other. "Right?"

Rook beams a triumphant smile and Ronin waves her through the door to go tell the garage guys to let her take the truck.

I wait until they are halfway down the aisle before I walk over and close the door again. Ford and I turn to Carson and he's smiling. He likes the fact that Rook won and we lost.

"Carson, look," Ford says. "You can be in the Club if you keep an eye on Ashleigh too. In fact, I think you should just come clean and tell these girls you're gay. You can be the gay best friend. Do their makeup and hair, paint their toenails, whatever it is that gay best friends do with girls."

"I'm not gay," Carson starts.

But Ford is not even listening. He's talking to me now. "If he keeps an eye on Ash and watches *Fight Club*, he's in." And then he pulls the door open and walks out.

I turn to Carson. "I'm not gay," he repeats.

"Carson, do you want in the Club or not? Just pretend, dude. You get to hang out with pretty girls, what's wrong with that?"

He glares at me in his nerdy tan suit. Tan. Who the fuck wears a tan suit? I try to picture Ford in a tan suit and almost laugh out loud. *No.*

"Fine, then. I'll pretend for now. But that's gonna cost you. I want a custom paint job for my Shrike Bike too."

I promised him a custom bike if he keeps his eye on Ronnie and helps me slip her a fake loan so she can start her own flower shop business. I'm not sure why Ronnie wants to sell flowers in a shop, she's never mentioned it before. But if she thinks it's better than being a tattoo artist, then more power to her. She can take that twenty grand I'm making Carson tell her came from the bank and blow it on shoes for all I care. I just want her to be happy until the trial is over and we can all breathe a sigh of relief.

"Deal. Now what's the plan for today?"

"Plan?" he asks with this pathetic stupefied expression on his face. "I'm planning on going to work."

"Not your plan for you, Carson. Your plan for Ronnie. And Ash." I stick that in since Ford will have a fit if I don't include her in the recon. "How will you keep them out of trouble?"

"Um…"

"I got it. Ronnie needs a new car, so you call her up later and tell her you wanna go car-shopping. That's good for one evening. We'll just have to take it day by day. Ronnie, she's a little bit unpredictable, ya know?"

He's shaking his head at me. "A little bit? Are you kidding? That girl scares the shit out of me. And her brother, man, that guy is like… like…" He huffs. "Well, just… Big. And he looks at me with that I'm-gonna-kill-you expression and you know what?"

Carson pauses, like I'm supposed to answer that rhetorical question. I give in. "What?"

"I think he really does want to kill me."

"Oh, for fuck's sake, Carson. Vic Vaughn is the least of your concerns. He's all bark, man. No substance behind that whine. At all."

"I dunno," he says.

Vic is not all bark. People think his name is short for Victor, but it's not. It's short for Vicious. What parent would name their kid Vicious? Fern Vaughn, that's who. That motherfucking Vaughn family has been the bane of Fort Collins for decades.

But they are pretty cool people once you're in with them. Carson just needs to be in. And there's no better way into the Vaughn family than taking care of their baby sister.

It's only then I realize Carson is still talking about Vic's killer attitude. "—and how am I gonna get Veronica to go car-shopping with me tonight, anyway? Huh? She's not very receptive."

"Simple," I say as I take out my phone and grab her contact. I press her beautiful face and listen to the phone ring. My heart beats a little faster as I wait for her to pick up. Three years later and she still makes my heart beat faster. The fourth ring ends and it goes to voicemail. "Fuck," I say to the machine. "Pick the fucking phone up, Ronnie. I own your ass." I press end and dial again, but get the same result.

"See," Carson says. "Even you can't contain her. But I know where she's at, she's over at the FoCo Cinema having coffee."

"How do you know?"

"She goes there every day at ten. How do you *not* know?"

I walk to the far side of my office, the side that faces the street, and peek out. And sure enough, who do I see? Ashleigh. Pushing that fucking stroller and flanked on either side by the red-vested canine face-eaters.

"She really does meet Ashleigh there?" I ask Carson.

He shrugs. "I dunno. I haven't had coffee with her in a couple weeks and Ashleigh is new in town. But I know for a fact that she meets Rook."

"Yeah, but Rook is going out to the farm today, so—" And just as the words are coming out of my mouth, Rook pulls the Shrike Bikes truck into a parking space out front of the cinema.

I dial the phone one more time, but I already know Ronnie won't pick up, so my feet are busting ass out of my office and over towards the back door that leads outside.

She thinks she can just ignore me?

Huh.

No.

# CHAPTER TWO

***Metallica's Breadfan*** is blaring in my earbuds and at least a dozen people sitting nearby are shootin' me the look. The music's not even full blast, so they can just move the fuck along and get their mid-morning coffee somewhere else. The Fort Collins Cinema is one of my haunts and that's the way it's gonna stay. I eat here in the restaurant four times a week and catch a movie at least twice a month. I'm a local.

So I'm banging my head a little, watching as the work crew paints the outside of the Strike Bikes building—which sits diagonal from the FCC—when my song is interrupted by a ding. I glance down at my phone, then ignore it.

It's Spencer. Again.

When he said he'd need me on call if I took the job as his personal assistant, he was not kidding. That mother dings my ass seven, eight times a day.

I continue enjoying my music, watching for Rook. Ever since she and Ronin got a place in Fort Collins, we meet here every day for coffee.

I see Ashleigh first. She comes now too. I'm not sure I like her, mostly because I'm not sure I like Ford, but the baby is cute. And I like her dogs, even if they are trained to eat the face off anyone who messes with her.

Ashleigh is one of those walkers. She walks every-fucking-where. They live all the way down Mountain Ave, across from the antique trolley station. It's like a couple miles away, and yet that girl walks. I live like two blocks away and every damn day I'm tempted to drive the car. I was gonna take it today, but I sold it last night. So I'm out of a car.

I suppose Ash has to walk those dogs sometime though. And the baby likes the stroller, so I don't judge.

Rook pulls up just as Ashleigh is hucking that humongo stroller over the curb and then they walk in together, making the bells jingle on the door. Ashleigh gets more looks than I do. She's got a stroller, two mean-ass-looking dogs with bright red vests, plus a baby.

And she's married to Ford Aston. That's like sixty-seven strikes against her right there.

She's way worse than me. I've got like ten. One for being a Vaughn. One for being a tattoo artist. One for being blonde. One each for being associated with Ford, Spencer, Rook, and Ronin. One for being poor. One for being mean. And two for having big tits. That's eleven, but who's counting.

Rook, she's only got two strikes. One for being Rook, since everyone knows her from the news. And one for being perfect in every way. Rook is so perfect, she makes people want to gag. But they can't. Because not only is she perfect, she's sweet. Not a mean bone in that girl's body. I've been doing my best to bitch her up a little, but she's a terrible student. She's polite and happy and she smiles. Like all the time. And since she and Ronin live in FoCo now too, we're all just like one big happy family.

Except I'm the odd one out since Spencer won't acknowledge me.

I unplug my earbuds and stuff them in my purse.

"Hey, Ronnie!" Rook chimes as they approach. "Sorry I'm late, I had—"

My phone rings and interrupts her. "Damn Spencer." I silence the call and turn the ringer to vibrate. "Sorry, Rook."

Ashleigh's dogs crawl under the table and one begins to pant on my ankle. The baby shoots me a gummy grin and I smile back. Babies are damn cute. I think Kate knocks off at least thirty-two points against Ashleigh, that's how adorable she is. "Hi, Kate!" I beam. She squeals at me. Rook and Ash disappear to go order coffee and my phone vibrates on the table.

Goddammit! I turn the ringer off, but a few seconds later the screen lights up with a text. *Answer your fucking phone, Bomb!*

I weigh my options and then decide to ignore the next silent call. In fact, I throw that damn phone right into my skull-covered Betsey Johnson purse.

The girls return and Rook chats us up about her new job as front door girl at the new Shrike Bikes showroom and garage. I glance out the window as she talks to get a visual of her in there being Miss Congeniality, but all I see is Spencer walking diagonally across the street. He's got a mean look on his face. In fact, he looks pretty fucking pissed off. Rook is still talking to Ashleigh—about what, I have no idea—so I stand up, grab my purse, and bolt to the back of the cinema where the back door leads to an alley.

It's starting to rain outside, and there's no way I'm gonna be able to run in high heels. So I slip my shoes off my feet and throw them in my purse. I start walking quickly down the alley, my bare feet splashing through puddles, and stepping on stones that make me wince. I look over my shoulder to see if anyone is coming after me and slam right into Spencer's rock-hard chest.

"What the fuck are you doing, Veronica? I've called and texted repeatedly, and you've ignored them all. When I gave you this job I told you you're on call."

He's got me by the wrists, and he's squeezing kind of hard. "Spencer, goddammit, you're hurting me, let go." I struggle against him. He squeezes even harder, then lets go and pulls me into his chest. He wraps his arms around me. I can't help myself, I give in.

It's starting to rain now and we're both getting wet. The drops are dripping down his face and for once he's got his sunglasses off and I can see his gray eyes as they crinkle with anger.

He starts walking, forcing me to step backwards, stumbling a little as I go.

"Spencer, what the fuck are you doing? You're gonna

make me fall!"

He doesn't let up, though. He keeps pushing and I keep stumbling backwards, his eyes still angry with me as I slam back against the brick wall of the building. He leans in close, his lips come towards my mouth and for a moment I fantasize that he'll kiss me.

But he never kisses me anymore. And he doesn't now.

"I'm only telling you once," he says with a snarl. "You do what I say, Veronica. When I tell you something, you do it. When I send you a text, you answer it." He stares hard into my eyes and his flash with anger, darting back and forth, making sure that I'm listening.

His chest is pressing hard against mine, forcing me back against the uneven brick wall. Anger consumes me. How dare he? How dare he burst into my day and start making these demands like he owns me. It's my turn to squint my eyes and look him dead on, the heat of my anger taking over.

"Spencer Shrike, I might work for you but I'm not your property. And if you think that paying me a salary means you get to order me around like you're the boss, you've got another thing coming. And maybe, just maybe, I don't need your fucking job. So if you think I'm going to put up with your—"

His lips crush against mine and my knees just give out. I'm weak. Whenever he touches me I am so, so weak. The heat flushes through my body and I know if I looked in the mirror I'd be red all over. His tongue presses against mine. Searching, probing, looking for everything he just demanded—and I respond. Goddammit, I respond, giving him exactly what he wants. His hands come up and cup the side of my head, threading his fingers through my hair and around the back of my neck. He pulls me up towards his face, making me stand on my tiptoes to try to keep the connection between our mouths. I want to touch him back, thread my fingers through his hair and make him as crazy as he's making me, but I can't even think straight while he's kissing me like this. When we come up for air, a fingertip traces along my jaw and the tip of my chin.

"Veronica," he whispers. "I am the motherfucking boss." His hand slips between my legs and his fingers find my sweet spot through my jeans. Goddamn, this fucking man knows everything about me. He presses against my clit and then releases, making me moan. "Say it back to me, Bombshell. Who's the motherfucking boss?"

I whine out a no, but he just palms my whole pussy and leans in, whispering in my ear. "Say it, Bomb. Or I'll take you right here in the fucking alley and prove it."

*Oh, God, is that a promise?*

"Why?" I whisper back. "Why do you do this to me?" Suddenly my emotions take over and it all becomes too much. I've known this man years. I've slept with him hundreds of times at least. His paintbrush has caressed the most intimate places on my body. I fell in love with him the first day we met. There is no man on this earth I want more than Spencer Shrike.

But…

"I can't do this anymore, Spencer. You're killing me. Every day you play these games with me, you're killing me. I can't take it anymore. I quit. I quit this stupid fucking job and I quit this stupid nonexistent relationship."

His fingers fist in my hair, yanking hard enough to make me moan. He closes his eyes and looks down for a moment, letting out a long breath of air. And it's only then that we realize it's starting to rain hard. He grabs my hand and starts leading me up the stairs under the overhang of the building's back door. He's still holding my hand when we finally find shelter from the rain in the empty alcove. I try to pull it away, but he holds tight.

"Please," I beg. "Please, stop torturing me." I want this man so bad it makes my heart ache inside my chest.

"Bombshell, it's more torturous for me than you will ever know."

"I don't understand you, Spencer. I don't understand. If you want me, just take me. I get it, you're guilty." He looks down when I say the word, but I'm tired of pretending that he didn't admit to me last week that he was a killer. "Spencer, look at me." I place my hand against his heart and push a little so that he sways backwards. "Why is it that Ronin trusts Rook, and hell, even Ford trusts Ashleigh, and they get to know all the secrets, but me, even though I've known you guys the longest, I get trusted with shit? I get nothing from you, Spencer. I'm no one to you. Why?"

His eyes search mine again, only now they look… pained. Why is he so confusing? "Because, baby, I love you enough to push you away."

The tears well up as the words come out and I sniff as I wipe them away. "Well, you're doing a really good job, because I am fucking out of here." I go to push past him, but he swings me back around and presses me against the wall.

"Just listen," he says in a low throaty voice. "Look at me, Ronnie. Because I'm only gonna tell you this once." He rocks his hips into mine, grinding his erection against me. And I am instantly flooding with wetness in anticipation. "I said fucking look at me."

I refocus, taking my attention away from the growing need between my legs, and stare him in the eyes. His emotions are coming through more clearly than normal, and while Spencer has never been a man to hide behind a facade of indifference like Ford, he tries to keep things on an even keel. But right now everything he's feeling… shows.

He cares?

And then, like he realizes I can see though him, he turns it off.

"Baby," he growls into my ear, "I'll give you what you want right now. But you gotta work with me here, Ronnie. If I give you what you want, you give me what I want."

I look out into the curtain of rain which is the only thing between our growing desire and the cars on the street outside beyond the alley. He's going to take me here, and he's not going to care who sees us.

"Tell me you want it," he orders. "You know how I work."

I do know how he works. Spencer can make me come

without ever touching me or uttering a single word. Because Spencer likes the details. Spencer wants to know everything I want, and he wants me to be crystal clear about it.

Details like… "My pussy is tingling, Mr. Shrike," I purr into his ear.

He grinds against me harder now, his breath becoming labored and heavy. This drives me wild, and he knows it. His breath in my ear is a signal we've had since the beginning. A signal that says *I'm ready for you, baby. Tell me everything. Tell me how you feel, tell me how I make you feel, tell me what you want, tell me how you want it.*

"I want it here, Mr. Shrike. Outside, in the alley. And I want it now."

His grinding intensifies even more now, and one hand reaches down to grab my ass while the other one unsnaps my jeans. "We might get caught, Bombshell," he says in that reasonable tone he always gets when I'm the one doing the dirty talk.

"We might," I agree.

"Mr. Harrison might open the donut shop door to throw out a bag of trash any second now."

"He could," I concede again, but my zipper is loose and my pants are sliding down my hips before the words are fully formed.

"Take me out, Veronica."

I unsnap his jeans and release his zipper just as quickly, then push his pants down just far enough for his hard cock to escape. My jeans are still around my hips and I let my arm drop so my purse can slide to the ground. My shoes fall out and one tumbles down the concrete stairs and lands in a puddle in the parking lot.

Both of Spencer's hands are reaching down inside my jeans so they can cup my bare ass and then suddenly he lifts me up. I bend my knees and raise my legs to give him access, pushing back against the uneven brick wall to keep me in position. He doesn't pull my jeans down so my legs are only open enough to give his thick cock access. I rest my calves on his shoulders and even through his leather jacket I can feel the power in those muscles.

Spencer is nothing but power.

He's gonna take me with no fanfare and no foreplay.

But with Spencer, the sex *is* the foreplay. It's not what he does, it's how he does it. It's not what he says, it's how he says it. It's not how I feel, it's how he makes me feel.

Spencer Shrike does not need to suck on my clit to get me ready. When I see him, I'm ready.

"Take me like this," I moan out in his ear. "Put your cock in me and just take me here, right now."

"Take you how, Bomb?" He eases his cock between my folds and I gasp as he pulls away. "Like this, soft and gentle?"

"No," I whine. "No. I want it hard. I want you to make me scream your name right now. I want to scream it so loud—" I lean in and purr in his ear in the softest of voices. "I want to scream your name so loud it'll stop traffic out there on the street. And—" I have to bite my tongue and stop talking for a moment. It's been so fucking long, I might make myself come.

His dick flirts with my entrance and he's holding me up one-handed now. My jeans are barely past my thighs, so I have to fight the urge to open my legs wide to invite him in. He's pressing me against the wall so hard, for a moment I have a slight panic about being able to breathe. But he can read me better than anyone and the pressure on my chest eases up just as his cock thrusts inside me and his hand returns to my ass, holding me steady. The angle of my hips and the fact that my ankles are practically next to my head make his thrusts painful, but it's the kind of pain girls fantasize about. Being filled up with the long hard cock of someone they love so much they spend every waking moment thinking of this.

His grinding evens out and we find our rhythm, my back arching and pushing forward each time he pounds me backwards against the uneven brick wall, our breath heavy with desire and effort.

I'm in ecstasy, I'm so close, even though his dick is nowhere near my clit, I don't need that with Spencer. His smell is enough to set me off. The thick corded muscles of his upper arms as he strains to hold me steady and fuck me at the same time—*that* is enough.

I'm about to explode when he pulls back and leans into my ear before I can whimper my protest. "Bombshell, listen carefully now, baby. Because I told you I was only gonna say it once, but sometimes it takes a good public fuck to make you hear me."

"Huh?" I'm all breathy and a little bit pissed that I'm not halting traffic from screaming his name right now.

"I'm the boss of you, Bombshell." He thrusts into me hard. Hard enough to hit the wall of my cervix and make me cry out in pain. "I'm the boss, aren't I?" He thrusts again and this time is even more painful, but at the same time, I can feel the orgasm building again. "Answer me, dammit," he says as he pulls out, leaving me empty and wanting.

"Yes, OK. You're the boss, Mr. Shrike." *Just keep the fuck going!*

He chuckles. "Good, baby. That's perfect." He eases back into me, softer this time. Slow, controlled back-and-forth movements that only make me ache for more.

"Harder, please," I beg.

"Now," he says through his heavy breath. "You're gonna be a good girl and do what I say, right?" He punctuates each word with a thrust and retreat.

I just nod. Hell, I'll agree to anything right now. I haven't been fucked since New Year's and that one I can't even remember. So it hardly counts.

"And what I want you to do is…" He leans into me, pushes himself as deep inside me as he can get and I swear, even though my eyes are open, everything goes black. My world is nothing but those little fuzzy stars you see just before you have the orgasm of a lifetime. His cock pulses inside me and he tugs on my hair and moans along with his explosion. His cock pulses over and over again inside me, his hot semen shooting out.

I push back, on the verge of something truly spectacular…

And then he pulls out and backs off, no longer supporting my legs so they drop to the ground.

"What the fuck?" I ask as his come spills down my thigh and collects against my jeans.

He pulls my pants up and then his own.

I'm stunned. "I was just about to scream your name."

Never—and I do mean *never*—has Spencer used sex against me. He's never been one of those guys to withhold orgasm to make a point. Until now, apparently.

"I told you," he says as he tucks his partially erect cock back into his jeans. "I'm the motherfucking boss of you, Bombshell. And I am not fucking around this time." He leans in, all the fun dirty talk forgotten. His orgasm forgotten. The flirty banter forgotten. "When I call that fucking phone, you fucking answer it!"

He's not behaving normally and this sets me back a minute as I try to button and zip my jeans back up. "I never got any calls, Spencer. Calm down."

He shoots me a nasty look. "You're a shit liar, Veronica. I can tell every time. You crinkle your nose when you lie."

"Do not. And what the fuck? Is this how you play now? You take what you want from me and once you've had your fill, you just leave me hanging? You're a total asshole. Especially after you said you never wanted to see me again. Only texts and phones."

He stares hard at me for a moment, his breath still labored from the sex. "I never said that, Ronnie. I said we only need to *communicate* with texts and phone calls."

I pick my purse up from the ground beside me, fish around and find my pack of e-cigs, and start puffing. Spencer drives me to puff. "What's the difference?" I say through a thick stream of vapor. "And if that's all you want from me, then why this… this… what the fuck was this *fuck*? I don't even have a word for it, you asshole!" I'm so upset with how this has turned out, I might cry right here, right now, in front of him.

"Ronnie, I need a place in town." He says this like…

like… like he didn't just fuck me in an alley and leave me wanting like a worthless whore. "Your job this week is to find me a place to live in town."

"What?" His words make my heart flutter and I have to place my hand against my chest to collect myself. "But… the farmhouse?" I've always pictured my life being lived out on that farm. Always. Since the day I met him three years ago, that's been my happily ever after and now he wants to sell it. I turn away and place my head against the wall.

It's over. My fantasy life with Spencer Shrike is over.

His strong hands grab my shoulders and turn me back around. "I'm not selling the farmhouse, Bombshell. Never. I just need a nice place to crash in town. That drive is killing me. So look around and find me something good. Set me up some appointments, and then text them to me."

"Oh." I'm hopeful again. "Do you want me to meet you there when you look?"

"No, babe. Just me."

Now I'm deflated. See, this is why I need to avoid him at all costs. He deflates me. He sucks all my air out. He collapses me into nothingness. I look down at my feet and concentrate on not being sad.

"And the next time I call or text, you answer. OK?"

When I look up he's already walking away and I'm feeling more used and dejected than ever.

"Spencer!" I call after him, desperate for one more interaction. "What's the budget?"

"No budget, Bomb," he calls out without turning back to me. "Just find me a nice place."

And then he rounds the corner and he's gone. And I'm left here, in this stupid alley overhang, looking like an idiot as the back door of the donut shop opens and I almost give Mr. Harrison a heart attack when he finds me there.

"Sorry," I say as I quickly hop down the stairs, pick up my stray shoe and stuff it in my purse with the other one, and walk barefoot out into the rain.

"Find him a house," I whisper to myself as I leave the alley and walk towards my street. Probably so he can share it with Carla the burrito bitch. I hate her. Why does she get a date with Spencer every damn week and I get nothing? I hate her and I hate him.

But a smile leaks out as my toes splash through a puddle on the sidewalk.

Because I will have the last laugh today. And I can't wait to see his face when he finds out what I'm doing.

## CHAPTER THREE

# Veronica

***By the time*** I make it back to my apartment, Rook is waiting for me in the Shrike truck, I'm sopping wet from head to toe, and my feet are fucking freezing.

"What the hell?" Rook says as she gets out of the truck and jogs over to me. "What happened to you? You just dashed out the back without a word."

We trudge up my stairs together, then I unlock and open the door and hold it open for her. I'm already wet, she's still fairly dry. Might as well keep her that way. I close the door behind me and hang my soaked jacket up on the coat hook. "Spencer was texting me all morning and I didn't answer, so when I looked out the window and saw him coming across the street, I panicked and ran."

Rook laughs. "That plan work out well for you?"

"Ha ha," I say as I walk to the bathroom. "I'm gonna take a shower because I'm fucking freezing. Then we can go."

"Sounds good," she calls back from the kitchen. "I'm gonna raid your fridge, mind?"

"Nah," I say back. "Go ahead. Be out in a minute." I head into the shower and start the water.

Spencer was right when he came over here last week. The *only* time he's been over here. He called it a dump. And it is.

Granted, my family home is sorta dumpy too, but at least it's from my relatives. The windows were cracked from baseballs me and my brothers threw. The linoleum in the kitchen is stained and chipped from decades of Vaughn feet walking over it. The banister is missing spindles because Vann got his head stuck between them when Vic was in charge, so Vic just pulled one straight out thinking he was gonna get his ass kicked if we couldn't all be accounted for when our dad got home.

Yeah, that's home.

But this… well, I lied to Spencer. I stuck up for this place because he made me feel poor and trashy. He was right though. It's a crappy place. The floorboards beneath my feet in the bathroom are probably all rotten with water damage. They sway when you walk. I might fall through the ceiling one of these days. Good thing no one is living below me. I have no idea what this place used to be. I've lived in Fort Collins my whole life, but I never paid any attention to these old buildings on this street. They were shops, I think. They look like storefronts with giant picture windows and mail slots on the doors.

The water finally runs hot and I peel off my wet jeans, toss them in the hamper, and then struggle out of my top and bra. I feel… *used*. And even though Spencer and I have had some pretty… interesting… sex during our relationship, it's never made me feel unclean.

I mean, he likes the dirty talk, so he's called me names during sex that would earn him a punch in the teeth any other time. I'm used to his particular brand of heat. But he's never used me like *this*. He's never used sex against me to get something he wants. That part of our relationship has always been normal.

Sure, I get a little hysterical when we fight. I've been known to throw a wine bottle or two at his head. But he's a good ducker. I've never actually hit him.

And he can predict my violence pretty well. He pins me down and dirty-talks me back into reality and then things are all good.

It's been a long time since he had to pin me down. And not because I've been rational. He just hasn't paid much attention to me for almost a year. After that altercation with Rook's ex, Jon, last summer, Spencer was almost back to his old self for a few weeks. We saw each other a couple weekends, he took me to Rook's birthday party at Antoine's studio, we fucked when we could manage to meet up, since we were living in two separate towns.

But then… after all that shit went down with Rook and Ronin and those weirdo human traffickers, Spencer was back to his distant self. And since that time, it's only gotten worse. We work less than a mile from each other. We should be having lunch breaks together every day. We should be living together out in that farmhouse of his, riding into town every day in his Shrike truck, drinking our coffee on the road as we chat about our day.

But things haven't turned out that way.

That thought alone is enough to start the tears.

I pull the ugly shower curtain back and step into my old and cracking tub and try to accept what my life has become. I should be thankful. Lots of people have it worse than me. I have a place to live, I have a job—two actually. I'm still working at Sick Boyz, my family's tattoo shop. Even though Spencer gave me this great job as his personal assistant, I can't just quit my tattoo job. I have regular customers who are depending on me to finish up their work. I'm booked solid three days a week for the next two months. And that's just the big pieces—the backs and chests I've been working on. I told all the guys with sleeves they had to go to one of my brothers or I'll be stuck there forever.

So yeah. It's hardly fair to complain when I have two jobs that collectively pay me almost fifty-five grand a year. That's not a bad paycheck for a twenty-three-year-old with no real prospects. I mean, I have an art degree, but come on. It's an *art* degree. How much did I expect to get out of that?

Plus, I have a great family. My dad and gramps are cool as hell. Yeah, they were mean bastards to the boys all growing up, but I was their little princess. The spitting image of my mother.

That makes me smile.

My mom died giving birth to Vann, my baby brother. Well, he's no baby now, he's seventeen. I was already six when he was born and my oldest brother, Vic, he was twelve. The twins, Vinn and Vonn—don't ask about the names, it's my dad's thing—were eight.

And my brothers might've challenged that princess side of me every chance they got, trying to toughen me up and teach me survival skills. But they love the fuck out of me. They are always there when I need them.

So check. I'm one lucky bitch. I should be happy. I should be grabbing this half-satisfied bull by the horns and riding the fuck out of it.

But I just can't get past Spencer. I fell in love with his ass the first night I met him and I even fucked him the next day. We were practically strangers. And that love has only gotten stronger. In fact, I might be on the verge of being obsessed with him.

"Ronnie!" Rook's knock on the bathroom door shakes me out of my funk.

"Yeah?" I answer back.

"Hurry, bitch. We gotta go."

I laugh at her calling me *bitch.* I taught her that. She couldn't make herself say it back to me at first, she thought it was an insult. But I told her, *That's what bitches call each other.* "Be right out."

I love Rook. I hope she never goes back to Denver. I want her to stay in Fort Collins with me forever. Rook is really the only great thing about my life right now. She's always down with my stupid plans to get back at Spencer and today just proves it—she's a keeper.

I turn the water off and step out onto the plush pink bath mat. The floor might be a mess, but I have my own stuff to counter it. I wrap myself up in a big thick towel and open the door. Rook is watching TV on the couch, stuffing her face with popcorn. "I'll only be five minutes," I tell her as I dash to my bedroom.

"Whatever," she calls back. "That'll be the day."

Yeah, and that would usually be right. I'm a primper. I take for*ever* to get ready. I dry my hair, curl it, brush it, curl it again. Then the makeup. I *luuurve* makeup. Like bad.

Then the clothes. I love clothes. I have my typical outfits. Tight low-scoop-neck t-shirts with the Sick Boyz logo on them. I wear those a lot with jeans. So much, in fact, it's like my uniform. They're comfortable and pretty.

I'm an eighties girl when it comes to fashion. I like big hair, tight leggings, stiletto heels, red lips, and tank tops under short jackets. And my big Betsey purse.

But today, I'm not about fashion, I'm about purpose. My last-ditch attempt to grab Spencer's attention. I sigh as I fetch a pair of jeans from my dresser. They are old and ripped in the knees. I slip them on and notice they are a lot looser than the last time I wore them. I like my jeans tight, so I almost take them off, but really, I'm in the mood for loose today. I grab a Shrike Bikes t-shirt. This one used to be red, but has faded to an almost grayish-pink color. It has a vintage pinup girl riding a WWII-style bomb. Over the girl it says *Spencer Shrike*, but the words below are what I love about it. It says *Bombshell Bikes*.

He made a bunch of different bombshell shirts specially for me back when he was trying out all his different logos. Now he uses the ravens and a few other things.

But this bombshell piece was like an arrow through my heart. It's like carving *Spencer and Ronnie sitting in a tree* on the picnic table in my back yard. Which I did the very first week we met.

I smile a little at this as I fasten my lacy pink bra and tug the shirt over my head. I slip on my old black Frye Harness boots and grab the leather jacket off the sturdy hanger.

I sigh as I look at it. And then I giggle. I stole this from him last year. Back when I could tell he was getting ready to leave me behind just as his business and body-painting careers were taking off. It scared the shit out of me and I wanted something more than a t-shirt that would keep me connected to him. Spencer never gave me a motorcycle jacket all painted up like he did Rook. And I do admit, I'm insanely jealous of that jacket she has.

But this jacket that I swear to fucking God I can still smell his musky scent on makes up for all that sadness and what I'm about to do today. Well, it's a defining moment for me.

I slip my arms into the smooth sleeves of the leather and put my hair up in a ponytail. The contents of my purse are exchanged into a backpack and then I walk out of the room.

Spencer thinks he can just boss me around, leave me hanging after getting himself off, and there's not gonna be consequences?

Yeah, right, buddy.

"Shit, Ronnie, took you long—" Rook stops talking as she takes in my outfit. I'm a girl who dresses for the occasion and Rook knows this. "No," she says. "You said you wanted me to help you haul it back to town on the truck, Veronica."

I tilt my head up and smile. "I know what I said. But I lied. Else you'd say no. But you already sold me the bike, Rook. It's mine. All I need is a ride out to the farm to pick it up."

My phone buzzes in my backpack and I grab it, hoping it's Spencer calling to apologize or maybe stop by after lunch to finish me off…

No such luck. "Carson," I say into the phone after I accept the call. "I've been thinking about that dinner invitation you gave me last week…"

"No, Veronica," he cuts me off. "That's not why I'm calling. I know you were looking for a car, so I lined up a friend of mine to show you some nice prospects tonight."

Silence.

"Uh, you know, so we can finalize the loan?"

"Riiiiight," I say back. "The loan. Ah… yeah. I do need a car." I eyeball Rook. "But I've found some transportation until I'm ready to buy another one. As for the paperwork, I've decided I don't need the loan anymore. I'm good, and a flower shop was never gonna be my thing, OK? Well, it's been nice knowing you, take care." And before he can say anything I end the call and slip the phone back into my pack.

"Spencer will fucking kill me if you get on that bike today, Ronnie." Rook picks up our conversation like Carson never even called. "It's wet out!"

I walk over to the front window and crack the blinds apart. "It's stopped raining already. It's supposed to be sunny today. Just a morning shower." I smile sweetly at her. Rook is a pushover, I'm not worried. When I told her I wanted to buy the bike, she said she'd give it to me. But I made certain I paid her what it was worth last night when I sold my car. Every cent I got from my Mini Cooper went to Rook. And I've got the signed title and the bill of sale in my wallet.

"Stop worrying. I told you, my little brother Vann and I took motorcycle classes together lasts summer. We're pros now. Besides, you're one to talk. You took off on that bike last year and drove it a thousand miles away and you lived."

"Yeah, Spencer and Ford came and hauled my ass back, too. They were not happy. Not at all. And Ronin gave me the kibosh on riding ever since. All three of them will kill me if I take you out there and let you ride."

"Rook, whose side are you on?" I exclaim. "It's hoes before bros, bitch."

She halts the rant about to come out of her mouth and laughs. "Hoes…" She shakes her head at that. "Ronnie, if you crash—"

"I'm not gonna crash, I told you. Vann and I have logged almost a hundred hours already. We've been on the sneak for almost a year. He's even got a bike halfway built at his friend's garage. He'll be riding it on his eighteenth in June."

She gives me a doubtful look. But all that was one hundred percent true. I hitch my pack over my shoulder, open the front door, and wave her through.

She accepts my invitation and I'm in. I am fucking in, baby.

My new life starts today.

Biker Bomb Ronnie.

# CHAPTER FOUR

***"What do ya mean*** she doesn't want the loan?" Fucking Veronica. Can't this woman ever just go with the fucking flow? Why does she have to make my life so complicated?

"You were standing right here, Shrike. She blew me off and said she was never interested in the flower shop idea anyway."

"Then—" I throw my hands up. "What the fuck is she doing?"

Carson checks his fingernails and suddenly he reminds me of a less cool version of Ford. "How should I know what that woman is thinking? I barely know her. She said she has transportation and she didn't need a car just yet."

"Trans—well, where the fuck did she get a car? I just saw her ass walking home less than an hour ago. How could she have picked up a vehicle in that time? Especially when I left her cold and wet"—very, very wet—"walking home barefoot in the rain."

"Just for the record, that's a dick move."

I raise my eyebrows. Charlie Brown is getting brave.

"Look," Carson says impatiently, "as much as I'd like to help you out, I told my old man I was at the dentist to come here this morning. I gotta get back to work. I'll stop by tomorrow and we'll talk ideas about my custom paint job. Later."

And he just walks out.

Fuck. I rub the stubble on my head. Bombshell is gonna send me to my grave, that's how crazy she drives me. I fish my phone out of my pocket and press her beautiful face. It rings through on the first ring. *"You've reached Ronnie Vaughn. I'm either working or playing…"*

I end the call and sit on the corner of my desk to think.

Ford comes back with a camera crew a few minutes later.

"What's up with them?" I ask, pointing to the three-man crew. "I thought they were Team Rook today?"

"Yeah, well, she told them she had to go to the women's doctor and if they tried to follow her, they'd each get, and I quote, 'a boot in the balls.' She took off from the coffee shop and left them standing outside."

I just stare at him. "So… she's got my truck. Ronin's out of town. She's conveniently got an appointment no one knew about. Ronnie's out of area and suddenly came up with her own mode of transportation. Something is not right."

Ford's already pushing the crew out of the office and closing the door while he dials his phone. "Ashleigh?" he says with some relief. "Have you seen Ronnie or Rook?" He listens to her for a few seconds and then pops off an, "I love you, be home at six," and ends the call.

They sorta make me gag. That's how sweet and considerate they are of each other. I can't stop the eye roll. "What'd she say?"

He shrugs. "Ronnie went with Rook to a doctor's appointment."

"Huh."

We stare at each other, both of us thinking that's all total bullshit. But then Director Larry comes in and drags our minds back to work and we drop it. Ford and Larry are busy setting up stationary cameras in front of each of the mechanics' bays, inside the paint room—we have our own in-house painter now—and in the showroom, behind Rook's desk.

Besides the new painter, we picked up a couple girls from CSU to run parts and do errands that Rook used to do. My payroll went from five to nine. Which may not sound like much, but three years ago I had zero employees, no real shop, no custom bikes of my own, and Ronnie and I were more together than not.

These days we're not together at all.

And it sucks. I hate it. I hate sneaking around behind her back, trying to get shit done, trying to keep my secrets.

Yeah, I admitted I was guilty last week when we talked, but saying it like that—all generic and shit, no details—it's not the same, because everyone knows the details are all that matter.

I walk outside and join the boys. The grand opening for Shrike Bikes is six days away. The painting crew had to wait until the rain stopped today, and now they are just finishing up the mechanic banners. The outside of the shop is all done up in black and red with a giant Shrike Bikes logo and a banner with each mechanic's name on their bay door.

They are all good guys and they've all been with me since the start. Only Ryan and I make the custom bikes. I use Fletch and Griff to assemble the stock bikes. They do a little customization—but no frame stuff.

All the guys are checking out the painting with me. They are excited and smiling. *We're big time,* those smiles say.

Yeah, we were on TV last year too, but this… This. Is. Big time.

I have to take a deep breath when Griff knocks me on the back and they all crowd around as we watch our names being painted on the side of a building.

And the reason I have to take a deep breath is because this is the dream, ya know?

I'm about to be living the fucking *dream.*

And it came pretty quick. I'm not even twenty-four years old yet. But that's not what's bothering me today. Today all I can think about are the mistakes I made to get here. And last week, back when I was bitching about Ronnie's dump of an apartment, she said something to me that really hit home.

She said, 'At least I got it honestly.'

It was like a stab to my heart. Because she's absolutely fucking right. I cheated my ass into this opportunity. Sure, I contacted the Biker Channel and pitched the show, but I name-dropped. My father stepped in, called up some of his old biker buddies. Got them to make calls.

And Ford. I told them I would get Ford Aston on board. I used our infamy to get the pilot. I let Rook sign the contract even though I knew she was only doing it to defy Ronin. Because I wanted Ronin to model with Rook on the bikes. And guess what? I got my way. I got everything I set out to get.

I used every bit of clout, reputation, friendship, and notoriety I had. And all of it was based on the fact that I'm a goddamned criminal. A murderer.

Alleged murderer to the public, but there's nothing alleged about what I did.

I pinch the bridge of my nose to stave off a headache and then look up when Ryan punches me in the arm. "Snap the fuck out of it, Shrike! This is *it,* man. The end of struggling. The end of sweating the payroll, the end of…"

I stop listening at payroll.

They have no idea. They have no fucking idea my net worth is over a hundred and fifty million dollars if you include what's left of my cut of the jobs the Team did a few years ago.

I stand out there with the guys as they paint my name on the last bay.

S. P. E. N. C. E. R.

I step back a few paces so I can see the whole thing. All five bay doors, the open-winged blackbird that spans the entire length. The skull and crossbones centered in the middle. The Shrike Bikes rocker above the skull and the tagline *Not Your Daddy's Ride* on the bottom rocker so that when taken together, the whole thing looks like the three-piece colors of a motorcycle club.

My mind wanders back to when I made this logo. Ronnie and I were on the couch in the living room, sweating our asses off in the midday August heat the summer after graduation…

### *Two years ago—Bellvue farm*

Her legs slip under my sketchpad and rub along the soft jeans covering my thighs. I've got a huge hole in the right pant-leg, and the flicker of heat that passes across my bare skin as she positions her legs makes me hard immediately. I stop sketching and rub my palm up and down her calf.

"Ooooooh," she purrs.

Her legs are so fucking soft and smooth. Either this woman is hairless or she shaves every day. "You're distracting me, baby. And you smell so fucking good, I can hardly stand it."

She sits up and wraps her arms around my neck, her legs staying put in my lap. "What do I smell like? Tell me again."

I smile at this. Why this turns her on, I have no idea, but it does. "Sugar, Bombshell. You smell like sugar." She licks the inside of my ear and I melt a little, letting out a deep breath. "I'm never gonna get this logo designed if you keep demanding my attention."

She grabs my sketchpad and tosses it over on the coffee table. "That logo is perfect the way it is, Mr. Shrike." Her back straightens and her tits push against my chest. "Pay attention to me," she begs in my ear, her soft breath floating across the sensitive skin.

I grab her ass, haul her up into my lap and squeeze her until she squeals. "You're being bad, Ronnie. I'm trying to work."

"I'm work," she pouts. "I need to be worked." She leans in to nip my neck and then she lifts her mouth to my jaw. "I need to be worked every day. I'm gettin' rusty."

"Ha," I chuckle. "I fucked you hard this morning, you're well-oiled as far as I can tell."

"No," she insists as her lips drift over to mine so she can make me respond when she begins to lick me. "I need to be oiled, but I'm far from well-oiled now."

She lets out another loud girly squeal as I toss her off to

the side, making her tits bounce when she hits the soft cushions of the couch. "Stay still, Bombshell."

*Fuck me*, she mouths silently. I lose control when she does that and she knows it. *Fuck me*, she mouths again. *Fuck me, fuck me, fuck me.* Over and over again.

She's wearing that little bombshell tank top I made for her. The one with the pinup looking suspiciously like her, sitting on a WWII bomb as it sails through the air.

I grab the hem of her shirt and rip it right up the center.

"Spencer!" she screams. "I love this tank top!"

I grab the cups of her lacy pink bra and rip that apart too. "I'll make you another one, baby."

"Oh," she gasps. "You are in so much tr—"

I pop the button on her Daisy Dukes next. It goes flying across the room. "You wanna get fucked?" I growl at her. "Lift your hips."

She shudders. She always shudders. Like what I do to her is a surprise each and every time. I wait for the swallow, but she tucks her nerves away and inhales.

I've fucked Veronica Vaughn like eleventy billion times in the past year that we're been dating. I've licked every inch of her body. I've fucked her pussy, her ass, her mouth, and her tits. We've done it outside, in the shop, on a bike—hell, on like a dozen bikes, at least—in the river out back, up on a ridge in the hills behind the property, in four public parks, on CSU campus—like every fucking building they have on CSU campus, minus the bookstore because we got caught before we finished, so it doesn't count—in the back of my truck, in the bathroom, kitchen, bedroom, basement… you name a place in the greater Fort Collins area, and chances are I've fucked my Bomb there.

But no matter what, no matter how many times I take her body, no matter how public the taking is, no matter how dirty the talk—the thing that turns me on the most about my Bombshell is the shudder that runs through her body each and every single time we get started. It's my drug, and I'm addicted to it.

That shudder says, *You rock my fucking world, Spencer Shrike.*

And my response, each and every time, are these thoughts. The ones running through my mind, and not the ones controlled by my dick. The memories we make every time I touch her.

*Fuck me*, she mouths again as she lifts her hips and I slip her shorts off. Her panties are so adorable. And this is what I love about Ronnie. She's a tattoo artist. She shoots better than I do after she took a bunch of marksmanship classes at my gun club. She's got moves an MMA fighter would envy. And she comes from a brood of siblings who would make just about anyone shit their pants if they ever met them in a dark alley.

But this girl—this girl is a fucking princess underneath it all. She's soft and sweet and pretty and she smells like a bakery.

She smells like a sugar cookie. She's like those little crystals of sugar on top, the ones that melt in your mouth.

"Fuck me," she says out loud now. "Fuck me."

I lean down and suck on her nipple, massaging her large breasts until she moans.

Piss on the logo, the logo can wait. I shift positions and lean down, her little body smothered by my large one. And now it's my turn to breathe into her ear. "Veronica Bombshell Vaughn, I'll never stop fucking you, baby. You know why?"

I wait for an answer and this throws her off her game. Her brows knit together slightly because I've changed the rules on her and I want a response. "Why?" she whispers back.

"Because you're mine, baby. And I'm gonna keep you forever."

"You promise?" she asks with a second shudder.

I have to close my eyes to let my body fully soak up that unexpected treat. "I promise."

My phone vibrates in my pants and I reach in my pocket and pull it out, hoping it's Ronnie calling me back.

It's not.

It's Ronin.

"Yeah," I say.

"Hey," he says back. "You seen Rook around? I keep calling and it goes right to voicemail."

"I think her and Ronnie are at the women's doctor together."

"Huh, why? Ronnie got a problem?"

"No, you asshole. Rook said she had an appointment."

"No," he counters back. We are like the Two fucking Stooges. "She never mentioned the doctor to me. I'm pretty sure she'd tell me that."

We just wait there in silence for a few seconds like dumbasses. "Well," I finally say to break the awkwardness. "I guess congratulations are in order. Way to go, she's probably pregnant and wants to keep it secret until she gets confirmation."

Silence.

"Ronin?"

But the phone beeps three times and the connection is lost.

## CHAPTER FIVE

***"He left you like that?"*** Rook says with shocked surprise.

"Yeah, can you believe the nerve of him? Got me all worked up, came on my leg, and then zipped me back up tight like he was wrapping a present to save for later."

"What a fucking asshole!" Rook is always on my side. I love her. "But like, what did he say? I mean, didn't you stop him and be all, 'What the fuck, dude?'"

I crack the window, pull out my e-cig and start puffing away. "Oh, you know. The usual caveman bullshit he always pulls."

"Pfft. Yeah, Ronin tries that shit too. I'm like, *No*."

"Oh, I love the caveman bullshit, actually."

Rook takes her eyes off the road and looks over at me. "You do?"

"Oh, fuck yeah. Spencer is one hundred percent caveman. So he was all, 'I'm the motherfucking boss of you, Bombshell.' And I was all—well, I was actually stunned silent that he was gonna leave me hanging." I take a puff and blow out a stream of vapor, making little smoke rings as I do it. "So I sorta just agreed with him."

"What? Veronica, don't let him walk all over you like that. God, Spencer, I dunno. He's hot and all but Ronin and I are like... *partners*. Spencer is too intense for me. He's bossy and... and *intense*. I would not be able to handle him."

I sigh. "God, why do I love that man so much, Rook? I

don't get it. He treats me like total shit. Like I'm garbage. And still, I'm practically wetting myself whenever he touches me." I puff and pout for a few seconds. "It's like I lose all control when I'm near him."

She turns the truck onto Spencer's private road, which he even named after me back when we first started dating. He lives on Bombs-A Way. It took months of paperwork and I have no idea how much it cost, but sure as shit, that's what the road is now called. It used to be Private Road 13, so Bombs-A Way is much better. And cuter.

"Why is he so confusing, Rook? I just don't understand him at all. I need to get away from him. Maybe I'll move to Denver when you go home." The thought of Rook leaving me is upsetting all of a sudden. "Are you guys moving back when the season's over? Or you gonna move to Boulder for school? Maybe I'll go to Boulder with you."

Rook sighs deeply. "I dunno about school, Ronnie. I sorta suck at like—all of it." She stops to laugh a little so instead of getting concerned that her dream of film school is going down the tubes, I relax and just listen to *her* problems for a change. "I mean, film school still sounds fun and all. I'd still like to do something related to movies. But I'm just not into the bullshit classes I have to take in order to get that piece of paper. I mean, I have that cool camera Ronin got me for my birthday. And I have a ton of money. Why can't I just start making movies? Why do I need to go to school to make movies? I know what I like to watch and those movies aren't bizarre artsy fucking bullshit. They're popular films that make millions. So can't I just make movies I like until I get good enough for people to take notice?"

I puff and ponder.

"Be serious with me now, Ronnie. Do you think you need an art degree to do what you're doing?"

I cough on the nonexistent smoke in my lungs. "To be a tattoo artist? I dunno." I shrug. "I was always an artist. Generally people who want to go to art school are already artists. They do it to make their parents feel better about their career choice. But in my case, I think I just wanted to prove that I was smart enough, ya know? Like I'm just as good as all those kids at CSU, even though I'm a Vaughn."

"Exactly!" Rook squeals as we pull into Spencer's driveway. "I think I just want the degree to prove I'm not trash. And back when Spencer was body-painting me he told me something. Something like—painting naked girls is his one true talent. The one thing he was born to do, the one gift he was given at birth. He said he did an internship with a famous painter or something, but basically he said he just knew how to do it. That's sorta how I feel about movies. I can make movies, I just know it. But what I can't do is college algebra."

I laugh at that. "I had a tutor. I'm not a math girl either."

She shakes her head and laughs with me. "Yeah, well, Ford's been busy with his new life and I'm too afraid to get another tutor after what happened with the last one."

Rook's math tutor last semester ratted her out to all kinds of bad people. Of course, he didn't understand he was helping the bad guys, but it's hard to let that shit go if you're the one on the receiving end of a plot to kidnap you and sell you to a Columbian drug lord.

"Hey, how come Ashleigh didn't come, anyway? I thought you said she was coming?"

"Oh, baby Kate was fussy. She's teething and stuff. Six months is a hard age. They start getting opinionated and demanding. Getting ready to crawl and assert some independence."

Rook says all that like she's a fucking pediatrician. I bet she read all those mother-to-be books back when she was pregnant, before she lost her baby to a terrible accident.

Rook parks the truck in front of the carport and shuts it off.

"Does it make you feel sad? When you watch Ford and Ashleigh with Kate?"

She looks out the window for a few seconds. You can see

the river in the winter because all the trees are bare. And there are a few deer over there looking for food. "You know," she starts softly. "It sorta does. And not just in the obvious ways. Ford and I are good friends. And Ashleigh is perfect for him. But we're not as close as we were. And the baby. God." She stops again and I'm tempted to change the subject so she won't have to face these feels. But she continues before I can do that. "Kate's so beautiful, ya know?"

Rook looks over to me now, all sad and shit. I nod. "Yeah," I say back just a softly. "She's very adorable."

"I'm going to the doctor after this," Rook blurts out suddenly.

"How come?"

"That was my excuse to get rid of the camera crew, but also—" She looks over at me, and for a moment I get the feeling she's afraid to tell me something.

"What? What is it?"

"I'm gonna have them remove my birth control implant."

"Yeah?" I smile big and lean over to hug her. "So—moving on?"

She shrugs. "I just look at Ashleigh and I'm a little bit jealous."

"Wait. You're jealous of *Ashleigh*? Why? Shit, Rook, from my end, you have the perfect life. Ashleigh's life is pretty good too, I guess. She's married and happy. Got the kid, the house, and the dogs, even if they are certified weapons. But you've got everything she has, plus you're *you*. There's no other Rooks in the world. I'd switch with you any day."

"What? Seriously, Veronica. Look at you. Your man calls you Bombshell for a reason." Rook laughs.

"Maybe. Except he's not my man. Is he? He obviously thinks I'm some sort of throwaway trash from the way he treated me this morning. And it's not anything he said, it's just—the way he walked away like it was nothing." Rook just stares at me, unsure of what to say. And that's the problem, there's nothing to say about it. Not really. It happened. He did it. "He thinks I'm nothing. So maybe it's time for me to walk away and think of *him* as nothing?"

She gives me a crooked smile as she shakes her head. "So that's why you've gone to all this trouble to get a Shrike Bike, you're wearing his leather jacket, and you took the job as his personal assistant? Not likely, Veronica."

And she's right. What the fuck am I doing? I'm just playing right into his hands.

I open the door and jump out, grabbing my pack and hucking it over my shoulder. "You said you had a helmet I could use?"

Rook gets out her side and meets me at the bike. "Yeah, it's down in my apartment. Come on, we'll go get it."

She keys the code on the door and it reminds me of the last time I was here. "Did you know Ford spent the afternoon with me on Christmas Eve?" I ask as the door clicks open.

She walks through the door into the kitchen and I follow her in. "This last Christmas? Really? He never said anything to me, and I talked to him on the phone that night."

"Yeah, he caught me coming out of Anna Ameci's with Carson, back when I had that one date with him. And he wanted to show me Spencer's office, to try to convince me that Spencer still cares."

Rook stops dead and I slam into her back before she turns around. "You were dating Carson?"

"Just that one time," I laugh. "I figured I needed to put Spencer behind me, right? And I wanted a guy who was like the complete opposite. Carson sorta fits that bill, right?"

"Well, uh, yeah. I guess. But it's a little overkill, don't you think?"

"Yeah, well, Ford, he's the perfect anti-Spencer. So seeing him that night—all nerdy and shit—I realized Carson was just a dweeb. Plus Ford showed me Spencer's office. Have you ever been in there?"

"No, what's in there?"

I walk off towards the hallway, then turn around and

beckon her. "Follow me and I'll show you."

"I don't have the code for the office, Ronnie."

"That's OK, I do. I watched Ford when he opened the door that afternoon. And normally I'd never remember a six-digit code, but this one is hard to forget."

"Why?" she says as I stop at the office and key in the code for the electric locking mechanism.

"Because it spells *Ronnie*."

I open the door and flick on the lights and she gasps, just like I did back in December when Ford was the one flicking on the lights.

"What the hell is this?" Rook asks as she makes a full three-sixty to take in the room.

"I have no fucking idea, Rook. That's what makes him all the more confusing. Ford said they call it the Ronnie Shrine and even though that might be a little bit flattering, it's verging on creepy for me. I mean, if we were together, then yeah. I'd like my man to have his office walls filled up with photographs of me naked and done up in these body paint costumes."

It thrills me that he looks at me like this when he's in here, and I'm a little bit uneasy about that thrill. Because there's not just one image. But six of them. All me painted up to look like different things.

She walks over to the cyborg image and her fingers reach up to touch it. "I was the cyborg too," she says softly. "God, I have to admit, Ronnie. I know he's your guy and it's probably weird that he painted me in all the same outfits as you, but that was the best summer of my life."

I sigh. "No, I totally get it. Because those two years he was painting me up instead of you—well, those were the best two years of my life as well. And I miss them. I miss *him* so very badly, Rook. It makes my heart hurt, ya know?"

She comes over and pulls me into a hug. "I know. But Veronica, surely this is a good sign. He has to love you, bitch."

I chuckle against her and then she joins in.

"He has to love you. You can't even see your tits or pussy

in these pictures, they're covered in paint. He has them on the wall because he wants to be surrounded by you. If he just wanted pictures of his work on the walls, Ronnie, he could've put me up there, because all those photos were taken by Antoine, they're stunning. And if he just wanted naked girls, he'd plaster porn up there."

She's right, but when I look back up at the images, instead of feeling better, I feel worse. I'm almost overwhelmed with the memories as they flood in…

CHAPTER SIX

***Three Years Ago—Bellvue Farm***

***"Come here,"*** Spencer says seductively as he reaches out for me. "I want to show you something, Bomb."

I place my hand in his as he holds the screen door open for me. I walk through and we descend down the front steps of the old farmhouse and start walking across the grass. We've only been dating a week, and even though I've been at his house almost every day, we've never been back in the shop.

But that's where he takes me now, and it's got my stomach all twisted up. Not because I'm nervous or anything. It's because I'm half a step behind him, so every few paces, his head turns and he flashes me this oh so fucking sexy grin. It even comes with a twinkle.

A few paces on he does it again, like he's a boy with a secret. And while I might not know exactly what that secret is, I do know what it's about. Sex.

Because Spencer fucking Shrike is nothing *but* sex. One hundred percent sex, one hundred percent of the time.

"Are you nervous, Bombshell?"

"No," I lie.

He chuckles as we reach the shop door. "Maybe you should be?" He stops here and pulls my face to his, his lips gently caressing mine for a second, then his tongue takes over and I almost melt right there in the driveway. I even have a flash of concern that I'll fall and skin my knees on the gravel.

But then his strong arms wrap me up and hold me steady

as he whispers in my ear. "I want to show you something, OK?"

I nod, because I lose all control around him. I'd agree to just about anything.

"You ready?"

"Yes," I whisper back.

He smiles and opens the door, waving me in.

I look around expectantly, waiting for something to happen, or at the very least for something to be different. But it looks the same as it did last week. Bikes. Some complete, like the Blackbird. Some in process, like the knockoff of the Blackbird he's building as his first custom Shrike Bike.

It smells like a garage, like all garages smell. It smells like home to me, because my gramps, my dad, and all my brothers are bike mechanics as well as tattoo artists.

Spencer closes the door quietly and then tugs me off towards a dark hallway off to the left. "This way, Bomb. I've got a surprise."

My stomach flips again. "What kind of surprise?" I ask, more curious than afraid. But I am a little bit afraid. It's dark in this hallway.

He stops at a door. "You'll see, baby." And then he takes his keys out of his pocket and unlocks the door, opening it wide enough for me to step through.

And I see the very last thing I ever expected to see.

On the far side of this drab prefabricated shop building is… something breathtakingly beautiful. A large glass-walled atrium filled with trees and plants, the air sweet with well-cultivated earth, young trees, and sunlight.

I walk forward into the room. "What's this?" I ask, astonished, twirling in place for a moment, trying to get a three-sixty view of the place. "It's like a greenhouse."

"It is a greenhouse. Only… a fancy kind. I told you this was my gran's place until I inherited it." Spencer stops to take a deep breath. "My gran was a botanist before she married my gramps. He died a long time ago, left her a bunch of money. They lived down in Denver, in the house I grew up in. And after he died my gran came up here to the farm and dedicated her life to plants."

When he looks back at me I'm smiling as I picture this. Our relationship is so new, I have no history on him yet. I know he's the heir to Shrike Bikes. I know he was in some trouble last spring and he got kicked out of the University of Denver, that's why he transferred up to CSU as a senior. I know he's hot. He's a bit on the controlling caveman side, and he's a spectacular lover.

I look up at the dome ceiling and I'm blown.

"It's weird, isn't it?" he asks, as he leads me to the center of the atrium, right underneath the geometric panes of glass that allow the sunlight to filter through and cover the ground in amazing patterns.

"What's weird?" I ask, only half able to pay attention to his words.

"Dedicating your life to plants."

This makes me look at him. "Is it? She must've loved plants, though, right? Like you love bikes and I love…" His eyes search mine for a few seconds and I'm suddenly completely off balance. I want to say *art*, but my mind says *you*.

He drops my hand and reaches out to touch the leaf on a nearby sapling. There are no fully mature trees in here, it's far too small to house them. But there are plenty of young trees. Some almost as tall as the ceiling, which would be about twenty feet if I guess correctly. And one tree that is bigger than the rest, right in the center of the place, surrounded by the most perfect sea of grass I've ever seen.

"*Aesculus glabra*," he says in a whisper.

I smile. Because seriously—Latin? This man is nothing but surprises. "What's that mean?" I ask, mimicking his low voice.

"Ohio Buckeye." He chuckles.

I study the trees more closely now, looking to see if they're all the same. "They're all buckeyes?" He nods. They have buckeye trees outside the student center on campus. That's how I even know about these trees. "This one is too big to be in here," I say as my eyes find the tallest tree and then travel all the way up to the ceiling where the branches are reaching for the sun. "What happens when it outgrows this room?"

When I look over at him, he's studying me, tilting his head a little. "What do you think happens?" And then something changes in him. It's small, not even something physical, but something… internal. Like my answer to this question is critical.

"There are only two options."

He smiles and nods his head. But he stays silent.

"Cut down the tree or tear down the building," I answer.

"Which do you think will happen?"

I look around at this beautiful place. The glass is a work of art in and of itself. They are not just rectangular panes, they are all different types of shapes. Triangles mostly, but some are square, some are circular, outlined by thick metal lines, similar to a stained-glass window, except all the glass is clear to allow the sun to shine through.

I look at all the rows and rows of potted plants, then a wall of hedges along one side of the room. My eyes take in the many saplings. Some are even out of the ground, their roots wrapped in burlap. Like they are waiting to be transplanted. There's a system of pipes with spray nozzles over many of the benches holding seedlings, and there's a workroom off to one side that looks like an office.

I look back over at Spencer. "You're going to destroy this room." I pause, because it's painful to even picture it. But then I look up at the tree and imagine how many years his gran must've cared for it to be so big. "How old is it?"

"As old as me," he replies as he looks around at the room. Maybe trying to come to terms with the fact that he has to tear it down to save this one life. "The crews are coming in next week to take everything away. I've sold all the plants." He points to the big buckeye. "Except that one, of course. It gets to stay forever. My gran lost herself in here. She never recovered when my gramps died before I was born. She really did dedicate her life to plants. When she died and left me this place I expected to have instructions, ya know?" He draws his gaze away from his tree and looks down at me now, his blue-gray eyes a little turned down with sadness. "But there was nothing in the will about the greenhouse." He shrugs. "I was sorta lost over it. I didn't know what to do, so I just kept paying her two gardeners and pretended everything was fine. The tree really needed to be set free a long time ago, but I guess she couldn't bring herself to destroy the room to save it."

"I'm sorry," I say. "I'm not sure what I'm sorry about, really. Maybe that you are the one who has to make the decision. Or maybe just because it's a sad story and it deserves an apology."

He inhales deeply and then lets it out slowly. "Yeah, but that's not really why I brought you here."

"No? Not to see the tree?"

He shakes his head. "No. I have a request and I'm hoping that you'll say yes, even if it sounds a little weird."

I just stare at him, waiting for it.

"Let me paint your body."

"Excuse me," I laugh. "What the *what*?"

He walks over to the office and pulls out a cart, then drags it through the grass, bending the perfect green blades and leaving tracks in the carpet of green. The cart is filled with painting supplies.

"You're serious? My body?"

He holds up a finger and walks back to the office and comes out with a portfolio. "Please, Veronica, have a seat." I think it's the formal use of my name that makes me obey, but I have to admit, I'm curious. I sit down in the thick grass.

Spencer lies down next to me, propping himself up on his elbow, and opens the black portfolio. "This," he says as he looks up at me with the most serious expression I've ever seen him wear, "is what I do, Ronnie. Besides build bikes and major in business in college, of course. This"—he pokes the clear plastic that covers the first photograph in the collection—"this is what I do. I paint naked girls."

I take the portfolio from him and look closely at the

images. They *are* beautiful, but they're naked. "You want to paint my naked body?" I ask, as I look back up to him.

"Yes," he says, holding my gaze. And then he breaks it and turns back to the page. "This was my model in France. I studied as an apprentice there a couple summers ago and that's where I created this portfolio. But I've been busy." He looks up at me sheepishly now, maybe embarrassed about all the trouble he's been in. "And to be honest, I'm a little picky about my models. They have to be perfect. Not like, perfect *bodies*, just… perfect for *me*." He stares at me. "You know?"

I look back at the book on my lap. These girls look like they are wearing clothes, but it's an illusion created with liquid color. Put the shadows in just the right places and things take on depth. Curve a line that should be straight, and suddenly it pops out of the canvas.

Spencer Shrike seems to be a genius at manipulating perspective with paint.

"You really are an artist? You weren't in my class just to pose naked for me?"

He laughs big now. "Well, yeah, Bomb. The whole reason I asked to join the class was to get close to you, that's true. But I *am* an artist. And next week I'll stop being a model and start being a student again. But what I want to know right now is will you let me paint you up in here and take some pictures so I can have them framed and shit?"

"You want to frame me? Naked?"

He nods. "I really do."

"Like… make me your art?"

"Yeah," he says, jumping to his feet, grabbing my hand and pulling me with him. His palms go to my waist and hold me tight, they pull me into his solid chest. One hand slips behind my ass and the other tips my chin up so I have to look him in the eyes. "Let me take you somewhere else today, Veronica. Be my canvas, be my fantasy. Come into my imagination for a little while, explore with me, let me take you somewhere magical. And when I'm done, I promise I'll bring you back."

"What if I don't want to come back?" I say, totally one hundred percent serious. "What if I like that journey? What if I want to stay gone with you forever?"

He doesn't answer, instead he leans in and kisses me. Not the hard crushing way he kissed me that first time. Not the sexy seductive way he does when he's fucking me.

But some totally different way that I'm not sure I can describe. I just know it's… *different.*

I come up from the kiss gasping for air. "When do we leave?"

"Right now, Bombshell."

"When do we come back?"

"When it's over."

"So you really didn't bring me out here to make love to me?"

"No, baby." He must read my disappointment, because he tips my chin up again. "But my paintbrush will."

I shudder.

And this is when I realize. I'm caught in his fantasy.

Spencer walked into my life, tipped me upside down, and shook the love right out of me.

My love spills out all over the place.

My love piles up at his feet.

# CHAPTER SEVEN

## Veronica

***"I've never seen*** this costume before," Rook says as she points to the framed picture on Spencer's large walnut desk. It's the magical one of me in the atrium.

I open my mouth to respond, but I stop before she realizes. It feels like a secret. Like that's a special place that only Spencer and I even know exists. The entire day was like a dream. A fantastical dream. That was the best day of my life. And even though I understood back then that it was gonna rank up there as far as memories go, three years later it is so much more.

I have no idea if Spencer ever brought another girl to his gran's atrium, but I doubt it. And just knowing that makes me feel special and sick at the same time. Like—why? How? How did we go from those perfect days during senior year to *this*?

My chest heaves with a sob and I turn and walk out before Rook catches on to my grief. The light flicks off as she exits behind me, and then I gather myself and wait for her at the top of the basement stairs.

She's got a pouty face on when she catches up with me. "You're sad?"

All I can do is nod, because if I speak right now, I'm gonna lose it and cry like a baby. Rook nods at me as she scoots past, then I follow her downstairs. When she opens the door, I brush past her hurriedly and flop down on her couch. We spent a lot of time together down here in her farm apartment. After she outed all those assholes involved in a human trafficking ring back in Chicago she was relentlessly followed by the media. And the weirdos. Like those awful people who picket the homes of dead soldiers. They marched around town with giant signs, declaring her a slave-trading whore.

And yeah, Rook was involved in some pretty insane shit back in Chicago. But she was just a kid who got caught up with an abusive man. He beat the shit out of her for years. You can hardly blame a homeless sixteen-year-old for being susceptible to a ring of powerful and abusive slave traders.

"OK, Ronnie," Rook says as she plops down on the couch next to me. "Spill, bitch. What's going on with you?"

I think it over for a few seconds, trying to find a good place to start. "You know how you said—" I stop, because it's unfair to drag her down into my wallowing bog of pity.

"Said what? Come on, just talk."

I take a deep breath. "All that stuff about Ashleigh. About being sorta jealous. Well… I feel like that too. About you *and* her. Because you guys both have what I want."

I feel terrible for admitting that, but it's true.

"Ronnie, I have nothing but Ronin. And I know this sounds flippant because believe me, I understand what it's like to have no money. But that money means nothing to me. It's just… there. I know I'll never be homeless and I'm not gonna starve. And if I wanted to run away again, I could. But that's all that money means to me. I have nothing but Ronin."

I look up at her and frown. "I don't even have Spencer to make it all OK. I'm just so lonely without him. I feel like fate is telling me to give up. Just let him go, because he'll never change. He's not the guy I thought he was. He's this… this… stranger. He's not the guy I fell in love with. I love that guy I met back in college. This guy he is now, I don't get it. And what makes it worse is that every once in a while, that other guy comes through."

I'm thinking about Spencer that night he was in my apartment. When he said he was guilty. He said, 'I am this guy,' meaning that guy who committed those crimes he was accused of.

But he didn't wait around for me to tell him what I

thought of his confession. Because it was a huge relief.

That criminal who got kicked out of school, who got off a murder charge on a technicality—*that's* the guy I fell in love with.

This guy today? This one who's all cold and distant and leaves me hanging in a back alley and treats me like trash? I don't like that guy. I'll take the killer over that guy any day.

Rook and I stare at each other for a few seconds and then she shakes her head and breaks away. "Shit, Ronnie, we are a couple of whiners, you know that?"

I nod. "I know that. I do. It's wrong to have so much and be so unappreciative. It's wrong, I get it. But I can't help it, Rook, I'm not fulfilled. I'm… unsatisfied."

"Holy fuck, that's the perfect word." Her eyes get wide and she puffs up her cheeks with air. "That's the perfect way to describe it. Time out from your pity party, I'm throwing one too. So last week when I was spending some time with Ashleigh before we did that—" She stops, like she caught herself saying something she shouldn't.

And this is when I realize that Rook is part of it. She's part of that shit the guys do. I let my head sink in my hands, totally defeated.

"Well… I was gonna take care of Kate for a few hours last week, so I went over to their house to meet her properly. She and Ford just got back the day before, so even though I saw her that night for the party—" Rook winces this time, realizing this mistake was even more damaging than the last.

God, that hurts. Because I wasn't invited to the Welcome Home Ford and Family Party.

"—and I was in their living room, looking around. Apparently that Pam is a whiz, because Ford and Ash's house looked like it came out of a magazine. Anyway." Rook shakes herself out of that thought and continues. "I'm sitting there just making chit-chat, right? Just, you know, feeling her out, getting to know her. So she tells me she was in grad school, like she's just about done with her master's degree in psychology, right? She's one research paper away from graduation. She's done all her studies, wrote like two hundred pages of notes, and it's some fancy-sounding topic—brainwave patterns of emotionally compromised children or some shit like that. Way, *way* over my head. So I ask her, 'You gonna go back and finish? Get that piece of paper?' And she's all… just as casually as you can imagine… 'No, probably not.'"

"Really?" I ask. "Master's degree—that's like a shitload of school."

"Yeah," Rook replies. "That's what I said. I'm all, 'Isn't it a waste of time and money to not finish when you're so close?' and she's all, 'Yeah, probably. But I'm satisfied. So I'm not going back.' And I tell you what, Ronnie Vaughn, I was so filled with jealousy for this woman, I could barely function for like thirty minutes. I mean, she's not really that pretty. She's cute, she's got a curvy body, her hair and skin are beautiful. And she's got big eyes and full pouty lips. So yeah, she's easy on the eyes. But she's not *stunning*, ya know? Not like the pets I've seen Ford with every once in a while before he got rid of them. Ashleigh never wears makeup, and her wardrobe—I'm sorry if this sounds catty, I'm just making an observation—but her wardrobe reminds me of my homeless days."

I laugh, I can't help it. It's all true. Ashleigh walks around this town with her mean-ass dogs, pushing a stroller, wearing t-shirts and leggings, with bright pink running shoes on her feet like she owns the fucking place. She could care less what people think about her. Like at all.

"And I'm seriously not saying this to be a bitch, OK? I like her, I love that baby. But she makes me feel so fucking inadequate."

I'm stunned, because in my mind, Rook—she's perfect. In just about every way. "Why?"

"Because she has everything I want."

"Aww," I say, leaning in to hug her. "I'm sorry, Gidget." That makes her chuckle but I know she's crying now. "Finish your thought, Rook, just get it out, bitch."

Rook sniffs and laughs again. "And it's not Ford, OK? I do love him as a friend. I still talk to him like four times a week on the phone and we've run the Poudre River trail a bunch of times since he's been back from New Zealand. I'm jealous because she's on the cusp of everything, ya know? Like, if she *wanted* to be a career mom, it's like six months of work, a licensing exam, and bam, she's a counselor. But she wants to stay home and be a mother instead. And my whole life I've watched girls get stuck at home with kids they couldn't afford and maybe even didn't want. They got left behind by the men who helped create that situation. So I spent all my teenage years pushing that away. And when I got pregnant with Jon, I was not happy. Not for a long time. But then the idea that I could relax and be a mother sorta grew on me."

I lean in and rub her back. Because what happened to her sucks. You should not have to lose a child like that when you're barely eighteen years old.

"And now I'm thinking I was wrong, Ronnie. Because Ash said something else after that. She said, 'I can go back any time I want. But I'm never gonna be this person again. Every day the baby grows bigger, my love for Ford changes in small subtle ways, my life gets better or worse, or more chaotic or less stressful. Nothing stays the same and I can't stop that. So I'm gonna enjoy what I have right now and not worry about tomorrow.'"

"Is that why you're taking your implant out today?"

Rook nods. "Yeah. Because you know what? Ronin rocks my fucking world. He's everything to me. And I guess it took me seeing it from another perspective to realize it. Because you know, Ford might be weird and a total dick to almost everyone. But he's a very black-and-white guy. He married Ashleigh and there's nothing in this world that will tear them apart from his point of view. Nothing but death. Because when Ford goes in, he goes all in.

"And I think all three of these guys are like that. I think Ronin's all in too. I just never noticed it or never accepted it before. And last year I had all these doubts about him. Who is he? Is he good? Is he bad? Will he hurt me? Will he leave me? But if I were Ronin, I'd be asking myself all those questions about *me*. Because I've been pushing him away since we met."

She stops and looks hard at me.

"And I'm so stupid to never have recognized it before. So I think from now on, I'm gonna pull him towards me instead. I'm gonna finish out this semester. Then I'll have a year of college under me and no one can ever take that away. So if I want to go back, I can. But I'm gonna stop thinking about what's next. I'm gonna stop and be satisfied with what I have for a while."

And now it's my turn to be jealous. I slump back against the couch cushions and pull my knees up to my chest. "I wish I was anyone but me right now, Rook. Spencer's not like Ford and Ronin. He doesn't seem to want any of the same things as me. Like, at all. And who the fuck, ya know? Who the fuck would've thought that Ford Aston would be married with kids before me?"

"Spencer loves you, Bomb."

I laugh at the nickname. I can't help it. It's so derogatory and sexist. But it makes me so happy to hear it. To know that's what he calls me, and only me.

"He loves you, it's just… he can't be with you right now."

I sit up immediately. "Why, Rook? Tell me why? You know something, I know you do. I want to know this. Rook, I *need* to know this. Why can't he be with me?"

She shakes her head. "I can't say, Ronnie."

"So much for hoes before bros."

"Ron, come on. It's about the trials, you know I can't say anything. It's too dangerous. I have to testify next week. And once that's over, things will be different."

Will they? I don't say it out loud, though. They all believe it will be different. Even Spencer said as much. So did Ford when he brought me here on Christmas Eve to show me Spencer's office. But different doesn't imply *better*.

"He told me he was guilty," I add quickly to see if she'll take the bait.

But she just shrugs. "I have no idea what that might even mean, Ronnie. Sorry."

I stand up. "Fine," I say amicably, but really I'm sorta pissed. I mean we are like BFF's. Sure, she says Ford is her real BFF, but you can't be BFF's with a dude like you can with your bitches. She should trust me. They should *all* trust me. I'm not a liability. I'm strong. I can fight. I can shoot. I'm a tattoo artist for fuck's sake. I'm sorta badass. Plus, I've been around for years. Ashleigh and Rook are brand new to this shit. I watched it all happen in real time.

But I'm not in the mood to fight with her right now. I just want to move forward at this point. "You said I can borrow a helmet? I'm going to the Harley shop down in Broomfield soon to pick up my own gear, so I'll bring it back when I'm done."

She stands and goes back to her bedroom, leaving me to wait. It pisses me off that everyone seems to know Spencer better than I do. Just plain pisses me off.

But I take a deep breath and tuck my annoyance away just as Rook comes back and hands me a black helmet with a full face shield. We walk back up the way we came and end up in the carport where her custom Shrike Bike sits under a blue tarp. She unfastens the bungee cords holding the tarp down and then pulls it off with a whoosh.

I sigh with happiness. I've seen this bike a million times, but it's never looked so beautiful. Rook said she picked this bike out on a whim, way back when she first met Spencer. Back before the STURGIS contract, before season one. Back when she was modeling for the TRAGIC stuff with Ronin.

But it's strange that she chose this bike, of all the bikes he had in the showroom back then.

Because this is the Shrike Blackbird.

The very bike he drew in my sketchbook.

The very bike I tattooed on his back.

The very first bike Spencer Shrike ever made.

And now it's mine.

## CHAPTER EIGHT

# Veronica

***"I'll follow you,"*** Rook says as she opens her truck door.

I twist the key in the ignition and start the bike and then nod out an OK. "I'm gonna take side streets to the DMV so I don't have to pass the shop or Shrike Bikes. So I'll cut out once we get back to town."

She sighs and points her finger at me. "Be careful."

I nod. "Yes, Mother." She gets in her truck and I pull away and go slow to let her follow. I realize I'm the only girl in a family of six men, but holy hell, does everyone have to treat me like an invalid? Because seriously, I'm way tougher than Rook and if she can ride a bike to Chicago alone, I'm pretty sure I can handle scootin' around town.

The dirt road is a bit muddy, so I am extra-special careful until we make it back on the main road that leads to town, but once I get there, I relax and let my mind drift.

Seeing that picture of the first time Spencer painted my body on his desk has triggered all kinds of memories. I have pictures of that day too, but I haven't looked at them in years. Since the day he gave them to me, as a matter of fact. I was sorta embarrassed to have naked pictures of myself. And I was very worried about my brother Vic finding out about the whole body-painting thing. He's very protective. The twins could give a shit what I do, and Vann is like my partner in crime. They've always babied him too—never stopped them from kicking his ass regularly all growing up, but still. He can relate to being told no all the time.

Eventually Vic did find out about the body painting. How

could he not? Spencer and I traveled all over the place doing contests the year after we graduated. But he never did see the pictures of the night in the atrium.

That day, that night, that experience…

That was not just body painting.

That was seduction, pure and simple.

***Three years ago—Shrike Shop Atrium***

"Take your clothes off, Bomb," Spencer says casually as he messes with an airbrush.

I just breathe and nothing more.

He cocks his head at me and squints. "You having second thoughts?"

My breasts rise and fall in rapid succession as the adrenaline courses through my body.

Spencer does not miss this. "You're nervous?" he tries again. I'm only capable of the most basic functions of living. Breathing. One, two, three more heaving breaths bring his attention back to my chest and then before I can understand what's happening, he's supporting my weight. "Ronnie, you OK?"

I shake my head, uncertain what just happened.

"Ronnie? Speak."

"I'm OK. I think. What happened?"

He leans down and kisses me on the lips and it's only then that I notice we're sitting on the ground. "I think you fainted."

"That's… stupid. I've never fainted in my life."

He kisses me again, just as softly. It's not a seductive kiss, even though I know for a fact I'm being seduced right this very moment. It's a casual kiss, the kind you'd give someone absently. Out of habit, with no thoughts of being denied or crossing boundaries. It's a kiss that says, *I'm here.*

My head spins again and I have to close my eyes and breathe deeply for a second.

"Veronica?" His voice has a little more concern now. "What's going on?"

"I'm not sure." Thoughts are racing through my head, fast and furious. Even though I know such thoughts need to be tucked away, lest I faint again, they surface and there it is. "I think I…"

"What?" he asks, leaning in close again. His lips caress my cheek this time and I'm dizzy.

"I think I *swooned*."

I expect a laugh, or a tease. Or maybe a kiss to wash away my silliness… but instead he says, "You know what that means, right?"

I force myself to look up into those gray eyes because I need this answer.

"It means you're in love."

"I am in love," I admit immediately, breaking every rule of new relationships in one fell swoop. "I'm afraid I'm a goner and you might be stuck with me forever."

He smiles the warmest, most adorable smile I've ever seen. On anyone. He's got the most amazing smile. It's soft, and caring. Such a contradiction to his hard body. "I've already planned our whole life, so I'm good with being stuck. But first, Bombshell, I'd like to get you naked. And then I'd like to caress you with my paintbrush until I turn your body into something magical. I'm gonna make you blush, Bomb. I'm gonna make you blush, and when we're all done, I'm gonna capture you on digital film and keep you with me forever."

Goddamn. This man has a way with words. How can his mouth be sexier than his… sex. I'm not sure, but it is. It very much is.

He gently moves me so I'm lying flat on the grass, my arms relaxed and my head lolling over a little with acceptance or surrender, I'm not sure which. And then he's unbuttoning my shorts. My eyes dart down to his hands and then back up to his face.

He gives me a soft, but very crooked, smile as he drags the zipper down.

I swallow.

"Lift your hips, babe."

I lift and he slides my shorts down, leaving my underwear on. My chest starts to rise and fall in that weird pattern again. He leans down to give me another comforting kiss. "Be still, breathe deep. I'm not gonna hurt ya."

"I know," I say quickly. "I'm not afraid."

"Your body says different, Bombshell. But it's OK. I'm gonna lead you through this, step by step. Now." He gently grabs my upper arms and pulls me towards him until I'm sitting up. "Let's take this off, OK?"

I nod as he slips my tank top up my stomach. And I swear, I try my best to not let it affect me, but holy hell. His fingertips drag up my ribcage, and I'm not ticklish much, but my head falls backwards and a moan comes out.

What the hell is happening to me? It's like I'm out of control. Fainting and moaning. And all the man's done is ask me questions and lift my shirt off!

Spencer leans into my neck once the moan subsides. "Do I make you hot?"

I try to regain some semblance of control, but I totally fail. So my words betray every empty thought in my head when I whisper, "I'm an insatiable inferno."

His large hands stroke my calf, then he grabs my foot and pushes it until my knee bends. He does the same thing to my other foot, and then grabs my panties and says, "Lift, please."

I swallow and lift.

His fingertips drag down my outer thighs this time, then tickle that little dent behind my knees as he hooks the panties over my kneecaps and lets them drop to the ground on top of my feet.

I wait for him to finish what he started and remove the panties from my ankles, but he doesn't. He leaves them there, a reminder that he just stripped them off me.

God, that makes me wet for some reason.

His hands reach around to my bra clasp, and then before I can even formulate how I might feel about being stripped of my last bit of clothing, my breasts fall free and he licks his lips. He pulls the lacy pink bra down my arms and I slip my hands out before he makes me keep it on. I'm still thinking about the panties around my ankles. Something about that is just so… so… sexual.

I wait.

He waits.

"Now what?" I ask.

"What do you want to do now?" he counters.

I reach down and slip the panties over my feet and then set them on top of the small pile of clothes.

"And now you're ready," he whispers.

"What am I ready for?"

He gets up from the grass, grabs my clothes, places them in the office, then drags his airbrush equipment over to the spot where I'm sitting on the grass. "Now, I fuck you with paint."

*Holy shit. He just said that.*

I'm so turned on, I'm starting to throb. He walks back over to the cart, tests the flow of paint on a piece of cardboard, and then turns to me. "You will never forget this day, Veronica Vaughn. For the rest of your life, whenever someone asks you what the best day of your life was, this will be in your top three."

"What about the other two?" I ask.

"We haven't made those memories yet, Bomb. But we will."

The air bursts out of the gun and flows against my lower leg. It's not a sexual place on the body, not really. But I have to stop myself from coming right then and there. When I look up at Spencer he's all business now, concentrating on his canvas.

I take my attention back to the paint. It's clear, or almost clear. But it's got some kind of glitter in it too. And as time passes and more and more of my skin is coated, I realize what he's doing.

He's making me… shimmer.

"Lie still," he commands in his alpha voice. "And spread your legs."

"Oh. God."

But he ignores my words and instead takes his light stream of air to the inside of my thighs. He paints them in long strokes. Long, agonizingly delicious, flutter-inducing strokes. Up and down.

He adjusts the paint flow and then a puff of air hits my pussy and I almost die. "Oh," I moan out.

Spencer's spraying never stops. The stream of air only becomes slower and more directed. Lingering over my clit for a moment, then moving off to the side, then down my leg again. I realize he's been doing the same places over and over and I want to open my eyes and ask him what he's doing.

But I don't need to. I know what he's doing.

He's fucking me with paint.

"Give in to it, Veronica. Just give in, baby."

And I do. I open my legs wider. I pull my knees up and slip my hand down to my stomach, but it's quickly removed.

"No cheating," he chastises me. And then he adjusts the stream of air so it's stronger and the delivery of paint so it's almost nonexistent.

My back arches as the nothingness reaches out and caresses my clit. One pass. I moan. Two more passes. I whimper again and again. Three quick bursts and I lose myself in the sensation. And then the air is gone, and Spencer's body is propped over mine, his mouth on my mouth, his tongue tangled with my tongue.

I orgasm in the atrium.

And only his paint and his mouth ever touches me.

I have Spencer's complete attention the entire day. After the erotic beginning, the conversation is easy and fun. He teases me and tickles me, on purpose and sometimes not on purpose. We laugh and when it gets past dinnertime, he stops and feeds me strawberries and holds a glass of wine to my lips. My fingers have been intricately painted with elaborate rings and the jeweled bracelets encircling my wrists are so detailed and beautiful, I wish they were real.

He's painted my face too. A fantastical pattern of barely-there pastels that have the same shimmer to them as the whole-body paint. He won't let me look in the mirror and even though I can guess that I'm some kind of fairy by the outfit, I really have no idea what he's doing other than making me fall in love.

"What are you thinking about, Bombshell?" he asks me.

I realize I'm smiling. Very big.

I turn my head so I can see him next to me, careful not to rub my painted cheek on the soft grass since I'm lying on my back. "You," I sigh.

"Then my plan is working."

"What's your plan? Keep me captive in this atrium all day, naked under the pretense of making my body your canvas?"

He smiles, like there's more truth in that statement than not.

"It's gonna get dark soon. Are there lights in here?"

He looks up at the ceiling and my gaze follows. It's only then that I notice that some of the branches of the large tree have been trimmed so the geometric patterns of the ceiling can be seen. He points. "All the light we need will come from the moon."

This statement stops my brain. I look over at him again and he's smirking. "What are you up to? You've certainly taken your time today." I lift my head so I can look down the full length of my body. "Is it done?" It could be, I conclude before I look back at him.

He says nothing, just smiles.

The minutes pass and I relax back into the soft grass. "It's such a shame this will all be gone next week."

"Nah," Spencer says as he stretches back next to me. He reaches for my hand and gently twines our fingers together. "It's gonna be here forever." For a second I think he's changed his mind about ripping down the building. But then he taps my head. "Veronica Vaughn, this place will live on in our fantasies. You will remember this place for the rest of your life."

I say nothing to that. Just accept that it's true.

A little while later the moon appears above us, but it's not fully dark yet. "Soon," Spencer whispers.

"Are we done painting?" I ask.

"We're done painting, baby. We're just waitin' on the moon now."

With each passing minute the moon travels closer to the apex of the atrium and the sky grows darker.

It's a full moon. And I realize that it's bathing me in its light.

Spencer stirs and then leans in and kisses me on head. "Stay here," he whispers. "Be right back." I tilt my head as he walks off into the little office room off to the side. He emerges a few minutes later with an armful of camera equipment, including a tripod, which he sets up a little ways off from where I lie still. He mounts the camera and presses some buttons which make a beeping noise.

And then he stands up and walks towards me, reaching down.

I take his hand, carefully, mindful of the paint. But he doesn't pull me to my feet, only a sitting position. I stare up at him and he puts his finger to his lips. "Shhhh," he breathes softly.

And then he lifts the hem of his shirt and drags it up over his abs. Over the muscles of his chest. Then, in one swift movement, over his head.

I've seen Spencer Shrike's amazing body plenty of times over the past couple weeks. He's been in display as our life drawing model in art class.

But with him standing here, in this magical room, bathed

in moonlight—well, I'm breathless just looking at him.

He unbuttons his jeans and drags the zipper down, the sound a break from the nighttime song of crickets against the backdrop of a flowing river on the other side of the glass walls. He steps out of the pants, completely nude, and then picks up his clothes and takes them back into the office.

When he comes back out he stretches out his hand again and this time he pulls me all the way up to my feet.

The camera beeps. Spencer leans into my ear and whispers, "Stay still now, Bomb. I need a long exposure time to catch the moonlight on your body."

As soon as the silence is back, it's broken again with the programmed click of the camera. It's positioned beneath us, looking up. And I realize that this photo will capture my shimmering body being held in the arms of Spencer Shrike in the moonlight, the view of the apex of the geometric glass over our heads, and the branches of the tree in each shot.

The shutter clicks and Spencer's hands come up to my throat and he kisses me. The beep sounds and we freeze, mid-kiss.

I can feel his breath inside me.

I feel nothing but him.

The camera shutter clicks and we change positions again. This time Spencer maneuvers me in front of him, one hand greedily squeezing my breast, the other flat against my throat as his mouth claims the tender spot on my neck, just below my ear.

Beep. Freeze. Click.

He turns me around again and now I can feel his thick hardness against my leg, but not for long, because he reaches around to my ass and lifts me up. I instinctively press my sex against his and wrap my legs around his waist.

Beep. Freeze. Click.

We move again. This time he eases inside me, and I throw my head back as he fills me up.

Beep. Freeze. Click.

I have never.

Been fucked.

So slowly.

In my life.

I have never felt every movement so clearly.

And who knew that an orgasm could obey the laws of moonlight photography exposure times?

I drag myself out of the daydream and turn into the DMV parking lot. I park the bike and take my pack off as I walk into the building. My phone begins ringing inside the pack. I check it.

Spencer.

Shit. I cannot talk to him right now. Not after I just relived those first few minutes in the atrium. I feel weak all over again. How the hell can this man affect me like this across time?

I need some fucking space. So bad.

I let it go to voicemail and then take a number and sit down in the hard plastic chair to wait my turn. It's not busy, so I don't expect it to take long. My phone dings a message.

*Did you find me a place to live?*

Shit. I totally forgot about my assignment today. I probably should find him at least one place to see. I text him back.

*Yes. Will send details later.*

My number is called and I go to the counter and ignore the next text. I've got everything in order, so I hand over my bill of sale, my insurance card, and my license. The woman doesn't even say hello, just does her thing and asks for her money. I hand it over and ten minutes later I'm walking back to my Shrike Bike with the biggest fucking smile I've had in ages.

It's really mine now.

It's all mine and no one can take it away.

I smile all the way back to my apartment. But when I pull up to the crappy building I'm accosted with trucks of construction workers blocking most of the alley and my parking space to boot. I weave the bike between the men and the trucks and park in front of my stairs. I slip my helmet off and a prickle goes all the way up my spine as my eyes seek the cause.

And there he is. Standing on the small concrete landing that serves as my front porch, his knuckles in mid-air, like he's caught in the process of knocking.

"Miss Veronica Vaughn?"

"Yes?" I answer back hesitantly. A man in a dark suit looking for me cannot be good.

"I've been waiting for you."

CHAPTER NINE

# Spencer

***Ford's phone dings*** as I enter the Shrike Bikes cafeteria where the guys are kicking back eating the catered lunch. That's one thing they really love about doing the show. Not that they don't love the money, everyone got a raise this time around. Hell, Rook is making a quarter of a mil and the boys are all pulling close to two hundred K themselves.

But men run on two things. Food and fucking. I can't help them with the fucking part, and they don't need it from what I know of their personal lives. But food—hell yes. We get fabulous lunches. Fort Collins might be podunk to most people living on the outside, but it's got a shitload of great restaurants that are more than willing to feed us for including their logo napkins in a shot on the show.

Ford chuckles as I walk up next to him. He's leaning against the white cinder block wall, smiling like a dumbass down at his phone.

"What's so funny?" I ask him as I walk up.

"Kate," he says, flashing me the picture on his phone. "She's eating apricots for lunch and she's got them all over her chubby face."

Jesus Christ. I have no idea who this Ford is. He's got baby on the brain these days. "It's two minutes away, why don't you just go home for lunch and spare the rest of us your pussy-whipped bullshit?"

"Because," he says, looking up at me, totally serious, "it's hard enough to leave Ash once in the morning. If I went home for lunch, I'd tackle her the minute I walked in the door and never want to leave."

"Oh, for fuck's sake." I walk away and go help myself to the food, then take my plate and cop a squat next to Ryan at the table with the rest of the boys. Ford and his family. He's only been back in town a week and I'm already starting to gag on his sickening happiness.

"You'll understand one day, Spencer. When you're tired of playing games with Ronnie, you'll see."

My fork stops midway to my mouth and I stare hard at him. "You better shut the fuck up, Ford." He eyes me, then the camera crew, who are not on a lunch break, and winces.

Luckily he's smart enough to drop it and not start spouting apologies.

"Hey." Ryan jabs me in the ribs to take my attention off Ford. "I thought you were gonna show up at the Sundance last Thursday? I took my date there, hoping you'd bail me out, but you flaked on me."

"Yeah." I look over at him. Ryan is a few years older than me and he came from a bike family too, only his old man lost everything in a high-stakes poker game a few years back. Ryan and I were already friends—we met at the Elvis convention in Vegas the year before and we hit it off right away. We both have bikes, tats, and an insatiable drive to make money. "I had to cancel on Carla. In fact, I'm just too busy to do the Thursday night dates anymore. I might still hang at the Cat Call on Fridays since it's close, but I'm not gonna do Saturday night dates either."

"Totally understand, man. You're hooked up big with commitments."

Ryan's tall and big, like me. But his tattoos tell a story I'm not sure I want to know about. His tats are nothing but violence. On a first look, they're just a bunch of retro WWII shit. Old-school stuff. Diving swallows, anchors that say Mom, pinups. But if you ever have a chance to look closely, you see that's not what they are at all. The swallow is dead and decaying. The anchor is attached to the foot of a drowning man. The pinup has a black eye.

He's had a difficult life. Family had a lot of money when he was small, but they were new money. And sometimes new money has no idea what to do with all their money. So they do all the wrong things with it. Like gamble away the family business. Or get hooked on meth and try to sell their kids on the black market. Luckily Ryan was already thirteen by the time that shit started going down, so he got his little sisters out of it by turning in his mother the night before the 'sale'. But that didn't stop the downward spiral for long.

"Yeah, but we should go out this week. Just the guys, maybe," Ryan says. "Celebrate a little, huh?"

"I'm in," Griff says. "I'm a free man again, why the fuck not?" He gets up to throw his trash away and then heads back into the shop.

"I'll go too," Fletch offers. He's the youngest. No steady girlfriend or nothing. He almost never hangs out with us since he heads down to Denver every weekend. "I'm sick of Denver." He finishes his last bite of lunch and then gathers his trash and heads after Griff.

Ryan and I both look at each other and smile because Fletch only gets tired of Denver when he's avoiding a girl. I'm shoveling some half-warm fettuccine in my mouth when the back door slams open and the cops come in.

"There he is!" that little fuck, Drake, calls out, pointing at me. "That's him. I want Spencer Shrike arrested for breaking into my shop!"

Holy fuck.

I look over at Ford and he's already dialing the phone. Ronin, I'm sure. Why the fuck do the cops have to show up when Ronin's out of town?

I take a deep breath and come out swinging—so to speak. "Hey, Drake! What's up, little dude?" I take my attention to the cops. It's a short chick with blonde hair and a big guy with… "Scott? You a townie now?" This is the deputy who busted Rook last summer for speeding in my Shrike truck. It was a major scene because he's the one who found out Jon had filed a missing person's report on her. We've never been close friends or anything—in fact, he sorta hated my guts until that little Rook incident. But he lives down the road from me, so I see him driving through Bellvue a lot. And he always flashes me the country wave when he passes now.

That's like the universal rural signal for *what's up*? Which means we're friends. Because if you're not friends, you don't country-wave people. It's the law.

"Yeah," Scott says as his little partner jots down notes. Of what, I have no clue, but the chick is getting busy with the pen and paper. Scott ignores her and walks up to me. "I had my name on the FoCo department waiting list for a few years. Full-time position finally opened up, so I took it."

"Hey, Barney Fife?" Drake says. "This ain't Mayberry. I want him arrested for stealing my bikes!"

Scott holds up a hand to me and then turns to Drake. "Mr. Cikes, we have a procedure, so why don't you go give your side of the story to my partner over there, and I'll handle Mr. Shrike."

Drake scowls up at him and then does a quick turn.

"OK," Scott says as he looks around, spies Ford, nods, and then takes in who all's here. "I know what you're gonna say. Talk to Ronin. But I don't see him and I'd like to just get rid of this little twerp." Ford walks up and stands next to me and Scott directs his talk to him as well. "So just tell me what you two were doing outside his shop last week and we'll call it good, OK?"

"We weren't outside his shop," Ford says, taking over. "We were parked down the street. And the last I heard, we still live in America. Where people are free to park on any public street they want."

"They were smoking a joint in the truck, ask them about the pot they were smoking in the truck!" Drake yells from across the room.

Scott rolls his eyes, but he's got his back to Drake, so Drake can't see. "Were you smoking pot in the truck, guys?"

We laugh. In fact, Griff, Ryan, and Fletch are all in the lunch room again now, and they laugh too.

We might be criminals guilty of a lot of bad shit. But we don't do drugs and everyone knows that.

Scott leans in. "OK, come on, guys, you know anything about this? I don't think you did it, but if you know anything—"

"He blames me for his bikes going missing," Drake yells again. "And he stole my shit to get even."

"Drake," I growl. "Your shit is shit. Look around, asshole, do you think I need to steal your crappy bikes? You're nobody. Those seven bikes stolen from my showroom are barely a blip on my bottom line. It's called insurance, dumbass."

He lunges at me, plows right through the little girly cop and sends her crashing backwards. The whole garage sucks in a collective breath as she skids across the polished concrete floor and comes to a stop against Ryan's leg. Ryan leans over and extends his hand to help her up. She's beet red with embarrassment, but she takes his hand.

And then Scott is slapping the cuffs on Drake. "You have the right to remain silent..."

We all just stand there as Scott pushes Drake out the door, leaving the little cop behind to wrap things up.

"Um," she starts. "I'm... sorry." And then she bolts out the door after her partner.

"What the fuck was that?" Ronin says from the doorway.

We all swing our heads in his direction. "Dude!" I laugh. "Insanity! Fucking Drake tried to say we robbed him or some shit. What're you doing back, anyway?"

"You got me all riled up about Rook being pregnant."

"Pregnant?" Ford asks. "Since when? She never said anything to me about being pregnant."

"Why would she tell you before she tells me, asshole?"

"Because we're best friends. She tells me all kinds of shit about you, Ronin."

Ronin is winding up to fight, so I stick my arm between them. "He's fucking with you, Ronin. You've known him for ten years, and every time you fall for his shit."

Director Larry bursts through the door now, and he's the

one who's all riled up. "Holy cow! This is gonna be the best season ever!" He claps Ford on the back and Ford bats his hand away and steps aside. "We got all that on tape. Even"—he looks over at Ronin—"the pregnancy. Holy shit, if Rook is pregnant, our ratings will go through the roof!"

Luckily Ford pushes Larry out the door before Ronin knocks his teeth out.

I grab Ronin's shirt sleeve and pull him outside. Scott and little cop are still busy arresting Drake in the parking lot, so we head across the street and start walking down Maple towards the shops so that the noise of lunchtime pedestrians and traffic drowns out our voices over any potential listening devices.

"We need to pull that bot out of that shop, like now, Ronin. This shit is getting crazy. I mean, who the fuck is in town stealing motorcycles? And why?"

"I dunno," he says. "But we might have the whole thing on camera from the bot. We can't risk going through footage parked in that neighborhood, so pulling it is the only option if we want to see who did it. I'll go scout out the area tonight. Alone," he adds. "You and Ford have already been made, so I'm the only option. Then we'll come up with a plan tomorrow. Let's just hope that little dick Drake doesn't suddenly get smart and sweep his place for bugs."

"Fuck."

"We'll figure it out. Just keep cool, man, OK?"

I look over at Ronin. "I'm always cool."

"Yeah," he agrees as we turn around and start walking back.

But I know what he's thinking. I'm not always cool. Because I'm the one who lost his cool and shot that fucker up in Boulder. I'm the one who had us all staring at a murder one charge and twenty years to life in prison.

And I'm starting to get that feeling again. That twitchy feeling that says a storm is coming. That says I need to prepare.

Because not only do I have to worry about keeping Ronin and Ford safe, now I have to worry about Rook. And Ashleigh. And Kate.

But thank fucking God, my Bombshell is safe. No one knows about us. No one knows how much I love her. And that's the whole reason I continue to break her heart, time after time after time.

I never want this shit we're in to touch her again.

# CHAPTER TEN

***"Well," I say back***, still standing at the base of the stairs. I should be walking up them, going inside. But this stranger has stopped me dead. "You found me."

He adjusts his coat. It's a long black trench, pressed crisp, and looks like it cost a million bucks. In fact, this guy screams money. And then he steps towards the stairs and descends. Slowly. Like he's trying to make an impression on me.

It's working. I'm just not sure what kind of impression he's leaving.

Handsome? Yes.

Intimidating? You bet.

Dangerous? Absolutely.

When he reaches the bottom he looks me over. Like, not just the look-over. I get that a lot. That look says *I'm a pervert and I'm imagining my dick between your tits right now.*

No. Not this guy. This guy gives me a look that says *pay attention.*

And right now that look he's giving me is making me wish he *was* just leering and looking for a mental image the next time he wanks himself off.

He stands there like he's waiting for something, and I have time to take him in. Short, styled brown hair. Green eyes. Expensive suit that looks like it was designed specifically for his body. Which is large, easily the same size as my brother Vic's. I bet he's got muscles for miles underneath those clothes. He extends his hand. "I'm Mr. Mansi, owner of this"—he waves another hand towards the building in a dismissive gesture—"lovely piece of property."

"Oh." I laugh a little with relief. "Got it. I signed the monthly lease with Mr. Golden when I rented this place. So sorry, I just didn't realize who you were." I look around at the chaos of workers and take stock the way Spencer taught me back when we first started dating. "Where is Mr. Golden?" I drag my gaze from the commotion and stare Mr. Mansi in the face. "I don't see him."

It's only then that I realize I'm still shaking his hand. For several seconds. He's looking down at our grip with an amused smile and I pull my hand back self-consciously.

"He's been… relieved of his position. I'm taking over from here. And that's why I needed to talk to you. He should not have rented you an apartment in this building, Miss Vaughn. The first floor is contaminated with asbestos."

I gasp. Holy shit, asbestos! That's as bad as hepatitis in my book.

Mr. Mansi puts a reassuring hand on my shoulder. "It's OK, it's not airborne. It's not been disturbed. But it needs to be cleaned out, and I'm afraid that means you can't stay here. You can't go back inside now until they're done. They've already started ripping it out. I've been trying to call you for several hours, and well, we couldn't wait any longer."

"Oh." I breathe out some relief. "OK, so how long will it take? I guess I can stay with my dad." He smiles an indulgent smile and all of a sudden I get it. "You're kicking me out, aren't you? For good?" I turn and kick the wall. "Goddammit."

"Your lease was month to month and—"

I shove my helmet on my head and walk over to my bike and swing my leg over. I'm just about to twist the key when he places his hand over mine. I look up at him and he's smiling. Asshole.

"Miss Vaughn, can you take the helmet off so I can explain your accommodation arrangements?"

"My what?" I echo through my helmet.

He knocks on the helmet and I slip it off and rest it in my lap. "My what?" I repeat.

"I own several apartment buildings in the area. I've arranged for one to be provided for you. Would you like to see it?"

"Uh…" What am I supposed to say? "OK," I manage after a few silent seconds.

"Come with me, I'll drive you there."

"No," I say with a small laugh. "I don't think so. I'll follow you on the bike."

He looks up at the sky and makes a face. "It's getting cold."

"I'm good," I assure him as I push the helmet back down on my head.

And then he nods and walks over to the alley. I start the bike and back out, then meet up with him at his big black Dodge Challenger. He revs the engine a little, making the whole car sway and rumble with power.

That is sorta hot.

He nods at me and pulls out slowly. I catch him checking his rear-view to make sure I'm following. We cross College Avenue and weave our way up a few streets, not far from Spencer's new shop. He pulls up to an underground parking garage and we wait for the gate to open for us. I follow him inside the dimly lit garage and he parks the car in a reserved spot near the door to the elevator. There's a few other cars, sporadically spaced. But the place is pretty empty. Everyone must be at work. I pull up next to him, shut the bike off and engage the stand, pulling off my gloves and then my helmet, before swinging my leg over the bike.

I feel sorta badass while I do this. I mean seriously, I'm riding a custom Shrike Bike. I've got my old faded blue jeans on. I'm wearing Spencer's painted leather jacket, and my four-hundred-dollar Frye boots are the biker icing on the cake. I'm like one hundred percent hotness. I know this because this Mansi guy's eyeballs never leave my body.

I wait for some sort of direction, but he waits too. "Well?" I finally ask. "You want me to live in the garage or what? Let's get this show on the road."

He waves me forward, then a beep sounds as the lock disengages and the doors to the lower-level lobby open. It's pretty nice in here. Couple couches off to the side. Nice tiles on the floor, a rug. The elevator dings and we both enter and watch the doors close behind us.

"This is weird," I say, mostly to myself, but also to the stranger who now has me alone inside an elevator.

"Apparently not weird enough to stop you from taking this ride," he quips.

"No, not that weird." I look up at him and I'm about to elaborate but the elevator stops and the doors ding out a request to exit. "Well, that was quick, at least."

"It's the second floor. I'm sorry, that's all I have available besides the penthouse. But at least it's not the ground floor. I'm sure you'd feel safer on the second story."

I say nothing to that. I'm not worried about being attacked. I mean, yeah, it could happen. And I'm a girl, so most men are a lot stronger than me. But I'm not just any girl. I'm Veronica Vaughn. I've been fighting boys my whole life. And maybe being alone with this guy is a bad move, but a whole shitload of people saw me leave my apartment with him. He says he's the owner of my building that is temporarily condemned for asbestos removal. I have no red flashing lights for this, so I'm gonna ride it out.

He stops at a door, pushes a key in, then opens it wide so I can enter. I do.

He flips on the lights as he enters behind me and I walk forward into a stunning apartment. "It's furnished?"

"This is the model for this complex. All the units are sold, save for the penthouse. So it's no longer being used. It hasn't been listed yet, so I'll hold off on selling until you figure out what to do."

"What to do? I'm not sure I follow. I get to go home once that whole removal thing is over and come up with an alternative place to live, right?"

He smiles one of those indulgent smiles people save for idiots and my blood boils. "No, I'm sorry. We're going to remodel the entire building. Your apartment was not for rent, but the *landlord*"—he practically seethes that word—"rented you the apartment, took your money, and ran off with it. It was a mistake. So you'll have to find other accommodations immediately." He pauses to assess my reaction, but I hold it in. "But feel free to stay here as long as you need to."

I'm just silent. What do I say? Thank you for kicking me out of my place?

He drops the keys on the table near the door. "Well, let me know if you require anything—"

"But… my clothes? My stuff? When can I get my stuff?"

That stupid indulgent smile is back. "We'll have to see how the decontamination goes."

My jaw drops. "What? But… I have, like nothing. No clothes, no—" I stop complaining because he's thrusting a credit card at me.

"It's prepaid, one thousand dollars. I'm sorry, Miss Vaughn. But I really need to go and take care of the penthouse. We're having an open house tomorrow and that coordinator is about as efficient and trustworthy as Mr. Golden, I'm afraid."

And just like that he turns to leave.

"But wait—" *Holy hell, Ronnie, get a grip. He's gonna think you're some pathetic loser who wants to jump his bones if you keep stopping him from leaving.* "My boss is in the market for a place. I'm not sure if he wants to buy or rent, but I need to show him a place today. Maybe I could just take him up there and you can show him around?"

"Now?" he asks, like this is the most stupid request he's ever heard. "I'm afraid I have pressing matters that require my attention. But I will instruct the doorman in the main lobby to give you access if you bring him by tonight. Otherwise he can look during the open house tomorrow like everyone else."

And then he walks out.

What the fuck just happened?

I live here?

I twirl around and take it all in. It's really beautiful. Maybe more beautiful than Rook and Ronin's apartment down in

Denver. There's an L-shaped beige couch complete with a myriad of throw pillows along one wall. A giant TV. Not like those paper ones they put up in furniture stores. It's real. There's a pretty coffee table complete with magazines and large colorful expensive-looking books.

I walk over to the French doors and peer out over the large square balcony. It's only the second floor, so I have a view of some trees. They don't have leaves yet, but they might in a few weeks.

Will I still be here by then? I'm confused.

I walk down the hallway peering into the first bedroom. It's decorated as an office. It even has a computer. Real, like the TV. There's a bathroom across the hall. Just a regular one with a tub and stuff. But then I turn left and walk on until I come to the master bedroom.

I don't gasp, I laugh. Because holy shit! It's the most beautiful thing I've ever seen. King bed, large dark wood dressers, another huge TV, and an *en suite* bathroom that has a large oval jetted tub and a separate glass shower.

My phone buzzes in my pack that's still slung over my shoulder and I fish through it, hoping it's Rook calling so I can tell her about this amazing turn of events.

It's Spencer. But I need to talk to him anyway, so I press his face. "Hey, I was just gonna call you with that appointment."

"You were, huh?" he asks, with, like, zero enthusiasm.

Does he have to be such a dick all the time?

"Yeah, I found you a penthouse in those new condos on Mason Street? Well, they're having an open house for the penthouse tomorrow, but I got you a private appointment tonight." I stop talking and get silence. "If you want it."

"Where have you been all day?" he finally says after several long seconds. "I've called a dozen times and it went straight to voice. You were out of area. Where were you?"

"Uh…" I scramble for my alibi. What was it? "Well, I sorta had a big day, Spence."

"That right?" he says in that voice that tells me he thinks

I'm full of shit.

"Yeah, my apartment, well, you're never gonna believe this, but—" I stop. Because that was not the alibi. It was Rook's doctor's appointment. "Um, well, I'll tell you if you want to see the condo." Silence. He's mad. Or suspicious. Or something. I'm suddenly so glad I'm at this place and not my old apartment, because I had nowhere to stash the bike over there. Here I've got it safely tucked away down in the parking garage. "So… do you? Want to see it?"

"Will you be there?"

Oh, what a dick. "Yeah, I'm the one showing it to you, remember?" *Asshole,* I add privately.

"The ones with the red roof?" he asks.

"Yeah, them. I'll meet you downstairs if you're coming."

"Be there in five."

And then I get the *I-hung-up-on-you* beeps.

## CHAPTER ELEVEN

# Spencer

***She sorta had a big day***? She sorta had a big fucking day? That takes her incommunicado?

Yeah, fucking right.

She's lying her ass off, that's what she's doing.

Ronin already called. He cornered Rook coming out of the women's clinic. And yeah, she had a doctor's appointment all right, but Veronica was not with her when she came out. So if Ronnie tries to tell me that shit, I'm gonna lose it.

How the fuck am I supposed to keep this woman safe if she's about as predictable as unexploded ordinance? I figured giving her an assignment today would keep her busy, but not *this* busy. She is most definitely up to something.

Maybe I shouldn't have left her wanting this morning?

Too late to worry about that. I flip the shades down, slap the half-shell helmet on my noggin, and climb on the bike. I kick it and then back out of the garage. Ryan peeks his head into the storage bay where we keep our rides to see who's leaving, and then flashes me a little salute and disappears.

I rev the engine and take off with a squeal. The Mason Street Condos are less than a mile away, so I'm already there before I can get any more thinking time in. I pull up to the front, then back the bike along the curb and shut her down.

The condo building is brick. Brand new—they just finished this complex last summer. I look all the way up to the penthouse. It's only eight stories tall, so it's not like some big high-rise. But in Fort Collins, eight stories is tall. I take off my helmet, leave the shades down, and climb the steps to the building. The door opens automatically and I find myself in the foyer of a luxurious lobby.

Ronnie is waiting at a desk off to the right, which in my opinion make this place look a little bit more like a hotel than a place to live. But what the fuck do I know about luxury living? Ford's Denver condo had a lobby too, and there was a doorman and a desk.

But that was Denver. This is FoCo.

The lighting is dim in here, so it takes me a few seconds of walking towards her to realize what she's wearing. I stride up, my boots making a dull thud on the polished floors, and look down at her as she talks, waving her hand at the guy at the desk.

I don't even see that guy. I see her. Wearing my fucking bike jacket. Wearing biker boots. Her hair is pulled back in a ponytail. She's sporting a backpack instead of a purse. She has a chipped nail on her right hand.

I completely ignore every word coming out of her mouth and grab the sleeve of her jacket. "What the fuck is this?" I ask, my eyes blazing.

Her words cease mid-sentence. "Uh…" She looks nervously at the desk guy. "You left it at my house years ago, Spencer. I've always had this jacket."

I figured that much. I know I left it there. But that's not what's bothering me. "Why the fuck are you *wearing* it?"

She gives me the I'll-get-you-back-for-this-caveman-shit-later laugh, and once more looks at the desk guy. "Spencer," she starts calmly. "Do you mind curbing the language? We're here to look at the penthouse."

I glare at the desk guy. "Let's do it, then." I need her alone anyway. I'm not gonna get any answers out of her with this guy hanging around.

He gives me one of those disgusted sighs most people reserve for guys who look like me, then hands her the keyless remote for the condo.

Veronica reaches for it with her dainty hands. "Thank you, Charlie." She beams at him. And then she turns and walks over to the elevators.

I give Charlie another glare, complete with eye narrowing and growling, and his eyebrows go to the ceiling in surprise. I turn and follow Ronnie, who is now holding the door open. I walk in and she clicks the remote and the penthouse button lights up as the doors close.

"I don't like that guy. In fact, I don't like this *place*."

Veronica sighs and shakes her head, but she says nothing. We stand in silence and I get angrier by the second as I ponder the limited reasons why she might be dressed up as a biker. She's scowling at the doors, pretending I'm not here.

The doors ding open and I follow her into the condo. It's massive. The entire floor. "How many square feet?" I ask as I walk over to the windows to take in the view of the mountains. Nice.

"Three thousand plus, two bedrooms, three bathrooms, office, formal living, formal dining, and a media room. The kitchen is this way." She leads me past the dining room and into the kitchen. "It's staged for an open house tomorrow, but if you're interested, I can see if Mr. Mansi wants to sell the furniture too."

Uh-huh. She wants to play tour guide with me? Pretend like this day never happened? I can play. "How you get over here? You walk?" I look her dead in the eye as she lies.

"Yes."

"Why you carrying a backpack? Just trying to make shit easier as you hoof it around town?"

"Uh…" She squints her eyes at me. She knows I'm trapping her. "Yes, actually. It's more practical. Carries more, too."

"Have you made plans to buy a new car?" I volley back.

"Yeah, my friend Carson is gonna take me looking later," she lies again.

"Did you know Rook went to the doctor today?"

She sighs in defeat. "What do you want, Spencer? You want me to say no? Yes? Which one is the right answer? You want to know what the fuck I did today? Huh? You want to know how I found this place? You want to know who Mr. Mansi is?"

"Yes, yes, and motherfucking yes," I reply as I pace the kitchen. "I want to know all that and more."

She smiles and I steady myself for the explosion.

"Well, Mr. Shrike, I've been a very busy girl today. And since I'm on the payroll, I guess I do owe you an answer."

I nod my head. "Damn fucking right you do, woman."

She laughs a little at my caveman impersonation. Bomb loves the caveman, so I'm not worried.

"Well, I didn't go to the doctor with Rook, nope. But I did see her today. She had to go out to your farm to pick something up."

"Hmmmm," I hum out as I start putting the pieces together.

"And since I had all that money from selling the car you bought me for graduation, I decided to buy her bike instead. And I actually did get an invitation from my friend Carson to go car-shopping with him, but I turned him down because I'm good as far as the whole ride thing goes."

"You bought Rook's bike? You bought *my* fucking bike? You *purchased* my fucking bike?"

She smiles a smile that's so big, the sun bounces off her perfect teeth and makes them sparkle. "I sure did."

I just stare at her. "Are you fucking insane? What the hell is wrong with you?" I pace the kitchen and rub my hands over the short stubble on my head. "Goddammit, Veronica! Seriously, what the hell is wrong with you?"

I turn back, waiting for an answer. But she simply smiles.

"You're gonna sell me that bike back."

"I am not," she says calmly.

"Are."

"Not. I bought it, I just had it registered, I have insurance on it. And I'm gonna ride the fuck out of that bike all damn summer."

I realize I'm going about this all wrong. All wrong. So I stop and take a deep breath. "Veronica," I say softly.

"Bombshell, listen—"

Smack! My face is stinging from her slap.

"What the fuck was that for? Jesus Christ, Ronnie—"

Smack!

I palm my face and stare at her. Her brows are knitted together, the tight muscles in her jaw are contracting, her little fists are clenching. "Don't call me that name again, Spencer. I mean it. We're done. You think you can use my body any way you see fit in the back alley of a donut shop, then walk away like I'm some piece of trash not even worthy of reciprocal pleasure?"

I spin on my heel so I can smile and she can't see me. She's pissed that I left her hanging?

No, that can't be all of it. She's had this day planned. She knew what she was doing before I showed up and fucked her in the alley.

She's still yelling at me, calling me names, insisting I'm a pig. But I tune it all out as I plan my next move. I only got one as far as I can tell. I mean, I can bring out the big guns, but it's not time for that yet. So this will have to do.

I turn. She's all red-faced, still spouting off about this and that. I walk slowly up to her and she points her finger in my face. I grab it and she gasps.

"What are you doing?" Her eyes are wide as I bring her finger to my mouth.

She swallows.

My other hand comes up and grabs her at the wrist so she can't break away when I start to suck on her fingertip. I bite it, and she tries to pull back, but I have her good now. "Come closer, Veronica. Don't back away," I say in a low rumbling voice.

"No," she gasps. "No. No, no, no. I'm not getting caught in your—"

I lick the length of her finger, then dip to the sensitive webbing of skin just above her knuckle.

"Ohhh, hell," she whines as my tongue flicks back and forth between her fingers.

"I can do more than this, Bombshell."

I wait for the slap, but she opts for the hard swallow again.

I push her gently over towards the granite-topped island in the middle of the kitchen. It hits her at the waist and she has to bend backwards, because I do not stop pushing. "What are you doing?" she whispers and looks around nervously.

"I'm gonna make it right," I say as I nip her finger again.

"Oh, God, Spencer—"

I lift her ass up and place her on the island, still pushing forward hard enough to force her to ease back. She resists placing her shoulders and head on the stone, but I let go of her finger and place my hands on either side of her, rubbing up against her tits.

"You're mad at me?"

She nods.

"For leaving you feeling like a whore this morning?"

She nods again.

"You want me to treat you like my princess? Like I care?"

She looks away at this part and my heart cracks a little. She wants that so fucking bad. I pull her up and kiss her mouth. I lick her lips and she opens for me, pushing back against my tongue. I know her mouth. I know her tongue. We don't kiss. We dance.

She moans.

"Veronica," I breathe into her.

"Spencer, please don't do this to me. I can't take it anymore. I'm at the end here." She starts to cry.

"Veronica," I say again as I undo her jeans and drag the zipper down. I pull her off the counter and hold her until she stands up.

She won't look at me. She can't tell me to stop because she wants it so bad, but she can't look at me either.

I put her back on the counter and then tug off her boots, letting them thunk to the hard tile floor.

She covers her face with her hands.

"Lie back, beautiful. And take your hands away from your face."

She obeys without hesitation but her face is red and her eyes are wet once she uncovers them.

I pull her jeans and her lacy pink panties down in the same motion, then let them drop to the floor. She stays still until I lift her by the shoulders and make her sit up again. "Open your legs, Ronnie," I whisper in her ear. She tucks her head into my shoulder, but her legs obey.

I scoot her hips to the edge of the counter and then slip my finger between her legs, tracing her opening until I get the shudder.

God, how I wait for that shudder.

"I love you," I say softly. She jerks her head back, her chest extended like she just inhaled and she's afraid to let it out. I look up into her sad blue eyes and say it again. "I love you, Ron. It's always been you, baby."

I say it because my Bombshell needs to hear those words so bad right now. She's so desperate for all my bullshit to be over, I am powerless to deny her.

My cock is free, pushing against her entrance when she starts to sob.

"Stop, Ron. I'm here," I say. I thrust into her all the way and she gasps and pushes back. I lift her up off the counter, then turn us both around and take her place, setting her gently in my lap. Her arms are wrapped around my neck like she's afraid to let go.

We sit like that for a few minutes. Her crying as silently as she can. Me feeling like a total piece of shit, whispering nice things in her ear. "I love you I want you. I want you so bad, Ronnie, you have no idea."

"I have no idea because you never tell me," she sobs.

"I'm trying to protect you. I need to keep you safe."

She stays silent after that, just keeping still as she gets herself together. And then, after many minutes of waiting, she begins to rock against me.

I smile.

She lifts up and eases back down on top of me.

My dick becomes rock hard with these small movements.

She moans. And then she lifts up farther and slams down harder, making *me* moan this time. She does it again and it takes every bit of self-control not to turn around and throw her down so I can fuck the sadness out of her.

I hold it together, letting her take control at the same time. This is Ronnie calling the shots. I want her to know she counts. What she wants matters. She pushes on my shoulders. "Lie back," she says with urgency. "Please, lie back. I'm so close."

I do as she asks and flatten my body out against the cold stone. She bends over my chest, her tits heavy on top of me, her golden hair spilling over her perfect shoulders as she moves her hips back and forth, dragging her clit over my skin, both of us so wet we're slippery.

"Oh fuck, Spencer!"

"Tell me you'll stay off the bike, Ronnie."

"No," she moans. "No, I love that bike, Spencer. It means so much to me."

I thrust into her again and she gasps.

"I want you off the bike, Veronica."

"No," she says as she continues her movements. The friction against my skin as she dips and rises is too perfect to argue with her, so instead I thrust upwards. Hard. Hard enough so that my balls slap against her asshole and that about drives me wild. I reach around and play with her back there, reaching down into her pussy to wet my finger, then slipping it inside a fraction. Just enough to make her clench against my cock and drive us both to climax.

I shoot into her as she whimpers, bucking and arching her back as she finds the release I denied her this morning.

The waves of satisfaction continue for several seconds and then we both sigh. I smack her ass and it echoes off the tall ceilings of the kitchen. I wrap my arms around her and hold her close so I can give her a squeeze. "No bike, you need to promise me. I'll go crazy thinking about you riding."

"Hello?" a voice calls out from the other room.

Ronnie and I bolt upright. Listening.

"Hello?" the voice says a little closer now.

I place her on the floor and pull myself together as she wiggles back into her jeans and starts tugging on her boots. I grab her panties from the floor and stick them in my pocket just as a man in a suit walks into the kitchen.

"Miss Vaughn?" he calls out again before he notices us.

I smile. When I look over at Ronnie she's wincing. Like she just got caught.

Hmmm… I walk over to the guy, who is looking at us like we just fucked on the ten-thousand-dollar slab of granite in a kitchen that does not belong to us.

"Did you find the place to your liking, Mr. Shrike?" he asks with clear disdain.

People have this thing about bikers with tattoos. Like they're better than us. Most of the time I let it slide. I know what I am. I know what I'm capable of. I know my true value. But for some reason, I hate this guy on sight. "Uh, yeah, it's real nice."

"And your condo is fine as well, Miss Vaughn? Or does it not meet your…" He looks over at me. "Specific needs?"

"Wait," I say, puzzled. "What condo?"

And now the suit guy smiles like he's got a secret.

"Oh, uh, Spencer," Veronica interjects. "This is Mr. Mansi, the owner of this building. Actually he owns my old apartment building as well—"

"What do you mean *old* apartment building?"

"Please, Miss Vaughn, it's Bobby." He smiles at her like he's making a claim and my insides go hot with anger. "She's moved into my building, Mr. Shrike. She lives in one of my condos on the second floor as of today."

# CHAPTER TWLEVE

***Oh, fuck.*** This is not gonna be pretty. “So, funny thing happens when I get home from the DMV today, Spencer. There’s all these construction workers…” My words keep spilling out of my mouth but all I’m thinking about is how this will go down. Spencer just fucked me in this two-million-dollar condo that belongs to a man who is looking a little too much like a challenger for my comfort level.

How did that happen? The guy was nobody an hour ago. He barely had time to show me into my new condo before he had to leave and now he’s giving Spencer the territorial look?

Neither of them are listening to me so I just shut up.

Mr. Mansi looks over at me. “I’m sorry to… interrupt. But Charlie downstairs called and was worried about you meeting your… boss up here alone.”

“Is that right?” Spencer says, puffing up his chest. “He was worried about me talking to my… employee?”

Oh God. There it is. So much for he loves me, right? I’m his employee. Why doesn’t he just fucking say girlfriend! Arrrggh! I’m so pissed off.

They do the silent, teeth-clenching bro-down for several seconds and I sigh and decide to just take over since apparently both of them have caveman tendencies. “Spencer’s not interested in the condo, Mr. Mansi, sorry to have wasted your time.” I turn to Spencer to tell him I’ll look for something else, but he cuts me off.

“Whoa, whoa, whoa. Who says I’m not interested, Miss Vaughn?”

“I’m pretty sure it’s out of your price range,” Mansi says

back. "But I have a friend with some economy units available across town. Perhaps you'd like me to put in a good word for you?"

Spencer smiles. I know that smile. I've seen it before. Usually it's during a fight with my older brother Vic and it almost always ends up with a trip to the ER. For both of them.

I eye Mansi cautiously. He looks like a guy who bails himself out with money, not fists. But looks can be deceiving.

"Besides," Mansi says with a grin. "I've decided to keep the penthouse for myself. It's no longer for sale." Then he looks straight at me and winks. "So you and I will be neighbors, Veronica. Maybe we can have dinner one night this week? Unless you have a boyfriend?"

His gaze never leaves mine, nor mine his. I wait for Spencer to interrupt and tell him I belong to him. That he and I are soul mates. That I'm his one true love. That he's loved me since the day he met me. That he just fucked me right here in this million-dollar kitchen that belongs to the man standing in front of him.

But he doesn't. So I suck it up and swallow down the sadness. "Yeah, Bobby. I'd like that. I've got some shopping to do now, so if you two will excuse me, I'm gonna get out of here. Spencer?" I finally turn to look at him and even though I didn't expect much, I expected something. Some expression of disbelief. A small tilt of his head to ask, *What the fuck are you doing?* Some twitch of his eye or a clench in his jaw to say he's gonna kill that motherfucker Mansi.

But he's got nothing. Pure poker face.

I wave. "I'll find you another place to look at tomorrow."

I walk to the elevator alone. Press the button. Take a deep breath. Enter as the doors open. Smile big as I turn to press the button for the second floor. And pretend everything is just perfect as the doors close in front of me.

And then I break down. Because that asshole did it again! I'm so sick of the fuck-and-deny I can't stand it.

In the few short seconds it takes for the elevator to reach my floor I'm a sobbing mess. The doors open and thankfully no one else is around as I bolt for my door. I push the key in, fling it open, and then slam it behind me.

I lean against the door for a moment, then slide down and slump to the floor.

I hate him. That's it. I'm so fucking done.

My face falls into my hands and I cry. After a few minutes I lie down on the dark hardwood floors and curl up in a little ball. I'm tired. I'm so tired of playing this game with him. I lash out and kick the door.

It kicks back.

Or actually, it knocks back. "Veronica?" Bobby Mansi's muffled voice comes through from the other side. "Are you OK?"

"Shit," I say, frantically wiping my eyes and standing up.

"I heard that. Open up, I just want to apologize."

I turn the handle and open the door. "Apologize for what?" I sniff.

He smiles a warm smile. "Interrupting. I'm sorry. I can tell you two are an item, even if he won't admit it."

"We're not," I insist.

He shoots me a doubtful look. "I'm not stupid, Veronica. May I come in?"

I wave him forward. "It's your place, why are you asking me?" He walks into the little foyer area and I close the door behind him. "Are you really keeping the penthouse?"

"Yeah," he says, turning. "I really am. I like it. I wasn't going to stay here. Normally I live on the West Coast. But I got some new business here that requires my personal attention."

I don't have anything else to say. I don't even know this guy. I don't know this place and the only familiar things I have right now are the clothes on my back. All of which remind me of the one man I desperately want to forget about.

Bobby waves me into the living room. "Want to sit down?" he asks.

I walk forward and stop when I get to the couch. It looks nice. But I'm not sure if it's comfortable. I've never even sat on it before and now I'm supposed to think of it as mine.

A hand is placed gently on the small of my back. "Sit, Veronica. There's actually a bottle of wine in the fridge. It was purely for looks, when people walk through the model. But it's not a bad year. We'll have a glass, how's that sound?"

I sigh and sit. The couch is comfortable. And then I look up at Bobby's expectant face and nod. "That sounds nice, actually."

Bobby walks into my new kitchen. It's an open-concept floor plan, so the kitchen is separated from the living room only by a granite island. Not quite as spectacular as the one I was just fucked on upstairs, but still a very nice specimen of stone. He uncorks the wine and there are even wine glasses in the cupboards. In fact, I think the cupboards are just as stocked with stuff as the rest of the place.

He comes back out and hands me a glass, then takes a seat on the chair opposite the couch and leans his elbows on his knees, expectantly, turning his wine glass. Like he's waiting for me to do something. Or say something.

I take a sip of wine instead. It's good. I take another. Then I guzzle the whole damn glass.

Bobby laughs and sits back in the chair, satisfied that I'm OK.

When I come up for air he gets up, exchanges my empty glass for his full one, then goes back to the kitchen and grabs the bottle. He sits on the couch this time. Not next to me, but not far away either.

My eyes dart back and forth without looking at him.

"Are you and Mr. Shrike dating?"

I take another long sip of wine. God, I so, so fucking need more wine.

"Because it looked to me like you two were having a romp in my kitchen."

Holy hell, what do I say to that? Wine makes it all better though, so I continue sipping.

"I asked him if he minded me taking you out to dinner."

I do look up now. I look him right in his brilliant green

eyes.

"He said, 'Be my guest.'"

My eyes drop and I give myself a refill and guzzle that glass too.

"Would you like to go to dinner, Veronica? Tomorrow night? Or is Mr. Shrike lying and the two of you do have a thing?"

My sigh comes out a lot louder than I expected. In fact, it's kind of a tipsy sigh. "No, we used to date. But it's been over for a long time. What we do…" I look Bobby in the eyes again and allow myself to swallow down the humiliation. "Everything we do… everything we ever did… was a mistake. That ship has sailed."

"But you still work for him?" Bobby asks.

Shit. I forgot about that. I'll probably have to quit, won't I? "It's a new thing. Do I need references to stay here?" I ask.

He hands me a small chuckle. "No, Veronica. I'm not interested in your credit score or your past landlords."

I nod. "Good, because that apartment was my first place. I've only got my dad as a reference. Or my brothers. And I'm pretty sure they don't count to a guy like you."

"Hey." He holds up his hands. "Don't judge me and I won't judge you. How's that?"

Is he sincere? I study him for a few seconds before deciding he is. "Well, in that case, I think I'll quit my job with Mr. Shrike and go back to the only thing I'm good at. Tracing line drawings on people's skin. But I won't be able to pay for this apartment." He puts a hand up like he's gonna tell me it's not necessary to pay, but I stop him. "I get it. The place is free. But it's not free forever. I'm not trying to discount your kindness or anything, but everything about my life since I left home has been one big mistake. I can't afford shit in the real world."

These words affect me in a way I never expected. Because I just admitted defeat. I went through all that soul-searching to come up with something I could do besides tattoo art. Even if I was never really serious about a flower shop in the first place.

Even if I just used that as an excuse to move on, move forward. It still stings that I dated a banker to try to get a loan. I sold my car to buy a motorcycle that is more sentimental than practical. And I spent all my savings on that cruddy apartment, only to have all my worldly belongings locked up and inaccessible. Probably irrevocably contaminated with fibers that will give me cancer just by breathing in their general vicinity.

Tears build in my eyes, so I get up real fast to make a break for anywhere but this couch with this man. I stumble from the wine and I'm about to go crashing into the glass coffee table when I'm caught in his arms. "Thank you," I mumble, pushing off him and regaining my balance.

My pack is over on the counter, so I walk over and fish out my phone and press Vic's face. Bobby Mansi watches me carefully as I put the phone to my ear and then he gets up and begins walking towards me just as the call rings through to voicemail. *"You got me. You know what to do if you want me to get you back."*

I end the call and don't leave a message. I forgot, my whole family is down in Colorado Springs for some tattoo thing. I have to work at the shop alone for the next three days. But no one comes in during the week anyway. Thursday nights get busy and the weekends are almost always packed. Everyone will be home Thursday afternoon, so I'll be fine.

"Problem?" Bobby asks.

"No, not really." I grab my pack and go sit back down in the living room. I take the chair this time.

Bobby waits over by the kitchen. "So, dinner tomorrow?"

"Sorry, I have to work in the shop until eleven at night. I'm just gonna have one of my girlfriends bring me a sandwich or something."

He smiles and nods. "OK."

I get up and walk over to the door since he's sending I'm-leaving-now signals. "Thanks a bunch for your kindness. Do you want me to drop the key off with that guy downstairs when I leave?"

"That would be fine." He steps through the door and then

hesitates, like he's gonna turn around. But then he changes his mind and calls out, "Nice meeting you, Veronica," as he walks down the hall to the elevator.

I close the door and slump back down on the couch, stretching out. I mess with my boots until I kick them off, and then before I know it, the day fades away.

# CHAPTER THIRTEEN

***"Rook's not pregnant,"*** Ronin says the next morning as he strides into the office, his hair mussed and his t-shirt wrinkled. He flops down on the black leather couch off to the side of my desk.

I shoot Ronin with my finger. "Gotcha. OK. We ready to discuss business?"

"Ashleigh is," Ford says. He shakes the *Wall Street Journal* a little to straighten it out as he holds it up to his face.

"Ashleigh is what?" Ronin asks.

"Pregnant."

"Ford, don't mess with the guy. He's got baby on the brain since Elise is due to pop out a niece. Not to mention you coming home with Ashleigh and Kate."

Ford ignores me. "She didn't pee on the stick yet, but I know she's pregnant." He turns the page of the newspaper.

"How?" Ronin asks as he leans over to my desk and grabs a coffee in the drink holder.

Ford peeks over the paper. "How does she get pregnant?"

"No, you idiot, how do you know she's pregnant if you didn't do the pee stick test?"

"Do you guys mind?" I interject. "I'm not ready for baby talk with my bros, OK? Let's just discuss what you found out last night, Ronin."

"She smells different," Ford continues.

"Different how?" Ronin asks back.

"Deliciously different. Like her pussy is candy, that's how good—"

"Enough," I bark.

"Rook got her birth control implant taken out yesterday," Ronin says, ignoring me. "That's what she was doing at the doctor."

Ford lowers the paper all the way to his lap so he can look at Ronin. "That's a step forward."

"Yeah, tell me about it." Ronin beams a smile at him.

"Hello? Anyone here besides me? You two whipped dumbasses do realize the jury selection starts today for the trial, reporters are in town in force, someone stole seven motorcycles from my shop and possibly robbed our friend Drake as well? Not to mention we need to get a military-grade robot out from *his* shop without getting caught. Like today. We don't have time to talk about candy pussy."

"Spencer," Ronin pipes up. "There is always time for candy pussy."

"And she makes this little squeal now." Ford keeps going, like I never said a word.

"What?" Ronin and I say together. I don't think I've ever heard Ford talk about sex before. He might make a comment in general. *I did this* or *she did that.* But he's never talked about a girl before. It's… strange. And while I'm no slouch in the fucking department, I'm not really into the shit Ford does. So I have to admit, I'm interested in what he's got to say.

Ronin turns to face Ford as well, so apparently he's interested too. "What kind of squeal? Because Rook, she does this little tongue thing right when we get started. Like, drags the tip over the edge of her top teeth, then licks the center of her lip. Fucking shit drives me wild."

Ford smiles a far-off smile, like he's picturing something. "It's more of a squeak, really. Like she's trying to hold it in and not let on that she's excited." He shakes his head. "She's always excited."

"Fuck. Is it lunchtime yet? I might take Rook home and make her do the tongue thing for me."

"I might need to take the whole afternoon off," Ford adds. "I do not believe in quickies. And if I get a squeak at the beginning, you can bet your ass it's gonna end up a scream at the end."

"It's only nine o'clock, you horndogs."

"Nine?" Ford asks. "That means Ashleigh is getting ready to walk to the coffee shop. I can probably catch her before she wakes Kate up from her morning nap." He gets up and throws the paper down. "I'll be back later," he says as he pulls the door open and bumps into Rook.

He pushes past her without a word and Rook is just about to ask what's going on when Ronin corners her. "Follow me, Gidget. I've got a surprise for you."

And then I'm alone.

What the fuck?

They didn't even give me a chance to tell them *Ronnie's* little tell. She does that shudder thing. When I touch her for the first time before we fuck, she shudders. And she closes her eyes for a second. That's how I know she's in the mood. Granted, I can make her shudder any time I want, but when she's really horny, all I gotta do is drag a finger down her arm and I get the closed-eye shudder.

I grab my phone from my desk and press her beautiful face. I don't expect her to answer, so when I hear her voice after the first ring, I feel… happy.

"How can I help you, Spencer?"

"Are you available today?"

She sighs. "Yeah, I already got you four apartments lined up to look at. I'm just pasting directions into the email right now. Be sure to check—"

"No, Bomb. Fuck the apartments. Are you available to *see me* today?"

She pauses. "See you?"

"Yeah, like, for lunch? Unless you're having lunch with that asshole from last night."

Silence.

I hate that I added that dig. I'm such a fuck-up when it comes to her.

"Ronnie?"

"I have to work at the shop. Everyone's down in the Springs until Thursday. I gotta open and close. So if you need anything else—like, shit that does not involve lunch—call me over there."

I get the three-beep hang-up.

That's just perfect. Just fucking perfect. Ronin is off screwing Rook. Ford is off eating candy pussy. And I'm stuck here with no one. And the worst thing is, I'm the only one who's worried about all the shit that's going down. Those two assholes are so busy with their women, they're getting sloppy and slow.

In fact, it's a good thing Ronnie and I are on the outs. Yeah. It's perfect, actually. Because now I can stop thinking about her and concentrate on my *job*.

I glance out the window that overlooks the bike bays. All the guys are anxious to get started on their projects. Ryan and I are both working on major deliveries, one of which needs to be completed in two weeks. But I'm waiting on the chrome guy and the upholsterer for the custom seat.

I stand up and look out the window behind me. This one has a view of College Ave. In fact, I can see the FoCo Cinema from my office. I like that. I can spy on Bombshell from right here and she'll never know, because I have a pair of high-powered binocs in my desk drawer and she likes to sit by the front window in the winter and outside in the summer.

The deafening roar of a badass bike makes me look left. It takes me several seconds to actually come to terms with what I'm seeing.

My Veronica.

On our bike.

She flashes past and I swear she flips me off as she passes. It's hard to tell because she could've just been adjusting her hand on the grips, but it sure the fuck looked like she flipped me off. She turns into a space in front of the cinema and parks the bike. A group of college guys are in line at the front coffee window and they all turn to look at her. I know they say something, because *that* one-finger salute is crystal clear.

I chuckle. Veronica is adorable. And I'm feeling needy right now. It sucks that Ford and Ronin get to have girlfriends while I have to squirrel away the feelings I have for Veronica to try to keep her out of the messed-up shit we're in. I'm not sure how Ford can justify it.

I mean, Ronin, I get him. He's got one thing on his mind and that's Rook. His job is lying to the police and bailing us out of shit. And right now, we're not in any shit legally. He's got nothing to do. Plus Rook works with us. She's here all day long.

Ford, he's a hacker, so I sorta get the feeling he thinks he's ten steps ahead of everyone at all times. Why worry? And I bet he is. Who the hell knows what goes on in that freak brain of his. He's practically employing his own private police force to protect Ash and Kate. And he's got those dogs.

But that's just not enough peace of mind for me. If I had my way I'd have all the girls locked up in here with us all day long. I'd stick a crib in the empty office on the other side of the shop and that could be Kate and Ashleigh's little room. Rook could run the showroom and Ronnie could just sit in here with me so I'd never have to take my eyes off her.

Plus, there's cameras all over this place. Not in here, this is the only private place in the whole building. But everywhere else is wired up for the show.

I sigh. They'd be so much safer here with me to keep my eyes on them. And that's *my* job. Yeah, I am the initial planner. Ford gets that genius brain to come up with original shit every now and then, but mostly I come up with the plans and he carries them out. I run security. I protect everyone, boots-on-the-ground style.

This is a waiting game. The trial officially starts today with jury selection but the witnesses are not supposed to start until next week. Apparently jury selection is an art and major players understand this and take their time. That's what our lawyers say, anyway. In the big-league trials—and this one certainly qualifies—jury selection is everything.

Rook is scheduled to testify next Monday. Day one.

Witness one. She is almost the whole trial. She recorded that FBI fuck Agent Abelli threatening to sell her. She filmed him torturing her ex-husband to death. She filmed him setting her house on fire with her in it. She had access to secret files that implicated more than a hundred people. More than one FBI agent. State senators, US Representatives, cops, a couple mayors, and a drug lord. And those are just the ones I remember off the top of my head.

Ford and I combed through each name before we put that last operation to free Ronin from jail in motion. But some of the names had no online database reference. Many were foreign.

Rook is the star witness. The only other evidence the federal prosecutors have, besides some questionable confessions from other members of the human trafficking crime ring, is the bank transactions. And all that was a setup by Ford. Except for the money transfer from the Columbian drug lord, every bit of it is fake.

And this worries me. Bad.

Because without Rook, the Feds have no case. And if the defense can pick apart those bank transactions, well, all that hard evidence falls apart too.

The guilt or innocence of Agent Abelli—and us too, since our stories are all wrapped up in each other now—hangs on the words of Rook Corvus and the hacking skills of Ford Aston.

And doesn't that make the both of them very attractive targets?

Ronin's truck pulls up in front of the cinema and Rook leans over and kisses him before getting out and walking inside where the girls meet every morning to have coffee. That must've been one hell of a quickie because it's only been about twenty minutes. Ronin backs up and makes the two-second trip across the street.

A few seconds later Ford pulls up to the cinema in the Bronco. He has to get out because Ashleigh has so much baby shit it takes two people to sort it out. Ford gets the stroller and then grabs Kate and puts her inside, while Ashleigh gets the dogs.

I have to shake my head at that. Why she puts up with his crazy dogs is beyond me. But I get why Ford does it. Those dogs give him peace of mind.

Me? I prefer guns.

Ford finishes up and then kisses his new wife goodbye on the lips and backs out. When I see them together, he's like a different person. Ashleigh and Kate make him different. Nicer, I guess. Because when he's with us alone, he's the same old asshole he's always been.

Ronin comes into my office and I turn around.

"Spying on Ron?" he asks as he grabs a bike magazine and plops down on the couch.

"Ford, actually," I reply back. "He just dropped Ash and Kate off."

The door opens again and Ford walks in, closes it behind him, and then just stands there looking between Ronin and I.

"What?" I ask, feeling nervous.

"Someone has contested my request to adopt Kate."

"Who?" Ronin and I ask together.

Ford takes a deep breath and exhales out the words. "Kate's father."

# CHAPTER FOURTEEN

## Veronica

***"I don't get it,"*** Rook says, confused. I take a sip of my coffee and wait patiently for Ashleigh to position Kate for nursing. Ashleigh looks a wreck. Her eyes are all red from crying and all the color has disappeared from her face. "I mean, how does a dead man contest an adoption?"

Ashleigh starts to cry silently.

Rook and I look at each other and she mouths, *Do something.* Like I'm good with this girlfriend stuff.

I'm not. I was raised by a pack of wild men. I had very few girlfriends growing up. In fact, I think Rook is the only girl I've ever been really close to. But Rook's the baby, so I take over. "Ashleigh, he *is* dead, right?" Rook's eyes go wide and she shakes her head no. I ignore her. If there's some sort of protocol for dealing with dead ex-boyfriends who contest adoptions by live husbands, I'm not up to speed. "I mean, he didn't, like, show up in person, right?"

"No," she says, sniffling. "It was a legal document served to me today. It came from a law office. Tony—that's Kate's biological father—Tony's name is not even on there. It says something like paternal objection. But that's not possible. He's *dead.*"

"Where's the papers?" I ask as Rook reaches over to rub Ashleigh's hand.

"Ford took them. He's calling the lawyers who are handling the case for us."

"What does he say?" Rook asks.

"He didn't say anything, really. Just that he'll take care of it."

"Well," I sigh. "I'm sorry this is happening. But if Ford Aston says he's gonna take care of it, I'd try not to think about it too much. If it can be done, he'll do it."

"Besides," Rook adds, "it's probably Tony's family who's putting up this fight. They think they have a claim, I suppose. Have you talked to them?"

Ash shakes her head no as she wipes the tears from her eyes. "No, they said they never wanted anything to do with me. They sent me nasty letters when I was in Japan after I found out Tony died. And now they go and pull this shit? I've been feeling so much better about things the past few weeks. I'm moving on, ya know? And then this happens and I'm right back where I was with the grief. I hate when people fuck with my life. I hate it so much. I didn't do anything, why can't they just leave me alone?"

Rook leans in and hugs her. "Ronnie's right. Ford will handle it. Ford always gets his way. They won't stop the adoption. He'll make sure of it. In fact, let's just go over there right now and see if he's found anything out."

"No," Ashleigh says quickly. "He's so upset, I can't see him right now. God, it's bad enough he had to put up with me and my sadness for the past two months, but this? It's like a slap in the face. He's been taking care of Kate like she's his own child since she was four months old and we finally get home to file the papers, and this happens. I swear to God, if I find out this is Tony's parents doing this to try to get a hold of Kate, I will lose my shit."

"Well," I say more to myself than anything, "if I were you, I'd call their asses up and ask them what the fuck? Ya know? Put them on the spot. Make them come clean and say what they want. Maybe they just want to make sure they get visitation or something? And then you guys can sort it out in like ten minutes and put it behind you." Both Rook and Ash are staring at me. "What? That's what rational people do. People like Ronin, Spencer, and Ford do the complicated shit. Who needs complicated when you have easy. I mean—"

"No," Ash says. "You're totally right, Veronica. That's brilliant." She perks up at my idea, but Rook is frowning.

"What?" I ask her.

"Ash, if Ford says he'll *handle* it, then you should just let him *handle* it."

"Why?" I blurt. "Are you so brainwashed by Ronin that you can't imagine picking up a phone and asking a simple question? I mean, come on, Rook. Not everything is a conspiracy."

Ashleigh is looking at me as these words come out, but she glances quickly over to Rook and her whole attitude changes. "Yeah, you're right. Ford can deal with it, I guess. Let *him* call them up and ask what the fuck."

My mouth drops open. "Are you kidding me? Ashleigh, seriously. It's a phone call. Rook, stop messing with her."

"Ronnie, there's things going on that you don't know about, OK? It's better to hand this off to Ford and the guys and let them figure it out. I'm sure Ford is hacking into some secret database getting information as we speak."

"So you're saying you two are part of the Team, but me, I'm not. So I can't possibly understand how complicated it could be to just call up people she *already knows* and ask them what the fuck they want with her kid? Is that about right?"

"What if it's not them, Veronica? What if it's some sort of trap?"

"What fucking trap? Why would anyone be using this stupid adoption to trap Ashleigh?"

Rook sighs, but she stays silent.

Ashleigh won't meet my gaze.

"Oh, yeah, OK. Once again, you two are in on the secrets but I'm not. You two are with the guys, and I'm not."

"That's not—"

Rook is interrupted by Ford and Ronin as they enter the cinema and walk over to us. "Come on, ladies," Ford says. "We're taking you home."

"Rook," Ronin adds, "you're staying with Ashleigh today until we take care of some business."

Ford gathers up Kate and calls the dogs to heel, while Ash frantically stuffs her things into the stroller. A few seconds later they walk out to the waiting Shrike truck out front. I look through the window and see Spencer at the wheel, but he's got his shades on, so I can't tell if he's watching me or not.

"Later, Ronnie," Rook calls out as Ronin urges her to hurry. "I'll see you later."

And then I watch them all pile into the truck and take off.

I look around after they're gone and everyone is staring at me. "What the fuck are you all looking at?" I slap a tip down on the table, grab my backpack, and walk out the door. The Shrike truck is stopped at the light at the corner and I can see them all talking inside the cab.

Then the light turns green and they turn and disappear.

Well, that's fucking awesome. I swing my leg over my bike and start her up. Fuck them. Just fuck them. I back out and head the other direction on College. A few seconds later I pull into a spot in front of Sick Boyz and turn off the engine.

I sit here for a few seconds thinking about how shitty I feel. They seriously just left me sitting there like some worthless garbage.

And that's two times in two days that I feel like worthless garbage.

And then I see him.

Bobby Mansi. He's coming out of the hardware store a few doors down, tossing his keys a little, like he hasn't got a care in the world. I bet he doesn't, rich bastard.

He turns his head and I look away real fast, pretending to mess with my bike before slipping my helmet off. When I look up again, he's standing right next to me.

"Miss Vaughn. I didn't see you this morning. How did you sleep?"

"Great actually. The couch was very nice." I wince internally at that stupid remark.

"The couch, huh? Well, I'm glad to hear it." He points up to the shop sign. "Is this where you draw lines on skin? Sick Boyz, Inc.?"

I look up at the old sign. It's been there since the sixties. We've had it repainted many times, but it's looking a bit weathered right now. And maybe for the first time ever, I feel ashamed that I work here. It's true I've never enjoyed it. Much, anyway. The blood, it really bothers me. But I've always been proud of what I do. I'm talented. I have clients come from all over the country to see me. Maybe we don't have our own TV show, but we're a good shop. I've always been proud of my family's strange talent.

But now, sitting here on a ridiculous motorcycle, all dressed up in yesterday's rebellious biker clothes. I feel... stupid. And small. And pathetic. Used-up, good-for-nothing trash. I don't answer Bobby. Obviously that question was rhetorical—I'm a tattoo artist and I'm sitting in front of a tattoo shop. This is where I work.

I grab my stuff, fish my keys out of my backpack, and get up to go open the front door. When I get inside I flip the sign from closed to open and break for the hallway that leads to the tattoo chairs. Bobby Mansi follows me.

I walk to the back of the building where we have a little break room. It's got a TV, a table that seats eight, and a small kitchenette on one side. On the other wall there's lockers. I dial the combination on mine and open it up. I grab my phone from my backpack and stuff it in my pocket, then shove the bag in the locker and slam the door closed.

Bobby Mansi is waiting for me in the doorway, his hands propped up on either side of the door jamb. "Sorry," I say as I duck under one arm and walk back to my tattoo room. "I'm not very good company right now. I'm here alone for the next few days and I have a client due in about thirty minutes, so I need to get things running."

I glance at him when I turn into my room. He's still in the door, but he's looking at me over his shoulder. "Something wrong, Veronica?"

I sigh as I look at him. God, this man is bordering on beautiful. I don't normally like the beautiful ones. Ford is sorta beautiful in his scary weird way, and his brand of handsome has never appealed to me. But Bobby Mansi. He's a definite maybe.

"Not exactly, no." I reply. "I'm just…" I have no idea what I'm feeling. All bad things. All things I'd rather not share with a handsome stranger.

"You're just… sorry you turned me down for dinner last night, aren't you?"

I laugh a little at his cleverness and look him over properly. He's grinning at me and his green eyes even have a little mischievous twinkle in them. "I didn't exactly turn you down, remember? I told you I have to work until eleven, so dinner is just not possible."

"Why do you have to work until eleven? Do you have appointments all night?"

"No, but we get walk-ins."

"But you own this place, correct?"

"Yeah. Well—it's family-owned."

"So close early. Close early and come have a nice dinner with me."

I sigh again. If only it was that easy. But then, he lives a comfortable life. He probably has no idea the struggles we have as a business. But I don't really know how to explain this to a guy who owns entire buildings, so I use an easy excuse. "I have no nice dinner clothes because my apartment was condemned. I don't even have time to go find some."

"We'll stay in. Have a nice dinner at my place. Wear what you have on, I have no complaints."

My stomach does a few flips at his suggestive tone. I feel a little guilty for even considering his offer, but then again… all my best friends did just leave me sitting in the coffee shop like I'm nobody. I mean, seriously—it's obvious that Ronin and Ford were worried about Rook and Ash. But me? No. Spencer could give two fucks about me. All he wants is the *idea* of me.

Why should I deny myself a nice dinner in the company of a good-looking man?

"OK," I finally say. "OK, I'll come. But I can't close too

early, we need the walk-in business. Nine, maybe. Is that too late?"

"I'll be back at nine to escort you home." And then he flashes me one more smile and walks back down the hallway. The bell jingles his exit and I let out a breath.

*Calm, Veronica. Be calm.*

But I can't be calm, because I just accepted a date with Bobby Mansi. And even though I did go out with Carson a couple months ago, it's not even remotely the same.

Carson is not my type. My type has always been Spencer. Even before I knew Spencer, my type was Spencer. And Bobby is not really my type either. I've never been into the rich guys. I don't know how much money Spencer has—more than me, but that's not saying much. He seems comfortable. I've never heard him complain about money, so I'm sure he's not sweating the downtown FoCo rent every month like we do to keep our shop running. But he comes off as a working guy. I like the blue-collar guys. They're very hot. That's my type. Working men.

But maybe it's time to explore new things.

Maybe it's time to let Spencer go. Maybe I've been holding onto this dream of being with him because that's all I've known for the past few years. Because we did so many cool and intimate things together and it was hard for me to accept that all that fun was over.

But just because I always do what I've always done doesn't mean I have to keep living life that way.

Yeah. I feel better already. I'm turning over a new leaf. Today is the first day of the rest of my life. I'm gonna reinvent myself.

So goodbye Spencer and hello Bobby.

## CHAPTER FIFTEEN

***I drop the girls*** and Ronin off at Ford's place, then Ford and I exchange my Shrike truck for the unmarked van we use to transport bikes. The same van we drove back to Chicago to save Rook last summer. We drive in complete silence across town to the apartment Ford has been renting since season one. He keeps some sensitive stuff over there.

As do I.

I glance over at him as we drive down College Avenue. Fort Collins is pretty spread out for being a small town. And it's not close to the freeway, the town itself is a good fifteen-minute drive west of the freeway, and since Ford's secret place is about as southeast as you can get and still be considered Fort Collins, it's a nice thirty-minute drive in lunch-hour traffic.

His fingers are flying over the laptop keys. I'm not sure what he's looking for, but ever since he came back from dropping Ashleigh off at the cinema, he's been eerily silent. Just tapping away on the one thing that keeps him totally sane. Access to information no one else has.

Ford has never filled Ronin and me in on what happened with Ashleigh and her baby, but he told Rook. She told Ronin, and Ronin told me. If Ford wanted it kept a secret, believe me, his mouth would've stayed shut. But he told Rook, and that means it's considered Team knowledge.

This whole mess is getting more and more complicated by the day.

"You finding anything helpful on there, Ford?"

"Lots," he huffs back. "But I need access to get answers."

He continues his typing and I give up on the conversation as I turn into his apartment complex. I head over to his building and park in an empty spot I know belongs to him. As soon as I put the van in park, he's out. I jump out after him and follow him up the stairs to the third floor, then walk through once he unlocks the door and enters.

The apartment is very generic. Just some basic furniture—couch, chair, lamps, tables—and that's pretty much it.

Ford heads straight to the bedroom where he hides the hard drive that holds his hacking scripts and I head straight to the one that holds what I came for.

The guns.

I have almost fifty of them here and this makes me happy in the same way bike sex with Veronica does. All the rifles and shotguns are propped up against two walls, lined up like good little soldiers. After that Boulder job went FUBAR I told myself I was done with the guns. I meant it too. I was done. But luckily it took me about five minutes to come back to my senses. You need three things to pull off the shit we used to do.

Access to information. We got that with Ford.

A tight-as-fuck alibi. We pull that off with Ronin.

And security. That's me. When we're on a job I'm the lookout with Ronin. And I protect us at all costs.

I do that last part with guns.

Guns are the only real equalizer when you're up against criminals as big as the ones we were fucking with in the past.

Ford was appalled when I started unloading all the guns last year. Especially after I killed our target. But that's precisely why I have so many guns.

The Boulder Mistake, as we call it now, was a life-changing event. Killing someone is not something I take lightly. I'm not an angry, violent man. I don't fight much, only when provoked or when Ronnie's brother gets on my ass too hard. I've tussled with Ford and Ronin a few times, of course. But that's just what guys do.

I played football in high school, I can take a beating. I'm

not afraid to fight. I have no problem pummeling the shit out of people. But it's not a habit I've developed. I'm pretty easy-going most days. And if I could go back and talk to my twenty-year-old self and tell him he'll be killing someone in the very near future, I'm pretty sure my twenty-year-old self would laugh his ass off.

I feel very little guilt about actually taking that asshole's life. Especially now that we know that motherfucker was as dirty as they come. He really was directly tied to all the human trafficking shit Rook was involved in back in Chicago. Even if we did manufacture most of that story she told the police to cover our asses and take most of that particular branch of the crime ring down, these people deserved to take the fall.

And call me God for making that decision. Call me self-righteous. Or morally superior, or smug. I don't care. I am.

I *am* better than those assholes we took out. My whole team is better than those assholes we took out.

So no, I'm not gonna feel guilty about killing that motherfucker. It was me or him.

I chose me.

And once we cross-checked the names of those guilty of buying and selling sex slaves out of Rook's unassuming suburban Chicago barn and found him on it, I felt even more sanctimonious.

It happened and I live with the consequences. But guilt isn't one of those consequences.

Looking over my shoulder for the rest of my life is.

And Ronin's. And Ford's. And now Ashleigh and Rook are included in this group too.

Sure, I fucked up. Given the choice, I'd choose to not have to kill people. So yeah, *we* fucked up.

And now that shit has come back into town to remind us. Give us a little homecoming queen wave from atop a parade-day float. 'Hello, boys,' that shit says. 'Remember me?'

Hell fucking yeah, I remember.

***Three and a half years ago***

Ford and Ronin flank me as we get out of the van and walk up the driveway. They are calm. Not me. I'm a fucking mess of nerves. I feel funny. Not like how we usually feel before a job, all amped up on the adrenaline of knowing we are about to commit a crime that will net us millions of dollars of untraceable digital money.

No. That's not how I feel at all.

I feel… wrong. "I feel wrong," I say out loud for the twentieth time.

"Just relax," Ronin whispers. "The father's out of town on business, the mother's up in Idaho Springs at some spa day thing. And Jennifer's in class and work after. She told me all this yesterday."

I know this. Ronin has said it over and over this morning, but I have this sick, sick feeling.

The beeps of the security alarm jolt me out of my unease and bring me back to what the fuck we're actually doing.

We're wearing work clothes for one. With the power company's logo on them. Our white work truck has a large magnetic logo on the side as well.

But even this is wrong. There are no teams of three in the power company. Not all in the same truck. It's a sloppy cover that I didn't think about until we got in the truck an hour ago. But now that it's popped into my mind, I can't stop thinking about it.

This is not what we normally do. We do not break into homes to rob people. We access bank accounts. We steal our money virtually. We cut our teeth on the stupid kiddie con scams we pulled out on the 16th Street Mall back in high school. And we knew that first drug dealer we took out over Mardee. But other than that, we've never even seen any of the marks in person.

"I want to abort," I say. But no one even hears me as the alarm beeps again when Ford disengages it.

A few seconds the door clicks open. Ford ushers us through, then closes it behind him.

Too late to go back now. At the very least we have to find the security room and get rid of the footage. That's about the only thing Ford could do virtually. Troll security company databases trying to find out which one monitors this house.

But it turns out none of them do. Sure, there's three signs in the front yard declaring they have a service with each one. But Ford looked good and hard until he finally concluded they have a private system. Which means all the footage is on site.

The house is impressive. Ford's loaded, so I'm used to old money. And Ronin's family owns Chaput Studios, a massive industrial building, so I know big time. But this house in the Boulder hills is something else altogether.

Old money says refined taste. Working money says nothing but the best as long as it's practical. New money says opulence.

This place screams extravagance.

"Jennifer mentioned once that his office was near the billiard room."

"Where the fuck is the billiard room?" I ask. "Next to the candlestick in the library? Do they have a Mrs. Plum here too?"

"Shut up, it's probably in the basement. That's where we have our game room," Ford snaps.

"And it's Professor Plum," Ronin adds, as he warily looks around for the basement entrance.

Ford finds it first. It's not behind a door like most normal houses would have it. No. It's a full-on grand staircase that has a slight spiral to it. The banisters are highly polished wood, and the stairs are soft carpet.

At least that muffles the sound of our boots as we descend.

"Ah," Ford says as we turn left at the bottom. "I knew this bastard would have on-site security." He points to a room that has a plethora of flatscreen monitors. We pass by those. "I'll come back on the way out and fuck it all up."

Yeah, I feel so much better now, knowing we're definitely on camera as we approached the house.

Ford finds the office and he and Ronin get to work on the accounts. I watch the hallway and try to shake off my unease. Ronin usually doesn't do this stuff, but he's the one who knows the girl who lives here. She's the reason we're doing this. We pick and choose our victims carefully. Only scumbags get the Team treatment. And according to his daughter, this guy has been molesting her since she was a little girl. Ronin said the girl, Jennifer, didn't share explicit details, but he got the impression it was graphic. She was drunk one night, Ronin was working his player magic, just trying to get laid, I'm sure. And this chick started spouting off some serious shit about her daddy.

Ronin let her talk until she passed out and then left. He said she pretended nothing happened that night, just passed it off as being out of her mind drunk—

The cocking of a shotgun blows my thoughts out of my mind and the stench of whiskey permeates the room.

All three of us whirl around and come face to face with the pedophile.

"In the corner," he spits, saliva dripping out of his mouth, his feet shuffling along the carpet as he approaches me.

He's wasted.

I put up my hands and back away, moving closer to Ford and Ronin. "We're from the power company—"

The thundering boom of the shotgun makes all three of us react. My hand goes to my gun, Ford and Ronin duck as part of the ceiling comes down on top of them, and then in the next moment, the drunk and I are face to face. His shotgun pointed at my chest, my 9mm pointed right at his head.

We squeeze at the same time. He flies backward from the kick, and I duck as the plaster crumbles off the wall behind me. This shit happens so fast I can't even register that I just blew the guy's brains out.

I slump against the wall, then slide down. The next thing I know, Ronin and Ford are standing next to me. "Ronin, you wipe everything down. Spencer, you go to the security room and locate anything that looks like a hard drive. I've got the money transferring now, I'll be in in two minutes. We're out in five."

Ronin and I just look at Ford, struck dumb.

"I'm not talking to myself, move your fucking asses."

Ronin goes into the adjoined office bathroom and grabs a towel, then starts wiping things down. We all have gloves on, but we came in here to get codes to steal money. We did not come prepared to clean up after a murder.

*Murder.*

"Move!" Ford yells in my face. "You can think about how bad you fucked up later. But right now we need to complete the job."

I walk out without looking at the dead guy on the floor. But I don't need to. Because the hole in his head and his brains splattered all over the beige carpet are etched in my memory forever.

I'm not even sure what happens after that. We do get the footage, and the money transfers all complete. We get back into the car and we're back at Chaput Studios before I snap back out of it. I don't even know how we got here.

I look over at Ronin. He's sitting in the middle between me and Ford, his expression as blank and empty as I feel.

I'm the official driver in all jobs but right now, Ford is behind the wheel. And I've never been so happy that he's the cold, emotionless asshole he's always been.

He's always said the detached getaway is his signature move.

And I guess he was right.

"You ready?" Ford asks as I realize I'm sitting in front of the rifles in his FoCo apartment, just staring off into space.

"I'm done and I'd like to get back to Ashleigh and Kate."

"Yeah," I say, clearing my throat. Fuck, I haven't thought about the details of that day in a long, long time. "I'm just gonna take some of these with me."

"Why?"

"Why?" I laugh as I grab the large duffel I use to move guns from place to place. "Because I have no guns in the new shop and shit's happening, Ford. I'm not sure how the adoption stuff is related to the missing motorcycles, but one thing's for fucking sure." I look at him as I stuff some guns in the bag. "It most definitely is, brother. It most definitely is. Jury selection starts today. Ronnie's apartment is suddenly condemned and she can't go inside—"

"What?"

"Yeah, some shit about asbestos. But this fancy guy shows up in town, claiming to own that new condo building over on Mason Street. He just happens to own the building she lives in right now too, so he gives her this free condo to live in while her place is cleaned up. Now you have this adoption shit and a dead guy coming out of nowhere. My bikes are missing and someone was trying to make Drake look like the perp. But as soon as we catch on, that shit morphs, right? Suddenly Drake's coming off squeaky clean because he's over at my place accusing me of stealing his bikes." I huff out a breath. "Convenient, right?"

I finish packing up the rifles and then crawl over to the handguns, all laid out in perfect order on the carpet. I pick up the .454 Taurus Raging Bull and weigh it in my hand. Ronnie might be able to shoot it, since we've practiced on the big guns a lot when we were first together. But Ronin never shoots. He can point a gun and probably hit his target, I've made sure he was trained. But he never practices. He's a ground fighter. Ford is a rifle man if he needs a gun. Point and spray is how he'll get the job done if it comes down to it.

"What do you think you're gonna do with that thing?" Ford asks, as he points to the Raging Bull I'm positioning inside the bag.

"Blow someone's fucking head off, what the fuck else would I do with it?"

He recoils at the imagery because that's exactly what I did to the Boulder guy. "I'm pretty sure that little .380 in your jacket will do the trick, Spencer. Don't get paranoid on me now."

"Ford, you do your job, I'll do mine. When you're in charge of the guns, you can choose the weapons." I zip up the bag, stand up, and throw it over my shoulder. "I'm ready. You got what you need?"

He nods and waves me out.

We drive back to town in silence. And that's a good thing.

Because right now the only thing on our minds is the job. Someone—hell, maybe a shitload of someones—is fucking with our lives. I'm not sure if it's Drake, condo guy, the scum involved in the trial, or one of the many, *many* people we've fucked over in the past. But one thing's for sure—it's all related.

And maybe this job wasn't planned by us. Maybe so far we've only been reacting to circumstance. Trying to piece the puzzle together bit by bit.

It doesn't matter. Because we're definitely gonna be the ones to finish it.

# CHAPTER SIXTEEN

***Guys like Chuck*** make me happy to be a tattoo artist. I've been working on his back piece for almost a year. He drives in from Kansas to get his work done. He's got at least four more appointments until he's done and since he can only get away from his job at the feed mill his family owns when production is slow—cows never stop eating, he always tells me—his visits are few and far between.

I finish the last of the shading I'm doing on the tribute to American horror he's got going on his back. If I didn't know Chuck, these images would scare the shit out of me. In fact, even though I'm the one who drew and inked the Pennywise, Leatherface, Pinhead, and Jason in his hockey mask on his skin, it still creeps me out.

I wipe down his back and then give him a nudge. "Hey, Chuck. You're done." Chuck gives me a snore. How the hell a man can fall asleep when I'm draggin' a needle across his back is beyond me. But he never has a problem.

Eh, I let him sleep. I don't have another appointment for a few hours. I leave him there and go back up front, and I'm just turning the corner when the bell above the door jingles.

"Ronnie!" Carson smiles brightly. "I just came by to see how you were."

"Um…" I pause because he's lying. Carson is so easy to read, it's pathetic. Maybe I'm just so used to the accomplished liars all around me, or maybe he's a terrible liar. But it doesn't matter. I can see through him. Almost everything he's ever told me has been a lie. And I'm not sure why he's lying. He's never asked me for anything, in fact he really was sincere about trying to help me get my own flower shop. "I'm good," I say back. And I'm just about to ask him what the hell he wants when the door jingles again and a crowd of people walk in.

Really? It's fucking Tuesday. No one ever comes in on Tuesday. I'm all alone and I get a crowd of… one, two, three… I count them up until I get to fifteen. Fifteen? Really?

The noise must wake Chuck, because he comes out from the back holding his shirt and rubbing his eyes like he needs to go back to bed pronto. I head behind the counter and ignore the crowd. Sometimes they just come in to look. This group might be here looking.

"What do I owe ya, Ron?" Chuck says.

"That's seven-fifty this time, Chuck. Should I put you in the book for two months?"

He eyeballs me as he takes his card out of his wallet. "Thought you was quittin', Ronnie? Your dad told me to switch over to Vic. You saying you'll do another appointment?"

"Would I leave you hanging?" I flash him a flirty smile but he scowls at me.

"Ya don't have to. We're at a good stopping place to switch over."

I stare at him as I internalize what he just said. It sorta hurts my feelings. I've been tattooing this guy for two years and to be honest, the thought of Vic finishing it just ruins my day. "No, I want to finish it, Chuck. Really, I do. It might be creepy, but I'm looking forward to doing Chuckie and Cujo next time."

He flops my head with his hat and I feel like a little girl again. "Kay, then. I'll call ya when the feeding season is over." Which means summer, since cows need to be fed in the winter.

I hand him his receipt and then turn to the nearest college kid waiting for my attention. "How can I help you?"

"We're the Kappa Gamma Gamma house and we all want to get matching tattoos." She beams at me like this is the most clever idea ever. "Today," she adds.

*Of course you do.*

Carson thrusts a clipboard with a sign-in sheet at the girl. "If you could all put your names on here to make a waiting list, then fill out these forms, we'll get you all scheduled."

I just stare at him as the girls saunter off to begin their list. "What?" he asks me as I continue to stare. "I figured you could use the money this group will bring, so hey, might as well make myself useful."

"Hmmm," I say. "Why are you here?"

"To help," he insists. "Don't you want it?"

We both look out at the girls. Their tattoo will be at least fifty dollars apiece, maybe even seventy-five. That's a lot of extra money for me, even after the shop takes fifty percent. "I have a scheduled appointment at three and another one at six. Do you think we can fit all these girls in before I need to close?"

"We can try, Bombshell."

"What?"

"What?"

"What did you just call me?"

Carson actually turns red. "Sorry, that's just… you just… you're like one of those… pinup girls, ya know? Sorry." He makes a break for it and goes to talk to the head girl to see what tattoo they want.

Bombshell, huh.

Suddenly Carson makes a whole lot more sense. I've been wondering why he's been all up in my face these days. Asking me about cars and shit. He's working for Spencer.

I turn away and walk back to my room. Smiling.

In fact, I laugh. I giggle. I get all sorts of stupid. Because Spencer—I sigh. God, I fucking love that man. He told me to date Carson last week. And I swear, I thought my chest was gonna crack open when he said that to me over the phone. It hurt like a motherfucker.

But Spencer is a sneaky fucking prick. A lovable, adorable, sneaky fucking prick.

I rip the plastic off my chair, then the machine and the

cord. In fact, I rip all the fucking plastic off. Even from the flatscreen. I find the remote and turn on the Biker Channel. I haven't watched it lately, but they run the promos for Shrike Bikes all the time. I'm only in one episode, the very last one, but my face is in at least one promo. I signed a release for it. They're not paying me, I was a pilot walk-on when Rook's ex came back and tried to kill her. He ended up shooting me instead, just a flesh wound, thank God. And even though Spencer told me I was never gonna be on his show when we had that big falling out last year, he was wrong. I am on his show.

I have to stop everything I'm doing so I can privately gloat about that.

I want to see that show. I'm suddenly excited. Life is good. My man loves me. He loves me so much, he told me to date someone else. He sent that someone else over to my shop to help me out since I was here all alone.

Carson walks into my room with the clipboard. "OK, fifteen girls. They all want a two-inch butterfly flower thing that looks kinda like this?" He points to a rough drawing on the clipboard paper. "Can you just whip up something like that and put Kappa Gamma Gamma underneath or… wherever. They said they want something a little customized, each one a little different, but the same sort of butterfly and the same lettering. So how much per tattoo?"

"Well, that's probably a forty-minute tattoo, but I don't want to rush it, so let's call it an hour and a hundred bucks, discounted to seventy-five for the group rate. I can do five today, the others will have to come back."

Carson nods his head as I ramble on, taking notes. Then he goes back out front and sends the first girl back. I don't get a lot of walk-ins most of the time, and hardly any of them are girls. Most of the girls go to the twins, so it's a nice change from my regulars. After we discuss the particulars of her design, she chats endlessly with me. And even though I don't point it out, she squeals when the Biker Channel runs the Shrike promo. She informs me that she saw Spencer Shrike standing in line at Big City Burrito. And she is excited about that.

I smile. He's very exciting, so I let it pass and don't even have a moment of jealousy

The next girl is more nervous and wants a smaller version of the last girl's tattoo. I adjust, as I always do, and give her exactly what she wants.

As much as I complain about this job, I do sorta love it once I get going. I like making art on people. The blood still makes me sick, but today, even that is muted.

This girl doesn't talk like the last one, and she's not even remotely interested in the Biker Channel, so every now and then, between the buzzing of my gun, I hear Carson out front. Chatting people up and quoting prices and hours. The bells on the door never stop jingling.

I finish this girl and have time to move on to the next before my regular appointment comes in.

My day is a blur of excitement. Almost an adrenaline high, like it used to be back when I first started working here my senior year of college. Back when my days with Spencer were always special, always ended with a fuck, a kiss, and the promise of more to come tomorrow.

God, I want to be that girl again. Back when the blood was just annoying. Back when sex was constant and wild. Back to the beginning.

I want to start over.

I need to start over.

CHAPTER SEVENTEEN

# Spencer

***Ford is eerily silent*** as I make our way back towards town from his secret apartment. I catch him blankly staring out the window several times. "You OK, dude?" I finally ask as we get back to College Avenue.

He doesn't answer. And he doesn't look OK, either.

When he called and told us he met a girl on the road to LA and was gonna ask her to marry him, we all thought he was crazy. Even Rook. Her, Ronin, and I sat down at my house and thoroughly talked out what it meant if Ford brought home a wife. Because regardless of what we thought about it, no matter how crazy he sounded on that phone that day, if Ford married Ash, then Ash was in. There's just no two ways about it. We discussed what she should know and when she should know it, and then we called up Ford and laid it all out for him.

Not that he needed our permission, but you know—the girl comes with her own set of problems. We needed to know what we were getting into if he made her part of the Team.

He told me about her family, but he left Rook and Ronin out of it. Ford has never seen Ronin as a friend. They've never been close and Ford's attachment to Rook does not transfer to Ronin.

Yeah, Ronin is part of the Team. But that's where it ends for Ford. He's not a sharing kind of guy on his best days with me, so he's never liked the fact that Ronin got to know shit about him by default.

Ashleigh's family has their own team going, it seems. Only on a much bigger, bazillion-dollar semi-illegal pharmaceutical business scale.

That sorta changes things. I mean, we've got a scam going here. We've fucked up a lot of people over the past few years. A lot meaning hundreds. Hundreds of important people are probably wishing they could find some way for all of us to disappear.

So it matters that Ashleigh comes from a crime family. It matters that little Kate has crime on both biological sides, and now her step-side too. Because people like them—people like us—we have long memories. We are a patient bunch. We never forget a favor or a betrayal.

And the only thing that became crystal clear since talking this out with Ford a couple months ago was this—we are small-time compared to the groups we're up against.

Teeny, tiny, minuscule time.

"Ford," I try again. "Look, man, I understand this shit's upsetting, but I need words, OK? I need to know what I'm supposed to do about this. If this is a huge problem, I need to know. We all need to know." He looks over at me, I catch it out of the corner of my eye, so I meet his gaze. "What? You're fucking killing me, dude."

"I know something."

"OK."

He's silent again after that.

"You care to enlighten me?"

"I don't want Ronin to know. I need him to stay out of it."

"Ford—"

"And Ashleigh. I don't want her to know either. I'm just saying, I've done something and I don't want them to know."

"But you're gonna tell me?"

"No," he says. "I just need to get that off my chest. Just in case."

"You're… involved in something?"

"Not exactly. But I know something. Something big. Something I probably should've shared, but kept to myself."

"And it's part of all this shit that's happening?"

"Possibly. I can't be certain. So I can't say anything, just trust me."

"Do you need me to do anything?"

"No, I just need someone to know—" He stops and looks over at me. "Just in case something goes wrong."

"Goddammit, Ford. We can't work like this. We—"

"Exactly," he interrupts. "We can't work like this at all anymore. Don't you see? We've got to stop this, Spencer. I can't be looking over my shoulder for the rest of my life, wondering when someone's gonna come back to fuck up my family. I need this shit to be over just as much as you do. Just as much as Rook and Ronin do. We need to stop."

"Well, this isn't the time to fucking stop, asshole. So I need to know what the hell is going on. I'm not gonna lie to Ronin. We need him."

Ford sits in silence, typing on his computer, and I swear to God, if I wasn't driving I'd smash that damn thing.

"Pull over."

"What?"

He waves his hand at the upcoming street. "Just pull over there. I need to show you something."

I turn off into a residential side street and pull over to the side of the road. Ford hands me his laptop and I take it automatically. "What's this?"

"Just read it."

I scan the page for a second. "What the fuck?" There's a picture of Drake Cikes. But that's not what makes my heart skip a beat.

It's the guy standing next to him. Davis Cooperson Smyth. Otherwise known as the Boulder asshole I murdered.

"What the fuck is this?"

"Drake. He's the illegitimate love child of one of Cooperson Smyth's sex slaves. His only son. Stood to inherit the entire estate. Until…"

It starts to make sense now. "Until we stole it."

"Exactly. He's got a motive, but not the skills, Spencer. So he's not the only one."

"Where'd you find this?" I ask, looking up at him.

"I used a virus—"

"Fucking Ford! What the fuck? You're gonna get us busted!"

"Relax, I was careful. I had help from a friend."

"Who? Because if we've got someone else who knows our business, we truly are fucked."

Ford squints his eyes and gives me a sly grin. "This guy has always known our business. I just never told you before. You think hacking into high-level databases is a solitary effort, Spencer?" He waits for an answer but I have no idea. "Well, it's not. Merc has had my back since high school. So he's cool. And besides, you do not want to know what *that* guy does for a living."

"So we're keeping this from Ronin? Why?"

"Just for now, OK?" He stops to see how much of a fight I'll put up. But seriously, if Ford's got some secret plan in motion, I have no choice but to go along. "If he starts pressing you for answers or you fuck up and let on that he's not as well-informed as he used to be—then feed him this info. Tell him about Drake and Ashleigh's past. That's our cover."

"We should not need to cover from Ronin," I huff.

"Normally I'd agree. But Rook can't know any of this if she's gonna testify. She's not a good witness, Spencer. Surely you can see that."

I can see it. Rook is a mess. We were so damn lucky she held it together last fall when she gave her statement. Ford and I grilled her for almost three days before we let her loose. But we held the cards back then. We had the element of surprise.

This time they're prepared for us.

So I drop it. If he doesn't want to let me in on the details of what he knows, then he's got a good reason for it. Ford is not impulsive. In fact, he over-thinks pretty much everything. Telling me this much was probably a huge concession on his part.

But keeping things from Ronin… that part is different. "Ronin's the bullshit detector. He's gonna catch on."

"Well." Ford huffs out a long breath. "Maybe it's time we all went our separate ways? If he finds out, maybe that's not a bad thing."

I'm not sure how I feel about that, so I let it ride. Ford is stressed. He and I have been friends since we were six and I plan on being friends with him when we're sixty.

But maybe some distance is a good thing? Once things are set right. Maybe we need to start new lives? Lives that include new teams filled with a wife and kids.

I think we're all ready for that.

I head into downtown and look over at Sick Boyz as I pass and laugh internally. Ford is upset, so I'm trying to be sensitive. But I can't help but smile because next to Ronnie's new Blackbird is Carson's car. And it's waiting-room only at the local tat shop today.

"What'd you do?" Ford asks. "Don't think I didn't catch that shit-eating grin as we passed Ronnie's work."

I'm glad my friend has snapped out of the somber mood he created, even if it's only to give me trouble about my nonexistent love life. "So Ronnie is holding down the fort at Sick Boyz, right? Everyone but her is down in the Springs at some tattoo thing. And she was bitching about her job last week, putting herself down, acting like what she does takes no talent at all and she's wasting her potential."

"Got it," Ford replies at my pause.

"So I called up a local sorority and told them I was the brother of a sister in their house and I wanted to gift them all a tattoo at Sick Boyz."

Ford looks over and smiles.

"You know, keep her busy and make her stop moping around. I get that she's got the blood phobia, but last week, Ford, she admitted that it causes her panic attacks."

"Really?" he says.

"Yeah, so I'm no expert in panic attacks, but I do know one thing. It's an irrational reaction to a rational situation. I mean, is that about right?"

Ford's father was a psychiatrist and he has a lot of

experience in the head-shrinking department. He knows about this stuff better than I do.

"Yeah, basically. I mean, there's lots of underlying reasons for it, but it's irrational, that's key."

"Right. So I figure this is not something she should be allowed to run from, ya know? I mean, you gotta get this shit when it's small. Nip it in the bud. Because she is one great tattoo artist. She's like world fucking class. I've told all my new famous biker buddies about Sick Boyz, and they plan on taking advantage of her skills once the show starts. They're going big-time over there. Soon. And if Ronnie really wants to quit, then more power to her. She can do whatever the fuck she wants with her life—as long as I'm in it, of course. But if she's running from this job because she can't breathe when she sees blood, well, that's bullshit. So I told the house girls I'd pay up to a hundred bucks per tattoo and sent Carson over to help Ronnie run the place until her family gets back on Thursday."

"Doesn't Carson have a job at the bank his father runs?"

"Yeah, but he's got a shitload of vacation time. That nerd never takes a day off. And he really does like Ronnie, as a friend, ya know?"

I turn left on Mountain and head to Ford's house. He's silent again. My plans for Ronnie can only drag him from his funk for so long. Maybe I'm not a parent, so I don't get the scope of love Ford has for that little girl. But it doesn't take a brain surgeon to understand that he's all sorts of torn up about the thought of losing her.

When I get to his house, I pull up in front, fully planning on dropping him off and getting my ass back to work. But Ford looks over to me and sighs. "You need to come inside and hear this, Spence." He pauses for a moment. "It's game time."

I throw the truck in first and shut it down as he exits, then get out and follow him up the front walk.

Ronin opens the front door before we get there, his face a mess of worry and stress. "Fuck," he says as he logs Ford's somber expression and the fact that I'm here with him. Because when we all get together like this over news, it only means one thing.

Bad shit is about to happen.

I follow Ford into the living room. Ashleigh is sitting on the couch, her feet all tucked up underneath her, leaning forward as Ford approaches and bends to kiss her cheek. He takes a seat and pulls her into a tight embrace.

"It's bad, isn't it?" she whispers. "Tell me, Ford."

"It's not so bad," Ford lies.

I look over at Ronin and he's got a puzzled look on his face. Ronin not only lies like a champ, he's a human lie detector as well. Somehow, some way, that guy learned to read body language. I'm not sure if it came from being a little kid in a house with a very dangerous man—his real father went to prison for murdering his mother in front of him and his sister—or if it comes from modeling with girls in some very sensitive situations. But Ronin can smell bullshit even when it reeks of roses.

And Ford is full of shit.

"The request came from a law office in town, but when I hacked into their system, the original request came from a law office in San Diego."

Ashleigh goes white. "My father? Or Tony's family?" she asks. But we can all see she's not even sure she wants the answer to that question.

Ford shrugs. "I can't be sure. When I hacked into the database at the law office in SD, I got anonymous." He pulls his wife in for another hug. "But listen, Kitten. Whoever it is, it's not gonna to work. You have sole legal custody of Katelynn. Tony's name is not even on the birth certificate. We're married, end of story. People can file all kinds of bullshit legal actions, it doesn't make them right and it won't help them win."

Ford waits for an answer, but all Ashleigh is capable of is a nod and a head tuck into his neck.

Poor Ashleigh. Talk about a girl who needs a break. She's had enough drama for a lifetime. And while all of us here are no amateurs when it comes to drama, Ashleigh's is so much more personal than anything we've been up to.

Plus, she's our weakest link. Yeah, she made it out of her mess with Ford's help. But she's recovering from a major depression, the death of her baby's father, and an attempted suicide.

Some muffled cries come from the hallway where the nursery must be, and Ashleigh springs into action. Rook eyeballs us, then follows her.

"That it?" Ronin asks, once Rook is out of hearing range.

"No," Ford says. "Something is very wrong," he says softly, so the girls won't hear. "Something is very, very wrong."

I take a seat in a chair, then lean forward and hold my head in my hands. "This is just one more thing, you guys. We're being set up right now. We're walking into a trap, I can fucking feel it."

"What trap?" Ronin asks. "I mean, I feel something's off too, but I can't put any of it together in a way that makes sense."

"It's Drake," I say. "I'm telling you, Ford. It's Drake. We need that bot back. Did you go scope that shit out last night, Ronin?"

"Yeah, locked up tight, dude. We're gonna have to get it out the same way we got it in. Drive it through the bay."

"We can't be seen over there again," Ford says. "We gave ourselves away the other night."

"What about Ashleigh?" I ask.

"Go to fucking hell, Spencer," Ford replies.

"Look." I take my case to Ronin. He's the final word as far as plans go. He can override Ford. "I get that she's sad right now, but she's the only option. She's the only one with no connections. We need someone to go over there and get that fucking bot out."

Ford scrubs his hands down his face. That's a losing gesture and I know I've won.

"She's on the Team," Ronin says. "She knows she's on the Team. She agreed to be on the Team. She's gotta do her job, Ford. Or we're gonna be blindsided. Hell, maybe someone *can* take your kid away. Maybe they're just biding their time until the shit hits the fan. Maybe—"

"Maybe," Ford interjects, "they started all this motorcycle bullshit, all this adoption bullshit, so they can distract us from the real issue."

"Which is?" Ronin asks.

"Rook," Ford replies. "Rook is the key here, OK? She's testifying next week. I think all of this has to do with Rook."

"Well, you're wrong," I counter. "I agree it looks fishy. And yeah, she's the obvious target. But none of this is adding up to Rook, Ford. All of it's adding up to your wife. Which means she needs to help us figure it the fuck out. You can't say no." He looks over at me and I stare at him hard and shake my head. "It's gone too far, Ford. You should've thought of this before we started."

"I'll help," Ashleigh says from the hallway. We all look over at her. "He's right, Ford. This probably is all my fault. I don't have any problem with the bot plan."

"He's wrong, Ashleigh," Ford says, standing up and walking over to her. "This is about Rook's past. This is about the guys we're trying to send to prison. This is about the man Spencer murdered up in Boulder. This is about stealing millions of dollars from people with long memories. This is not about you."

"Well," Rook says from behind Ashleigh. She's holding the baby and when I look over at Ronin he's got a painful expression on his face. Probably thinking about the baby she lost. "If we're a Team, then it's about all of us. And if we're a Team, then we stick together." She looks over at Ford. "Ashleigh can do this, Ford. It doesn't matter who's involved, she needs to do her part, just like we all need to do ours."

Ronin looks over to Ford. "Well?"

"Ford," I say. "We'll do it tomorrow at dinner. It will be light out, for fuck's sake. Daytime. Drake's complex will be busy with workers. One and done, dude. In and out."

"If this goes bad and something happens to Ash or Rook, I will have your ass, Spencer."

I squirm in my seat a little. He's serious. If something happens to his wife, something ten times more terrifying will happen to me. "I'll put the shine on this plan, don't worry. I'll make it airtight. We're gonna win this. I haven't figured out the game yet, but I will. We're gonna win this and then we're gonna put all this shit behind us."

I take my time scanning the room of faces. Meeting each gaze for a few seconds before moving on. I end up back at Ford, then look over to Ronin one last time. "We're gonna put this behind us and we're never gonna look back. Is this clear? I don't care what new bullshit comes our way. I don't care who tries to fuck us over. I don't care if we lose all our money and can't pay the fucking rent. Once we fix our mistakes"—I look over at Rook—"once we put the bad guys away"—I settle on Ashleigh—"once we make it clear that you belong to us… we're out. Forever. Because while Rook has Ronin and Ash has Ford, I have no one. I've kept Ronnie away from all this bullshit for a reason. And that reason is so we can spend our lives together. And I'm done waiting. It's my turn to get what I want."

I pause to see if anyone has anything to add.

"We're in agreement, then? One last job."

"One last job," they all reply together.

I get up and walk out of Ford's house and get in my truck before they see the look on my face.

Because that's what they all say, right? Just one last job to make things right.

And we all know how that ends.

That one last job just fucks it all back up again. That one last job is usually the opening scene of a very long, fucked-up movie. That one last job always, always ends up with someone dead.

I'm just hoping that the dead guy at the end of our story isn't one of us. Because if one of us dies, this will never end.

## CHAPTER EIGHTEEN

***When I get back*** to the shop there's a big-ass black Mercedes waiting in the parking lot. I park the truck out back with the rest of the guys and go inside. This should be interesting.

As soon as I turn the corner that leads to the showroom I see our guest. A tall, blonde woman with bright blue eyes.

She's chatting up Director Larry. Which is weird, because first of all, Director Larry isn't in charge of shit in my shop. And second, Director Larry hates people. That's why he's the director. He sits on his ass in the control room calling the shots. But this Larry is smiling at the tall blonde.

"Can I help you?" I ask, as I walk up to the counter. She's standing on the other side, like she's a customer. She's wearing a very fancy short yellow dress with brown stiletto boots that go to her knees.

Yeah. She's definitely from out of town.

"We're not open to the public, Ms.—"

"Li-Montgomery," she replies as she extends a dainty hand in my direction.

I pinch the bridge of my nose and then scrub my hand down my face. "You're Ashleigh's sister?"

"That's right," she says in a curt tone, probably pissed off that I didn't kiss her hand or some ridiculous shit like that. "And you are the infamous Spencer Shrike."

I throw my hands up. "Guilty." She narrows her eyes at me, probably wondering if I just admitted to my crimes or if I was joking. I don't elaborate. "Like I said, we're not open to the public. And Ford and Ash live down the street. If you want, I can call them up and let them know you're in town."

"That's not why I'm here, Mr. Shrike."

I wait a few beats. "Well, you gonna spit it out or what? I'm fucking busy."

She scowls and narrows her eyes further at my swearing.

"Lady, I'm in a really bad fucking mood. I got a lot of shit going on, so if you have a reason for being here, start talking. Otherwise, get the fuck out of the shop."

She straightens her dress a little and softens her expression, allowing for a small fake smile. "Have I offended you?"

I sigh, because it's the only way I can suppress the eye roll. "Ford told us all about you, so cut the shit. He said you tried to take his kid away and I'm—"

"That child is not his, Mr. Shrike. Surely you can string a few simple facts together. That child is not his."

"So you're the one fucking up his life? Trying to contest the adoption?"

She smirks at me now. "That would not be me. Ashleigh already called me. She was quite unreasonable."

"Mmm-hmm." I nod at her. "So you live in town now? Or you just happened to be in the neighborhood? Or maybe you're psychic and you knew the adoption would be contested? Which of these is true?"

She throws me another knowing smirk and now my paranoia is kicking into high gear. "It doesn't take a psychic to see this coming, Mr. Shrike. It only takes intimate knowledge of the man Ashleigh thought she was in love with since she was a little girl."

"The dead guy."

"Well, some think he's dead. But dead men do not file legal actions to prevent their infant daughters from being adopted."

"Right. So who filed the papers? You? Your father? Tony's parents? Because if this fucking guy is alive, he won't be for long."

"Why's that, Mr. Shrike?" And then she leans in and whispers. "Killing is the way you handle all your problems now? The first one's the hardest, but it gets easier, doesn't it?"

I recoil back from her words. "Honey," I say in my normal voice. "You have no idea who I am or what I do. And this conversation is over."

"Wait, Mr. Shrike." She grabs my upper arm as I turn and this makes me stop and look her in the face.

"Do not fucking touch me," I growl, shaking her hand off my arm.

"I don't know if he's alive," she continues, like I never even spoke. "But I do know something isn't right. And life isn't as perfect as it looks from the outside with you and your… Team."

"Yeah, well, that's life, eh? You always gotta fight for it." I walk over to the front door, unlock it, and push it open. "Thanks for stopping by. I'll let Ford know you're in town in case he wants to get together."

She walks through the door like she owns the place and makes her way to the car. The driver's side door opens and a guy gets out and walks around to let her in the car.

Not the back, curiously. The guy settles her in the front seat.

"Her husband," I say out loud.

"I feel sorry for him," Ryan says behind me.

I turn around and let out a long breath. "This shit just gets better by the day."

"Yeah? Well, I got some more bad news. The Feds came by earlier looking for Rook. Apparently there's a new witness for the defense. A cop buddy of Jon's from Chicago."

My stomach flips.

"He says he tried to help Rook years ago. Found her at the house all black and blue. His name was not on the list of people tied up in that trafficking shit, so I guess he's clean."

I wait for it.

"He's gonna testify that he offered Rook a way out, money, a shelter for battered women. A job."

I turn away, shaking my head.

"She turned him down. And by this time, she was already well aware that they were selling girls in their barn."

I've never talked to Ryan about what happened to Rook. I've never talked about it to any of them. And they never asked. We're a business. They work for me. I do not share personal details about my life with the mechanics. But everything he just said, except for the new stuff about the witness, is public knowledge. And if the Feds came in and talked freely to a guy who looks more like a criminal than the man on trial, well… then this shit is all over the news by now.

"Camera crew was here too," Ryan adds to deepen the blow. "Scott is useful as a townie cop, he ran them off. But they're not far. He called me a little while ago and said they regrouped at the courthouse."

I put up my hand and walk away. The place is deathly silent, the only sound the echo of my boots across the polished concrete floors. Everyone is staring at me as I pass. Fletch and Griff. Larry. Two camera crews. I swallow hard and walk into my office, closing the door and flipping the blinds on the window so no one can see me.

I sit in my chair. This executive fucking leather chair that screams success.

And I swear to God, the only thing I want right now is one more carefree summer day with Ronnie.

***Two years ago***

Her tan is almost as golden as her hair as she lies face down on the beach, the midday sun blazing down on her perfect body. She's topless, but that's OK. This beach is private. The look on her face… I chuckle to myself as I walk towards her with a couple of ice-cold beers in my hands.

"How can you afford this?" she asks, looking around with wide eyes.

"I got a deal," I say back.

And I guess I did. This island was reserved last year before my team and I were busted for murder. We were spending some of the money we stole. Not a lot. But enough to reserve this island for Ronin and I to celebrate our graduation.

Of course, all that other shit went down and yeah, I haven't even talked to Ronin in over a year. But I'm the one who made the reservation, the money came from my account. My Bombshell has never been to the Florida Keys, so here we are.

I drip cold water from the beer bottle on Ronnie's back and she jumps, turns, flashes me her giant tits, and then turns over on her back and reaches for the beer. She lifts her head just enough to take a sip and then burrows the bottle into the sand and relaxes back again.

"Happy?" I ask.

"So, so happy," she replies, her eyes closed.

"You love me for my beach access, don't you?"

She wiggles a little in the sand, smiling and blushing. This is a game we play. *You love me for…*

"I love you for your big cock."

I bust out laughing. "You love me for my bikes, don't you?"

"I love you for your talented tongue on my pussy."

I shake my head this time. "You love me for my farmhouse, and my redneck trucks, and my beat-up barn, don't you?"

She sits up this time and I reach for her tits.

"Yes, yes, yes," she purrs.

I pull her into my lap and lift her breast to my mouth and suck. "Yes," she says again. "The farmhouse, the dirty-ass barn, the redneck trucks, your tongue, your big cock, your perfectly muscled Greek-god body, your money, your tattoos—even though I'm the one who did them—your brain, your business sense, your bikes…" She pauses to laugh. "And the way you fuck me with paint every now and then."

I release her nipple from my mouth and go to work on her lips. They are soft and lush. Plump, even. I bite the lower one and she laughs into my mouth.

"Do it again," she whispers.

God, this woman says the most normal things in the most seductive way.

"Devour me, Spencer."

My hands leave her breasts. One slides up her back and slips under her hair to palm her neck. The other dips down between her ass cheeks. She squirms against my hand as I pull her pink bikini bottoms aside. I slip a finger into her wetness and begin with long, slow strokes.

"Easy and soft," I say as she buries her head in my neck and begins to suck. That shit drives me crazy. She makes my whole body erupt in sensations that no woman has ever made me feel. It's not just horny. It's a whole other level of desire. It's love.

"Baby," she whispers.

The Bombshell likes to talk during sex now. When we first met it was like pulling teeth to get her to say anything but *yes*, and *oh my God*. But now…

"You're so hard for me, baby," she whispers. I like the whispers. She pulls away from my neck. *Fuck me*, she mouths silently.

I love the silent *fuck mes* even more.

But I shake my head. "Hard for me, baby? That's amateur shit. That's week two shit. I'm looking for graduation-day shit."

She bites her lip and then the tip of her tongue begins to caress the center of her upper lip. "Do you know what I thought about when you walked up on stage at graduation?"

"You were proud of my academic accomplishments?" I tease.

"I thought about your cock, pressing against your jeans under your black gown. I thought about how my mouth was caressing it a few minutes earlier as you took me in the car in the parking lot."

"Did you think about people watching us?"

"Mmmm," she hums against my neck. "I saw a man peeking in the front windshield of the truck. He grabbed himself."

"Fuck, did he really?" I'm sorta appalled.

"Spencer," she laughs into my ear. "Stop, I need a fuck. How can I earn a fuck if you refuse to let me be serious?"

I lift her off me and lay her down in the sand. "Did you really see a guy watching us?"

"Yes."

"Did it turn you on?"

"Yes, as long as you were the only one touching me, his watching for a few seconds was… exhilarating."

"We're probably being watched right now."

She cranes her neck up to look around. We are on a private island, but it's small and there are many other small islands nearby. Not to mention boats constantly traveling between them.

"Should we go inside?"

She shakes her head and bites her lip. "No, baby. I'm not done with my story. There's something else I never told you about graduation day."

"Oh, you're holding out on me, Bomb. You wicked, wicked little tramp."

She shushes me with a finger. "Now listen," she says, once more in her dirty-talk whisper. "Because I was very bad that night."

I lift my eyebrows. "I know, Rons. I was there. We fucked in the back yard, under the moonlight."

"Mmm-hmm. But I had a camera hidden away in the trees."

"Are you serious?" I blurt, once again breaking her sexy seduction.

"Spencer!" She smacks me on the arm. "Stop!"

I seize her tiny wrists and lean into her mouth. "Are you telling me we have a sex tape and I haven't watched it yet?"

She laughs. "Do you want to watch a sex tape of us?"

My hands wrap around her face. "Yes, baby. Did you bring it?"

Her nod starts out enthusiastic and my heart races as I picture all the dirty things we did in the backyard that night. But then her yes turns into a no. "What? Yes or no, Bomb. You're killing me here!"

She leans over and grabs her beach bag, pulling out a little video camera. "I never made a sex tape of that night. But I'd like to make one now. In full daylight. On this beach." She looks around for boats and they are all far away. "I don't care who sees you take me, Spencer Shrike. I'm yours. Only yours. They can look, but they can't touch. I want to talk dirty for you on camera. I want you to record my screams as your cock unloads inside me. I want to film you eating my pussy, and then turn the camera on me and film my face when you make me come. I want—"

I grab the camera and turn it on, then hand it back and take my shirt off. "Action, Bombshell."

## CHAPTER NINETEEN

***Yeah, those were*** the good old days. When Ronnie and I could just kick back on a beach, drink beer, and think about nothing except fucking and what's for dinner.

My daydream is interrupted by a knock on my door. "Spencer?" Ronin calls as he opens it a crack. "Can I come in?"

The boys must've warned him about my mood when he came in the shop. "Yeah," I say back.

He opens the door, enters, and then shuts it behind him. "They've got a new witness."

"I heard," I mumble back.

"Rook's gonna come off looking pretty bad."

"Yup. That's about how it's looking right now."

Ford bursts through the door, no polite can-I-come-in knock from him. "Ashleigh's with Rook in the lunchroom. Kate's asleep." He paces the room a few times and then stops and looks straight at me. "I'm feeling paranoid, Spencer. I'm feeling trapped. I'm feeling like we're being set up."

Ronin flops down on the couch and bends over to hold his head in his hands.

I stare out the window. "Ashleigh's sister was just here. Talking shit about Tony and his parents. She didn't say who's behind the adoption thing."

When I look back at Ford his expression says it all. That look says he's scared. That look says this shit is not pretend.

Ford's got it all right now. A wife he loves and who loves him back. A beautiful baby to take care of. A big house in a quiet neighborhood filled with designer shit. A job working with all his favorite people. And if there's one lesson the three of us have learned, the more you have, the more you have to lose.

It's scary as fuck. And isn't it better to have nothing? Isn't it better to have nothing to lose than to have everything, and know it's all gonna disappear?

I think it is.

"Rook's testimony," Ronin reminds us. "What's she supposed to say when this guy says she chose to stay with Jon?"

Silence. What can she say?

"We're so fucked," I say. "She's never gonna convince anyone of anything. Do you remember how many times we had to have her go over the details when we pinned all this shit on Abelli in the first place, Ford? And there was no one to cross-examine her." I look over at Ronin and he's pale. The truth of what we're into is finally sinking in. For all of us. "Last fall, Ronin? That was just a statement. It was pre-school shit compared to what they're gonna do to her next week when she takes the stand."

"We only have one option," Ford says. "She needs to tell the truth. Whatever the truth is about why she stayed, Ronin, that's what she needs to say. That's the only thing she's got left. We need that jury to buy her story about Abelli and Jon one hundred fucking percent, otherwise we're all going down. Otherwise all that shit she said about what happened in Boulder is back on the table. And if the jury decides we're lying about what happened in Boulder, not only might this asshole walk, but the Feds might think we're the ones behind all this shit. Not Jon. Not Abelli. Not that fuckup in Boulder. Us. And how fucking ironic would it be for *us* to get pinned with *their* dirty shit?"

We're silent again. "What's the truth, Ronin? Did she say why she stayed?" I hate to ask it—I mean, I'm on Rook's side—but you know, when someone comes and says they want to save you from an evil monster, most people get on board with that.

I look over at him when he doesn't answer.

"We could say she was psychologically traumatized," Ford

offers.

"She probably was," I agree. "But that doesn't make her a reliable witness. We need that jury to buy into a lot of fucking lies. A lot of fucking lies. And her name is on that property, Ronin. She was half owner of the property where those girls were being sold. And then this witness comes in and says he tried to help her get away and she said no?"

I'm quiet to see if Ford will fill in the blanks for me, but he doesn't. "Ronin." I wait until he looks up at me. And God, it breaks my heart to see him so defeated, but he needs to hear the truth. "She's going to jail if that guy testifies." I look over at Ford and he's got his hand over his mouth as he listens. "She's going to jail for a long fucking time. We need a goddamned miracle at this point."

Ronin pulls his phone out and texts someone. He waits for a reply and then sits back on the couch. A few seconds later there's a knock on the door.

"Come in," Ronin calls.

Rook peeks her head in, then swallows hard like she knows what's coming. She slips in and closes the door behind her. Ronin stays silent and even I'm beginning to squirm.

"Should I sit?" Rook asks.

Ronin looks up at me. "We can't just sit back and take it, Spencer. We gotta try, at least. So she's gonna talk and you're gonna find the holes. Got it?"

I nod.

Ronin turns back to Rook. "I want all of it this time, Rook. Not the bits and pieces you've told us so far. OK?"

She looks terrified, but Ronin grabs her hand and pulls her onto his lap. "Gidget, we're on your side. OK? We're not gonna judge you. But we need you to be honest with us, because if we don't get this perfect, we might *all* go to jail."

He stresses *all* and when I look over at Ford I can tell he's picturing what might happen to Ash and Kate if he goes away to prison. At least I've kept Ronnie out of this. If I go away, yeah, she'll be upset. But she's independent. She's a fighter. A survivor. Ronnie will be sad, but she'll be able to move on. She won't fall into a depression and be left with only her criminal family to rely on. And Rook in prison? God, she'll never make it.

"Understand?" Ronin asks Rook.

She buries her face in his neck and nods.

"Now," Ronin says as he lifts her off his lap and sets her down on the couch next to him. "Tell us why you stayed when that guy said he'd help you. Were you pregnant?"

"No," she says in her small, scared voice. "It was after I lost the baby."

"Were you scared?"

She shakes her head again. "I was scared," she says, contradicting her body language.

That's not gonna fly at all. The jury will pick up on things like that. The defense will jump on that shit so fast. And it's intuitive. Whether people know it or not, they pick up on the lies with these small cues.

"I was scared," she continues, "that Jon would find me if I left. Come take me back and be even more violent. But the truth is—" She looks over at Ford, then me. "I was embarrassed that I was in this situation to begin with. I was embarrassed that I let him turn me into that person I was back then. I was ashamed that I was part of this sleazy underground world of sex slaves. Even if those girls were there willingly in the beginning and I was duped into believing they were all there because they liked that stuff, I was ashamed to be part of it."

Ronin looks over at me.

I just shake my head no. Not good enough. "I get it, Ronin. It makes sense. And they can call in experts to testify that Rook's reaction was normal, because it is. After years of abuse like that, her mind was not right. But we don't want experts convincing the jury she's OK. We need *Rook* convincing the jury she's OK. We need them to trust her. And this explanation makes her look weak and stupid."

We sit in silence. Each of us thinking about her mistakes. About all our mistakes.

"I thought he'd do the same things to me," Rook admits a few seconds later. "I thought that guy was lying and he was gonna take me somewhere far away and sell me. Or rape me. And yeah, Jon was a monster. But he was the monster I knew. He made me have sex with him and he beat the shit out of me, but he never let anyone else abuse me. So I thought this cop friend was just another one of Jon's business associates. I mean, probably deep down I knew he wasn't. But the paranoia took over and once that idea got in my head, I couldn't get it out." She looks over at me. "I swear to God, Spencer, I know it's sick, but I just figured I was better off understanding my place in Jon's world than taking a chance on this stranger. I didn't want to go through that again. I didn't want to have to accept that my life was changing and it was only getting worse. I could deal with the fact that one man raped and beat me, but anyone else doing it but Jon would break me completely. I just couldn't take the chance that he'd be nice."

Ronin pulls her close and wraps a protective hand around her head. Then he looks up at me with questions in his eyes.

"Better. That's better. Much better than the first one. It's still a pretty bad answer, but it makes her look sympathetic instead of weak."

"Pam." All our heads collectively turn to Ford as he talks into his phone. "Find me the best witness prep specialist you can. I need them delivered to Fort Collins by Friday." He stops to listen. "It doesn't matter. We'll cover all costs." He presses end on the phone and then lets out a deep breath.

"I don't want to cheat," Rook says. "I don't want to have to lie to win anymore."

I agree. And I think Ford and Ronin feel the same way. We can't go on living like this We can't. This shit needs to be settled.

"It's not cheating," Ford says calmly. "The defense is using the same tactics. And I'm sure the Feds will have you talk to witness prep anyway. We're just gonna get our own. To protect our interests only and fuck the rest of them. OK?" He looks over at me, then Ronin. "Because those guys in that courtroom do not give two shits about Rook and how this will affect her. They want to win. And if they have to make her look like an evil slave seller and put her behind bars in the process, they will."

No one says anything after that, just a few awkward moments of silence.

"OK, on to new business," Ford says. "Enough of this 'we're out' crap. We've got a new job going down tomorrow, Spencer, come up with a plan."

It's absurd. It's just totally absurd to talk about honesty and truth in one breath and then plot out how we're gonna slip a spy cam out of my competitor's garage in the next.

But fuck it. We're in. We're in deep. And we've only got two choices… sink or swim.

Rook looks at Ronin. Ronin looks at me. I look at Ford.

We start swimming.

## CHAPTER TWENTY

***Once everyone gets*** back to work I call Carson.

"My man," he says over a cacophony of girly voices. I've known this guy like one week and he's changed so much I barely recognize him. "What's up?"

"What's up with you?" I ask back. "How's things going over there?"

"We're so busy," he says in a whisper. "She's got so many customers, she barely has room to breathe, let alone think."

"Is she pissed off at being so busy?"

"Nah, she's enjoying herself. I can hear her laughing back there right now. And she's not using the plastic. Too distracted."

Now this is the best news all fucking day. I get that dealing with the blood is a serious thing. I understand that she's at risk of getting a disease if she's not careful. I want her to be safe. I want her to continue to provide exceptional care to her clients. But she's overdone it. That plastic shit needs to be over. She needs to stop being paranoid and just enjoy herself. If she wants to quit inking people up, that's fine. But she should not make that decision based on an irrational fear.

"So she's happy?" God, I just want her to be happy.

"Hold on."

There's some background noise and then I hear Veronica's voice. She's joking with her customer.

"Can I help you, Carson?" she asks in her sweet voice.

"Just wanted to let you know your next regular is here. That's all."

"Oh, good. Tell him I'll just be a minute."

"Will do, boss." A few seconds later he comes back on the phone. "See? She's having a good day, Spencer. This was a great idea. It's been nothing but butterflies and flowers. Except for that horror show who showed up earlier. But it's fine. This next guy probably wants something demonic too, but after him there's two more butterflies waiting."

"Perfect, man. I owe you some chrome on that bike."

"And my own custom logo. And a t-shirt with my logo."

"You're pushing it now."

"Nah," he says back. "You love her. And I just told you she's happy, so you love me now too."

"Well, keep the bromance on the lowdown, eh? Later."

I end the call before he can reply and lean back in my luxury chair, my hands behind my head. I sigh. He's right. I love her and I love everything that makes her happy. I hope that when all this shit finally settles she realizes that I've always had her in mind. I hope she knows that I only pushed her away to protect her.

I only have to look at Ford. He's starting to realize how vulnerable Ash and Kate are, and this confirms that I did the right thing keeping Ronnie away from my fucked-up life. I only have to look at the fear in Rook's eyes today. She knows she's going to be ripped apart again next week. She knows that all her mistakes will be out in the open. And she knows that some of the things they're saying about her are one hundred percent true and it could land her in prison.

And she probably knows that there's a part of her that deserves to be punished for standing by and letting women be sold on her property. Just like I know there's a part of me that deserves to be sent to prison for murder. And that's not even counting all the fucking money we stole.

But Ronnie is clean. Ronnie is perfect. And that's almost funny considering that most of the people in this town think she's some feral girl from a trashy family. But she's never been arrested. She's never been in trouble. She's never had to lie her way out of a tight spot. She doesn't get drunk and dance on tables at the Sundance. She doesn't cheat people. She might be loud, and devious, and she might plot to piss me off every chance she gets. But she's never hurt anyone.

And that's sorta cute. Out of all of us, Veronica Vaughn—tattoo artist, deadly shot with a .45 at forty yards, and loud-mouth e-cig smoker with big hair and bigger tits—is the only one of us who's squeaky clean.

If I get arrested next week because Rook can't handle the stress of testifying, I'll ask Carson to take care of Bombshell for real. He's gone above and beyond for me in the Bomb department. And she's got her family. Her brother Vic will make sure she's OK.

I go back out to the garage and start getting my shit together for the bike we're delivering to the first big client in two weeks.

We might not make it that long.

This dream of mine might be over before it even starts.

CHAPTER TWENTY-ONE

# Veronica

***When I'm finished*** with the last girl for the night, I walk her up front and plop down on the couch while Carson rings her up. Most of her housemates have left, but the ones who were tattooed today wait for her outside in front of the shop. One blonde girl notices her paying and then the group of them swarms inside, chattering away like girls do, lifting up the back of her shirt to see the bandage. One girl carefully pulls on the tape so they can check it out, and then they *ooh* and *ahh* at it.

Yes. I feel quite pleased with myself. Today was fun. I did my three regular guys. That back piece on Chuck from Kansas, the final art for a chest piece on Stew—that one took a while because I had to take all sorts of pictures to put in my portfolio—and then my last regular was Dave from town.

Dave's been coming to me since before I actually worked here. When I look at him I see the last four years of my life inked up on his body. Most of my regulars have a theme—like Spencer's blackbirds or Chuck's horror movies. Stew has naked girls. He's got naked strippers, naked acrobats, naked clowns, naked Playboy bunnies, and his chest piece is actually a stage full of saloon girls. There's just tits everywhere on that guy.

But Dave is different. Dave's theme is all war scenes. Today was just some shading and fill-in stuff. He's still got a few months before his work is done.

Since most of my clients are men I don't get a lot of butterflies and flowers. Each of these girls today wanted something a little different even though they all said butterfly with flowers. One wanted a bitchin' death's-head moth instead of a butterfly. I do those a lot, that's a very popular tattoo. One girl wanted a fantasy butterfly. One wanted a regular butterfly but caught in a Venus fly-trap.

And now that it's eight forty-five, I'm dead-ass tired but one hundred percent content.

But it's got more to do with Carson calling me Bombshell than the ink I did today.

"Well," he says as all the girls pile through the door and the place becomes silent, "you pulled in almost four thousand dollars today so far. That's a decent take, right?"

"So far?"

"Yeah, you're open until eleven, aren't you?"

"Oh, yeah. Well, four thousand dollars is a decent take. My dad takes half, so two grand for me. That's incredible." And it is. It's weird too—a few weeks ago I was stressing about coming up with a down payment on my crappy apartment. And now it seems like money is just dropping out of the sky for me. "Well, I'm beat and my date's gonna be here any minute to follow me home, so—"

"Date? What date? You're open until eleven."

"Yeah, usually. But my new landlord asked me to have dinner with him tonight and I said I'd close early. So…" I walk back to the break room and Carson follows. I wiggle out of my scrubs and Carson almost has a panic attack until he realizes I'm fully clothed underneath. I stuff my scrubs in the washer and pull out some clean clothes I left here a while back from my locker. They're just old jeans and a sweater, but it's better than the clothes I've been wearing for two days. When I look back at Carson he's got his chin in his hand, like he's thinking very hard about what to do next.

I leave him standing there and go into the bathroom to change. When I come back out, still pulling on my boots, he's still standing in the same position. "Something wrong, Carson?"

"No," he says too quickly. "Nothing. It's just… how well do you know this landlord? You've never mentioned him before."

"Oh, I just met him yesterday."

"Oh, the apartment thing, right."

I smile at him. "Yeah, how'd you know about my apartment?"

"Uh…"

I was gonna let him run back to Spencer, but he's screwed up twice now, and that's just sloppy. "Spencer knows him. Bobby Mansi? So when you go report back tonight or tomorrow or whenever it is that you check in with the bossman, you tell him that's who I'm having dinner with."

Carson laughs. "I don't know what you're talking—"

"Carson? Just for future reference, only Spencer calls me Bombshell. So you know what? If you're suddenly on the Team, along with Ashleigh and Rook, then you better get your shit straight. Because if he gets hurt because you fuck up in front of the wrong person, I'll make you pay."

"Veronica, please. I have—"

"Don't act like I'm stupid, OK? I know he sent you here. I might not know the details, but one of those girls talked about a hundred-dollar limit and mentioned that someone was paying for their art. So save it. That was obviously Spencer."

"OK." Carson puts his hands up. "OK, yeah, it was Spencer. And he sent me over here to help you out while your family is out of town. But please, don't mention it to him. He was very clear that you should not know he was behind all this stuff."

*All this stuff,* I repeat back to myself. All what stuff? But I don't get a chance to ask, because just then the front door jingles and Bobby calls out, "Veronica? You here?"

"Be right there!" I point to the back door. "Out, Carson. I won't say anything if you come back tomorrow and help me again."

"Deal," Carson says as he heads to the door. "Oh, and

one more thing. While you were busy some girl came in, not from Spencer's offer, and wanted you to paint her body for her boyfriend. Not tattoo it, but paint it. She said you're like famous for that or something."

"Body painting? *Me*?"

"Yeah, and she said she wants it done in edible paint. Like frosting or something. She and I looked it up online, they actually sell that stuff. So she placed an order for you and I made her an appointment in two weeks. She left a hundred-dollar deposit that I put in the drawer." And then he gives me a little salute. "We'll talk more tomorrow."

Edible body paint. Why have I never thought of that before?

"Veronica?"

I turn around and Bobby is standing in the doorway, his arms on either side of the door jamb, just like he was this morning. "Sorry," I say quickly. "I was just saying goodbye to my new receptionist." I have a private laugh at that characterization of Carson. He probably pulls in a hundred grand a year with his bank job and he spent the day with me, checking in sorority girls for tattoo appointments.

"You look happy," he says with a suspicious tilt of his head.

"I'm not allowed to be happy?"

"Sorry," he grins. "I've only known you two days, but you've been pretty upset each time we talked. What's changed? Your employer treating you better?"

Hmmmm… suspicious guy number two. I bet Spencer has paid this guy off as well. I bet Spencer is behind the whole apartment being condemned and my awesome new digs.

He's gonna pay so bad for doing this to me.

"Well…" I sigh deeply and lower my eyes. "No, he's not been very nice to me today at all. But I've been looking forward to this dinner. It's been so long…" I let my words trail off to see if Bobby catches my drift.

"Long?"

"Yeah," I say in my best pouty bombshell voice. "Long. Since anyone paid much attention to me."

"Spencer Shrike ignores his girlfriends? I find that hard to believe. He comes off as a player to me. Kinda like the rest of his gang."

Gang? Ronin and Ford? That's above my pay grade so I ignore that remark. "I've heard he treats his girlfriends nice too. He dates the cashier over at Big City burrito every week. You should ask her if he's a good boyfriend. Because when I was dating him, he wanted to fuck me and paint and that's about it."

Bobby's eyebrows hit the ceiling and I do a little mental cheer.

"Yeah, I *know*," I add. "He dates the bartender over at the Cat Call Club too. She's totally his type. He used to make me pole dance for him all the fucking time. Like every night."

"Really?" Bobby unconsciously leans forward.

"Yup. Fucking, nude body painting and pole dancing. That was the extent of my relationship with Spencer Shrike." I smile sweetly. "But that was a long time ago."

Bobby nods slowly and I wonder if he'll be a total copout like Carson, or…

He walks slowly towards me, his eyelids half closed as he takes me in. He stops a few feet away, and I look up into his eyes, then swallow hard at his heated stare. "Veronica Vaughn," his deep voice rumbles, betraying a building desire. "Are you trying to play me?"

I clear my throat as he steps closer. Well, I guess he's not the type of guy who runs away from a little *femme fatale* action. "Should I be offense or defense?" I snap back.

"Offense, Veronica. Always, *always* be offense." He takes another step closer and then wraps his hand around the back of my neck, pulling me towards him.

Oh, shit.

"Hmmm," he growls in my ear. "You better be careful, Bombshell," he whispers. "I'm not what you think." He dips his head down, and my gaze drops to his mouth as my tongue sweeps over my lips. "Do you still want to have dinner with me?"

I drag my eyes away from his mouth, even though he still hovers close and when my chin tips up, there is a fraction of a moment when he rests his forehead against mine.

"Are you trying to scare me off?" I ask in a hushed tone.

"Yes," he says, his grip on the back of my neck growing tighter.

"It's working." My chest is heaving now and he can't stop the downward migration of his stare. Curse my big tits.

"Good," he says as he releases me and backs off. "Good. Because I'm not a player, Veronica. I'm just a practical guy who gets the job done."

*What job?* I think it, but I don't say it.

"So I'll ask you one more time, Bombshell. Would you like to come over for dinner?"

I pause, breathe, then pause again. "Just dinner?"

He laughs and the smile I found alluring this morning is back, the scary dark side I just witnessed gone. "Veronica, if I ask you to come for dinner, then I'm only asking you to come for dinner. I don't deal in pretenses. I deal in truth. And I expect truth in return. So let's try this again. Are you in a relationship with Mr. Shrike?"

"Why are you so interested?" He's fishing, I realize. He thinks I know what they do in their little Team business.

"Yes. Or. No."

"No," I say honestly. "I told you, I was, but now I'm not. Not for a very long time now. He broke it off with me more than a year ago."

"Why?"

I huff out a laugh. "I don't think so, buddy. If you want someone to feed you information, use the internet like everyone else."

"What if I give you something in return?" He steps forward again.

"Like what?" I know it's all kinds of wrong, but I can't help myself. I am getting all sorts of weird feelings about this guy, and none of them are the fun and flirty kind. I need to know what the fuck is going on. "You've got the hot and dangerous vibe going for you, but I'm not interested in a pity fuck."

He laughs again. "No, Bombshell. I—"

"And why are you calling me that? That's a real nickname I have and you should not—"

"Shhh," he says as his fingers silence my lips. "It's rude to interrupt."

I smack his hand away. "It's rude to shush someone too. Especially if you touch them."

"I thought you said you were scared of me?" he smiles.

"I'm over it. I might be a girl, and I might look stupid and helpless because I have big tits and blonde hair. But I don't go down without a fight."

"I bet you don't, Bomb."

"Mmmhhmm. They always think my feistiness is cute at first. And if you call me that name one more time without explaining how you know about it, I'm gonna walk away."

"What makes you think I care if you walk away?"

"Because I'm a bottom feeder, Bobby Mansi. I know desperation when I see it. You need me for something. It's not dinner, and apparently it's not a fuck either. So that means you want info on my ex." I pause for a moment to see if he denies it, but he stays silent. "Or maybe it's got something to do with Rook, or Ronin, or Ford."

His face is impassive.

"Or"—I play my last card—"Ashleigh and Kate."

He cracks a grin. Not a seductive one, or a scary one, or a challenging one.

No. His grin says *bingo*. I called it.

"I know a lot about you, Bombshell. I know a lot about your friends. And to be quite honest, most of those details bore me. All except one."

"Ash."

"Ashleigh Li Aston."

I wait for more information but none comes forth. He holds his cards. "Come to dinner," he commands.

"And if I don't?"

"Then goodbye."

"Are you going to hurt her?"

"Does it matter?"

"Of course it matters! She's my friend!"

"I'm not here to hurt her. I'm here about something else."

"The baby?"

"She's part of it too, but no. That's not the main reason I'm in town."

Damn. I'm so fucking curious. "Why should I trust you?"

"You shouldn't. I'm not a very good guy."

I scoff and turn away now. I'm done. I grab my leather jacket from the locker and slide into the smooth lined sleeves, then grab my helmet and my backpack. "OK, well. I'm just gonna take your advice then. If you don't mind, I need to lock up." I wave him forward.

"After you," he insists.

I swear to God, I expect him to gag me with chloroform as we walk back up front, but he doesn't. I flip the lights off as we exit, then turn the key in the door lock and check to make sure it's engaged. When I turn to walk to my bike, he walks with me.

"Come to dinner."

I snort this time. "Why? I'm not giving up information that might hurt my friends."

"I said I'm not here to hurt her. I'm not here to hurt any of your friends. I'm here to help, actually. And Veronica"—he grabs my arm before I can step off the curb and get on the bike—"they *need* my help."

It's not so much the words, but the way he says them that sends a chill up my spine. "Why? What's going on? I know something's going on. What's happening?"

"They don't tell you?" He still has a hold of my arm, but he drops it and ponders his own question. "You're not involved at all, are you?"

"No, I have no idea what they do. You're asking the wrong person. They don't tell me shit. I'm really not Spencer's girlfriend."

And that's when the real smile comes out. "I'll follow you back to your condo. Dress for dinner, and I'll come to your door and pick you up in an hour."

I say nothing.

But he follows me when I pull out onto College Avenue, and even though I could go home to my dad's house, Bobby Mansi has me freaked the fuck out. My dad's big, empty house with no locking doors or windows is the last place I want to be tonight.

Winning the game of life is all about the devil you know. So I'm gonna hang with him. Get all the info I need, and then take this back to Spencer tomorrow. Maybe then he'll see I'm not some helpless girl who can't be trusted with secrets.

## CHAPTER TWENTY-TWO

***A little while later***, after Ryan and them have all gone home, the camera crews are packing shit up in the control room and Ford and Larry are discussing the particulars for tomorrow's filming. Rook and Ronin come back to the office. She's been getting the front showroom all squared away while Ronin hoofed it around downtown looking for local businesses that want to get in on the big opening day and supply food and shit.

Rook plops down on the couch. "Kate just woke up from her nap. Ford sent a car to get them, should be here in a few minutes."

I nod at her and look over at Ronin. He's peeking through the blinds, looking out at the street. There's been people hanging out in the parking lot all day. I'm not sure who they're hoping to get a glimpse of. Me? That's just weird. More likely they're looking for Rook. In fact—"Reporters, you think?" I ask Ronin as I stand next to him and peek out.

"Probably," he mumbles. "Even if they're not legit, everyone's got a camera phone. Everyone thinks they're just one YouTube video away from Grumpy Cat greatness." He lets go of the blinds and they snap closed again. "You got a plan?" he asks as Ford and Ashleigh come in. Kate is squirming in Ashleigh's arms and it's painfully obvious both of them have been crying.

"I do have a plan, and it's not dangerous at all."

"Good," Ford says. "Because I'm not happy that Ash

needs to be the bait. Not one bit."

"Well, her bait days are limited, Ford," Rook snaps. "She's gonna be all over the news next week, so relax until we hear what we're doing."

Go, Rook.

"OK." I take over since I'm the planner. "Tonight we're gonna send Ashleigh out to Drake's neighborhood. She's gonna run out of gas and pull into the parking lot. Call a cab and go home." I look at Ford as I say all this and since he doesn't stop me, I look over to Ashleigh for acceptance. She gives me the nod. "Tomorrow, just before Drake does his usual dunchtime getaway to the Cat Call, when the whole fucking world is up and about and we're in plain sight, we're gonna send Ashleigh back with a gas can. While she's busy getting the gas in her car, me and the Shrike Bikes boys will take a little run over to Drake's and start some shit. Our new BFF Scott the townie cop will show up—"

"Wait." Ronin stops me. "Scott's on board?"

"Not yet, but he will be. Just let me handle it. So Scott's gonna come by a few minutes after we arrive, we're gonna start some shit. Ford will be up on the roof of the building across the parking lot, keeping an eye on Ashleigh and driving the bot out of the bay. Ashleigh will pick it up, stick it in the car, and leave."

"How's Ford gonna get on the roof?" Rook asks.

"He's gonna stay the night up there. Keep an eye on the place tonight. Ronin, you and Rook need to go out in public while this is all going down tomorrow. I think you should go to church. It's only three blocks from your apartment, so you can walk. And it's right across the street from the courthouse, so no one is gonna follow you in and bother you. When the shit's all done, we'll text you and I'll have Ryan swing by and pick you up. This also makes Rook look sympathetic for next week's testimony."

I pause to gauge reactions. "Questions? Concerns? Comments?"

Everyone looks at each other, but nothing more is said.

"OK, then. Ryan's got an old piece-of-shit VW that he drives in the winter. That's what Ash will drive tonight. We can't afford to fuck up the details, so Ashleigh really will have to run out of gas, coast into the lot, and then wait for a taxi. Ford, we need to siphon out the gas and then you can calculate the exact volume of fuel we need and how far she has to drive on that tank to make it to Drake's place."

"The approximate gas mileage for a seventy-four VW Beetle is close to twenty miles per gallon, so she'll have to coast over there on fumes."

"Damn, Ford," Rook says with a smile. "How do you know this shit?"

Jesus Christ. I shake my head at him and shoot him a look.

"I once read the owner's manual during Right to Read Week at school—"

"Enough, Ford." Fuck. He shuts up and I continue. "OK, so I think Ashleigh should go home with Ryan so Ford won't be seen driving her around later. You never know who's watching." I wait for Ford's tantrum. In fact everyone waits for Ford's tantrum.

But he stays silent and I swear to God, he is so lucky.

"You're OK with that, Ashleigh? Ryan's a good guy. He'll cook you dinner. It's just for a few hours."

"What about Kate?" she asks with a frown. "Who's gonna watch Kate if Ford is up on the roof and I'm busy doing all this stuff?"

I'm just about to open my mouth when Rook blurts out, "I will! I'll watch her tonight. She can stay at our place."

"OK, yeah. That's a good idea," I say, looking over at Ford for a reaction to this, but he stays silent. Just calmly looking at Rook, who is tickling a now-smiling Kate under the chin. "OK, we're set." I get out my phone and text Ryan. A few minutes later he texts back a little picture of a upturned thumb. "Everyone goes their separate ways and we regroup tomorrow out at the farmhouse after the fake throwdown."

We all stare at each other.

"Don't we have a goodbye chant? Like, *All for one and one for all?*" Ash asks with a smirk, apparently at ease with things now that Rook is gonna watch Kate and this plan is stupid simple.

"Yeah, sure we do," Ronin says. "Ours is, *No good deed goes unpunished.*"

No one laughs. But I'm pretty sure it wasn't a joke.

Ashleigh and Rook leave first, talking about Kate's needs for the night. And Ronin follows.

Ford arches one brow at me and I shake my head. He follows Ronin out and I'm just about to grab my jacket when my phone buzzes. Carson. I press his face. "Yeah."

"First of all," he says, gasping out each word and totally out of breath, "this is not my fault."

I get a sinking feeling in my gut. "What's not your fault?"

"I mean," he says, ignoring my question, "I ran after her, OK? I ran all the way down Mason from Sick Boyz, to her condo. Left my fucking car and everything, because I wasn't sure where she was going and I didn't want to lose her around the first corner, so I ran."

"So she went home? She lives in that condo right now, Carson."

"No—yeah, I mean, I know. But it's not where she went, but who she went *with.*"

"Who?" I ask, but I already know the answer.

"That Bobby Mansi guy. She says they have a date."

That motherfucker. He wasn't kidding when he said he was gonna ask her to dinner. I had to feign indifference to keep the charade going, but I am so fucking jealous. I can only imagine that this is how Ronnie feels every time I pretend to go out on dates with other girls. If she's gonna leave me for this new guy, well—she's not gonna get the chance. I'm gonna make damn sure of it.

## CHAPTER TWENTY-THREE

# Veronica

***There is no music*** in the elevator, so the silence hangs between us and even though I'm not looking at Bobby Mansi, I feel him. I feel his stare. It's hot. Not an I'm-getting-wet kind of hot, just a make-me-uncomfortable hot.

I swallow and clear my throat, thankful that I'm only on the second floor when the elevator beeps and the doors open. I step out and turn back to him, unsure and uneasy. "I'm just—"

"One hour," he says, pressing the code for the penthouse. "I'll be back in one hour. You clean up." His smile is something close to genuine, and I hesitate just long enough for the doors to close on my confused face.

I walk down to the condo door, unlock it, and step inside. It's dark and I have no real idea where the lights are, so I feel around on the nearest wall for the switch.

The room illuminates and I step forward. What the hell am I doing here? It doesn't even make sense. My stomach rumbles and reminds me that I haven't eaten all day. I go into the efficient kitchen decked out in granite counter tops and stainless steel appliances, and pull open the fridge.

A bowl of strawberries and a bottle of red wine.

I'm not really a wine person, but I find a corkscrew in a drawer and start drinking that shit out of the bottle. I grab the strawberries and set them on the counter top, then slide onto a plush barstool and start feeding myself.

Damn, this is like the best meal in the world.

My phone buzzes a text in my backpack. I jump down, fish it out, and read. *Don't get comfortable. Clothes in the bedroom. You have fifty minutes.*

I text back. *Who is this?*

*Ha ha,* he returns.

At least he has a sense of humor. I walk back to the bedroom and type a simple *OK* as my response at the same time.

When I get there, all I see is the dress, laid out on the bed. Black. Short. Sexy. Then the black fuck-me boots. Damn, this guy has my style down. There's some packages of expensive makeup that never in my life have I ever owned. I'm happy with the Cover Girl shit they sell at Target most of the time. And next to the makeup is a basket filled with hair products.

I sigh. This is a new feeling for me. Being taken care of like a woman. I'm not complaining about my dad's parenting skills, he was not terrible at it. But no one has ever just… supplied me beauty things.

I love it. Like, I mean, I *really* love it. I hate struggling and even though lots of confusing things have happened in the last week, lots of really great things have happened too. Like today at the shop. I never once thought about the blood. I was too excited that Spencer sent Carson over to help me. Too thrilled with the fact that he's had Carson leading me around, keeping some sort of big-brother eye on me. How long has that been going on? I'm not sure, but I think it's new. Spencer just started paying attention to me last week when he found out I moved out of my dad's. That's when everything changed. And this Bobby guy has my curiosity up. I'm pretty sure he's not gonna try to fuck me tonight, even though all of this appears to be leading up to a fuck.

No. That's not why he wants me to come to dinner.

My phone buzzes again and I glance down. *Forty-five minutes,* is all it says.

I'm not actually sure why Bobby Mansi wants me to come to dinner, but I'm curious enough to find out.

Ten minutes later I'm clean. Twenty minutes later my hair has been blown dry and my head is dotted with hot rollers. Thirty minutes later my makeup is done. Forty minutes later I'm wearing the dress and I'm trying to get the fuck-me boots on. They are not so fuck-me accessible without a zipper. Spencer would never waste time trying to get these fuckers off. Nope. I'd be sleeping in them.

This makes me smile. Like so big. God, to be sleeping with Spencer in fuck-me boots again. I'd do almost anything to make that happen.

A knock on the door pulls me from my mini daydream and my heels click in that sexy whore-in-a-porno way as I walk down the hall to answer the door. I pull it open and put my hand on my hip because I'm feeling a little sassy right now. "You are one punctual guy. Is that your best quality?"

If I was answering for him, I'd have to say no. That is not his best quality. Because he's standing in front of me in a dark suit that looks like it cost more than my ex-Mini Cooper, his hair is coiffed back the way the magazine models are wearing it these days, and he smells like sex.

"It might be," he says seriously.

Yeah, that fuck-me scent he's wearing is as much about me as these fuck-me boots are about him.

Weird.

"I'm ready."

He smiles and then points to my head. "Not quite."

"Oops, BRB." Oh God, I'm so embarrassed. I left my rollers in. I do the high-heel tip-toe run back to the master bath and start taking the pins out. My hair rolls down my back in loose bouncy curls and I take an extra minute to fluff it up properly, then let out a deep breath and walk back down the hallway, grabbing my leather jacket off the barstool.

Bobby eyes it suspiciously. "There's a nice coat in this closet," he says, pointing to the door off the small foyer.

"I'm good," I say back as he guides me out of the condo with a gesture, but not a gentle hand on my back like Spencer does. That's another flag. Not a red one, but it's at least a yellow. Because he's got me all dressed up for a date, he's feeding me dinner in his penthouse, and there's an underlying air of romance about things.

And yet… there's not.

It's strange, but I don't have much time to dwell, because the elevator doors open and I'm once again waved, but not physically guided, into the large living space. It looks just like it did yesterday, so I'm not awed or anything. This kind of luxury is pretty, I like it. But I'm a small-town girl at heart. I'd never be happy with a condo as my forever home.

"Please," Bobby says as he motions to the table set up in front of the terrace windows. The view is black, with just a few twinkling lights from houses, because we're facing the mountains. Out here the view is real. The view is nature. It's got nothing to do with how the colors light up the darkness and create a beautiful facade that covers an ugly city.

When my eyes adjust to the low light the other view comes into focus. Stars. I'd never trade my starry nights for a valley of lights.

Bobby pulls a chair out for me and I sit as he pushes me back in. "You have nice manners," I say absently as I take in the table.

"Thank you. I come from a prominent Italian family. They were big on manners."

"Were? You don't see them?"

He seats himself across from me and shakes his head, essentially ending that line of conversation. So I just take in my surroundings. I've been to fancy parties with Spence, mostly having to do with Antoine and Ronin. Their parties are productions. So I've seen a fully decked table before. But those people are like family. Their brand of opulence has never felt intimidating.

This brand does. This table says this man is serious about his fine dining.

I can hear people in the kitchen, so I know we're not alone, and that eases my nerves a little.

"Hungry?" Bobby asks.

"Yes, I really am. I didn't have time to eat today. We were busy from the minute I went in until the minute I left. I'd still be there working right now if you hadn't come to collect me."

He smiles as he grabs his napkin from the table and places it in his lap.

I do the same, sorta embarrassed that I didn't do it immediately. My manners can't compare to his. I mean, I *have* manners. I'm not some Honey-Boo-Boo backwoods, trailer-park redneck. But I'm pretty close. We are most definitely considered white trash around this town.

"Nervous?" he asks.

"Yes," I say back truthfully. "I'm not sure why I'm here."

He smiles as a waiter appears and fills our glasses with a deep red wine and sets down some bread in a pretty silver basket. "You're a beautiful single woman. I'm an attractive single man. It's a simple deduction, don't you think?"

He lifts his glass and takes a sip of wine to hide his smile.

I fidget in my seat and blow out a long breath, desperately wishing I had brought my e-cigs. I want one. Bad. I settle for a hard swallow and a mental pep talk. "I don't think I'm here so you can fuck me tonight after you feed me a delicious meal."

He laughs and sits back in his seat, crossing a leg over a knee and taking another sip of his wine. Totally at ease with my complete unease. "Is that so?"

I nod. God, this man can't be much older than me—I'd say twenty-eight at the most—but he makes me feel like a child.

He caresses the edge of his wine glass with a fingertip, eliciting a sharp ting from the crystal. "Then why do you think I brought you here?"

I stay silent, wondering how much I should say. I actually do have a theory, but it's pretty far-fetched.

"You must've thought about it, at least? Why would I ask you to dinner if not to get you in my bed afterward?"

"Well…" I look away. I guess this is it. It's kinda exciting, but at the same time, terrifying. "You want me for something."

He tilts his head in the slightest of nods, urging me to continue.

"You know I'm friends with… interesting people. People who have a lot of information, which," I quickly add, "I have no knowledge of. At all. So if you're looking for some insight into what they're doing, or what they did in the past, or whatever, I have nothing to give you. I'm not that close to them."

I sigh and look away. It sucks to admit it, but it's true. I'm an outside friend, not an inside team member.

"Yes, I can see that from the way Spencer Shrike treats you."

*Yeah, thanks a lot, asshole. Thanks a bunch for reminding me I'm nothing to him.* I mean, I had a great day fantasizing that Spencer cares, and now this jerk has to come in and hand me a reality check.

"They're a team, those guys. Ronin, Spencer, and Ford. Right?"

"Yeah. And Rook."

"And Ashleigh Li?"

I can only shrug at that. "I dunno much about her. I'm not even sure I like her. I never liked Ford much, but Rook loves him hard, so I try. But I'm not sure what kind of woman would marry a guy like Ford, to be honest. It bugs me."

"Is he mean?" When I look over at Bobby, he's got an eyebrow arched up in confusion. "He doesn't come off as mean. An asshole, yeah. But from what I've seen, he's not mean. But maybe I'm wrong?"

I'm careful with my answer because for some reason, I think this really matters. I think that if I say Ford *is* a mean guy, this might change something. It might change Bobby's opinion of Ford. My opinion might actually matter.

Huh, that's refreshing.

"No, I don't mean it like that. I don't mean he's beating her or anything. But he's a weird guy."

Bobby visibly relaxes.

"Why are you so interested in her, anyway? It is Ashleigh that you're mainly interested in, right?"

He takes a long sip of wine before answering. "I have my reasons."

"Yeah, well, if you want me to supply you with any more information, you're gonna need to tell me those reasons."

Bobby's laugh is both lighthearted and terrifying at the same time. "Veronica, we both know you don't have any information. Spencer Shrike has gone out of his way to distance himself from you for years. You're not on the Team, honey."

I throw my napkin down on my place and push my chair back to rise—but his strong grip on my wrist holds me in place. "Let go," I demand calmly.

"No, Veronica. Sit back down, we're not done."

"Look, I'm not sure who you really are or what you really want, but I'll tell you what. I'm not gonna sit here and let you hurt me. So let the fuck go of my wrist or I will take you down."

"Is that—"

I hammerfist him in the forearm, yank my wrist free, spin on my fuck-me heel and whack him in the side of the face with my other fist. I step back and wait for his attack.

He sits in his chair as the redness creeps into the cheek I hit. "So you're a fighter," he says matter-of-factly. I say nothing. "That's all I needed to know."

And then he waits. It's my move. I can walk out or ask the question he just set up.

I opt for the question. "Why?"

Now he does stand. His napkin falls to the floor and for some reason I fixate on it for the second it takes for him to get close to me again. He grabs my upper arm this time, but instead of pulling away, I let him pull me close.

Close enough to whisper in my ear.

"I'm not on the Team either, Veronica. I'm not trying to hurt your feelings. I just need to know if you're a free agent."

"Free agent?"

"Because I'd like you to be on *my* team."

The waiter clears his throat and we both look over at him. He's carrying a tray of covered food.

"Please," Bobby says, and this time he does guide me with a hand on my back. "Please, eat. We'll talk. And then I'm going to take you somewhere and test you."

"What?"

He pushes me forcefully back towards my seat at the table. "If you sit and eat, Veronica, you will get all the answers you require."

"Hmmm…" I know that trap. All the answers I *require*.

"Sit," he commands. "You're in, I can see it. So stop with the posturing and be patient."

I allow him to seat me again, and as soon as he's back in his place, the waiter approaches with the tray of food. My stomach growls and then practically screams as the lids on the silver trays are lifted and I'm presented with a delicious Italian feast.

"I'll eat," I say as I pick up my fork and dig in. "But I want more than the required answers."

When I look up from shoveling another forkful of creamy pasta in my mouth, Bobby's stare is rigid and flat. "You'll get the answers I choose to give. But I assure you, everything I tell you will be the truth. I do not lie. I don't believe in lies. If I can't tell you the truth you want to hear, then I believe in silence."

"We're gonna kill someone, aren't we?" I say offhandedly as I keep shoveling in the food. But it's hard to miss the silence that follows *that* question.

## CHAPTER TWENTY-FOUR

***I do my best*** to ignore the fact that Bobby Mansi practically admitted he wants me to help him kill someone, but after we sit in silence for about ten minutes, he begins to explain.

"I am here for one purpose," he says as he caresses his wine glass. "I have a goal. There are many ways to achieve that goal, and yes, one ends in killing someone. Will you have a problem with that?"

I continue chewing. Slowly. Methodically. I dab my mouth with my pretty napkin and then set it back down in my lap. I reach for the wine and take a small sip. I can tell Bobby Mansi is not used to being made to wait. But I continue to take my time, crossing my legs, leaning back, and folding my hands in my lap. "I'm not killing anyone. I'm not a murderer. So yeah, I actually do have a problem with that."

"You won't be killing anyone, Veronica. Unless I need help. Then, if you agree to be on my team, I'll expect you to have my back. That's something we need to get clear right now."

I reach for the bread and pick off a small piece and pop it in my mouth. Why can't I ever get a normal date? Why do I only get asked out by the Spencers and the Bobbys? Am I that unapproachable that the only men who want to date me are criminals? Why does my first real dinner date in three months have to turn out to be an invitation to murder?

There must be something wrong with me. I'm pretty. I've

got a nice body. I've got a college degree, and yeah, I'm a tattoo artist, but seriously? And this Bobby, he doesn't even like me. He wants me to be his backup in some crazy scheme. He's playing on the fact that I'm not part of Spencer's secret team. He's hoping I feel left out, alone, vulnerable, and desperate.

And he's right. I feel all those things.

"Will you have my back?" he asks again.

I don't know what to say. Seriously. What does a person say when she's asked if she'll protect a man who might be trying to kill someone?

"Do you trust me?" he asks when my silence continues.

That's an easy one, so I just answer. "No. Why should I trust you? I don't even know you. You blow into town with money and buildings and offers. And I'm supposed to what, just jump at the chance to play cops and robbers with you? I mean, please. Give me a little credit."

He smiles big at that, and his smile, good God. It's quite nice. He's a dark guy—Italian, he said. He looks Italian. His hair is thick and just shy of jet black. The shadow on his chin is just short of panty-dropping, that's how sexy it is. And his eyes are bright with excitement.

"Do you have a girlfriend?" I ask suddenly. I need something from him. Something personal to ground me. Help me form an opinion.

"No, I don't have time for girlfriends."

"What do you do then? I need some details, Bobby. Give me something."

"I'd like you to go for a drive with me, Veronica. It's an hour east of here, in an empty field. You and I will be alone. But"—he stands and walks over to a case on a buffet table along the wall, opens it, pulls out a FN Five-SeveN and holds it out to me—"you can have your gun now."

I just stare at him. Is he serious?

"You gonna take it? Or just look at it? You know what this is, Veronica?"

"I know what it is." I'm huffy about it, but fuck him.

"Don't talk to me about guns like I'm a girl."

He shakes the gun a little, a signal for me to get up and take it from him. I push my chair back slowly, then rise and walk calmly across the room and accept the gun. I pop the magazine out—fully loaded with all twenty rounds—then check the chamber—empty. "It's nice."

He laughs. "Nice, yeah. It's nice. So, would you like to accept my offer to test for me?"

"You want me to shoot for you? Right now? In the dark?"

His smile fades quickly. "The job's happening tomorrow. I need to know if you're on board tonight, otherwise I need to plan to go solo."

"I need more information."

"Come with me now and I'll tell you everything you need to know."

"Not everything, just what I need to know. Not good enough."

"I'm paid to complete missions, but I'm also paid to keep secrets. I'll tell you all the details you need to do your job, just as I was told all the details I need to do mine."

I look down at the gun. It's more than nice. Much more than nice. Expensive, both to buy and to shoot, because the ammo is unique. A cone-shaped projectile that acts more like a rifle cartridge than a bullet. My heart thumps a little at the offer. I feel like I'm in a movie. My life is morphing into something interesting and dangerous before my eyes. It's far better than sitting around pining for Spencer.

I look back at Bobby Mansi and nod. "OK, I'll go. But I'm not making any promises until I hear the details."

Sixty minutes later we are still driving. It's eleven thirty at night, it's dark as hell, and I'm truly in the middle of nowhere. I have lived no fewer than ten rape/kill scenarios in my head. But that's ridiculous. I've got a gun. A very powerful gun.

I'm sure Bobby has one too. Somewhere on him. But it's not in his hand with his trigger finger resting alongside the barrel, like mine is. I flicked that safety off and loaded a round into the chamber as soon as I got in the car. Bobby was walking around to get in his side after holding the door for me—those rich-boy manners again—so he didn't see me do it. But I'm sure he knows I'm ready to shoot his ass, should the need arise.

I've never shot a person but I've shot a hundred thousand rounds, at least. Spencer and I used to go shooting once or twice a week back when we first met. We'd spend the entire day at the gun club. I took a lot of shooting classes. I'm a better shot than Spencer is.

I still have a gun club membership, paid in full every year thanks to my ghost of a boyfriend. In fact, I'm still on his account. We just never go together. I'm not sure he even goes there at all—he has his own range on his farm. It's just the back side of a dirt hill, but that's all you need.

Bobby and I sit in silence the whole ride. I guess he's not a music guy because he never turns it on. And when I steal some glances over at him every few minutes, his expression is distant and serious. Like he's thinking very hard about things.

My grip on the gun tightens. God, I hope to hell I'm not setting myself up to be killed.

The car slows and we turn off on a dirt road. We bounce around on it for about a mile, then he stops and cuts the engine and we both get out. "We're here."

I look out at the total darkness. "How the hell are we gonna shoot targets in the dark?"

"You're on the clock now, Veronica. Be quiet, watch, and then do as you're told."

My brows go up into my forehead. *Jesus. Blunt much?*

He opens his trunk and rummages around inside a duffel bag, then produces a contraption that looks like a bunch of laser pointers taped together. He sets it down on a table—table? I guess we're actually somewhere legitimate. And then turns it on. Ten laser beams shoot off into the distance and rest on some sort of vertical platform. The points of light create a line of red targets.

"Shoot them," he says in his all-business tone.

I check my barrel to make sure I've got a round in there, then lift the gun, sight the first dot and move my finger to the trigger. I pop off ten rounds, and with each release the pinprick of light blinks to signal I hit it.

I stand back and lower my weapon. Smiling.

God, I love shooting.

Bobby says nothing, simply moves the target slightly and then the pinpricks of light are farther away. "Twenty yards. Go," he says.

I pop those off in rapid fire, then disengage the mag and hold it out to him. He gives me a smile this time, then hands over another loaded mag and moves the lasers again. "Let's just get to the good shit, shall we? Fifty yards."

I slip the new mag in, load the chamber, and disengage the safety. I fire all twenty rounds this time, starting over from the end after I hit the last dot. I pop the mag out and wait.

"You missed."

"Only twice." I shrug. "I'm not gonna apologize for missing two shots out of forty. I'm standing in fuck-me boots and it's dark. Be reasonable."

I catch his smile in the dim starlight.

"OK, I did my part, now you tell me who you really are. Let's start with your name. I know it's not Bobby Mansi. No one is stupid enough to come to town with an agenda to kill someone and use their real name. So spill."

He hands me another loaded mag and I take that as a sign of trust. "Let's see how much you've figured out first, then I'll see if you need to know anymore."

"That wasn't the deal."

"Adapt, Veronica," he says dryly.

I shake my head and walk over to the car, leaning against the hood. The engine is warm and that feels good in the cold night air. My legs are bare, so I slide up and take a seat. "I think you're Tony. I think you're Ashleigh's husband. You're not dead, obviously, and you want your baby and girlfriend back. You're here to kill Ford."

He laughs. Like, a real *that's-fucking-funny* laugh.

"And I gotta say," I continue, "I'm not sure I can kill Ford. He's weird. But I'm not gonna kill Ford. Or watch your back while you kill Ford. I might even like Ford. He's growing on me. I love Kate. And he loves Kate. So I'm gonna have to decline. If you try to kill Ford, I'm on Team Ford."

When I look up at him he's smiling at me. "You done?" he asks, his eyebrows raised in amusement.

I shrug. "I'm done."

"That's some imagination you have, Veronica."

"What's your name?"

"Bobby."

"What's your other name? The name your friends call you?"

He tilts his head at me as he thinks and then shrugs. "You can call me Tet if you want. My associates call me Tet."

"Tetrahedral? Tetra?"

"No. Tetro, like tetrodotoxin."

Okay. "That poison-puffer fish stuff they eat for fun in Asia?" I have to turn my head so I can giggle privately. Because, come on. It's a little dramatic, right? I compose myself and turn back. "Are you a good witch or a bad witch, Tetro?"

He puts a palm out, asking for my gun. I hand it back to him and he reloads. The look on his face when he lifts his eyes from the weapon reminds me of a predator and I'm instantly sorry I gave the gun back.

"I'm number six. In between poison mushrooms and mercury."

I have no idea what that means so I just drop it because I'm not in the mood to get weird with a guy who has a deadly poison for a nickname in the pitch-black middle of nowhere and is holding my gun.

He hands me a scope, moves the lasers to another area

downrange, then raises my weapon and turns back to me. "Ninety yards. That's max limit for this gun. Watch carefully."

I raise the scope to my eye, adjust it a little, find the targets, and then he fires, one after the other. And with each shot the laser blinks.

He lowers the weapon, hands it back to me, and then walks over to the trunk and grabs a green canvas sack. "Here," he says, holding the sack out to me. I take it and my arm almost drops to the ground because it's so heavy. I lean down and open the drawstring to peek inside. It's far too dark, so I reach in and feel around.

Boxes of ammo. And magazines for the FN Five-SeveN.

OK. He's got my attention.

I look up at him and from this perspective, he looks every inch a killer. *What the fuck was I thinking?* My heart starts to beat wildly at the prospect of what he might expect me to do and it's like he can read my reaction on my face. Because he leans down, grabs my shoulder, and pulls me close.

"Bomb," he says in a very serious voice. *Oh God, we both have dramatic mobster nicknames.* "I've got a few more details for you, are you ready?" He urges me to stand.

I try to push back but he holds me firmly. "No, I think—"

"I'm a soldier."

Oh shit, here it comes. I'm gonna get everything I asked for and then some hardass is gonna stalk me and kill me because I know things I shouldn't. Dammit.

"But not the legitimate kind." One arm wraps around my shoulder and then I'm turned so I'm facing him. A hand slides into the curve of my waist and rests on my hip, just a little bit underneath my jacket.

I almost forget to breathe.

"Usually I work alone. We all work alone. But I need a partner for this one. I've got two girls involved."

My eyes flick up to his. "Rook and Ash?"

"Plus a baby."

"Oh, shit."

"And I need you because your friends, Bombshell—your friends are in *a lot* of trouble. And I don't give a shit about this trial, what they did, why they did it, or how they'll fix it. All I care about is my mission. I owe someone. This mission is how I pay them back."

"Revenge?" I'm out of my mind scared to ask that, but I ask it anyway.

"I need you to help me get the girl and the baby, Veronica," Bobby says, ignoring my question. "I came to town for Ashleigh and Kate."

I drop the gun and cover my face with my hands.

"I need you to watch my back when I take them, you understand?"

I stare up at him for a few seconds. His face is dark. He comes off as menacing and intense. But even so, I was brought up in a family where making demands was met with more demands. I'm well-versed in the art of negotiations. "I can see what you get out of this. I'm your ace, right?"

He nods, but even in the dim light I can see him squint as he tries to figure out where I'm headed with this.

"So what do I get?"

He chuckles. "You get to participate. On my team."

"Do I look some dumb blonde who's so hard up for attention I'll agree to anything just to get it?" I huff out a laugh. "Sorry, poison pufferfish. There's got to be something in it for me."

His hand goes to his chin as he ponders my answer. "You love that guy? Spencer Shrike?"

"What's it to you?"

"You want something from me or not, Veronica? If so, cut the shit. I'm about to make an offer."

He waits. Ball's in my court. "Yeah," I say after several silent seconds. "Yeah. I love him, OK? He's the only guy I want."

"Well, that trial? That testimony by your friend Rook

they're all hanging their futures on? It's not gonna turn out the way they think. It's fixed, Bombshell. They're all gonna be charged with murder, obstruction, perjury, and grand larceny next week. And in the case of your blue-eyed friend? Human trafficking. I've seen the order. Your girlfriend is walking into a trap. She's gonna be caught in lie after lie after lie as soon as she takes that stand."

"What?" Holy fuck, my heart is beating so fast, I feel like I have to hold it in my chest with my hand.

"But I can make it go away, Bombshell. I can." He smiles down at me. It's the most diabolical smile I've ever seen. "I have latitude to…" He stops to laugh under his breath. And then he turns his head and gives me a sidelong glance that sends chills up my spine. "To take care of things in my own way. And if you help me tomorrow, I'll take care of that trial and your dream relationship with Spencer Shrike can begin."

I gulp. "And what if I don't?"

"You will, Ronnie. Because if you don't, your boyfriend dies."

## CHAPTER TWENTY-FIVE

***It's three AM*** when he drops me off on the second floor of the condo building. I give him a curt, I'm-a-professional nod and walk out calmly. But as soon as the doors close behind me, I lean back against the wall and try my best not to hyperventilate.

How the fuck, Veronica? You are one stupid chick. *Oh, a pretty gun. That's exciting! Sure, I'll be your backup, you mobster-slash-soldier who isn't legitimate.*

I breathe in and out for a few seconds. I get the panic attacks all the time at work, so I'm pretty good at getting it under control.

Whewwwww. I blow out a long breath and wait for my heart rate to calm down. Then my phone vibrates and I squeal and jump as I put my hand over my heart again. I check the text message. *Go inside, Veronica. I need you fresh later.*

I look up at the ceiling and yup, sure enough there are cameras up there, hidden in those little black dome things that Rook always points out to me where ever we go. She's paranoid of cameras after her first reality show experience.

I smile and do a little salute. I don't want him to see me so vulnerable. I hate being vulnerable. And you'd think a girl carrying a loaded FN Five-SeveN and two hundred rounds of those pointy cone-shaped cartridges packed inside ten extra mags would feel powerful.

But guns don't make the girl. And I don't feel powerful.

I push the key in the lock and open the condo door. It's

dark, so I fish around for the light switch. Find it. Flick it.

And… nothing. No lights.

Strong hands reach out and grab my arms, wrestling me backwards, slamming me into someone's hard chest. "What the—"

My mouth is covered and the gag is tied behind my head. I bend over, ready to fuck this person up with some stealthy jujitsu, but my wrists are pulled together and bound behind my back before I can even attempt a move.

I scream, but it comes out muffled and then the hood is thrown over my head.

I'm dragged down the hall to the bedroom and this is when it all becomes real. I kick. I fling my feet wildly, but the man just picks me up and carries me to the bed, throwing me down hard enough so I bounce.

My legs kick out again as I try to scramble away, but those hands are on my ankles, not squeezing hard, but just enough to make me—

"Argggghhhh," I moan. Oh shit, that fucking tickles. "Stop," I try to say through my gag. But his hands go behind my bare knees and I lose it. I wiggle because I'm really getting tickled now. I wiggle so much I almost get away.

Lips begin to kiss my neck and chills erupt down my whole body.

"I love the shudder, baby. Did you know that every time I come at you for a fuck or a tease, you shudder for me? Do you shudder for anyone else?"

Spencer.

I can't answer because I'm still gagged and hooded.

He leans down and buries his face in my neck, and then inhales deeply. "Veronica Vaughn, why the fuck do you smell like guns?"

The light on the bedside table flicks on and the hood is removed. Spencer is smiling down at me. I can't help it, I smile too. Right through my gag. And then I start making noises that should clue him in to take the gag off, but instead he puts the hood back on and lowers himself on top of me. His body is hard. Every inch of Spencer is hard. He's like a rock or a mountain. His arms are positioned alongside my body and he spreads his legs so he's straddling me.

He bites my lip.

"I like you gagged, Bombshell. It's refreshing to make you be quiet. Don't get me wrong, I love your slutty mouth, especially when it seals around my cock, sucking me until I explode down your throat. But right now, I'm gonna talk business and you're gonna listen. You got it?"

I nod. I'm all for his brand of talking. When Spencer talks business, my panties need changing. It's been a long time since I had a proper Spencer fuck. A long, long time. That alleyway halfer and the penthouse quickie do not a fuck make.

"Did you go shooting tonight?"

I nod and he leans down to kiss my neck. Oh God, here it comes. I'm already wet.

"Did you go on a date tonight?"

I shake my head. That was not a date. I thought Spencer's idea of a date was pretty bad, but Bobby or Tet or whatever the fuck his name is—yeah, that was not a date. A job interview is more like it.

"You look hot, Bombshell. What were you doing?" Spencer pulls the hood off and slips my gag down. "Answers, *now*."

"I did have dinner with the landlord. Pasta. It was really good, he's got a private chef up there, have you ever hired a private chef for a date?"

"Ronnie, cut the shit," he growls at my rambling.

"He took me shooting after."

"Why?"

"To show off." I'm not gonna tell him shit. Tet made that very clear on the ride home. No information about the job was to leak out. Like at all. Because if it did, Spencer was a dead man. I love Spencer so right now I'm gonna lie like the professional I've suddenly become. "And try to impress me after I challenged him. He thought I was some stupid girl who didn't know her pink .38 from her Walther P99."

This makes Spencer laugh and his eyes crinkle up in the corners.

"Untie me."

"Yeah, right. I'm not done. Did he try anything?"

"Yeah," I lie. "He kissed me."

Spencer frowns. "Did you like it?"

"Yes, it was"—I pause to stop the laugh, because Spencer's jealousy is all over his face—"um, well. Sweet, I guess. Gentle."

He smiles. "Sweet, huh. So you like it gentle, Bomb?"

"Sometimes."

"Do you want it gentle now?"

"Untie me."

"Answer me." He sits up on his knees and pulls his shirt over his head.

I moan. I'm not even embarrassed to admit it. "I need this. I need this bad. I need it to be long, and slow, and rough, and dirty, and fast, and hard, and every way you want to give it to me, Spencer. I need you. I need you to love me *right now*. Whatever the reason is that you've been ignoring me, been pushing me away, just stop. Please. I need you."

He gently grabs my shoulders and pulls me forward to untie my hands. Then he finds the hem of my dress and pulls it up and over my head. He throws it off to the side of the room and then looks down at my fuck-me boots. "Those," he says with his eyebrows raised, "will need to stay on."

Do I know this man, or what?

He reaches around and unclasps my bra, his fingers lightly dragging across my skin as he pulls it over my shoulders and down my arms. My head falls back and my mouth opens to let out a moan.

He goes for my panties next. His fingers hook inside the elastic and he pulls. I wrap my arms around his neck so I can lift my hips and he leans in to bite my lip and slip me some tongue before backing away. He gives me the crooked I'm-gonna-make-you-scream grin, and then his mouth is all over my body. His lips suck on my breast and he palms them from underneath, forcing them to push up my chest. "Suck, baby."

My tongue darts out and licks my nipple and he goes wild, growling against my skin, his mouth stealing the bunched-up tip away. He flicks his tongue against it, then bites.

I squirm because it's painful, but he holds me still. "He kissed you, Bombshell?" And then he pinches my other nipple.

Oh, shit. "Ow!" I squirm away.

He pulls me back and resumes his task. "He kissed you? Did you slap him?"

"No," I reply through the stinging sensations shooting up my breast. "Ah! I punched him in the face!" I laugh it out. "Spencer, stop. You jealous caveman. I'm not your girlfriend, remember? *You should date Carson*," I squeal again. "Stop!"

My nipple is released and I take a breath.

"I am a jealous caveman, and don't you ever forget it. You're *my* Bombshell. And if that asshole wants to come into my town and think he can fuck with my woman, I'm gonna have to set him straight."

I eye him carefully, trying not to read too much into what he just said. "Do you want me?"

"I've wanted you since the day I laid eyes on you. You know that."

"Sometimes I forget, Spencer." I say it softly, so I don't hurt him. I'm done playing games. I just want to settle. I just want *us* to settle. I trace his lips with my fingertip. "It's so hard to remember what it used to be like."

He stares at me for a few seconds, his expression unreadable. "Maybe you need a reminder, then, eh?"

*Fuck me*, I silently mouth. *Fuck me, fuck me, fuck me.*

He says nothing, but his hand does. It rests on my thigh, squeezing gently, and the wetness escapes my throbbing pussy. "Tell me, Bomb. Tell me what you want."

I grab his hand and guide it to my sex, my fingertips

holding his fingertip. I stroke myself with his finger. Back and forth. And then I slip inside myself, the walls of my pussy slick with want. His finger follows, pushing mine in further.

"Tell me, Ronnie."

I melt at the name. He's got so many names for me, but Ronnie—that's the one that says *I love you.* I gather up the wetness on my finger then withdraw it and brings it to his lips. "Suck me, Spencer." His tongue darts out and laps against my finger. And then he dips his mouth down to mine and gives me a taste as well.

I taste like lust. I taste like want. I taste like greed.

He watches my tongue as I lick his finger. "I've said every dirty thing imaginable to you over the years, Ron. We like it like that, don't we? The dirty talk."

I nod. "We do."

"You know what else we like?"

My head shakes out the slightest no. It's been so long since he's looked at me like this. So, *so* fucking *long* since he's had any kind of real conversation with me. So long since he's said all the dirty things that tell me he loves me. I need it so bad. "Tell me what else we like, Spencer."

His smile is small and crooked. Almost sad as he reaches over and laces his fingers in mine. "We like to hold hands too, don't we?"

Oh, God. That was not what I expected. I swallow down the tears and nod.

He watches me struggle and then frowns and lets out a sad sigh. "We like to watch TV, too. Don't we?"

I nod again. "Adult Swim and *King of the Hill.*"

He laughs for real at this. "Yeah, baby. You appreciate the cartoons like no other woman I know. What else do we like?"

A tear slips out and rolls down my cheek. His finger automatically swipes it away and then he presses his mouth into my ear and says, "Shhhh. Don't cry, Ronnie. Just tell me what we like, so I can remember. Because I've lost my way, baby. I'm worried about so many things right now, I'm afraid I might've forgotten why I'm doing all this. Why I'm hurting you so badly. Why this Bobby guy gets to take you out when I can't. So tell me, remind me why I'm doing this, Ronnie. Tell me what we like."

"Trees," I blurt before the sobs come out.

"We do like trees. You love me for my buckeyes, huh?"

That makes me giggle, but his expression remains serious. "Yeah," I whisper. "We love the buckeyes. And we love beaches."

"I love being on the beach with you, Bombshell."

I can't stop the tears now, they just stream down my face. "We like puppies, too."

"Pound puppies, right?" He leans down and kisses my head. "We like to save them, huh?"

"Yeah," I say as I wipe my nose.

"We're gonna get a shitload of pound puppies once this is over, baby." His gray eyes are darting back and forth across my face, studying me. "Tell me what else we love, Ronnie."

"We love the country. And we're gonna live on the farm."

He leans down and kisses me gently on the lips. "Absolutely live on the farm. I'd never leave the farm. What else?"

"And have Sunday dinners with your parents."

"Together," he adds with a sigh. "For once. We're gonna do that together. Keep going. Tell me all the things we like. Tell me all the things we're gonna do when this is over, Ronnie. I want to hear it all. I want it burned in my brain when I leave here."

"Line dancing."

"We love the fuck out of line dancing, Bombs. I'm gonna take you dancing every week when this is over."

He leans off to the side of me, resting his hand on my stomach and his head next to mine, making it clear that none of this is about sex. Or my body. Or our lust. He makes it clear that every bit of this is about *us*. Our dreams, our lives.

"Do we love kids, Ron?" he asks, so, so serious.

"I think we do, Spencer."

"That farmhouse has a lot of rooms. We're gonna need to fill them all up. There is nothing worse than a big empty house."

"We hate empty houses, huh, Spencer?"

"Can't stand them, Bomb. Our farmhouse will be busting at the seams with rowdy kids and pound puppies. Do we like boys or girls, Ronnie?"

"We like girls. You need a pack of princesses running around in ballet shoes."

He's silent for a long time after that. Maybe picturing it like I am. My eyes begin to get heavy. I want nothing more than to make this moment last forever, but his body pressed up against mine makes me content in a way I can't even explain. He makes me feel safe and protected.

"I never cheated on you, Bomb. I took those girls out to trick people into thinking I didn't care."

"Oh." I'm not sure how to feel about that.

He turns towards me and one hand comes up to cup my face. "I don't want you to get hurt. I don't want my mistakes to come back and hurt you. I'll die if something happens to you." His eyes stare into mine and he swallows. "But I'm the one who's been hurting you with this plan. And I just want you to know, Ronnie. I'm sorry. I'm sorry," he says again. "It's just… we're in a lot of trouble, baby. And I hate to bring you in on it like this. But I don't want you to think I never cared if something happens and I never get a chance to tell you—"

He stops and I'm crying all over again. I hug him close and bury my face in his chest. "Nothing's gonna happen, Spence. It's not, OK?" I look up, sniffling. "I love you too. And I feel the same way. I'd do anything for you."

He kisses me on the nose and then scoots down the bed and starts taking off my fuck-me boots. "You're gonna drive a minivan, Ronnie. And all my princesses will go to Catholic school. They'll wear those little green and blue uniforms, Bombshell. And my daughters will wear *pants*, every fucking day. No tartan skirts for my little girls."

I laugh at that and sigh as I picture it. "I'd do anything to make that dream come true. Anything."

Spencer wraps me in his arms and holds me close. "I love you, Veronica. I love you more than I love myself. More than I love Ronin or Ford. More than the Team, Ronnie. I love you more than the Team. Much more. And I just need you to trust me a little bit longer, OK? I just need to keep you safe. I'll tell you everything once it's all over. But I can't tell you anything right now, babe. Do you understand me?"

"I do, Spencer."

And I really mean it. Because Bobby-slash-Tet and I talked the whole way home from the test. And he told me things tonight as well. Things I'm probably not supposed to know. Things Spencer would not *want* me to know. Things that need to be done to keep our dream alive.

I love Spencer just as much as he loves me and that's why I'm gonna be Bobby Mansi's backup. I have a job, and just like Spencer, I'll do whatever it takes to make sure we all come through the other end alive.

After a while Spencer's hands find their way back to my body. We're all talked out, so we show our love in different ways now. We show our love with kisses, and eye contact, and light dragging touches across bare skin.

Every movement is slow.

Every gesture is tender.

Every word is soft.

And if I didn't know what was coming, it would be the perfect happily ever after.

# CHAPTER TWENTY-SIX

## Spencer

***Leaving Ronnie in bed*** might be the hardest thing I've ever done. I look at her one last time in the dim glow of approaching dawn outside. Her golden hair is spread out on her pillow, her little hands all tucked up under her chin like she's cold. I pull her close one more time. She's a heavy sleeper, but she grumbles and gives me a snuggle before wiggling away and turning over.

I wish I could just steal her away right now. Run away with her. Some tropical island where we'd live naked, brown from the sun, carefree with no one else around. And if I had met Ronnie first instead of Ford and Ronin, I would. I do love her more than the Team, but my Team is in this mess right now because of me.

Yeah, Rook has a lot to do with it as well, but now that our stories are intertwined—for the sole purpose of saving my ass—it's not about Rook's mistakes anymore. It's all about mine. I'm the one who killed the Boulder dude. I'm the one who told Rook to cover for me with the story she told the police last year.

And yeah, Ronin and Ford were there when I pulled the trigger, and Rook is responsible for those human traffickers being linked to us in the first place. But everything all comes back to me. We stand together, so if we lose, we're all going down. We all played a part.

But I'm the only one who's really guilty. I can't just up and run away with Ron. I have to clean my mess up or one day it will come back and kick my ass. I know this. I saw it happen when I was sitting in the Denver Detention Center, waiting to be processed over to Boulder County, and I was stuck in this cell with a guy who was also in for murder one.

***Three and a half years ago***

"You got a girl?" the guy asks from his side of the room.

I don't even look up. "No. Not really. A bunch of them, you know." It just sorta comes out. My mind is spinning from my current situation.

Because we are fucked. That detective in Boulder got a hold of Ford's computer and sure enough, he found a way inside Ford's protected shit.

How the fuck did they breach his shit? I don't get it. It was locked up tight. In fact, it wasn't even on that computer. It was being held on a remote server. I don't know all that shit Ford does to keep his data private, but I do know for a fact that nothing's actually *stored* on the computer. Nothing is local. Which means these guys got into his system, traced his ass through the cloud, and then broke in.

My breath comes out in a long controlled exhale.

I'm so fucked.

"That's good, son," the older guy says. "Because they always get you. They always get you in the end."

I look up at him now. He looks Mexican but his Southern drawled English says he's not, he's about forty or so, and his green tats tell me he's no stranger to prison. All the knuckles on his left hand have x's on them. "What?" I've got no interest in hearing this asshole's version of Life Lessons Learned in the Joint. I just want him to shut the fuck up.

"Your loved ones? You got loved ones? Mommy and Daddy?"

I shake my head at him. "Dude, my family is not gonna be my downfall, take my word on that one."

"No? Why's that? Because you innocent?"

I take a deep breath and go back to my own thoughts.

"And that's not what I meant, anyways. I meant, if you've got someone close to you, too close to you, then they *sees* that, you know?"

*Sees* that? The grammar lapse conflicts with my previous opinion about his English. "See what?" I ask, frustrated with the talking but unable to stop myself from asking. Being locked up will do that to you. I've been here three days already, and this asshole's blathering is not my idea of enlightening conversation.

"See you love someone. They sees that, then they use it to take you down."

"The cops?" I ask, confused by both the bad grammar and what he's actually saying.

He laughs at me. "Them cops is the least of your problems. The ones you work for. Those ones. They keep records of your family."

I just stare at him. "What?"

"You're still learning, pup. But if you want to stay in this business, you better figure that part out right quick." The dumb Mexican routine drops the longer that sentence streams on and I realize he's been playing me these past few days.

I sit up and pay attention.

"That's right, kid. Now you're learning."

"What the fuck are you talking about?" I look up at the ceiling, at the cameras. I'm pretty sure they're keeping a nice peeled eye on me right now.

"The cops ain't the bad guys, pup. It's the bosses you gotta worry about."

I stare at him for a few seconds, looking beyond the ugly tattoos, the weathered brown skin, and the fact that he smells like he's been homeless for years. And when I finally do that, I see him for the first time.

I see him because I recognize him.

He is some other Team's Ronin. As sure as shit, I see it. He's some Team's liar and he's here because it's his job to take the fall.

"Is that all?" I ask him.

He gives me a small smile. "Let me offer you a piece of advice, OK, son?" He stops, but I give him nothing but silence. Silence is the only safe way out of this situation. "Keep the ones ya really love far, *far* away."

I'm just about to reply when the door buzzes and both of us jump a little. It slides open and two guards appear. "Shrike?"

"Yeah." I blow out a long breath as I get to my feet.

"Charges have been dropped. We're moving you through outtake."

I walk forward, then look back at the Ronin and give him a nod. He nods back and I walk through the doors.

I never saw the guy again. Not in person anyway. But I did see him on the internet a year later. *Drudge Report* ran a headline about a mob job gone bad and an unidentified victim with x's tattooed on his knuckles.

He was the mark in that hit and not two weeks before that his wife and kids died in a freak carbon monoxide accident while they were sleeping.

It freaked me the fuck out. I had just pitched the Shrike Bikes pilot to the Biker Channel. I sucked up to Ford and got him to commit, then called Antoine to feel him out for the photography. I had always planned on using Ronnie for that show. I wanted to make her life special, give her a taste of the better life, as she liked to call it. A life where she could shop and play without worrying about money.

I wanted her to be my model. So bad. Painting Ronnie's body is the most erotic thing I've ever done. Man, she turns me on like nothing in this world.

But that guy. His words were burned in me. So I told the

Bomb no. I told her I wanted a new girl. Some professional model. Someone taller, dark hair. Thinner. I told her I wanted the anti-Bomb to be my Shrike Bikes girl.

I hurt her with those words. I've never seen a more hurt look on her face. She broke it off with me and I played the bruised boyfriend for a week or so, telling anyone who'd listen that she's a bitch. But every night I drove by her house. Sometimes I'd sit up on the roof of the little candle shop across College Avenue from Sick Boyz and spy on her. You'd be amazed how far you can travel on the rooftops before you have to hit the streets.

And she dated a few guys. I held my jealousy in check, because it never seemed to go anywhere. I followed her relentlessly for months. And then slowly I let her go. Redirected my attention to Rook, and the two brothers I'd been missing for years, as we all got back together for the STURGIS contract.

But when Veronica Vaughn showed up as Operation Jon was in full swing… when she came out of that building smelling like guns with blood dripping down her side… when Rook told me she's the only reason Jon didn't get her that day…

Ronnie wasn't hurt. I knew she wasn't hurt. That bullet skimmed her, it was a scrape. But that's not the point. The point is, my world touched her. My fucking world *touched* her. And Ronnie pulled out her little pink gun—it was a Walther P99 that day, but every gun I picture her with is a pink .38 Special—fully loaded this time, and went in shooting just like I taught her.

She got knocked on her ass that day. Jon really did a number on her. When we got back from Sturgis she was all black and blue. And that shit really hit home. I lost all my resolve. I wanted her back. I wanted her back so bad. I kept her closer to me that month than I had in more than a year. I took her to Rook's birthday party and I fucked her every chance I could.

Until the bullshit came back in full force. *Again.*

It's like these mistakes we made will never end. It's like the past has me by the balls and it has no intention of letting go.

This trial is our last chance to put this that Boulder shit to rest.

Rook. *Rook* is our last chance to put this shit to rest. Rook needs to just get up on that stand and lie her ass off. She needs to stick to the story she told last year. That's the only way this will end and Ron and I can be together.

If we can just get past the trial…

## CHAPTER TWENTY-SEVEN

***My phone vibrates*** in my pocket as I take the stairs down to the garage where my bike is. Rook. *We're having coffee at Shrike Bikes today, park in back and the crew will let you in.*

OK.

Yeah. Today has nothing in common with yesterday. I thought this week and last week were totally different, but today and yesterday are like two different dimensions. Yesterday I was Veronica Vaughn, tattoo artist. Today I'm Bombshell the Assassin's Assistant.

I still don't know who Bobby—Tet, or whatever the fuck his name is—will be killing. And actually, he never said he was killing anyone, but he never denied it either. And he left me with the impression that silence is a valid answer for a reason. It means the question is important, he's just not giving me an answer.

What he did tell me was that he's part of a secret organization—aren't they all?—and he's here to complete a job that somehow involves Ashleigh and Kate.

*And Spencer,* I remind myself. Bobby didn't elaborate on the whole you'll-help-me-or-your-boyfriend-will-die thing, either. And I'm too chicken shit to ask outright. Because I'm not sure I want to know the truth.

What if Spencer is part of this guy's business? Spencer told me he was guilty that night last week. But he never said of *what*—just everything they said about him on the news that year we met was true. But that's ludicrous. They said a lot of shit that I know for a fact wasn't true. Like he came from an abusive home. That was said once. I looked up all the reports after he left that night. That's definitely not true. And they said he knew Ronin since they were six, but that was Ford. They got that wrong too. So Spencer is exaggerating. He's not guilty of *everything.*

But some of the stuff rings true to me. I know they've conned people. I'm not sure who it was, but Spencer and I were out once with some friends of his from Ronin's old neighborhood in Denver, and I heard mention of con jobs. Drug dealers, they said. But I'm not sure conning drug dealers is a bad thing. Spencer does not do drugs. We've never smoked a joint or anything. We drink beers when we're out together. But he's not a partier and neither am I.

Spencer is all business. His life pretty much revolves around his work. Be it painting, or bikes, or the show.

So murder? Yeah, they said it on TV. And yeah, I'm pretty sure that's what Spencer was referring to the other night when he said he was guilty. But murder? I just can't see it.

Spencer is a calculating guy. He's a thinker. He's calm and rational and he plans everything. He makes lists and keeps spreadsheets. He's not a guy who just goes off and murders someone.

He's a gun fanatic, sure. He's got guns stashed everywhere in the house. And whenever I asked him why he needed so many guns, it was always the same answer. 'You might only get one chance to save your life with a gun. Keep one on you and keep one next to you.'

I've been packing heat since the first day I met him and went to his shop to see the '56 Blackbird. After our very first dirty fuck, Spencer loaded me up, set me on the back of his dirt bike and took me out to the gully he uses as a shooting range on his property so he could show me the basics.

But even though on the surface he looks like he's half-crazed about these weapons, he's not. He's very disciplined. We've been in several confrontations while traveling and even though I know he's always got a gun on him, he's never, ever pulled it out. Ever.

The gun doesn't make the man. That's what he always said. The gun doesn't make the man.

I palm the FN Five-SeveN through my jacket, just to quadruple-check that it's there. It's not big, and it's not heavy, not even when it's fully loaded, so it fits nicely in my inside pocket.

I straddle the bike, snap on my helmet, and start her up. I ease back out of the parking space, then give her a little gas on the throttle and stop at the gate. I don't have an opener, or the code to get back in here, but the gate must be on an automatic trigger, because it opens for me after a slight pause.

I pull out on Mason Street and barely have time to shift into third gear before turning on Maple and pulling into the lot behind Shrike Bikes. There's a lot of cars and bikes here, but the door opens before I even shut the engine down. I get off and walk over to the open door, taking off my helmet.

"Rook and Ashleigh are in the front."

I don't really know Spencer's mechanics since they were never part of the biz when I was around, but I have seen Ryan enough to know his name. I smile and walk past as he lets the door close behind me. "To the right," he says, pointing.

I walk down the hallway, go through a steel door, then come out in the showroom. I can hear Rook and Ashleigh talking in a room behind the counter, and the whole place smells like coffee.

I really need some coffee.

"… so I have to piss on the stick tonight."

"No!" Rook exclaims as I enter the little room behind the showroom desk.

"Oh, hey, Ronnie," Ashleigh says as she hands Kate a baby cookie.

"You're pregnant?" I ask.

"She doesn't know yet. But Ford's asking her for a test to check." Rook waggles her eyebrows at me. "They've been bareback for months."

Great. That's just great. I'm gonna help a man abduct her tonight, and she might be pregnant.

"Coffee, Ronnie?" Rook asks, handing me a cup. "Spencer got me this new coffee machine and outfitted the store room as my own personal space."

"Why?" I'm confused. And jealous. Why the fuck does Spencer do everything for Rook? I'm insanely jealous every time he pays attention to her, even after he told me how he really feels last night.

"The boys don't want us having coffee across the street until things die down," Ash says. "Why do you have that look on your face?"

"I don't have a look," I reply defensively. "I'm just confused, that's all."

"Ronin is crazy thinking about the reporters."

"Yeah," Ash joins in. "And Ford, holy shit, he's off-his-meds insane over this stupid job tonight."

"Ashleigh," Rook chastises.

I walk over to the fancy coffee machine and press the button for coffee, then take my time adding cream and sugar. I can't hear them whispering behind my back or anything, but I can almost feel the looks and hand gestures.

When I turn they're both smiling big. Like I just caught them doing something bad. I ignore them and plop down on the couch.

"Spencer came in happy this morning," Rook offers.

"Well, he got laid last night, so I guess that's why," I reply back, uninterested. All I'm thinking about is tonight. How am I supposed to help Bobby/Tet do this job when Ashleigh is pregnant?

"Earth to Ronnie," Rook says as she snaps her fingers in front of my face.

"Huh?"

"I said, are you two back together?"

Are we back together? We can't be back together, because then my loyalty belongs to him. And I can't choose him over this job, otherwise his life is in danger. "No, I'm seeing someone else. This Italian guy from my building. He owns the building, actually. He owns the other apartment building too, but there's asbestos in that one and—"

"Whoa," Rook says. "What are you talking about?"

"Did you say Italian guy?" Ash asks, her face pale with worry when I look over at her.

Yeah. That's a dead giveaway. Does she know this guy? Maybe, maybe not. But she's worried. I know her Tony came from the mafia, Rook spilled that part to me as soon as she found out. Damn, I wish I had a picture of Bobby. Or a picture of Tony. "Hey, we should go to your house for coffee, Ash. Let's go now."

"No," they both say together. "We're not allowed out of the building today," Rook says.

"Until later anyway," Ashleigh explains.

Rook shoots her another look and it's pretty clear they are in on the job Bobby was referring to last night. I just sulk on the couch for the entire hour after that, saying pretty much nothing. My mind is racing at top speed, trying to justify kidnapping my friends.

The ends justify the means. That's what Bobby said last night. Yes, it's horrific and terrifying, but the end justifies the means.

Of course, he never told me the end. I laugh out loud at that and both Rook and Ash stop talking to shoot me a look of concern. "Sorry," I say quickly.

They continue to talk until I get a text from Carson telling me I'm late to open the shop. Holy hell. I get up, say my quick goodbyes, and then head for my bike. Three minutes later I pull up in front of Sick Boyz, more confused than ever.

Because I might be trading the lives of my friends for Spencer.

How does one choose between friend and lover?

My shoulders sag as I get off the bike and greet Carson. I open the door, flip the sign to open, and then head back to my room as Carson talks to me from the register.

I don't hear any of it though, because all I can think about is how I'm on the wrong side.

I'm totally on the wrong side.

But it doesn't matter.

Bobby Mansi made it crystal clear. If he dies, I'll lose everything. Because he won't fix the trial until his mission is complete. And I'm not even sure what that mission is, but I need to be on board. Because if Rook testifies… all my friends go to jail.

CHAPTER TWENTY-EIGHT

# Spencer

***"Hello? You dumbasses still there?"***

Ronin and I just look at the phone on my desk. I'm so fucking distracted today about Veronica, I should just go home. I loved her being here in the building this morning, but now she's at work and Carson, damn. That guy is a lot of things, but a hero isn't one of them.

"We're here," Ronin says. "Just… processing."

"Yeah," I reply. "Say it again. Because I'm pretty sure you just said you saw Ashleigh's sister drive by six times."

Silence from Ford means he's irritated. He's pinching the bridge of his nose, gritting his teeth so hard his TMJ will be acting up tonight, and closing his eyes, sympathizing with himself about having to deal with stupid people. "You're giving me a headache," he says calmly.

"Well, you're giving *me* a headache," Ronin replies. "So just explain why the fuck we should care that Ashleigh's sister is here. Is she the one behind the bike theft? Is she the one behind the sudden appearance of the new witness in the trial? Is she filing for adoption of your kid?"

"No, Ronin," Ford says in his *why are you on this team* voice. "But she's a wild card we can't afford to discount. What if this bitch does something unpredictable?"

"As in what?" Ronin asks. "She's gonna swoop in and save Ash from an out-of-gas car while we're in the middle of the job? I'm not following."

I have to bite back the cringe as Ford remains silent.

"OK, I'm back to surveillance. Spencer, you owe me for this. I am not recon for a reason." The three quick beeps says the call has been ended on the other side.

"What's he so fucking strung out about, Spence?" Ronin asks, turning to me. "It's like he's having a conversation with himself. I don't get it. Is the new family compromising him or what?"

"I don't think that's it, Ronin. He's just worried about Ashleigh doing this job. He doesn't want her involved, but we've got no choice."

"Yeah, well, this is the part I'm not getting. OK? It's a pretty fucking simple job. Get dropped off in a taxi, fill up the tank with two gallons of gas. Start up the car. Wait for you and your crew to show up and distract everyone. Ford drives the bot out, Ash picks it up. She drives away. What am I missing?"

I wait a beat too long and Ronin is on to me. He starts shaking his head. "You better come clean, Spencer. I swear to God, if you two are keeping shit from me, I will flip the fuck out."

"That's not it," I say calmly. "That's not it at all. It's just…" This is not a lying pause. Ronin taught me this pause. It's an *I don't want to tell you the truth, but the truth is coming out anyway* pause. "It's just we're not one hundred percent sure who all the players are." And this is not a lie either. That's the whole fucking reason we're doing this job, right? To get the players lined up like soldiers.

Ronin's brow furrows. He's not buying it and like the inexperienced liar I am, I keep talking. "What if there's someone else involved? What if Ashleigh's sister *is* the one behind all this? What if all this has to do with Ford and not Rook? What if we've been targeting the wrong enemy?"

"You know something and you better fucking tell me right the hell now."

"Ford thinks Ashleigh's father is the one behind the stolen motorcycles."

"But why?"

The fact that Ronin is still asking me for answers and not filling them in himself tells me he thinks I'm lying. I might not be the liar on the Team, but the liar has been one of my best friends for ten years. I know him. He knows me. We know Ford. And all of us can *feel* there's something wrong with *us* right now.

"It's a distraction, I guess." I shrug my shoulders, but it's lame and even I know it so I play my last card. "Ford never told you, and dude, I'm sorry for keeping it from you all this time, but Ashleigh's family ties are big-time…" I search for the right word. "Big-time corporate mobsters, I guess. And the guy she was engaged to, Kate's real father, that guy comes from the actual Italian mob. Not some low-life rank either. But like the fucking Godfather's son."

I wait for Ronin's reaction but he rolls a hand at me to keep going.

"And the Godfather and Ashleigh's father, Damian Li, they hate each other. They both do business in San Diego. Ashleigh left the US for college and met up with Tony, the Godfather's son, in Japan. Tony joined the military, became a SEAL, and then got blown up on some mission. Stop me if you've heard this."

I wait but Ronin is not amused because he has not heard this. Not one bit of it, and now that he realizes I have, he's only gonna get angrier.

"Ashleigh went a little insane when the death of Tony and the birth of Kate pretty much occurred simultaneously, left Japan on this whacked-out road trip, and may or may not have tried to kill herself by falling asleep in a broken-down car during a blizzard. Ford unwittingly saved her, took her to LA thinking she just wanted to have words with the guy who left her hanging and pregnant in another country, not realizing Tony was dead, and then Ashleigh's father came and forcibly took Kate, threatening to incarcerate Ashleigh in a psychiatric facility if she didn't give the baby over to her sister to be adopted."

"Shit. Holy fuck. Why didn't Ford tell me?" Finally Ronin is processing.

"That's not all, dude. Ford lied his way into Damian Li's home, then married her on the spot using some legal loophole only California has, called a confidential marriage license. The woman who performed the ceremony is still hiding in Australia, that's how terrified she is to face Li."

"So," Ronin says, finally ready to fill in the blanks. I do my best not to breathe a sigh of relief. "We're not only dealing with corrupt FBI and politicians who think keeping girls as sex slaves is OK, but also a double-crossed corporate criminal, and maybe even a real-life mobster, both of whom are related to Ashleigh and Kate. Well, that's fucking wonderful. And you guys didn't think to tell me this earlier?"

I relax a little, because he's playing along right now, but that doesn't mean he's on board. I'm dealing with our liar. And even though this was kept from Ronin and this is all one hundred percent true as far as I know, none of this shit is what Ford does not want Ronin to know. *Or me,* my nagging thoughts add, as if I needed anymore bullshit on my plate.

"Of course we thought of telling you, dickwad. But we figured you had enough on your plate with Rook's problems. But now we're second-guessing ourselves. Maybe Rook's not the problem, maybe Ashleigh is."

All of that was true. Every word of it. And Ronin knows this, so even if he's still suspicious, he has to let it ride.

"What about the new witness for the trial?" he finally asks, after several seconds of silence. "How's that play into it?"

I throw up my hands because I actually have no idea. "He's just another witness. I mean, look, the defense has a team of very accomplished lawyers. Of course they can find a witness to substantiate their claims against Rook. It's not that unusual. Right?"

"And Drake?"

"Ford found something when he was doing his computer thing back in his apartment. Drake, it turns out, is the illegitimate son of our friend the Boulder pedophile."

"What?"

"Yeah, so shit's starting to make sense, right?"

He shakes his head at me, angry as all fuck. And I don't blame him. If the tables were turned, I'd be raging. "Then why keep it from me, Spencer? That shit's not cool. At all."

"Rook," I say as he stops his pacing and looks over to me. "Rook cannot know anything else. She's a terrible witness, Ronin. Too much information is just as bad as too little."

Ronin paces the room a few times. He looks over at me, then stops in front of the window and peeks through the blinds. There's people outside again, but they are not in the parking lot today. I hired security to rope it off. They are out by the sidewalk with their signs. And really, who gives a fuck about some picketers at this point? We'll deal with them if they come too close. Right now we're dealing with two mobsters, the FBI, two teams of lawyers, three girls and a baby we're trying to keep safe, and the possibility of the Team breaking up over these lies I'm telling.

Those people outside are not even on my radar.

I look back at Ronin and he's not taking this too well. His eyes might be looking out the window, but his mind is a million miles away. His mind is on Rook.

Just like Ford's mind is on Ashleigh and my mind is on Veronica.

We can't do this anymore. We have way too much to lose. But that's a talk for another day. Today, Ronin needs to just go along. That's it. Just go along. So I start talking again. "She's not even involved in this, Ronin. Rook is the babysitter, right? You're gonna be with her the whole time. You're gonna take a nice walk to church with the baby, sit inside for a little while. Talk to the peeps in there if they ask questions. Then get in the car I send and meet us out at the farm to regroup. Ashleigh is the one taking the risk. Ford is the one who needs to be worried, not you."

He looks over at me and then opens my office door and

walks out without another word.

I sit down in my chair and sigh.

This is it. This is the end. This Team is over. And as much as I want a normal life with Ronnie—I'm fucking sad at the thought of leaving my brothers behind.

And if I'm honest, I'm scared to leave them behind as well. We've been through a lot. We've stood up for one another through so much. I've known for many years, even back when we were fighting, if I needed anything, I could just call. But when you've got babies and women involved, that answer is no longer automatic.

Because we've all got new priorities now.

And as much as I want all this shit to be over so I can move on with Ronnie and have a normal life… I'm sad.

# CHAPTER TWENTY-NINE

***My morning goes*** by like that. I have the sorority girls and one regular today. I do butterflies and flowers, then work on the 3D robotic parts I've been tattooing on my regular's arm for the better part of six months. Today is the last appointment, and I should be thrilled, because this shit is art. This tattoo will find its way into magazines, will be all over the internet the second the redness goes away, will win competitions if he decides to enter—it's that awesome.

This tattoo will be famous for another reason. Because the arm it's inked on belongs to a drummer for an up-and-coming Denver band. They had a single featured on iTunes last Christmas and they're almost ready to put out their first full-length CD. And he wants to come back and have me do the other arm next month.

I told him yes. What could I say? No? I'm quitting? I'm a quitter?

I'm not a quitter, so I told him yes. I scheduled it for May, the day he comes back from a short small-venue tour in California.

But my mind is really not on tattoos right now. My mind is constantly wandering over to Rook. And Kate, and Ashleigh.

Because in two hours, I'm gonna be involved in something horrific.

I swallow that down, because even if it goes perfectly, even if I save Spencer's ass by doing this, the second he finds out, he's done with me. I'll never be his friend again, let alone his girlfriend.

The phone in my pocket buzzes and I jump, dropping the machine I'm cleaning into the stainless steel sink in my room. Shit. I remove my nitrile gloves—I might be distracted enough to forgo the plastic on the chair and shit, but I do not fuck about with cleaning without some heavy rubber gloves. I lay them on the counter and turn the water off, then fish out my phone.

*Twenty minutes. Do not be late.*

Oh, God. My stomach is in knots.

"You OK?" I spin around and Carson is looking at me with a worried frown. "You look freaked out."

"No, I just have a date with that guy again. So I need to go. Thanks a bunch for your help. I'll probably be OK tomorrow. Vic and my dad will be here at two, so you don't need to come in." He's about to protest, but I put a hand up. "Carson, believe me, you do not want to come in. All those clichés about dads, daughters, and shotguns… well. They're cliché for a reason. Some fathers really do that shit and mine is one of them."

He looks at me for a few seconds, but then he nods and drops it. "OK, then. Call me and we'll go car-hunting. Spencer is still really adamant about you getting a safe car."

This makes me smile. My Spencer. He cares about me. He wants me to drive safely. "OK, sure." I say it but I don't mean it, because after tonight, Spencer will want nothing to do with me.

I go back to cleaning my machine and getting it ready for the autoclave, and Carson takes the hint and lets himself out the front door. I throw the bagged parts of my machine into the sterilizer and then walk down the hall and lock the door, leaving the neon sign that's flashing open to the outside world on. I parked in front tonight, but I'm not taking the bike home. I'm walking. It's not even six o'clock, but it'll be dark soon, so I grab my pack and hoof it out the back door.

The condo building on Mason is only about a mile away,

so I take off at a jog. I glance over at Shrike Bikes as I make my way across Maple, but there's nothing going on over there. Everyone is in position for that secret job they're pulling tonight, I suppose. By the time I make it to the building I'm sweaty and out of breath. I have no key to get inside the security door, but I don't need one. The place is unlocked.

I pull the door open and step in. My stomach sinks. Because it's dark too. And deserted. Something is wrong.

Have I ever seen anyone besides me, Bobby, and the doorman here?

No. Never.

I swallow hard and go to the elevator, but when I push the button, it stays dark.

My phone buzzes again. *Get in position now, Veronica*, the text says. I look up at the camera domes and give a hesitant nod.

I pull the door to the stairs open and climb up to the second floor. I'm just about to pass the exit to my condo but my curiosity gets the better of me and I leave the stairwell and head to the closest apartment. When I turn the handle I expect the door to be locked—or maybe I *hope* the door is locked. But it's not.

I open it and my suspicions are confirmed. No one lives in this building but Bobby Mansi and me. The condo is empty, the floors are unfinished concrete, there's no kitchen, only the plumbing sticking out of the walls.

My phone buzzes again. I check the ceiling for cameras and pull the door closed as I exit and then make my way back in to the stairs and resume climbing. I don't look at the text until I'm upstairs in front of the penthouse door.

*Service terminated.*

Wonderful. I hope to fuck this phone will still record, because I'm not gonna be part of this with no record to save my ass if it all goes wrong.

When I walk inside this time, I *am* stunned. Because everything is gone. Even the kitchen. Just bare concrete. And something tells me that if I went to my apartment downstairs, it would look the same way. I bet my real apartment has mysteriously been vacated of all asbestos workers and is one hundred percent normal as well.

Who has the money and resources to play this kind of game?

The insistent buzz of my phone jolts me out of my pondering. *Later, Ronnie,* I tell myself. But right now, I need to make sure Bobby Mansi comes out of this alive. Bobby's instructions were to hide. But what the fuck? He never said the place would be dismantled when I got here.

*Think, think, think, Veronica.* I walk over to the stairs that lead up to the rooftop deck and kick open a grate that covers the lower steps. A door slamming in the hallway near the elevator jolts me out of my stupor and I drop to the floor and wiggle into the small space.

I grab the screen and pull it in front of me. I can't fasten it or anything, but here's hoping that doesn't matter because Bobby walks into the room with a tall blonde girl and a guy who looks exactly like him.

I aim the phone camera at them and press record.

"I saw her over there, Tet," the new guys says to Bobby. The new guy pushes the gagged, bound, and blindfolded woman to the center of the room. She stumbles, but Bobby reaches out and grabs her arm before she can fall.

"Don't, Cy."

A few small whimpers escape past the woman's gag, and this is enough to anger the new guy. Are they twins? No. Bobby looks older than this guy. But they definitely look like brothers, they are that alike. "She better shut the hell up or believe me, I'll put this bitch down like a dog."

He's got a gun—the same gun I have, in fact, the FN Five-SeveN—and he pushes it under the woman's chin. Bobby slaps the gun away and pushes the brother back. "I'm fucking warning you, Cy. Do not fuck with her."

"This bitch has it coming and I swear to God, if this shit

goes bad, she'll be the first to get hit."

"And you'll be the second, brother, so use some of that control they spent all these years beating into you for once. It's not her fault you're in this position. It's yours. So keep with the fucking plan and do not stray."

The new guy is wearing all black. He looks like an assassin. Bobby said he was a soldier, but he's still wearing a suit. He looks like a businessman.

The woman is about the same age as him, maybe mid-to-late twenties. She's wearing a fancy dress and some brown leather boots. Only they don't say *fuck me*, they say *envy my credit card.* Bobby leads her over to the fireplace, which has a ledge about knee-high as the hearth, and carefully urges her to sit without speaking. She's got earbuds in her ears and the wire leads down to an MP3 player strapped to her arm like joggers wear. So she can't see, talk, or hear. Bobby ties her feet together and then backs away.

"You do your job your way, and I'll do mine," the guy in black says. "And fuck that brother shit. We're nothing, Tet. Nothing. You chose them over me and I'll never forgive you."

Bobby says nothing, just stares at his angry brother, his jaw clenching a few times. The fist not holding a gun is pumping. Like he's got the urge to hit this Cy person, but is restraining himself. "You grab the Blackbird and the Duchess, I'll get the Kitten."

"And the Bomb?" the angry guys asks.

I have to stifle a gasp, because shit, that's *my* mobster name. That guy wants me.

"The Bomb is out. I had her picked up at work. Her bike is still in front of the shop, but she's been taken to her old apartment. Leave her out of this."

"I'll get her too, if you fuck up," Cy says. "I'll get all of them if you fuck this up."

Bobby nods. "Sure. Sure you will." Then he turns and walks back to the stairs, his footfalls fading away with him. It takes the new guy a few seconds to follow, but he does.

And then the heavy stairwell door slams closed and I'm alone.

With hostage number one.

# CHAPTER THIRTY

## Spencer

***I sit at my desk*** for the rest of the afternoon. Ford calls again at four thirty. Ronin left with Rook and Kate. Ashleigh left with Ryan. He's already dropped her off at the gas station down the road. Ford's got five pairs of eyes on her alone, so we're both watching a silent feed of her in real time. I watch the cab pull into the gas station parking lot, and then head out, grabbing my new helmet off my toolbox as I walk past and enter the back garage. The guys are all waiting. They know something is up, but they keep silent. In fact, it's so fucking quiet in this garage with no camera teams around or Director Larry barking out commands, it makes me uneasy.

"You guys don't have to come." I stare at Ryan when I say it.

He smiles at me. "Just shut your trap and start your bike, Shrike. Let's go rile Fonzie up."

We all kick the bikes over at the same time and the garage is alive with the thunder of power. I push the button on the opener and the doors lift up. We wait until they are halfway, and then the four of us pour out of the building looking every bit as badass as we sound. The crowd that was out front is running our way and Ryan gives them a little salute as the door closes behind us and we exit out onto Maple Street, then stop for the light at College.

We've got the attention of the entire downtown. Heads are peeking out of doors, a line of people waiting for coffee at the FoCo Cinema across the street all turn round simultaneously, and when the light turns green, car alarms go off from the noise we're making. We cross College and head down Riverside.

I tap the Bluetooth attached to my ear and wait.

"I'm here," Ford says after a few seconds.

"Keep me updated," I say back. I'm not sure if he can hear me over the roar of the bikes, but that's the best I can do at the moment.

"Scott's on alert. He'll start driving over in eight minutes. Ash just pulled up in the cab. The whole garage is looking at her. Fonzie is making his way over, asking her if she needs help. I need your ETA so I can talk myself out of going down there and kicking his ass for talking to her."

"Five minutes," I say back.

"Well, hurry the fuck up."

"Where's Ronin?"

"I'm here," Ronin says. "We've got Kate and we just left our apartment building heading south. We'll be inside in about… five."

"Any trouble?" Ford asks Ronin.

"Not right away, but yeah. The cameras are practically jumping out of the bushes right now. But I've got it covered. We're a block away now. You OK, Rook?"

Ford and I stay silent as we try to hear her answer, but we can't catch it.

"Hey, back off!" Ronin yells to someone in their vicinity. "I've got a camera too, asshole." Ronin goes quiet for a second and then speaks low into his phone. "I can see your security, Ford, so we're good."

"If those reporters touch Kate, I'll kill them. What's your ETA now, Spencer?"

"We've arrived, you freak. Can't you hear us coming?" Because I can—our bike noise comes through the ear piece connecting me to Ford. "Let's start some trouble."

"Ashleigh is still filling her tank. Hurry, Kitten," Ford urges her from afar. "Fonzie is looking your direction, Spencer.

Here he comes, get ready."

The four of us pull up into the industrial complex driveway that winds around the various buildings and then make the left turn that leads to Cikes Bikes. I still have to shake my fucking head at that shit. There was no name under that picture Ford showed me of him and his pedophile father, so I bet that's not even his real name. Asshole.

Drake and his team of seven or eight are all walking down the driveway once we turn into their little parking lot. I look past him at Ashleigh, who is still messing with the gas can.

The boys and I stop and rev our bikes, letting the douchebags come to us.

"I've got the bot into the bay," Ford says in my ear.

"We're inside the church," Ronin adds.

"We're a go here too," I chime in. I nod my head at Fonzie as he comes up talking shit. Ryan and I look at each other and smile and then Griff and Fletch shut their bikes down and get off.

Another look at Ryan tells me he knows what's up, so I let them take it from here and watch Ford drive the little bot over to Ashleigh. She's got the trunk open and then she races to the bot, scoops it up, and puts it in the trunk.

And that's when Fonzie decides he wants to fight. He swings at Fletch, but Griff knocks him back and then all eight of those posers are on my two guys. Ryan and I are off our bikes, throwing punches, when the cops show up. Scott is ordering us to stop on his speaker, but the only thing I care about is that Ashleigh weaves that piece-of-shit Beetle in between our chaos and drives off.

"Mission accomplished," Ford says. "Now get out of there and we'll meet at the farm."

Everything is a blur after that. People are pushing me, Fletch and Griff are still trying to throw punches, and Ryan is talking to Scott calmly.

"Shrike, what the fuck is going on?" Scott asks.

"Hey, we pulled up to check things out and these assholes

just attacked us."

"Yeah," Ryan says. "I've got it all on film."

Fucking Ryan might be my new number one.

Scott watches the video for a few seconds and then takes out his cuffs and makes a grab for Drake. His little blonde partner catches Fonzie before he can slink away from Scott, and slaps the cuffs on him.

"Paybacks are a bitch," I say under my breath. But Fonzie catches it and lifts his chin a little as he sneers at me.

"You best remember that, Shrike."

"OK, we got a problem here," Ronin says in my ear. "There's a mess of fucking reporters inside the church now. We need that car."

"I've lost Ashleigh," Ford says, just as Ronin finishes.

"What?" we say together. Both Scott and Ryan are looking at me funny.

"I've lost contact. The car stopped in an alley, two blocks east of downtown. I'm on my way, maybe she ran out of gas again."

"Call her, Ford," I say out loud, even though both Ryan and Scott can hear me clear as day. I hold my hand up to their questioning looks.

"I did, she's not answering."

"I need that car, Spencer. We need to get out of here. I've got Rook and Kate in the bathroom."

"She's not here," Ford says.

"What?"

"Rook?" Ronin calls. "Rook?"

"What the fuck is happening? Ford? Ronin?"

"Ashleigh's gone," Ford growls.

"Rook and Kate are gone too. I put them in the bathroom and they're gone!"

I look over at Drake and he's smiling. "Paybacks, Mr. Shrike, are always a bitch."

I lunge at him, swing mid-leap, and my fist crashes against the side of his jaw. His head swings in this exaggerated motion, almost like I'm watching in slow-mo, and then we both hit the ground. I sit up, straddle his chest and start whaling. "Where the fuck are they!" I pound on his face, one punch after the other. "I will kill you—"

My oxygen is cut off as an arm wraps around my throat, and then I'm being dragged off Drake.

Scott leans down, rolls Drake over and picks him up off the ground. It's only then that I realize the person holding me back is Ryan. I stop struggling and he lets go. "That motherfucker," I say, walking towards Scott as he lifts Drake up off the ground. "That mother—"

Scott's hand darts out and catches my fist before it connects with Drake's face again. "Get lost, Spence. Now."

"Come on, dude," Ryan says. "We gotta go."

I shake my head and point at Drake. "If you have them, Drake… if you're involved, just remember your own famous last words. Paybacks aren't a bitch, man. Revenge, now *that's* a motherfucking bitch."

Scott whirls Drake around and pushes him towards the open door to the backseat of the cop car, but Drake plants his feet and calls out over his shoulder.

"You best be thinking about revenge, Shrike. Because it's about to jump up and bite you in the face."

And then Scott pushes down on his head and shoves him into the car, closing the door behind him. He points to me. "Get out, now. Or I'll arrest you too."

Ryan pulls me back to our bikes, and I go through the motions. My mind spinning. Ashleigh, gone. Kate, gone. Rook, gone. I pull out my phone and press Ronnie's face.

It doesn't even ring.

But the operator tells me that this phone is no longer in service.

## CHAPTER THIRTY-ONE

# Veronica

***I breathe erratically*** for several seconds and I swear to God, if I have a panic attack now, I might as well just give it up. *Come on, brain. Work with me here.* I'm scared, but I cannot afford to freak out like this. Everything in my body is telling me to run away. To hide, call for help, get the hell out of here. My heart rate jacks up just thinking about these possibilities.

But that's feeding into the panic. I'm safe here. Bobby and that other guy are gone. I know they're not coming back right away, I know the plan. I'm safe here. Running away would actually make things worse for me.

So I take a deep breath and move the screen aside so I can squirm my way out from under the stairs.

The woman is crying. Her chest is heaving with the effort because it's almost impossible to cry with the restraints she has on her mouth, not to mention her hands being tied behind her back make it more difficult to breathe. And I can sense that she's feeling this limitation. Because I'm feeling it right along with her.

I get to my feet and walk over to her, then pluck an earbud from her ear and lean into whisper. "You're OK," I tell her. "You're gonna be OK." Bobby was adamant that Ashleigh's sister be contained. In fact, his exact words were, 'She's a wild one.'

She cries harder so I just replace the earbud and she tries to talk through her gag. I think she's begging me to let her go. But that's one thing Bobby was very clear about. Do not let them go unless I hear shooting. Because if I hear shooting, the game is over and things got messy.

I'm not sure what that means. Messy. But I don't need to be Ford to figure out it's bad.

The woman is not placated by my words, in fact, she's more distressed than she was before because I probably scared her. She begins to hyperventilate, her breath coming in gasps though her gag, and I almost have my own panic attack with the thought that she might die.

Fuck that. I go back over to her and pull the gag down her chin, letting it hang loose around her neck.

She gasps for breath, making all kinds of strange sounds as she tries to get more air inside her body. "Please," she gasps between her hitching breaths. "Please, let me go!"

I pull the earbud back out and lean in so she can hear me. "I can't, now stop being so loud. They might be close by and if they come back here and see you, the whole plan will be ruined."

"My father is rich," she pleads with me. "My father will pay you to let me go. Lots of money. My sister's husband, Ford Aston, is rich too, he can pay you right now, he lives here."

Oh, fuck. "What's your name?" I ask in a whisper.

"Amber Li," she sobs out. "I'm Amber Li. I'm Ford Aston's sister-in-law. I can pay you, please, just don't let him get me!"

"Who?"

"Tony! He's a bad guy, whatever your name is. He's bad. I tried to tell Ashleigh, I tried to warn her. But she fell for all his charms."

*Tony.* "The dead guy?"

"You know him? You know me? My sister? Tony's not dead," she insists. "He's been hiding for months. He lied to Ashleigh—"

"Wait." I cut her off. "Amber, listen to me. There are two guys here, how would I tell which one is Tony?"

"Two? Oh, God, no. He's gonna kill him too! He's gonna

kill all of us!"

"Who, for fuck's sake? Who?"

She's panicking now. Her breathing is coming in long draws and uneven gasps.

"Amber, please. They'll be back soon and they're bringing my friend and Ashleigh and Kate. I need to know what to do!"

"Do they look like brothers?" Her voice is low now, but it might just be that she's having trouble forming words through her trembling lips.

"Yes, like brothers!"

"Oh God, he's gonna kill him, he's gonna kill me, he'll kill you and your friends and who knows, he might even kill Ash and Kate. Oh God!"

I slap her. Hard, right across her face. She recoils and begins to choke on her panic, so I slap her again, and this stuns her silent. "Look, bitch, I need to know what the fuck I'm up against. Which one is which? How can I tell them apart?"

"Tony is the mean one. The animal. The killer who's been trained since he was a little boy that revenge is the only answer. And right now, we're all on his list. We're all on his hit list because every one of us is standing between him and his property."

"What property?"

"Ashleigh and Kate."

I slip her gag back up and scoot away once more.

Holy fuck.

What the hell is happening? Is Bobby really Tony? Did that asshole lie to Ashleigh and fake his own death? And I just spouted off my theory to him last night and he never answered me.

My panic attack is back in force and so is Amber's. We sit there together, sucking up air like it's our last dying breath, and I can't take it anymore. I grab my phone and bolt down the hallway. There are still walls in this place, not like the condos downstairs. So there are rooms. I try the first door and the handle turns. I push it open and enter, closing the door behind me.

I bend over at the waist and try to calm down, but that's one of my panic attack defenses. So I do the opposite. I stand up straight and hop up and down, trying to raise my heart rate with something legitimate, instead of the irrational flood of fight-or-flight adrenaline that is now coursing through my body.

After several minutes of hopping my rate evens out. It's still fast when I count, but I've got a legitimate reason for it now. I'm not in a blind panic, I'm doing a mini-workout.

I stop hopping and notice my surroundings.

It's not dark in here, but not because there's lights on nor is there light from outside filtering in through the curtains because there's no windows. It's light in here because I'm in the security room and there are walls and walls of monitors, but every one of them is white with static. They've been disconnected because after tonight, this place obviously never existed. I'm the only record of what's happening.

I am not cut out for this shit.

I don't think Bobby is Tony. I think the other guy is Tony. That guy had killer written all over him. Bobby… he fed me a nice dinner. He was understanding and he gave me a chance to save Spencer and not let him walk into a setup blind. He gave me the chance to protect him. All I have to do is make sure Bobby comes out alive. That's it. Just have his back and things will be cool.

I have no idea what I'm doing. I'm so fucked.

That mean guy with Bobby already said he was looking for me. Bomb. That's me. And the mean one was the one grabbing Ashleigh and Kate. Blackbird and Duchess, he said, but I'm pretty sure Duchess is a name Ford calls the baby.

And then I hear her. The loud, incessant crying of a very distressed Kate.

# CHAPTER THIRTY-TWO

***Ford storms into my office*** and takes a swing at me. I duck and swing back. He lands a fist on my jaw, spinning my head a little, and then I see red. I throw him down on the ground and land on top of him. He locks an arm around my neck and I get him in an armbar, ready to crack that shit if he doesn't let go.

Ryan and Ronin pull us apart.

"I told you," Ford says as Ronin pulls him off to a corner. "I fucking told you if she got hurt, I'd fuck you up, Spencer."

"She's not the only one missing, asshole! Rook is gone and so is Veronica, so don't fucking pin this shit on me! Besides, what the fuck happened to that security team you had on her? Huh? How's their failure my fault?"

"It's your motherfucking job!" he snarls back. "My job is hacking. Ronin's job is lying. Your fucking job is security! I did my job and you fucked it up *again*!"

Ryan extends his hand and I let him pull me up. Ronin offers the same courtesy to Ford.

We all look over at Ryan and he shakes his head. "I'm out, I get it." He backs out, closing the door behind him.

"My security is gone," Ford finally admits.

"Gone? How?"

"Like they were never there. Someone infiltrated my fucking team."

I feel little vindication over this admission. The facts don't change. It doesn't matter who's at fault, the girls are still missing.

Ford paces one side of the office while I pace the other. Ronin stands in the middle, calm. Calmer than he should be since Rook is missing. "What?" I ask him as I pass by. "Why the fuck are you so calm?"

He huffs some air at me. "Because one of us has to think clearly, Spencer. Look, I don't have all the info here, OK? You two know something I don't. What the fuck is going on with this Drake guy, Spencer?"

"I fucking told you, Ronin, he's the fucking son of that Boulder bastard. He was about to get cuffed back there by the little blonde cop he knocked over yesterday and I said, *Paybacks are a bitch*. And then he said, *Yeah*, or *You better remember that*, or some shit like that. Meaning I'm the one getting paid back." I point to my own chest to emphasize.

"By who?"

Ford makes for the door and I grab him by the arm. "Where the fuck are you going?"

He glares at me and shakes his arm free. "We have the bot. We're gonna find out right the fuck now who's behind this shit. And then, I swear to fucking God, whoever took my girls will be dead by tonight." He stops and looks at Ronin, then me. "I'm not fucking around."

And then he's gone.

Ronin looks over at me and swallows. "What the fuck is going on, Spencer?"

"Dude, I swear, I have no fucking idea. But Veronica's phone has been disconnected."

"Maybe she's just tired of you bugging her, maybe she just got it changed?"

"No, I was with her last night, OK? We had a really good night. I told her to be patient, this shit was almost over. She was good, we were good. And now she's missing too."

"This just makes no sense, Spencer. Rook's testimony, Ford's daughter, your girlfriend. None of these things are related beyond the fact that they're all our girls."

I swallow and inhale deeply. "Yeah." That hurts. So fucking bad. Because all these years I've been trying to protect Ronnie and now look. She might be killed because of me.

Ford comes back in, slams the bot down on my stainless steel desk, then opens his laptop and takes a seat in my chair. He types and then pulls up the bot's memory card via Bluetooth.

We wait as the footage loads. Ford drums his fingers on the desk, refusing to look at anyone. Ronin peeks out the window facing the street. I'm frozen in place, my worst nightmare coming true.

"Here it is," Ford finally says after many long silent minutes. "Drake came in two days ago, bitching about the theft?"

"Yeah," I say as I go around the desk and squat down so I can see the monitor. Ronin flanks Ford's other side, and we watch the footage run in fast-forward. It's not the best spot for the bot to be parked—it's got a fifty-five-gallon drum on one side of the bench it's parked under and the guys in the garage pile shit up on the other side for a lot of the day. But every night, the shop is picked up and the camera has a clean shot of the bay that houses Drake's bike. His schedule is annoyingly consistent, and the bot's camera goes into sleep mode after eight minutes of no motion detection. It stays dark all night, every night until…

"Two nights ago," Ford mumbles as his fingers type on the keyboard. "That's after he says the bikes went missing. No fucking bikes went missing. Everything goes quiet around eight, like usual, but it comes back to life at ten thirty." We watch the monitor as he slows it to real time. There's three sets of feet walking by, but they are too close to the bot to see faces.

"Come on, come on," Ronin says impatiently. "Fucking fast-forward until they move back, Ford."

Ford obliges, and the footage gives us absolutely nothing. The screen goes blank again.

"Fuck," Ford says. He fast-forwards again to get to the

next day, which is yesterday. Same thing, there's nothing out of the ordinary at all. Just customers, mechanics. Drake working on his bike. We keep watching in fast-forward until the screen goes black and then Ford speeds it up again.

"Whoa, whoa, whoa," I say. "Back it up. I saw a flicker."

Ford rewinds and yeah, sure enough, at three thirty last night the camera comes on.

And this time we can see exactly who it is.

"Bobby Mansi," I mutter. "That guy on the left is Bobby Mansi, Ronnie's new landlord."

Ford looks at me and shakes his head. "Well, that guy on the right? That's Tony Fenici. Ashleigh's dead husband."

The door bursts open and I've got my gun out and pressed against Carson's head before I even process who he is. "Fuck, Carson, you almost got yourself shot!"

"Sorry, Spencer," he says, all out of breath. "But shit, you guys need to get over to that penthouse where Ronnie lives, because I followed the Bombshell over there after work, and dudes…" He pants a little as he tries to catch his breath. "All your women are over there with some pretty nasty-looking guys with guns!"

Ford is up before Carson even stops talking but both Ronin and I grab an arm and wrestle him back to the chair.

"Stay focused, Ford." I point my finger down at him. "We don't fucking rush in to anything. And right now, they've got your wife and baby, so the last thing we want to do is go in unprepared."

"I'll kill that motherfucker, Spencer. I swear, I will kill that motherfucker."

"Understood." I swallow hard and clap his shoulder.

"OK," Ronin says, turning to Carson. "Tell us everything you know."

So he does. And Carson Reed instantly jumps from prospect to Team member.

And then there's only one thing left to do.

I get the guns.

# CHAPTER THIRTY-THREE

***I dart down the hallway*** to an empty closet and slip inside. There's nothing in here, no hangers to rattle and give me away. So I try to calm my racing heart. I open it a crack and push the record button on the phone just as the elevator doors open. He must have a key that makes them work.

The baby is sniffling but her crying has stopped. Rook is holding her tightly to her chest, her eyes covered with a blindfold. Her mouth is not gagged and her hands are not bound, though. She needs those to hold Kate and whisper calming words to her to keep her from wailing in protest at what's happening.

The baby recoils in terror when the man I think is Tony leans in and talks to her. "Katelynn Fenici, you're mine, little girl."

"She's not yours," Rook growls back in protective mode. The guy belts her across the mouth. Her head snaps to the side. Blood drips down her lip and Rook spits it out on the floor. It misses the guy's boots, but just barely. "That's all you got, asshole?" she snarls. "You hit like a girl." He hits her again and this time Rook stumbles to the side, her lip split open good. "You can hit me all you want, it doesn't change a thing. This baby is not yours."

Tony pushes a gun in Rook's back and give her a push. "Walk forward," he barks.

"I'm not walking blindfolded with a baby. I'll fall and she's the one who'll get—"

The guy pushes Rook hard enough to make her stumble forward. I almost gasp as she begins to fall. Tony plucks the baby right from Rook's arms and then she crashes forward, landing hard on her side. Tony leans in and says something to Rook, but I can't hear anything over the panicked wailing of Kate.

He thrusts the child back at Rook and Rook wraps the baby in her arms protectively, bringing her close to her chest as she tries to calm her.

Tony walks over to the large windows and looks out, then turns back to Rook. "If she moves," he says to no one, "shoot her. You hear that, Rook? You move, you take off that blindfold, you get up and try to escape, my two guys will shoot you." He kicks her in the leg and then goes back to the elevator, which still has its doors open. Like it requires a command to do anything at the moment.

I can't see Tony as he gets in, but a few seconds later the doors close and the room is quiet.

"Rook?" Amber says from across the room. I almost forgot she was here. And she's got her gag off! If that guy had seen that—

"Don't talk to me."

"There's a girl here, not two guys. She's hiding somewhere, and she's not going to shoot you. Come untie me."

"Shut up!" Rook snaps. "I don't even know who you are."

"I'm Kate's aunt, Amber. I'm Ashleigh's sister. And I'm telling you, there are no guys here, just a girl who is gone. She told me I'd be OK. But right now that guy who just left is going to get my sister and then he'll come back up here and take Kate and kill us both. He's an animal. So if you want to live, if you want that baby to live, then you need to get your ass over here and untie me so we can escape."

Rook lifts herself up cautiously, waiting for the command to sit back down, but when it doesn't come, she stands all the way up and coos into Kate's ear. "You're OK, baby. We're gonna get out of here now, OK? Go see your mommy and daddy." She removes her blindfold and looks around. I duck back into the closet as her eyes swipe past the room. Then she runs over to Amber and removes her blindfold.

Amber sighs with relief. "Untie me. We need to get the hell out of here before he comes back."

Rook sets baby Kate down on the bare floor and goes to work on her bonds. When she's done untying her, they both stand and Rook takes the baby again. "We need to get outside," Rook says. "We can make a run for Shrike Bikes."

They both run to the stairs and pull open the door, listening for footfalls or voices. They must not hear anything, because they both disappear inside.

I follow them. I get up, tiptoeing as silently as I can in my Chucks, and get my gun out. I check the chamber to make sure I'm ready, and then I pull the door open and follow them down the stairs. They go slowly, Rook desperate to keep Kate from crying, her pleas and Kate's complaints dead giveaways to anyone who comes in here looking for us. I'm still two flights above them when I hear a small squeak from the door directly below me.

I freeze.

The door closes quietly. Kate is loud now, and Rook cannot contain her crying, so the man below me takes advantage and leaps down the stairs, once, then again. Rook is screaming, Amber is screaming, Kate is screaming… and I'm already standing in front of Tony Fenici, pointing my gun at him before I even have a moment to think about it.

I aim for his chest and fire. The bullet hits the wall and shatters the plaster.

He turns at me and I duck back. A bullet whizzes up the stairwell and hits the ceiling. Heavy footsteps thunder down the stairs and Kate's cries diminish as Rook and Amber exit through the door to the garage. Tony follows them, jumping over the railing to save himself some time, and I'm right on his tail.

Fuck Bobby Mansi, I'm on Team Rook right now.

Tony slams the door open and exits and three seconds later I follow, my gun ready.

Tony grabs Rook and she loses her grip on the baby. I watch in horror as he takes possession of the hysterical child just as a car pulls into the garage. A door swings open and Ashleigh is out and running towards us.

"No!" I scream.

Tony whirls around, and Rook grabs Kate, just as Bobby takes a shot at me. I duck back inside the stairwell as the cinderblock crumbles off to the side of my head.

What the fuck was that? Am I on his team or not? And how did he miss me? He shoots that gun like he was born holding it.

"Ashleigh!" Bobby yells. "Stop right now!"

But Ashleigh doesn't stop. She's running full-on towards a fleeing Rook who has her child.

Until Tony turns to face her. And then her feet stop. Her face contorts in confusion. Her mouth opens. Her eyes widen. Her hands come up to her mouth as she tries to process what she's seeing.

And then she drops to her knees and her world comes apart.

## CHAPTER THIRTY-FOUR

***We get over to the*** Mason Street condo just as a black car pulls into the garage. When they move through the gates, Ronin, Ford and I jump out and leave Carson in the truck. We book it to the gate before it closes and enter the garage just as Ashleigh falls to the ground. At first it looks like she's hurt, and I look around wildly, trying to figure out where the threat is.

"Ronin," Ford says in a low voice. "Kate's on the far side of the garage with Rook. Get them. I need to speak to Ashleigh."

"Tony, Tony, Tony .." Ashleigh's small voice keeps repeating.

And this is when I figure it out. Ford knew. Ford knew Tony was alive and he never told Ashleigh.

Ronin takes off just as Ford enters the garage. I follow him in and even though I'm pissed he kept this secret from us, it hurts my heart to hear Ashleigh say the name of her dead lover in front of him.

Ford's shoulders slump as he takes in the scene. And I can only imagine this is his worst nightmare. Like Ronin watching Rook take the stand and admit her part in that human trafficking ring.

Or me, after all the sacrifices I've made to keep Ronnie safe… to find her hurt because of my past.

Watching Ashleigh come to terms with this new reality is Ford's version of hell. He just stands there, waiting to see how it will play out.

There's movement on the far side of the garage—not Rook and Kate, they've disappeared inside the stairwell. Someone else. Another woman.

"Ashleigh," the blonde calls out. "Stay away. Please, Ashleigh! Stay away from him!"

"Ashleigh," Tony says in a tone one uses for children who are acting irrationally. "Come here, baby. It's me, Ashleigh. It's me. I'm here." And then he opens his arms. "Please," he begs. "We have to go."

I walk the wall. No one is paying any attention to me. All eyes are on the girl who holds all the cards. "You're dead," Ash manages. Her breathing is suddenly erratic, like she's overwhelmed with what's happening. She clambers to her feet, swaying back and forth a little, and Ford takes a few steps forward. "You're dead!" she repeats, louder and a little more forcefully this time. Like she needs to talk herself into it.

"No, Li Li," the very much alive Tony replies. "No, baby. I'm not dead. It was fake. It was fake. I had to make it look real, I had to make everyone believe. It was the only way to get out of my contract."

"What?" Her hands go to her head and she grabs fistfuls of hair, like this makes no sense to her.

Tony moves forward. But Ashleigh retreats several steps, stumbling until she backs herself against a cement pillar.

"You're dead!" she says again, only this time she's on the verge of hysterics. "I'm seeing things. Ford!" she yells.

"I'm here, Ashleigh," Ford says, and then all eyes are on him, like a target.

Tony takes a shot at Ford, but it misses. A warning shot. But I duck behind a pillar, just in case. My gun is ready, but for some reason, I'm so very, very calm.

"Stay where you are, Aston, or the next one goes through your head." He extends his hand towards Ashleigh again. "Come on, baby. Just take my hand, Ash, and we'll get out of here and go home."

"Home?" Ash says, like she's confused. "You're dead,"

Ashleigh says one more time. "I saw your grave. I went to Texas. I drove in a blizzard. I went to LA. I took a very long trip to go see your grave."

"Empty," he says. "It was an empty grave, I made sure you knew that. I made sure there was nothing in that grave so you'd know. I told you. I told you, Li Li. I'd never leave you. And in your heart, you knew I was alive, right? You felt me, you knew I was alive. You knew it was empty. I'd never leave you, Ashleigh. Never."

Ashleigh starts to cry and Tony moves forward again. I'm not sure if I should stop him or not. When I look over at Ford I can feel his pain just by watching the expression on his face. She might walk away from him right now. He might lose everything.

She lets Tony approach this time and then he's got her wrapped in his arms. "We're leaving now," he says in her ear.

"Ash," the blonde woman I now recognize as Ashleigh's sister calls out. "He's a bad man, Ashleigh. He's a bad, bad man. Please, listen to me. He's a paid assassin, Ashleigh. He was never in the US military. OK? He was never a Navy SEAL. He's a soldier all right, but not the kind who protects people. He's a killer. I've been trying to tell you for years. Remember when I dated James? Tony's brother? He's bad too, but at least he knows better than to drag a woman into his world. Please listen to me, Ashleigh. Please do not let him take you, because you will sell yourself into this organization if you go. You'll sell Kate into this organization. Is that what you want?"

Tony stares at Ashleigh's sister like she's the devil, and every second she speaks, I expect him to shoot. But in a weird way, he almost looks relieved. He looks down at Ashleigh, his eyes begging her to accept these things as true and still want what he has to offer.

Ashleigh starts to cry uncontrollably. "Why?" she asks, looking up at the first man she gave her heart to. "Why did you do this to me? How? How could you do this to me?"

Tony's face hardens with her words. "I did this for us,

Ashleigh. So we can be together! If I hadn't died, then I'd still be a slave to the organization. And I'd never be able to have you and Kate." He grabs her face and holds it steady, forcing her to look him in the eyes. "I did this for us! For our family. Say it back to me, baby. Tell me you understand. Tell me you know I did this for us!"

Ashleigh shakes her head. "I thought you were *dead*."

"I'm not dead, Li Li. I'm not dead. We're together now. Everything's OK now."

He grabs her hand and tries to lead her away, but she plants her feet firmly on the ground and resists. She pulls her hand free. "I almost killed myself."

"Ashleigh—"

"I almost killed myself! I was almost locked away in a psychiatric hospital, that's how depressed I was after hearing you were dead. I was going to fall asleep in a parked car during a blizzard. I wanted to *die*." She backs away again and then her eyes search wildly until she finds Ford. He's out in the open still, in full view of everyone. Just standing there, like he's got a great big bullseye on his chest. "Ford saved me," she finally says.

"I'd do it again, Ashleigh," Ford says. "I'd never walk away from you, Kitten. Ever. Not for any reason. Never. We'll do it together or we won't do it."

She turns back to Tony. "I'm married," she admits in a calm voice. "I'm married to my soul mate. I'm happy. I'm happy I'm alive and I'm happy with my life. I can't walk away from Ford. I'm not walking away from Ford. I'm not coming back to you."

Tony reaches out, a pained look on his face. And then in one swift move, he's got Ashleigh by the throat. He pulls her next to his body and a shot rings out.

Veronica, of all fucking people, is shooting at Tony. She hits him in the back three times, but he's got armor on. The shots jerk his body, but he stays standing. Ford rushes towards Ashleigh, and I cover him, shooting at Tony's feet. Ford grabs

Ashleigh's arm and swings her out of the way. Tony points his gun at Ford's head, and then Ronnie shoots again, and a distracted Tony pops off several shots in that general vicinity.

I'm aiming, but Tony makes one more mad grab for Ash and she's back in his clutches. The gun goes to her head. "I'll kill her, Aston! Stay the fuck back, or I'll kill her!"

Ford drops the gun I gave him back at the garage, his hands in the air. "You don't really want to hurt her, Tony. If you love her, you'll let her go."

For a second I think Ford's soothing voice will work, but then Ashleigh's sister is running towards her screaming. "No, you bast—"

Tony fires several times and the woman takes a shot to the chest. She drops to the ground and then Bobby Mansi comes out of nowhere, his gun pointed at Tony.

"I'll kill her, Tet," Tony says, pushing his gun into Ashleigh's temple as she sobs, calling out to Ford. "I'll fucking kill—"

One, two, three, four shots ring out and Tony's head explodes, four times over.

Ashleigh wiggles free and makes a run for Ford. Bobby Mansi stands over the fallen Tony, emptying round after round after round into the dead man's chest. When he's out of bullets he drops the gun on the ground, looks over at me, and then says as calmly as you can, "Better call an ambulance."

"I think he's dead, man," I say back.

"Not for him, Shrike. For her." He points to a body near the stairwell and my whole world begins to spin.

Because my Ronnie is laid out on the ground in a pool of blood.

# CHAPTER THIRTY-FIVE

***Chaos***.

That's my world right now.

"Ronnie?" You'd think I'd be screaming it, but it's a whisper. "Ronnie, baby?" I'm kneeling down next to her and my only thought is how pissed she'd be if she knew so much blood was covering her body.

"It's a flesh wound, Spencer," Ford says as he shakes me.

No. Oceans of blood do not pour out of a flesh wound. My hand goes to her arm where the blood is pulsing out in a river.

"She must've been shooting at him when it hit her. The cartridge nicked the brachial artery in her upper arm." Ford pushes me out of the way and then grabs a belt being offered by Carson and loops it around her arm, up near her shoulder. He pulls it tight and Veronica lets out a moan.

"Ronnie?" But that's all I get from her because at that moment—the moment when I realize this might be the last thing I ever hear from her mouth—my world goes silent.

I watch. I'm an observer as Carson talks on his phone. He's hysterical. Rook and Ronin are trying to calm a screaming Kate. Ashleigh's kneeling down over her sister, her tiny hands pushing against Amber's lifeless chest as the blood seeps out and puddles up on the ground.

She's dead.

Ashleigh and I come to this realization at the same time, and then she's up on her feet, looking around wildly. Bobby

Mansi walks forward calmly, she falls into his chest and they embrace. He hugs her hard, his hand wrapped around her head as Ashleigh sobs for her dead sister.

Sirens sound off in the distance.

I watch them like this until the embrace is broken by Bobby. He holds Ashleigh out at arm's length and begins to talk. Her tear-filled eyes are locked with his as he takes her face in both his hands. His lips move as he talks, and Ashleigh's head bobs up and down in agreement.

They both look over at Tony's body, then to us. To Ford, who is still working on Veronica like he's some kind of military field medic. He's barking orders to Carson and then Ford presses a phone in my hand and I take it automatically. When I look down I realize it's filming.

It's Ronnie's phone. Disconnected from service, but the camera still functions.

I look back to Ash, but she's alone now.

Bobby Mansi is standing over Tony's body. He drops another weapon on the ground that looks identical to the first, and walks calmly to the elevator, where he inserts a key and the doors open. He steps in and turns.

I catch his eye just as the doors close and he shoots me his finger.

But it doesn't come with a wink.

Flashing red and blue lights take over from there. Carson is running towards the cops, yelling for them to bring an ambulance.

There are half a dozen cops surrounding me, yelling for me to drop my gun. I look down at it and my hands let go automatically. It clangs to the concrete and then the next thing I know Ronnie and I are on our way to the hospital. I sit in the ambulance, silent, stoic, as the medics work on my Bombshell.

They are shining a light in her eyes, lifting up her eyelids, calling her name.

She's not responding.

I watch the lips of the medic at her head. *Lost a lot of blood,* they say.

The ambulance stops and I'm pushed out the doors. I can only watch as they maneuver the stretcher out of the back and wheel her into the ER. I try to follow but the cops are there again, they have me by the shoulders. And normally I'd fight back or protest or something. But I feel like I'm in another world right now.

"Ronnie," I say softly as she disappears behind the ER doors.

I'm ushered to a police car in the parking lot, cuffed and put in the back. And none of this matters. The only thing that matters is Veronica.

I sit here for how long? I have no idea.

It feels like hours before I spot Ronin outside the car. Ford is here, too. Our team of lawyers. Scott comes over to my car and opens the door. "Come on, Spence," he says softly.

"Don't talk to me like that, Scott." I finally find my voice. "Don't talk to me like I need your sympathy."

He helps me out of the car, uncuffs me, and then slips Ronnie's phone into my palm and closes my hand around it. "We never saw this," he says.

Ronin jogs over from the huddle of lawyers and grabs my shoulder. "She's OK, Spencer. She's in surgery. They have to repair that vessel. But she's doing OK."

I nod, still numb. Doing OK and OK are not the same thing.

All these years of trying to protect her mean exactly shit to me right now.

What a waste of life. What a fucking waste of life.

"Come on," Ford says. "We can wait inside." We all follow him and end up in a small waiting room on the second floor.

We sit in silence and it's only then that I realize Ford and I both are covered in blood. Ronnie's blood.

It's past midnight before a doctor comes into the waiting room. "Who's a family member here?" he asks.

"I am," I say. "She's my fiancée."

"Mr.—"

"Shrike. Spencer Shrike." I can barely meet his eyes. I'm terrified of what they'll tell me.

"She's stable, Mr. Shrike. She came in with a tear to the brachial artery—"

I stop listening and sit back down, my head in my hands, wanting so badly to cry with relief. I replay those words over and over in my head. *She's stable.* It keeps me from falling apart. It becomes my mantra. The only thought I'm capable of.

Ford takes over, asking questions using words I've never heard before. When the doctor leaves, he sits down next to me and puts a hand on my shoulder. "She's OK, Spence."

I can't look at him. I'm so fucking messed up, I can't look at anyone.

"There's no nerve damage that they can see so far, the repair went better than expected, and she's being moved to a room right now. You can go see her in a few minutes."

Ronin sits on the other side of me and puts his hand on my shoulder too. "The trial is off," he says.

"What?" I look up at him.

"Yeah, that's why they cuffed you and we had to call the lawyers. Apparently Agent Abelli is dead. They suspect poisoning, but they won't know for sure until they get the toxicology back."

I want to laugh but it's not funny. I want to feel relieved. Ashleigh belongs to Ford, Tony really is dead now. Veronica was shot, but she'll be OK. And Rook won't have to testify next week.

We're saved.

But if this is victory… I'm not sure I'm cut out for it.

"It's over," Ford says, like he's reading my mind. We've been friends for eighteen years. I've done everything with this guy. He's saved my ass so many times. But today… he saved Ronnie. A few more minutes and she would've bled to death.

"I owe you, man," I tell him as he gets up and goes over

to the dark window. Just contemplating for a few moments before looking back at me.

We stare at each other for a few seconds and then he smiles.

"No, Spencer. We're even. It's over now. Veronica will be fine. Rook will not have to testify. And Ashleigh and Kate are mine. All three threats neutralized."

Ronin and I look at each other and I know him well enough to read his mind, just as Ford read mine.

*Did Ford plan this?* we ask each other.

But Ford turns away and just stares out the window. "Ashleigh peed on the stick earlier while she was waiting to play her part."

We wait for more information but when he turns back to face us, his triumphant smile tells us all we need to know.

CHAPTER THIRTY-SIX

# Merc

***I'm checking out*** the coffee shop in the historic section of downtown Cheyenne when the call comes in. I answer it through the cigarette in my teeth. "You're late, asshole. Report. I got a recon job going." Tet huffs, a response that tells me he's just as annoyed at having to report in to me, as I am that he's late about doing it. "Job ended last night, so shut the fuck up and report."

"You know he's dead. I already filed my report with the boss." He lets out a long breath of air and now I realize he's smoking. Tet's a reformed smoker—this is a tell for him. He's stressed. But hey, if I killed my brother yesterday, I'd be smoking something a lot stronger than a cigarette, that's for damn sure. "So we're even now. Call it, Merc. This job is over and my debt to you is cleared. Your buddy got his girl and my backup got the trial canceled. As far as I can tell, you probably owe me a favor now."

I click my tongue, ready to talk some shit. But then the girl comes out of the bar across the street. "My target's here. So I'm gonna make this quick. Ford was not happy. At all. No one authorized you to hire a partner. And sure as fuck no one authorized you to hire Spencer Shrike's fucking girlfriend."

He exhales more cigarette smoke and laughs. "She swore up and fucking down they were not together. I even asked him, repeatedly, if they were together. He never said a word. So as far as I'm concerned, Veronica was fair game. She was qualified and willing. End of story. It's Shrike's problem for keeping their relationship secret. And Ford's problem for wanting the hit in the first place. Besides, she lived."

I consider my next move, letting him stew a second. Tet was born into this organization. He's been in it from the beginning, but from what I can tell, he's about ready to check out as well. The only question is—will he do it the easy way and let himself be killed off like his brother? Or will he do it the hard way and fight his way to the top, taking the whole thing down as he climbs?

My bet's on number one.

"Well, I'm tired," he says, almost answering my question. "They're sending me to the beach. To relax." He laughs loudly at this and even I smile. "For some downtime, see if I'm salvageable with a few weeks of rest."

"Huh. Well, they wanted Tony dead too, so what's their problem?"

He's quiet for a few seconds. That's too long in this business when everything we do is based on quick reflexes.

"I lost someone when I took him down."

"Yeah." He sure the fuck did. Amber Li-Montgomery. I don't know Ford's father-in-law, but I'm the one who did all the digging when Ford was plotting to steal Ashleigh out of his house. So I know how upset Li probably is right now that his golden daughter was gunned down by the son of a ruthless enemy. "Li's gonna be pissed."

"Fuck Li," Tet says. "I loved Amber, Merc. I left her behind so she'd be safe. Her husband was my number one bodyguard. He's been looking after her for years. Until fucking Tony showed up." He hesitates, and then exhales some more smoke. He's really puffing tonight. "I failed my last psych exam."

Well, that's my cue. "My mark's leaving, gotta run." I end the call and toss the phone on the seat next to me as I watch the girl hanging on her piece-of-shit boyfriend outside the bar. I'm not interested in Tet's state of mind. Not one bit. You gotta be crazy to do a job like this. And I've never pretended to be sane, but I'm really not in the mood to be reminded of it at the moment.

Because if I had just fucked up a job, caused the death of a major crime boss' daughter, got a civilian shot, and then used my get-out-of-jail-free card to poison a former FBI agent while he was sitting in jail waiting for trial, leaving sloppy clues all over the fucking place? Clues that practically scream, 'Yo, it's Tet. I'm killing people here.' And they wanted to test me? Evaluate my mental stability?

Yeah, I'd sure as fuck fail that shit too.

I let out a breath and try to forget about Tet. He's a big boy, not my problem.

I only have one thing on my mind. It's not Ford's hit. A hit I owed him because of that job I fucked up last Christmas.

And it's not Tet clearing my debt with Ford by killing Tony.

It's this fucking girl across the street.

Because her father owes me *big*.

And I'm here to collect.

# EPILOGUE 1

# Spencer

***Seven Months Later***

***It's a beautiful October day***. Well, for a few hours it is. Colorado likes to play with the temperature quite a bit, but sometimes we get lucky and get a seventy-five-degree afternoon that comes out of nowhere.

I take full advantage of this day, lying in my hammock under the buckeye tree behind the shop. What used to be the shop. I tore it down and built a new garage attached to the house so Ronnie doesn't have to park her minivan outside. Besides, that shop was blocking the view of the tree from the house. And now we can see it and the river from the living room.

The screen door slaps closed and I turn my head to watch Ronnie walk across the grass to where I'm at. She's waddling these days. Her belly is already big and round even though she's only five months along.

She smiles at me as she approaches, and then sits her ass down next to mine and lies back with me. We sway a little and I wrap my arms around her. "You love me for my hammock, don't you."

She giggles.

I reach down to the ground and pick up a buckeye and hand it to her.

"And your buckeyes," she says back.

"What should we eat tonight?" I ask her as I kiss her on

the head and slip my hand underneath her maternity shirt to rub her belly.

"Hmmmm. Probably hospital food."

"What?"

"Rook called," she says as she turns her head to see me. "Ashleigh's in labor."

I sit up and scoop her up in my arms. "Holy shit!"

"Calm down, caveman. You're as bad as Ford. They just left for the hospital, these things typically take a long time."

I ignore every word as I carry her to the house. "Ford has got to be crazy. He needs support." I set her down when I get to the porch steps and smack her ass. "Get ready, Bomb. We gotta go."

She walks off towards the stairs to change or whatever she's gotta do to be ready to meet Ford's new baby. I'm new to all this shit, but I love the fact that Ford's gotta be the guinea pig. Every fuckup he makes, I take notes. Then I avoid that shit at all costs.

Like that dumbass told Ashleigh she should try natural childbirth. Yeah, he had to sleep on our couch for three nights.

I immediately asked Ronnie how soon she could get the drugs to make the process easier for her. She gave me a man massage that night.

I proposed to Ronnie in the hospital while she was still groggy from the drugs they used to surgically repair her artery. Twice my Bombshell was shot at because of me. Twice she lived.

I'm done. I told Ford and Ronin we're all done. And they had no complaints. We need to quit while we're ahead, and ahead simply means we're all still alive.

That's a win-win-win for everyone.

Ronin proposed to Rook last month at the party Antoine threw for her twenty-first birthday. They moved back to Denver as soon as Shrike Bikes season two filming ended. Ronin is the marketing manager for Chaput Studios and Rook is making a documentary on the inside lives of erotic models.

We got picked up for a third season, but Rook says she's done with the reality show stuff.

I don't blame her. Even Ronnie has lost interest in that shit. She's all about babies now. She gave up tattooing. Not because of the blood and not because she did actually have a little nerve damage from the gunshot wound that sometimes interferes with her inking. She gave it up because she started a new business. Edible body art.

This is the brain child of Carson Reed, if you can imagine. I added on to the Shrike Bikes building and gave them their own little studio. She paints people with colored sugar now.

I stop in there at least once a week to fuck her with frosting. That shit gives candy pussy a whole new perspective.

I'm still building bikes, mostly because I love building bikes. But if that show was canceled tomorrow, eh. I'm fine with it. I have a new definition of success these days and it has nothing to do with reality TV.

My idea of success is Bombshell's fat stomach. I smile at her as she comes back down the stairs with her shoes and sweater on.

"What's got you looking so guilty?" she asks.

"Not guilty, Bomb. Just happy."

She leans up and wraps her arms around me. "I love you for your smile."

I kiss her head. "I love everything about you, Veronica Vaughn. And that wedding day can't come soon enough for me."

She sighs. "I know, me too. But I'm not getting married while I'm pregnant. Ashleigh never had a real wedding, so I'm trying to talk the girls into a triple wedding next spring."

"I'll see what I can do on my end." I'm so pussy-whipped. But so are Ford and Ronin. These girls mean everything to us. If they want us to dress up in suits and tell a shitload of people we love them… well, we're on board.

We drive into Fort Collins talking about Ford and Ash. They don't know what the baby's sex is, Ford wanted to be surprised, so this is pretty exciting. When we get to the hospital I hold Ronnie's hand up to the maternity ward and then we stop at the nurse's station to get the room number. I'm just looking around when Ronin comes down the hallway. "Hey," he calls out. "Ronnie, the room's down here."

"Where's Ford?" I ask Ronin as he walks up to me.

Ronin points down a narrow hallway that ends at a little alcove with a large picture window that overlooks the mountains. "I think you should go talk to him. He's freaking out and Ash is starting to ask what's wrong."

"OK, I'll meet you guys in there." I kiss Ronnie and then walk down the hallway towards Ford.

He's got his hands in his pockets, his chin up. Like he's just taking in the view and not having a baby today.

"Hey," I call out when I get close.

He doesn't turn, so I just walk up next to him and wait.

He swallows hard. So hard it's audible. Something is wrong. "It's genetic, you know."

"Huh? What's genetic?"

He lets out a long breath of air. "What's wrong with me. It's genetic."

"Dude, there's nothing wrong with you."

He looks over at me and I can see the fear on his face. "Spencer, you've always said that. And I just want you to know, I appreciated that you treated me like I was normal my whole life."

"You *are* normal—"

"No," he interrupts. "I'm not. I'm defective. And all these months with Kate, parenting a child who accepts love and touch like all other children, well…" He breathes deeply again. "I'm just afraid, Spencer. That this baby will not let us touch it. I'm afraid the baby will be like me."

I squeeze his shoulder but I don't know what to say so I opt for technical stuff. "You don't know it's genetic, anyway. You have no clue what caused your issues."

"It is genetic, Spencer. I've studied everything about my

symptoms since I was eight years old. I've cross-referenced every research paper done on neurological touch syndrome." He throws me a sideways glance. "I even coined the term for it. I have commandeered grad students at the medical center in Denver to figure this out. But these things take *so* long. I've run out of time. The baby is coming today."

Ford looks over at me now and God, I feel so bad for him. I try to give him a smile but he looks away.

"The baby is coming today and I have no answers. I've failed."

"Ford?" Ronin calls from the hallway. "She's ready, dude. Ash wants you with her."

I grasp his shoulder again and squeeze. "Come on, it's time. There's no sense in worrying about it now, you're gonna know soon enough, right? I mean look, Ford. You really need to learn to just… let go, man. I get it, you're worried. But you can't control everything."

"Says who?" he asks, all serious.

"You're such a dick. You know that? But you're not defective. You're just… a special snowflake."

I get a real laugh out of him for that remark.

"Really, Aston. Think about it. God would not put another Ford on this Earth. There's no way he'd do that to humanity."

Ford laughs again. "True." He turns to look at me. "God is so damn serious. He needs to learn to go with the flow."

It's my turn to laugh and I clap him on the back. "Right. Come on, it's time to meet your kid."

He turns and walks down the hallway. I follow him as far as the waiting room where Ronin, Rook, and Ronnie are waiting. Kate's at home with Ford's mother, so it's just the Team here today.

Ronin and I pass the time drinking coffee and talking shit about the Broncos on the TV while the girls talk about babies. Rook's not pregnant, but she's almost ready. I can tell because she's never looked so happy. She wasn't the world's greatest model. Or the world's greatest student. But Rook is a damn good filmmaker. She entered her first short in a film festival and got an honorable mention.

She's figuring it out. And that's all you can ask for, really. Just an opportunity to figure it all out on your own terms, in your own way.

About an hour later a nurse walks up. "Aston family?" she asks, looking down at her clipboard.

"Yes!" we all say together.

"You can see the baby now." The nurse beams a bright smile at us and then walks off.

But my stomach is doing a little flip inside. Like I'm nervous as all hell. I want to take a moment to figure out what it means, but I have no time. I wipe my sweaty palms on my jeans and grab Ronnie's hand. She's excited, as is Rook. But both Ronin and I are worried about Ford. That short walk down the hallway feels like miles, and when we finally turn the corner and enter the room, I realize I've been holding my breath.

The girls rush in first. They are chatting and squealing with Ashleigh, who is looking pretty tired, but she's beaming a smile at us.

My eyes scan the room until I find Ford. Sitting in a chair next to the bed. Holding a little blue bundle with dark hair. A little blue bundle that is sleeping happily in his father's arms.

"It's a boy," Ford says softly, like he's trying not to wake him. He leans down to kiss the baby's cheek. "And he's perfect."

I'm not sure, because Ford is holding the baby close to his face. But I think I see a tear.

I nod and shoot Ford with my finger. "Just like you, dude. He's perfect just like you."

"What's his name?" Rook asks excitedly. Neither Ford nor Ashleigh ever disclosed the names they were throwing around.

"Rutherford Aston the Fifth, of course," Ash says.

And then Ford looks up at me and Ronin and grins. "I shall call him… Number Five."

We all laugh. Fucking Ford. My serious friend is a major goofball. I pull Ronnie into a hug and whisper in her ear. "Just picture it, Bomb. Kate and Number Five growing up with little Princess Shrike. They'll be friends from birth."

"They'll be a team, won't they?" she says, her beautiful face smiling up at me.

"They will, Bombshell. The old team might be gone, but a new one was just born."

EPILOGUE 2

# Five

***Six years later***
***First day of school***
***St. Joseph's, Fort Collins***

***I tap my finger*** on my tooth and Kate reaches out to slap it away. I frown up at her. She's still taller than me even though we are in the same grade now. They made me skip first grade after my IQ test came back.

Can't a man just enjoy himself? Relish in being six instead of being rushed into the realm of seven-hood?

I resume my tapping, but not on my tooth. Kate says that gives me away. Tells people I'm nervous. So she won't let me do it anymore. So I tap my toe inside my shoe. No one can see my toe tapping, so it's OK.

I glance over at my father as he talks to Sister Nemesis. I know I'm not supposed to hate people, but Sister Nemesis tries my last nerve. She has so many rules. And honestly, I've been reading since I was two. Why should I have to sit cross-legged on the carpet and listen to stories like kids who can't?

They figure moving me up a grade will help that. But they'd have to move me into college to satisfy my academic pursuits here in this little school. That's not gonna happen. I'm gonna make sure that never happens.

And as if on cue, I hear it.

The low rumble of Uncle Spencer's nineteen sixty-nine Camaro. My heart thumps with excitement as he pulls up to the curb on the far end of the playground. "Be right back, Kate," I call out as I rush towards the car.

Aunt Bombshell is gathering up the backpack from the backseat and then…

I see her.

Princess Shrike.

I waited all last year for her. And they think they can just shoot me up a few grades and keep her out of my reach?

Never!

I sigh as I take her in. She's got on her little blue and green tartan skirt and her white shirt is pressed smooth. Her long blonde hair is up in two flowing pigtails. She looks over at me and waves and my heart flutters a little.

She's mine now. Ha ha ha.

"Aunt Ronnie." I beam up at the Bombshell after she kisses Princess Shrike with a sappy tear in her eye. "I'll take it from here." And then I grab her little pink hand and lead her down the sidewalk to the playground.

Her parents follow, but they make their way over to my mom and dad now, so I relax a little. I look down at my best friend. "Are you nervous, Princess?"

She stops walking and puts her hand on her hip. "You're not allowed to call me that, Ford. My name is Rory. You have to call me Rory!"

I nod. "Sure thing, Princess. And it's Number Five. Now, are you ready?"

"Yes," she says with a smile. "I can write my name and I know my address."

"Hmmm." I'm not impressed. "In how many languages?" My toe begins to tap inside my shoe again. This might be more difficult than I thought.

"What?"

"Princess Rory, I can see my work is cut out. We will meet every day at lunch and you will learn French. That way you'll know what the grownups are saying when they are talking about secret things."

"Why do I need to know secret things?" she asks innocently.

The bell rings and kids begin gathering their things for class.

I lean in to her ear. "Because, Rory. You are on the team now. So we gotta stick together. It's all for one and one for all. Now listen," I say as I grab her hand again and begin walking her inside the building. "I'm a whole five months older, so I'm the boss of you, Princess. OK?"

"You're not the boss of me," she says in her sweet little Princess voice. "My mom says I'm the boss of me."

"No, your mom is wrong. Every team needs a boss, and that's me. Because I'm the smartest. You're the youngest, so I'm the boss of you."

She continues to argue with me all the way to her classroom, and then all the parents are there, interfering with my plans of playground domination.

But I'm not worried.

Because Kate, Number Five, and Princess Rory are gonna take this podunk school into science fair greatness.

You. Just. Wait.

# End Of Book Shit

***WELCOME to the End of Book Shit***. I'm kinda cheating on this new EOBS because I actually wrote this in 2015 right before 321 released. But it was such a cool afterthought about the series, and it was on my book blog, not even my JA Huss blog, so practically no one saw it.

So I'm resurrecting it for your pleasure today!

Spencer is in every single book in the Rook & Ronin series. He comes in late in Tragic, but boy does he make an impression. He scoops Rock up when she needs a friend, and just when you start to think this might turn into a triangle, Spencer Shrike does a 180. He's not what he appears to be. But then again, that was the whole point of the series.

Sometimes when I'm writing a later book in a series I recall a little detail in an earlier book that changes everything about the story. This happened with Spencer and Veronica in Bomb. That novella is supposed to be the first book about Spencer, but instead it introduced Veronica the Bombshell Bomb—Spencer's long-time love-interest who has been dumped.

In Bomb I start from the beginning and take you back in time to the day Spencer first saw Veronica on their college campus. He proceeds to woo her, and they end up back in his garage where he reveals his customs bikes. Well, he's only got one custom bike at that point in his life.

That bike he shows Ronnie sort of existed in Tragic, but only as a casual detail. Spencer takes Rook to his bike shop where he has lots of custom bikes. This is his future. He's Big Time now. He's got a showroom filled with motorcycles he needs photographed. He wants something from Rook, and he's willing to offer up something big to get her on his side. So he offers her a custom motorcycle.

Rook picks a Shrike Bike resembling a classic Triumph motorcycle that is just sitting in Spencer's shop, so that's the bike he pretties up for her and presents to her in Manic. The bike ends up being called the Shrike Rook. But it used to be something else before Rook claimed it…

I'm pretty sure no one ever thought about that bike again except me. Because when I had to go back to the time when Spencer was first dating Veronica, Spencer was in Veronica's family tattoo shop asking her to give him ink. He drew the tat he wanted and it caught Veronica by surprise. Spencer was surprised too.

The Shrike Rook appears in Tragic, Manic, Panic, Slack, Bomb, and Guns. If I had really planned it better, it would've been in Taut as well. :) But I didn't plan that bike at all. I pulled that classic Triumph design out of my memory for its first appearance in Tragic. I knew a guy once… he had one. But I had no idea Triumph made a model called the Blackbird when I decided to name Rook after a black bird. I had no idea that the Shrike Rook was modeled after the Triumph Blackbird when I put that random memory into Tragic. And the way the whole thing came full circle didn't even hit me until I was writing Bomb and I realized what I had set up by accident.

I think that's the best thing about writing a series like this. Moments when all the little back story details add up to something BIG just because you're making it all up, and most of what you make up is based off things you already know.

The motorcycle means a lot to Rook. It's her one true possession in Panic—something she takes with her on her final quest to put her past behind her. It means a lot to Bomb as well. She has her first Spencer experience on the half built model and she wants it back in Guns. And to Spencer, because it was the first bike he ever built—it was a symbol of his future, what he was capable of.

I resurrected that bike when I wrote Mr. & Mrs. I didn't plan it then either. I had Oliver and Kat up in Five's motorcycle garage, and Oliver was looking for some sexy times on a bike in true Shrike fashion, and Kat points to a dirty old thing propped up in the corner. And when she wipes the dirt off the tank and they see what it is… well, that's when I saw what it was too.

I swear to God, I just stopped and thought about that for a second. How that bike came back over and over again. How it turned into much more than a bike for so many characters.

And there it was, out in a garage in the middle of the Caribbean just waiting for me to find it.

I think it's the little things like this that makes the story come alive, and even though I didn't really plan it out that way, sometimes it's better to create by accident.

I think that might be the quote they put on my gravestone.

"She created stuff by accident."

I'm OK with that.

Julie
JA Huss

# End Of Book Shit

***Oh, my fuckin' God***, I forgot how cute Five was in this! So anyway, this is the End of Book Shit, commonly called the EOBS. Now back to Five. .

So I just now, like just two seconds ago, finished formatting this eBook for Guns and two things happened at the end of that.

ONE – MERC! Haha! I totally forgot he was in this book! So I make these headers for the chapters, right? And I click on the next chapter, ready to put in either Spencer or Veronica and it's MERC! I laughed out loud at that. Then I quickly went and made a new header for him, slapped it in, then got back to Spencer's epilogue.

Then FIVE! Double surprise!

I know it's stupid since I wrote the books, but shit, you guys! It's been almost five years since this series started and almost exactly four since I released Guns. And in that time I have published too many books to count. But they are definitely counted in the dozens at this point. So… it slipped my mind.

Which is also funny, since Five has been on my mind a lot these days. The audiobook for the Five book came out about three weeks ago and then the Mr. & Mrs. audio (which also features Five's POV) came out last week. So I've been listening to those, enjoying them a lot, and yeah.

So how the hell did I forget! I dunno, but it was a happy

surprise when Merc and Five showed up at the end of this book. I hope you guys felt that way too.

I had no idea what I was doing when I started that story about down-on-her-luck Rook meeting erotic model Ronin. I already said in Ford's new EOBS that I'd planned on him being the bad guy and had no plans on continuing the story after Panic. So none of this came out the way I thought it would when I started Tragic – holy fuck, I'm so glad I didn't know what I was doing. I'm so glad I just did my thing back then. I'm so glad I found all you fans (and you can't fool me, I know most of you reading this now probably already own several copies of this book with different covers and End of Book Shits!) because I don't think you can plan something like this. I really don't.

The Rook & Ronin Series was, and always will be, the number one way in which readers turns into JA Huss fans. Sure, I know lots of you started with 321, or 18, or Taking Turns. But fans go back and start from the beginning when they find me. They go back to Tragic and take the whole messed-up journey into the future.

One more guy I had no clue about was "Bobby" who, if you've already read The Company books, you already know is not really Bobby, right? He's James Fenici. So during this series I found Merc, James, and Sasha. All of whom would come back with their own stories and consume my writing life for the next year and a half.

And what do you know, all these characters are back again because Johnathan and I are doing The Company TV pilot stuff. And Five found his way into the Mister series and then got his own book, and then threw the best wedding ever in Mr. & Mrs. This world is crazy. But crazy good sometimes. Fate, man. That's all I can say about this series. It was meant to be.

I just put up a blog post today on the HussMcClain site because today was the last cover reveal for the original Sin series that Johnathan and I are writing. And I was talking about covers in that post and how they go through trends, which is why I felt the need to update this covers on this series, and then, of course, I had to update the EOBS too. Not to make you guys buy it again (thank you, though, if you did! I really appreciate it!) But because they needed a fresh look. Fans still love this series so much (as do I) so I don't want it to get left behind.

And it's funny because Johnathan and I have created this new world with the Sin books. It's in Vegas, not Colorado, but I've been to Vegas so many times over the past few years, it feels very familiar to me. Like London these days. Which is where I'm headed in four days for the RARE London's Calling Author Event. I emailed my editor RJ last week, who lives in Bristol, UK, and it went something like this, "Hey Bitch! I'm gonna be in town next week. Show up at our usual place and see me!"

Well, not exactly like that, but very close. Because I stay at the same hotel near St. James Park every time I go there. I know the neighborhood now. I know where the restaurants are, I know exactly what I'm gonna order at the Blue Boar Pub (Yes, that's an Anarchy Series reference and that's where it came from!) and I know how to get to the park, and the post office, and Big Ben, and Westminster Abbey!

It's familiar. Like these characters, like Fort Collins, Colorado, like the Rook Shrike, like St. Joseph's school, like College Avenue. Even if you've never been to Fort Collins you probably have a picture of Shrike Bikes in your mind. And Sick Boyz Inc. And Anna Ameci's Restaurant, and Big City Burrito…

I created a world in Rook & Ronin. One I never wanted to leave behind. Right now I'm doing that same thing with the Turning Series books. That series is over but I just started a new spin-off series called Jordan's Game and those pesky Turning people just can't keep their noses out of thing in the new story!

You can't really plan for a fictional world to take on a life of its own. You can do your best to make it real, and vivid, and interesting. You can fill it will cool people, and cool places, and intriguing plots. But you can't really know it's gonna be "real" when you start. You just do your best.

And about six weeks back Johnathan and I were talking about our new world and our new characters and which of them might need a spin-off book. We have a few in mind but we have so many ideas for NEW books, would we really want to write about them? And I said something like, "You never know. We might be writing these characters ten years from now. You just can't tell."

You really can't. I hope the Vegas Sin books are as real to you as Rook & Ronin. I know I'm already living in Vegas. I might even want to visit Pete's. ;)

And I hope all these worlds I've created go on living for a while.

Because to me, these people are real. These places are real.

The places, and people, and weather, and culture all add up to something. Another character in the book called "Setting". And I know most authors don't view their setting as a character, but I always have. Ever since Junco I've written the "where and when" as just another character in the story. What, where, and when in Tragic is just… eh. You're really just getting to know that place. So yeah, you like Coor's Field and you like the zoo… but eh. And when I took you up to Fort Collins in Manic you were like… Bellvue who? What the fuck?

But it grew on you. Like the St. James Park neighborhood in London for me. And now we're in Guns and you know all these places. You recognize them. They MEAN something to you. You know the ride from Spencer's farm into town is long. You know Ford's house on Mountain Avenue is across from the City Pool. You've had coffee in the FoCo Theatre with Rook and Ashleigh. And you probably petted her face-eaters, because fuck it. You know Ford's dogs are highly trained and you can trust them not to eat your face at the coffee shop.

So thanks. Thanks for coming over to my side of town. Thanks for stopping by. Thanks for coming back.

Wanna keep going? There's more books to read.

The next series about these people is called The Company. It picks up where "Bobby" and Merc left off. After that it's Meet Me In The Dark, then Wasted Lust.

And when you're all done with those, I've got a sweet surprise for you called Happily Ever After. Don't forget about that one!

Julie
JA Huss

# About The Author

***JA Huss never wanted*** to be a writer and she still dreams of that elusive career as an astronaut. She originally went to school to become an equine veterinarian but soon figured out they keep horrible hours and decided to go to grad school instead. That Ph.D wasn't all it was cracked up to be (and she really sucked at the whole scientist thing), so she dropped out and got a M.S. in forensic toxicology just to get the whole thing over with as soon as possible.

After graduation she got a job with the state of Colorado as their one and only hog farm inspector and spent her days wandering the Eastern Plains shooting the shit with farmers.

After a few years of that, she got bored. And since she was a homeschool mom and actually does love science, she decided to write science textbooks and make online classes for other homeschool moms.

She wrote more than two hundred of those workbooks and was the number one publisher at the online homeschool store many times, but eventually she covered every science topic she could think of and ran out of shit to say.

So in 2012 she decided to write fiction instead. That year she released her first three books and started a career that would make her a New York Times bestseller and land her on the USA Today Bestseller's List eighteen times in the next three years.

Her books have sold millions of copies all over the world, the audio version of her semi-autobiographical book,

Eighteen, was nominated for an Audie award in 2016, her book Mr. Perfect was nominated for a Voice Arts Award in 2017 and her book Taking Turns was nominated for an Audie award in 2018.

She also writes book and screenplays with her friend, actor and writer, Johnathan McClain. Their first book, Sin With Me, will release on March 6, 2018. And they are currently working with MGM as producing partners to turn their adaption of her series, The Company, into a TV series.

She lives on a ranch in Central Colorado with her family, two donkeys, four dogs, three birds, and two cats.

If you'd like to learn more about JA Huss or get a look at her schedule of upcoming appearances, visit her website at www.JAHuss.com or www.HussMcClain.com to keep updated on her projects with Johnathan. You can also join her fan group, Shrike Bikes, on Facebook, www.facebook.com/groups/shrikebikes and follow her Twitter handle, @jahuss.